MED CENTER

Two Novels

VIRUS and FLOOD

MED CENTER

Two Novels

VIRUS and FLOOD

DIANE HOH

SCHOLASTIC INC.
New York Toronto London Auckland Sydney
Mexico City New Delhi Hong Kong Buenos Aires

Virus, ISBN 0-590-54322-9, Copyright © 1996 by Diane Hoh.

Flood, ISBN 0-590-54323-7, Copyright © 1996 by Diane Hoh.

12 11 10 9 8 7 6 5 4 3 2 1   5 6 7 8 9 10/ 0

Printed in the U.S.A.   01

This edition created exclusively for Barnes & Noble, Inc.

2005 Barnes & Noble Books

ISBN 0-7607-6338-0

First compilation printing, January 2005

CONTENTS

She needed him to live!

Upstairs, the nurse at the desk didn't want to let Susannah into Sam's room. She pointed toward the door. "You see that sign? It says DO NOT ENTER. It's for your protection, Miss Grant."

"Oh, for heaven's sake!" Susannah cried. "I've already been exposed in ER, before we knew what anyone had. I am *going* in to see my brother. I'll suit up. I'll even wear goggles. But I *am* going in there."

And she did. The nurse gave in. There *were* advantages to being Samuel Grant's daughter.

Feeling strange in the weird protective gear, Susannah sat beside Sam's bed, holding the hand that hadn't been pierced with an IV needle, talking to him in a low, steady voice. He lay perfectly still, his face ashen, his eyes closed, the monitor at his head reflecting a steady zigzagging line that reassured Susannah. As long as that line wasn't flat . . .

MED CENTER

CENTER

VIRUS

chapter
1

~~\/\~\/\/\~\/\~\/\~\/\~\/\~~

Hot. So hot. Every inch of her being roasted over hot coals. Her skin, when she touched it tentatively, felt as dry as dust, and her eyes burned as if she were staring directly into the sun.

She didn't understand it. Like most of the other day-camp counselors in the lush, heavily treed playground at Grant Med Center, she was wearing white shorts, a red tank top, and sneakers. The temperature hadn't yet gone above eighty, and there was a cool breeze that ruffled her long, sleek blonde hair and set the only unoccupied swing gently swaying.

The breeze should have cooled her body, but it hadn't. Not a cool spot from her toes to the top of her head. Not a drop of saliva remained in her mouth. It felt full of wool. If she had been required to speak, she was certain no sound would have made it through that arid thickness.

She couldn't be sick again so soon. She had thought she was completely over that rotten bout with the flu. It couldn't come back now. Boring old school was finally over, and summer was here. Why couldn't this have happened while classes were still in session? Maybe she'd have missed that last fatal geometry test and been spared her mother's endless lecture about the importance of a good education. If the flu was going to hit her again, why hadn't it done so then? Until a few days ago, she'd felt fine. Or was it a week ago? She wasn't sure. How could she think with her brain on fire?

A spasm of coughing seized her as she moved slowly, wavering slightly, to catch the toddlers whizzing down the sliding board. The spasm caught her off guard. She'd had others, the night before and again this morning, but this one was the worst by far. In seconds, she was doubled in half, as if someone had delivered a blow to her stomach. Her hands went to her mouth. Her knees bent under the strain of one hoarse, body-wrenching cough after another.

The children at the very top of the sliding board, awaiting their turns, stared, wondering what was happening. She wasn't their favorite counselor, always whining about something or other, but she was okay. So they waited for someone to come to her aid.

The boy who did was tall, dark-skinned, handsome. Fortunately for the girl, Will Jackson was a paramedic, not yet on duty at Med Center's Emergency Services. He knew the signs of serious physical distress when he saw them. He had come to the playground to deliver his six-year-old nephew, but stopped en route to the oversized, crowded sandbox when he saw what was happening. Calling out the girl's name, he rushed over to her, at the same time waving commandingly to two other counselors standing near the monkey bars to join him.

The three ran together to the girl's aid.

By that time, her knees had given way completely. She sank to the ground, still wracked with the agonizing coughing. Her hands went to her chest in a desperate effort to remove the iron bands squeezing the breath out of her. A moment later, her eyes rolled back in her head and, face scarlet, she toppled sideways, landing gently in the soft, sand-filled pit at the foot of the sliding board.

The coughing stopped. She let out a little sigh of relief and closed her eyes, her fevered body going completely limp.

When Will Jackson reached her, the other two counselors right behind him, a vivid scarlet rash had sprung to life on the girl's chest, clashing with the red of her tank top.

"Call Emergency!" Will barked, waving a hand toward the tallest of the cluster of brick buildings encircling the playground. "Get an ambulance!" He crouched beside the stricken girl. "Something is really wrong here."

He was right.

Something was very wrong.

In the far south end of Grant, in a small building that could only be called a shack, pre-cariously perched on a slope above the riverbank, a young man in T-shirt and jeans prepared to leave for his summer job as a window washer. His efforts at leaving some sort of order behind him were desultory. Even on good days, he tended to leave his coffee cup sitting on the table, the brown liquid coagulating into a sticky residue by late afternoon when he returned. He never made up his narrow cot in the tiny back room of the shack, figuring he was just going to mess it up again that night, anyway, and he washed dishes no more than once a week, usually at that point when he could no longer find a clean glass or coffee mug or spoon. That was on good days.

But today was not a good day. On this partic-ular Monday morning, Jenkins Rue was feeling like a tennis ball at the end of a long match be-tween champions. He knew it was his own fault. He'd stayed out late both Saturday and Sunday nights, dancing his boots off at The Music Room, a club downtown. Couldn't tear himself away, and now he was regretting it.

It was way too hot for so early in the morning. What had happened to the usual cool breeze from the river? Bad enough he had to live in this hellhole. Was a little breeze too much to ask for?

If he didn't show up at work, he wouldn't get paid. He needed that money. The only way he was ever going to have a chance with someone like Tina Montgomery was with a college degree hanging on one of his walls, and that took big bucks. It wasn't as if he had parents to hand him a tuition check, like Tina did. Hell, her parents could *buy* her a college if they wanted to. His, on the other hand, had crashed their Harley into a tree ten months ago. They hadn't been wearing helmets ("Not cool" his mother had said) and they weren't the type to buy insurance. If his grandfather hadn't left him this old fishing shack, Jenkins Rue would be living on the streets.

Man, this headache! Felt like his brain had swollen to three times its normal size. Weird, too, because Tina had complained about having a bad headache last night. He'd thought she was just trying to get rid of him. Maybe not. Were headaches catching? His throat hurt, too, and he couldn't stop hacking away like a heavy smoker, which he wasn't. Tina had been coughing, too.

Damn. He couldn't afford to get sick.

Maybe once he got outside, the fresh air would take care of it. If it didn't, he'd down a couple of aspirin and go to work, anyway.

Without combing his thick mass of shoulder-length, light brown, curly hair, Jenkins Rue left the riverbank shack for his window-washing job.

He made it to work at the University Health Club without slamming into a tree or another vehicle.

His window-washing routine never varied. The health club on Mondays. The rest of the week he spent at Med Center, doing whichever of the eighteen buildings he was assigned to. Jenkins wished he were doing the lab today. Although it was huge and took forever to do, it was only two stories high. With his stomach so queasy and his head splitting, he wasn't keen on taking the scaffolding up to the top of the eighth-floor fitness center. But this was Monday.

Coughing hard, Jenkins wiped a brow that burned beneath his hand, and stepped onto the mechanized scaffolding, grasping the side railing with both hands after he had pushed the button to send himself skyward.

He was between the second and third floors, directly above a wide cement driveway, when a wave of dizziness assailed him and he staggered sideways a step or two. If he hadn't been coughing so hard, he would have righted himself easily and regained his footing.

That didn't happen. The spasm was much worse than the preceding ones. It watered his eyes and made breathing difficult. Dizzy and disoriented, Jenkins made a fatal mistake. Instead of taking a step or two back to the right, he mistakenly attempted to step to his left, sending his left foot completely off the platform into empty space and tilting Jenkins off balance.

Two and a half floors above the driveway, he flew out into the air, seemed to hang there for a fraction of a second, and then plunged straight down, arms and legs flailing.

A red-and-white ambulance, with the words GRANT MEDICAL CENTER printed on its sides in huge, black, block lettering, sped away from Emergency Services and raced through town, turning left at the end of the driveway, toward the day-care center.

Its siren screamed throughout the early morning quiet of the city of Grant, Massachusetts, without pause until it reached its destination. Then it died abruptly.

chapter
2

Susannah Grant had been trying for ten minutes to get the attention of her father, Samuel Grant II, a tall, distinguished-looking man with thick white hair and keen blue eyes, wearing an impeccably tailored gray suit over a two-hundred-dollar white shirt and a red silk tie. He sat in his customary place at the head of the long, oval, antique table in the dining room of Linden Hall, the family's elegant stone and white-frame mansion. He wasn't responding to his daughter because he was deeply engaged in conversation with his son, Samuel Grant III, sitting on his father's right.

Susannah, sitting opposite her twin, glared at both of them. Basketball scores! Heads bent, leaning earnestly toward each other, they were talking about the past weekend's athletic events as if the discussion might bring about an end to world hunger. They seemed totally unaware of Susannah or her mother, Caroline, who poked listlessly at her fruit cup at the opposite end of the table.

Susannah turned in exasperation to her mother. "Why do I always feel, when I'm sitting at this table, that I've suddenly become invisible?"

Caroline glanced up, her beautiful face a blank. Deep blue eyes, the same exact shade as her children's, were distant, as if she'd just awakened from a dream. "Did you say something, dear?"

Susannah sighed in defeat and reached up to brush a thick wave of blonde hair away from her forehead. Her irritated gaze returned to father and son. "I wouldn't want to interrupt the most important sports discussion held in the state of Massachusetts in this century, but I need to ask Dad something."

Caroline nodded vaguely and said, "Yes, of course. Go right ahead, dear." She returned to her grapefruit and orange wedges.

Susannah sighed. No help there. Temporarily giving up, she sat back in her chair, glancing around the dining room as she waited for a lull in the conversation that excluded her. It was a pretty room with cobalt blue walls and shiny marble floors. An imported crystal chandelier was centered over the table, which easily seated twenty people. Baskets and vases of brightly colored summer flowers, courtesy of the efforts of Paolo, the gardener, were perched on the sideboard and on a long, low table behind Sam. The early morning sun, streaming in through a wall of French doors leading to a stone terrace, striped the gleaming hardwood floor.

Susannah's eyes moved to survey the people in the room. Sam was so good-looking, Susannah decided, watching him, that he could easily have been in the 100 Most Beautiful People issue of one of those popular celebrity magazines. A recent cover had featured a young man — hadn't it been one of the Kennedys? — who wasn't any better-looking than Sam. The only difference was, that guy had had dark hair and eyes, while Sam's hair was sun-streaked blonde, like hers, and although they were not identical twins, he, like she, had their mother's brilliant blue eyes. Minus the faint look of sadness.

Nothing sad about Sam. Life of the party. And why not? If anyone in Grant, Massachusetts, had the world by the tail, the heir to the Grant fortune certainly did. Girls, parties, fun, money. The story of Sam's life.

If we were identical, Susannah thought not for the first time, I'd be gorgeous, too. And I'd be tons of fun, like Sam. Not only do we not look that much alike except for coloring, but our personalities are as different as Mother's and Dad's.

Caroline Grant sat at the far end of the table, as if, Susannah thought, she'd been banished there for breaking a house rule. Something Caroline would never, ever do. Even at seven-thirty in the morning, every auburn hair was in place, makeup perfectly applied, and she was fully dressed in pale blue silk, looking every inch the wealthy, well-bred wife of the most powerful man in town.

So why didn't she look ecstatically happy?

Although Susannah's mother seemed remote at times, she always functioned perfectly as the head of their busy household. She kept herself fit and trim, entertained beautifully, and was popular with the other wives of Grant "society." If she found a spare moment, she quite often spent it trying to persuade her only daughter to cultivate more friends. Susannah interpreted that to mean "Try to be more like Sam" and ignored the advice. She loved her brother, but his hectic life of fun and games wasn't for her. She loved dancing, but she also liked quiet times with friends, and walks along the riverbank that bisected the city of Grant. Secretly, she believed her mother would have preferred a quieter lifestyle, too. But there were parties to go to, charitable affairs to organize and attend, entertaining to do. If her mother had wanted to stop and smell the roses, she'd married the wrong man. She should have married Paolo, the gardener, instead.

Through the sparkling glass of the French doors, Susannah could see, far below, the mass of eighteen red brick buildings, some ivy-covered, some tall, some shorter and wider, that made up the world-famous medical complex known as Med Center, where she did volunteer work in Grant Memorial's Emergency Services. Surrounded by the city of Grant, the vast, sprawling complex was almost a city in itself. She yearned to be down there, where she was the happiest.

Suddenly impatient to get going, Susannah said quickly, "Dad, can I take the Jeep today?"

Without lifting her head, Caroline corrected automatically. "May I, dear, not can I."

The forkful of omelet halfway to Samuel Grant's mouth paused in midair. He frowned at his daughter, as if he'd forgotten she was sitting there and was startled to hear the sound of her voice. But it was only her request that caused the frown. "The Jeep? I bought that for Paolo, Susannah. It's strictly for running errands, hauling supplies, and off-road driving to check the property." He smiled tolerantly at her. "It probably smells of fertilizer. What's wrong with your own car?"

He had given her, for her sixteenth birthday, a sleek, silver Benz convertible. Susannah hated it. Only two people fit in that car. If she wanted to include a third person — Kate Thompson, for instance, or Will Jackson — where would she put them? Neither was small enough or contortionist enough to cram into the tiny space behind the leather bucket seats.

Not that she spent that much social time with either Will or Kate. But that didn't mean she didn't want to.

Her father never would have bought Sam such a small car. Instead, Sam had a top-of-the-line van, also silver, loaded with the latest automotive features. In it, he hauled the basketball team from his private day school, the soccer team, the squash and jai alai teams. If it was a sport, Sam played it. And if he played it, he excelled at it.

His twin excelled at no sport. She played softball and basketball well, and was a fairly good dancer. But she didn't excel. "Nothing's wrong with my car. Except what I've said all along. It's too small, Dad."

Samuel Grant laughed, showing perfect white teeth, startling in a face so deeply tanned. Although as head of Grant Pharmaceuticals he was a very busy man, he found time for enough golfing, swimming, and tennis to maintain the physique of a man half his age. "Well, I could have given you a Caddy, Susannah. But what would you want with a car that size?"

She knew perfectly well what he meant. He meant that she wasn't the Cadillac type. *He* was. He fit into big, expensive cars. So did her mother. And Sam would, when he was older. But not her.

"I'd rather have the Jeep," she forged on stubbornly. "I already checked with Paolo. He doesn't need it today."

When her father had given in, Susannah excused herself, a needless gesture since no one paid any attention to her departure, and left the house.

Her disgruntled attitude left her, as it always did, when she was outside. Tall and slender, her long, wavy, pale hair caught up in a neat French braid, Susannah stood with her hands on jeaned hips, looking down at the city below. Her eyes lit up as they always did when they focused on Med Center, the sprawling medical complex.

She couldn't wait to get down there. There was life in the dozen and a half buildings set on velvety, rolling green lawns among huge old maple and oak trees. *Real* life. There was, of course, death, too, and heartache and tragedy. But she preferred to think of the center as a place of life and hope. She called the complex MC for short, which she wrote as "Emsee" when she sent letters to her maternal grandparents in Florida.

The Grant family had made their fortune in railroads. Since World War II, they had made a new fortune in pharmaceuticals and surgical instruments. The family, over the one hundred years since the hospital had been founded, had been the main financial contributor to Med Center.

To Susannah, Emsee was the very heart of

Grant, Massachusetts. Without the complex and its companion, Grant University, no blood would flow through Grant's veins, no oxygen would reach its lungs or brain, and it would wither and die.

Grant Memorial, the tallest building in the complex, was where she did most of her volunteering, in the ER. She was happier in that building than anywhere else on earth. And proud. She was proud to be a part of it. Wherever she was in town, whatever she was doing, when she heard a siren split the air, she knew the staff at Emergency would hear the sound, too, and all would be on the alert. Traffic accidents, heart attacks, floods, fires, explosions, whatever, the best medical staff in the world would do everything in their power to keep the incoming patient or patients alive. Even when the injuries were minor, requiring only medication, sutures, or a bandage and reassurance, Susannah was glad to be a small part of the process.

She climbed into the Jeep, feeling the sun on her face. It was the pace of Emsee that she loved the most. Day after day, the admissions at Emergency came in fast and furiously, handled with what Susannah thought of as "controlled chaos." When the EMTS arrived with an ambulance, they barked out vital statistics at a breathless pace, and nurses and orderlies rushed with the gurney into a treatment room. What followed was a mad, noisy, adrenaline-fueled race to save a life before the "Golden Hour," the period that could make all the difference between life and death for a critically ill or injured patient, could expire. And yet there was a purposeful design to those frenetic, tension-filled moments, a concerted effort to put together the pieces to the medical puzzle in time to save a life.

They were busy in ER even when the emergencies were mostly minor. On any given day, ER could have as many as ten people in the waiting room, five or six, even seven in various treatment rooms, and more patients lying on gurneys or in chairs awaiting X rays, exams, or stitches for minor cuts.

"Never a dull moment," Will, a busy paramedic, often said as he ran past Susannah alongside one of the wheeled stretchers.

He was right. If Emsee was the heart of Grant, Massachusetts, then Grant Memorial's ER was the heart of Emsee, and that was where Susannah wanted to be.

She put the Jeep in gear and drove, faster than she should have, down the steep, winding hill to Med Center.

At the University Health Club, an ambulance screeched to a halt, and Will Jackson and two other paramedics jumped clear.

Jenkins Rue was conscious and able to tell them that he had fallen.

Will glanced up at the building. Jenkins had fallen almost three stories. How could he still be conscious?

He had no neck pain, he said, but his left elbow jutted out oddly. Dislocation, Will told himself, kneeling beside the victim. And his left femur was clearly fractured. Not a clean break, either. Jenkins was going to need surgery and he could probably kiss his football career good-bye.

Will began reading off statistics. "Pulse 92, respiration 18, blood pressure 118/70." He would not normally have taken the patient's temperature at that point until they had the cervical collar on and light traction applied to the leg. But when his hand came in contact with Jenkins's skin, he knew immediately that the heat of it wasn't only from the hot sun. "He's hot, man," he said to his partners, "burning up."

When they had done the best they could with the injured leg by dressing the open wound and applying gentle traction, they immobilized the possibly dislocated elbow with a well-padded pair of ladder splints and carefully, gently, transferred the patient to an aluminum scoop stretcher before putting him on the gurney.

"When you call in," Will told his partner as they climbed aboard the ambulance, "mention the temp, okay? It's 102. They'll need to know that." He wasn't nearly as concerned about Jenkins's injuries as he was about the high fever. The leg was going to need surgery, and the high temperature complicated things.

Contact with the hospital by radio brought orders for an IV of normal saline for Jenkins and the application of antishock trousers. Because of the leg injury, the trousers were to be applied only to the uninjured leg and the abdomen. It would have to be done carefully.

When that had been done, Will's partner completed the cursory physical exam. No evidence of chest injury, yet the lungs didn't sound clear, as they should have.

"I think he's probably got the flu," Will said.

Hospital staff members were standing by when they arrived at Med Center. A nurse took a new set of vital signs as they hurried along the corridor with the gurney, and Will quickly pointed out the unusually high temperature. The temp was important. Because Jenkins wasn't in any danger of bleeding to death and the initial examination in the ambulance hadn't detected any sign of internal injuries, the fractured leg in itself wouldn't be given high priority. But the temp would.

The nurse thanked him and urged the orderly helping her to "Hurry it up!"

Will watched as the stretcher raced down the hallway toward a trauma room, and wondered what the chances were that Tina Montgomery and Jenkins Rue were suffering from the same illness.

chapter
3

On the east side of the city of Grant, in a neighborhood known as Eastridge, where the homes were small enough to fit into the Grant mansion's sunroom, Kate Thompson raced around the sunny, clean but disordered kitchen on Persimmon Drive, getting ready for her shift at Med Center, where she, like Susannah, worked as a volunteer in Emergency Services.

Strong, athletic legs ran from counter to table to kitchen drawer and back again, carrying an empty coffee cup and toast-crumbed plate to the sink, tossing her paper napkin into the yellow wastebasket, straightening the blue-flowered plastic tablecloth and wiping it free of crumbs. In front of the small mirror just inside the kitchen door, a purple pick raked its way through a fringe of bangs over dark, long-lashed eyes. There was a minor adjustment to thick, black, cornrowed hair. A dab of plum lip gloss followed, a flick of blusher to high, sharply angled cheekbones, then a pair of heavy wooden earrings of Kate's own design were hurriedly

20

thrust into her earlobes, and she was done. Jeans and a white T-shirt were acceptable work gear at Emergency. Sneakers instead of sandals on her feet. Safer footing on the slippery white tiles.

Kate was one of the few volunteers actually allowed into the treatment rooms at ER where the cases in need of instant, expert care were brought. She and Susannah Grant. They had been carefully selected by the Director of Emergency Services because of their grades at school, their interest in medicine, and because, after being interviewed by two psychiatrists at Llewelyn T. Grant Psychiatric Hospital at Med Center, the Director had been assured they could handle whatever came their way.

Kate hadn't been the least bit surprised by the results of her own evaluation. She'd never had much doubt that she could handle the more gruesome aspects of trauma work. But she'd been knocked out when she heard that Susannah Grant, of all people, would be working alongside her. *The* Susannah Grant? *Princess* Grant? For that was how Kate had thought of her, until she got to know her. Blonde and blue-eyed, of course, as all princesses must be. The Grant girlfriend, who didn't even attend public school with the rest of the masses, looked like she'd faint at the first sight of an artery spurting the red stuff.

But she hadn't. Kate had to admit, however reluctantly, that Susannah had handled every horror that had come into Emergency since they'd become volunteers with cool, calm efficiency. Hardly batted an eye, although sometimes her peachy skin turned a shade or two paler if the damage to a victim was particularly gruesome.

Kate had found, also reluctantly, that she really liked Susannah. The girl might not be a barrel of laughs, but that was basically just shyness, Kate felt. This particular Grant, fancy-schmancy mansion or not, was no snob, even if the house she lived in did actually have a *name*. Whoever heard of naming a *house*? Linden Hall. Sounded like one of the buildings on the University's campus.

And Abby O'Connor, someone Kate had met through Susannah, was okay, too. Not that the three of them were best friends or anything. When they did go to the mall or a movie together, Kate's friends from Eastridge who saw them together had plenty of choice comments to make about "those white-bread girls you've been hangin' around with."

Oh, well. Who said life was supposed to be perfect?

Too bad the staff and other volunteers at MC couldn't see how smart and capable Susannah Grant was. It made them nervous to have Samuel Grant's daughter hanging around the place. Stupid. Susannah's father didn't *run* the complex. That monumental job was the responsibility of Caleb Matthews, parent to the biggest snob in town, one Miss Callie Nose-Up-In-The-Air Matthews. You'd think *she* ran the place.

Scooping her heavy shoulder bag off the back of a kitchen chair, Kate left the kitchen. At least Susannah had three allies at Med Center. There was Kate herself, and Kate's mother, head nurse in Emergency, and Will Jackson, a close friend of Kate's. They'd grown up together. Kate suspected that her parents had always hoped she and Will would become more than friends. Hadn't happened. Will's interests lay elsewhere these days. Kate was around Susannah and Will enough to feel the vibes. Not that they'd ever made a move toward each other. Maybe they never would. Life was tough enough without *that* particular complication.

Kate couldn't very well say, "Oh, go for it," which was pretty much how she felt, when neither had confided in her about their feelings for each other. That was *their* business, not hers.

Waiting at the corner for the bus to Med Center, she wondered what kind of mayhem and misery they'd see on this sunny, warm June Monday. It should repel her, she knew that. But it didn't. Partly because along with the mayhem and misery came miracles. She'd seen them with her own eyes. The heart attack victim who died on the table and was resuscitated, promising with great fervor that he would never, ever smoke a cigarette again. His wife wept in gratitude. The teenager whose arm had been ripped from his body by an auger while he was farming, the limb brought to the hospital in a plastic trash bag filled with ice cubes by his very sharp mother. The arm had been surgically reattached by a brilliant and skillful team of surgeons. Kate had seen that boy later, in Rehab. He'd been moving *both* arms, his eyes shining with relief and pride. He might have to quit the wrestling team, but at least he wasn't going to spend the rest of his life with only one arm. The tiny baby in Neonatal ICU, weighing no more than two and a half pounds and looking decidedly unfinished in his Isolette, his red, wrinkled form hooked up to half a dozen wires and tubes. Everyone at the center, nicknaming him "Peanut," had followed his progress. He'd gone home after two months, weighing slightly over five pounds. He was still a little peanut, but he wasn't blind and had no congenital defects, like some preemies. A lucky peanut.

It was endings like that that kept Kate enthralled with Med Center, and daily strengthened her resolve to have a career in medicine. A surgeon, maybe . . . orthopedic? The reattachment of that boy's arm had truly been a miracle. She would do something like that some day.

"Need a lift?" a voice called, and Kate pulled herself away from the image of herself striding down a white corridor, a stethoscope around her neck. She knew the boy leaning out of the old red truck's passenger window to address her. Damon Lawrence. A friend of Will's all through school until Damon dropped out. He was almost as gorgeous as Will, and she'd had a terrible crush on him when she was ten.

"No, thanks." Kate's voice was cool. She'd never heard of Damon getting into any trouble, but she couldn't forgive him for quitting school and ruining his chances of ever leaving Eastridge. He'd had good grades and was a super athlete. Could have had a scholarship, maybe. Why had he quit?

"Oh, come on, Kate," he pleaded, grinning at her. "I never see you anymore. You're always hiding out there at Bones 'n' Blood." His name for Med Center. Kate hated the nickname. Damon wasn't the only one who spoke that way about the complex, she knew that. There *were* people in Grant who resented the Grant family's wealth and power. Many of them extended that resentment to include Med Center.

"Wait till you need us," she retorted. "You'll change your tune fast enough." Hadn't she seen it happen with her own eyes? Someone who had bad-mouthed MC repeatedly would be brought into the place screaming, maybe bleeding, or doubled over in pain, and by the time they left, they couldn't say enough good things about the staff and the care they'd received.

Damon cocked an eyebrow. "Me? I'm healthy as a horse."

"And just as stupid," Kate said, turning away from him with a careless shrug. "Or you'd still be in school."

The grin disappeared. Muttering something Kate couldn't hear, he jerked away from the window and stomped down hard on the gas. The truck roared away.

What a waste! she thought angrily.

A few minutes later, the big blue-and-white bus arrived at the curb with a puff of smoke to pick up Kate and carry her off to Med Center.

chapter
4

Because Abby was teaching an early aerobics class in the Rehab building at Emsee, Susannah didn't have to pick her up as she usually did. She drove straight to the medical complex.

She never ceased to be awed by the very size of the place when she drove in through the open double gates at the entrance to Emergency's parking garage, a gray stone structure ten stories high. She stood at the back entrance to Emergency, glancing around with pride and the excitement that always overtook her when she left her car and was actually on the grounds of Med Center. The dozen and a half brick buildings of varying sizes were devoted to every area of medical care, including the Walter E. Miller Burn Unit, the Hazel Williams Neonatal Center for Infants and Children, the Psych building, and, to her left, the enormous Oncology building, where new strides in cancer treatment were made every day. There wasn't a physical problem that couldn't be treated at Med Center, and treated with the very best of care. And if there *wasn't* a treatment, it was very possible that the lab at Grant Pharmaceuticals, a long, low building nearly hidden from view in a thick grove of trees behind the complex, would come up with something.

Susannah was just turning to enter the building by its back entrance when she heard an approaching siren. Her heart began to pound as it always did at the sound. Someone whose life was in some way endangered was on his or her way to Med Center. She always wondered, as "incoming" arrived, if they realized, in their shock and pain, that they were coming to the right place. The absolutely right place.

She pushed the double swinging doors open and hurried inside, grabbing a smock off the rack beside the nurses' station as she passed it, signing in hurriedly, and then glancing around for some sign of Kate. She was already busy in one of the treatment rooms, Susannah saw through the glass windows, feeling a pang of envy. Kate was rushing around from table to counter to supply cabinet as a team of hospital personnel worked on a patient. Everyone in Emergency trusted Kate Thompson implicitly. Maybe it was because her mother was ER's head nurse. Whatever the reason, Kate had been asked to help in ten times the number of trauma cases that Susannah had.

Susannah knew that wasn't likely to change.

Not as long as she was Samuel Grant's daughter, and she expected to be that for the rest of her life.

The double doors burst open, and the EMTS raced in pushing a gurney, an IV held high above the patient's head.

Susannah ran ahead of the rushing gurney to fling open the double doors to a treatment room, then stood back and watched as the paramedics ran inside pushing the wheeled cart. Urgent calls went out over the PA system for staff. Susannah remained in the doorway as doctors and nurses came running and the paramedics barked out statistical information about the patient's condition: blood pressure, heart rate, temperature.

Susannah heard "temp, 104," and thought, Oh, wow, there's trouble. 104?

She knew the first moments after a patient arrived at Emergency were the most critical. Every second counted. Sometimes, no matter how prepared the staff was or how efficient, there were not enough moments and they lost the battle. Not often. The entire medical complex had one of the highest patient survival rates in the world, even in Oncology and Cardiac Care. Cancer and heart patients had the best chance of beating their illnesses at Med Center. The ER's survival rate was even higher.

Susannah caught only a glimpse of long, fever-matted blonde hair under the oxygen mask as the gurney raced ahead of her and came to a halt in the middle of the treatment room. The resident on call shouted, "Let's get some fluids into her, stat!"

Stat. Faster than immediately. Susannah nodded. Of course. With a fever that high, they would have to pump fluids into that girl fast.

The young doctor, a resident, took a quick look at the patient and asked the paramedics, "Any history? How long has she been sick? Parents here?"

"She collapsed on a playground. No family around. Will Jackson was going to get in touch with them, but he got called out on a run to the health club. Looks like flu to me, though."

"Get her parents!" the resident ordered. "I need a history."

Then, everyone gathered around the table began calling out statistics and orders at the same time. It was impossible to make out what they were saying, but Susannah knew the gist of it. Fluids in, stat, to combat the patient's dehydration. Dehydration in a human being could be fatal. Take some blood! Type and cross-match! Race the samples to the lab! Pay attention! Do as you're told, no questions asked. Hurry, hurry! No mistakes, this is a *life* in jeopardy here.

A new IV was set up beside the table, then a needle appeared, the first of many. Into the patient's left arm. Taped in place. Then more needles. Some to give aid. Some to take blood. And all the while, poking, prodding, lifting the patient's limbs, testing for mobility, rigidity, examining her eyes, her mouth, her ears, poking, prodding, searching for clues. A nurse repeatedly called to the patient in a loud voice, "Tina? Tina, can you hear me? You collapsed at the playground, Tina, you're at Med Center. Can you tell me where it hurts? How long have you been sick?"

Tina? Susannah knew a Tina. Tina Montgomery. They attended the same private day school. Jenkins Rue had a mad crush on her. But that couldn't be Tina Montgomery on that table. That Tina was strong and healthy. Susannah had seen her the night before, dancing with Jenkins. She hadn't looked sick. Not from a distance, anyway.

Still, that looked like her hair. . . .

More needles, more orders shouted from the attending physician, nurses running from table to supply cabinet, more poking and prodding of the patient. The orders came fast and furiously: aspirin, a refrigerating blanket, alcohol rubs, all designed to bring the dangerously high temperature down.

"Here!" a voice next to Susannah said, as two vials were thrust at her, "get these to the lab, stat!"

Thrilled to help, Susannah whirled and ran. And although she heard another siren die outside the entrance as she ran, she knew there was no time to stop and find out what else was happening. She kept going.

When she returned, another gurney was rushing down the hall toward her. Will Jackson, wearing his navy blue EMT jacket, ran along beside it. She knew better than to ask him any questions as he raced by. But she glimpsed anti-shock trousers on one of the patient's legs and guessed that the other leg was too seriously injured for confinement. She caught a glimpse of a face that looked as if it had been caved in with a heavy sledgehammer. Drying blood, the soft look of a broken or fractured cheekbone, the puffiness around the eye. If the patient had fallen, he or she must have landed face first.

Trusting the staff to handle this newest emergency, she returned to Tina's treatment room. She stood in the doorway, watching. The work at the table continued just as it had when she left. "Temp, 103," a nurse called out. Down one degree already, Susannah thought with satisfaction. The blanket was working.

When she glanced over her shoulder, the second gurney had disappeared, that patient already in good hands.

Her reaction inside a treatment room during an emergency was always the same. At first glance, it looked like complete and utter chaos. As if no one in the room had the foggiest notion what they were doing. All of the people gathered around the patient shouted at the same time. Two people might be barking out orders for X rays, or a tube down the patient's throat or nose, while someone else called for a chest line or ordered oxygen, or, in extreme cases, a "crash cart" to shock a stilled heart back into action. Still other voices called out vital statistics repeatedly. People scurried around in rubber-soled shoes collecting thermometers or oxygen masks or tubes or IV equipment, while others brought bandages, antiseptic solutions, hypodermic needles, whatever was needed to help the patient.

Although the treatment varied depending upon the state of the patient, the pace was always the same: rushed, frenetic, dizzying, just as it was in this case. Susannah thought of it as miraculous. In the midst of this horrendous, hectic scene, with everyone talking and shouting at the same time, with so many hands reaching across the patient for one piece of medical equipment or another, a life was being saved.

Incredible. That was always her first reaction.

Her second reaction was a fierce yearning to be a more important part of the process than she'd been so far. Was that ever going to happen?

"Miss Montgomery?" A nurse standing at the head of the table called to the patient in a loud voice, "Miss Montgomery, can you hear me?"

Susannah's eyes widened. That really *was* Tina Montgomery on the table.

She remembered then, her mother commenting at dinner one night last week . . . or was it the week before . . . that Tina had the flu. Mrs. Montgomery had told Caroline that Tina was being stubborn about seeing a doctor. Caroline, Susannah remembered now, had been concerned that Tina wouldn't be well enough to model in the Auxiliary's upcoming fashion show. Maybe she wouldn't. This looked a lot worse than a simple case of the flu.

As far as Susannah could tell from where she stood in the doorway, the nurse got no response from the stricken girl.

The tall, heavyset man in white, whom Susannah knew as Dr. Jonah Izbecki, said over the hubbub, "This girl hasn't stopped coughing since they brought her in. Get X Ray down here, stat!"

Because she was standing right beside the wall phone and because she wanted to help, Susannah whirled and picked up the receiver.

And realized she didn't have the faintest idea

how to call X Ray. No one had ever explained the interhospital phone system to her, and no operator came on the line. There were three-digit numbers next to each button, which did her no good at all since she didn't know which number referred to which department.

Kate came through the doorway just then, heard the order for X ray, and immediately sensed Susannah's dilemma. Without taking the receiver, which would have been humiliating for Susannah, Kate quickly reached up and punched in three numbers. Flushing with gratitude, Susannah ordered a portable X-ray unit and hung up, vowing to ask Kate to explain the code to her when (if?) they had a free moment together.

The X-ray order was a little puzzling. What did you X-ray when you suspected a case of the flu? Nothing. But Tina *was* still coughing, a hoarse, wrenching sound that bounced off the white walls. So it had to be Tina's chest that Dr. Izbecki intended to X-ray.

Maybe Tina had pneumonia. That could sometimes be a complication of the flu, especially if the patient ignored the symptoms as Tina had.

If what the patient had was a simple case of pneumonia, it could be treated and conquered with antibiotics. In someone as young and normally healthy as athletic Tina, pneumonia wouldn't be fatal.

But a simple case of pneumonia, Susannah thought with a stirring of uneasiness, wouldn't explain why Dr. Izbecki stepped away from the table just then and said, looking down at Tina, "I don't like this. I don't like this at all. This girl is very sick. She should have seen a doctor long before now. Are her parents here yet?"

His first two sentences seemed strange coming from a man who dealt with accidents and illness on a regular basis. He couldn't like *any* of it, could he? Was it just Tina's delay in seeking medical help that was bothering him? Or was there something else?

An orderly rushed in just then, pushing the portable X-ray machine. Susannah shoved the strange comment out of her mind, concentrating instead on the efforts to care for Tina Montgomery.

Two more doctors arrived, summoned by phone by Dr. Izbecki's nurse. One of them ordered Susannah to "go fetch this girl's parents!"

It wasn't much, but it was something. Susannah turned and ran again.

The first person she saw as she left the treatment room was Will Jackson. Still wearing his navy blue EMT jacket, he was leaning against the buttery-yellow wall in the hallway and sipping a cup of hot coffee. "How is she?" he asked Susannah.

"I don't know. Were you on the run that brought her in?"

"No." He shook his head. His dark eyes regarded Susannah seriously. "But I was at the playground delivering my nephew Benjamin when Tina collapsed. Coughed her lungs out and then just caved. I've never seen anything like it, and that's the truth. When I took her pulse, her skin felt like hot lava was running through her veins. I followed the ambulance in my own car, but the minute I got here, I had to go out on a run. So I hadn't heard how she was doing."

Susannah didn't know Tina Montgomery very well. Tina's father had a really important position at Grant Pharmaceuticals, which Susannah's father owned and ran, and the two families belonged to the same private country club, but Susannah spent little time there. Even if Tina's best friend at school hadn't been Callie Matthews, someone Susannah couldn't stand, she knew that she and Tina never could have been friends. They weren't the same kind of people at all.

Still, Susannah had no wish to see Tina in such dire straits. "I think she had the flu last week or the week before," she said to Will as she began to move on down the hall toward the visitors' waiting room. "Tina's mother told mine. Maybe it came back."

He shook his head negatively again, this time more emphatically. "This isn't the flu. Or if it is, it's a whole new strain, like that swine flu thing a few years back. I've never seen anyone this sick from the flu. Uh-oh," he added, "here come Momma and Poppa Bear."

Susannah turned her head to see a well-dressed couple advancing toward her. The woman was short and too plump for the tennis whites she was wearing, her blonde hair too long and curly for her age. The man was much taller, also slightly overweight, dressed for business in a gray suit. He looked angry, and as they moved up the hallway toward Susannah, she heard him say to the woman at his side, "How could you let it get this bad? The only thing I ask you to do is take care of our daughter, and you can't even do that right? Playing tennis, day and night, is *not* parenting! Meanwhile, my child has fallen so ill that she has to be taken by ambulance to the hospital! And I have to be dragged out of a very important meeting."

Then Astrid Thompson came out from behind her desk and in one smooth, calm movement, stopped the pair from continuing any further, spreading her hands in front of them to act as a barrier. "Mr. and Mrs. Montgomery," she said quietly, "if you'll just wait right here, Dr. Izbecki will be with you shortly. Why don't you have a seat right over there?" She pointed to a cluster of comfortable-looking upholstered chairs and thickly padded blue benches in a wide alcove filled with plants and a table holding a large, silver coffee urn and stacks of white Styrofoam cups.

The VIP suite, Susannah thought dryly.

"Izbecki?" Mr. Montgomery asked. "Listen, I don't want some newcomer with a strange name taking care of my little girl. You get me Joe Landis! Get him down here right now. He's a friend of mine. He'll know what to do for Tina."

"Dr. Landis is a neurologist, Mr. Montgomery," Nurse Thompson answered calmly, taking Mrs. Montgomery's elbow and ushering her gently but firmly into the alcove. "Your daughter doesn't need a neurologist. And Dr. Izbecki has been with us for nearly ten years. I'm surprised you aren't familiar with his name. Your daughter is getting the very best of care. Please don't worry." When she left to summon Dr. Izbecki, Susannah went back to stand beside Will.

She always felt secure when Will was around. He was the youngest paramedic at ER, but he was always so professional, so calm and efficient, reassuring patients in a gentle but firm voice as he ran alongside the gurney to a treatment room. She had come close, many times, to telling him how much she admired his work, but each time she'd hesitated, afraid it would sound patronizing.

She had no way of knowing that praise from her would have made Will Jackson very happy.

"Who was the second incoming? The run you were on?" she asked him quietly. "I heard the ambulance and caught a glimpse of the patient, but I had to run to the lab." She said the last part proudly, glad that she'd been of some use.

"Jenkins," he said grimly.

Susannah gasped. "Jenkins Rue? What happened? He didn't crash on his bike, did he?"

"No. Fell from a scaffolding at the health center. Fell more than two stories. To cement. One leg's a mess, and he could have a head injury."

Susannah's left hand flew to her mouth. "Oh, God, is he . . . is he . . . he's not dead, is he?"

"Wasn't when we brought him in. Pulse thready, though, and I wouldn't want to guess at how many broken bones he's got. But he was still alive. Funny thing, though," Will added, crumpling his cup and tossing it into a nearby wastebasket, "his temp was 103. And that couldn't have been from the fall."

On Susannah's left, the noisy, hectic efforts continued in Tina's treatment room, while behind her, in another hallway, she could hear the same kind of sounds from a different room.

She knew now, her heart sinking at the thought, that what she was hearing was a concentrated effort to keep a friend of hers, a boy

named Jenkins Rue, who owned just about nothing, from losing the one thing he *did* own, free
and clear. His life.

Telling Will she'd see him later, she turned and
raced down the hall to see if she could help. No,
not "if." Not this time. This time, she *was* going
to help.

chapter
5

Jenkins's room, when she entered, was even more chaotic than Tina's had been. There were at least eight people working on the patient, their hands moving rapidly around his body. Susannah saw blood on the jeans that had been cut away to reveal the injured limb. That was no simple fracture. If he was hoping for an athletic scholarship to college, what would this injury do to his chances?

"Blood pressure falling!" someone at the table shouted. "Eighty over sixty!"

Susannah knew the falling pressure could indicate serious internal injuries. A sharp request for more units of blood quickly followed. A nurse rushed to obey the order. One of the doctors ran to the wall phone to summon an orthopedic surgeon. Susannah recognized the name. The damage must be really bad if Jenkins needed surgery on the leg, instead of a simple setting of the bone, and a plaster cast.

Susannah hesitated just inside the doorway, not sure what to do to make her presence known. When a nurse ran over to the wall to make a call, Susannah said quickly, "If he needs blood, maybe I could give it. Let me do something. I want to *do* something." The nurse nodded, made her phone call, and hung up. But before she returned to the table, she gave Susannah a long look and asked, "You know him?"

"I know who he is. He's not going to die, is he?"

"Don't know yet. Here," she said, handing Susannah a clipboard. "Pay attention to vitals and write them down on here when they're called out. Don't make any mistakes, okay?"

Her stomach churning anxiously, Susannah gripped the board and ran with the nurse back to the table.

Jenkins was unconscious. Tubes and wires ran from his body to various pieces of medical equipment. His skin was chalky, his eyes closed. The entire right side of his face was bloody and beginning to purple, in sharp contrast to the whiteness of his skin. But it was the leg that had suffered the most damage. Susannah had to steel herself to keep from gasping at the sight of the pulpy, bloody mess. Two doctors were working on it at the same time, while two nurses tended to blood pressure and respiration. The very second they called out a new figure, Susannah immediately printed it on the chart in her hands. Her fingers clutched the pen so tightly, her knuckles turned white. She was terrified of making a mistake.

Intent on what she was doing, she jumped, startled, when the orthopedic surgeon who had just arrived barked, "This kid's burning up! I can't operate until he's stable, but the leg won't wait that long."

A hurried, animated discussion between the two doctors began as to the best course of treatment. They continued to work as they argued, and Susannah continued to write down Jenkins Rue's vital statistics as they were called out.

While Susannah worked in Emergency at the rear of the building, a petite, pretty girl wearing a white halter-neck dress and high-heeled white sandals, shiny blonde hair swinging around her shoulders, an unpleasant downturn to her full, pink mouth, hurried with a sense of purpose across the spacious lobby at the front of the building. The pink-smocked woman at the reception desk called out as she passed, "Hello, Miss Matthews. Stopping in to see your father?" She received no response.

Callie Matthews, giving no sign that she had heard the greeting, continued to click-clack in her heels straight to the elevators. She took one of the cages up to the tenth floor. Her father, Caleb Matthews, Med Center's Chief Administrator, and his staff, occupied a suite of offices there that took up all of the tenth and eleventh floors.

Callie loved visiting her father. Nowhere else, not even in their luxurious split-level stone home on the outskirts of Grant, did she feel as strong a sense of power as she did when she stepped out of the elevator onto the thick, copper-colored carpeting. Facing her were dark-paneled walls hung with framed pictures of Grant ancestors and former Med City administrators. Her father's picture would be on that wall one day. In the meantime, the thought that her very own father *ran* this huge, eighteen-building complex known and respected all over the *world* made her feel much taller than her five feet plus one inch.

Of course, she thought as she marched along the hallway toward the door with her father's name on it, there was a downside, too. He was hardly ever home. And her mother was too sick most of the time to be any company. She tried. On her good days, they went shopping and sometimes to the Club, although Althea Matthews, a victim of chronic kidney disease, had long since stopped playing tennis or swimming. Mostly, she just sat, looking even more yellowish and wan than usual in the midst of all the other tanned, healthy mothers.

Callie never would have told anyone, except maybe Tina, but one of the reasons she visited her father so much was, it made her feel better to see how healthy he looked. At least one of her parents wasn't sick. He was losing his hair, and she loathed his choice of ties, always unbelievably garish in color, but he was healthy. Hadn't been sick a day in his life.

So she dropped in as often as she could, even though she knew it sometimes annoyed him because he was so busy. She understood that, because just *think* of all he had to do, running a health complex that last year treated 25,000 patients, performed 14,000 operations, and treated 58,000 patients at Emergency Services. A new patient was admitted every twelve minutes at Med Center, and a new operation begun in the Surgical building or in Emergency every thirty minutes. While she understood how unbelievably busy that made her father's job, she still had a right to see him.

Callie's lips curved upward. Her *father* was the boss of this huge, busy, very important place!

His secretary, Lindsay Cutler, wasn't at her desk outside of his office. Inside taking dictation, maybe. Didn't matter. If she had been there, she wouldn't have tried to keep Callie out unless Caleb was in a very important meeting. Maybe because he knew how hard it was for a teenager to have a semi-invalid mother, her father really did try to make time for her whenever he could. And tall, beautiful Lindsay (incredibly *healthy* Lindsay) had her orders. She was to allow Callie free access to her one healthy parent whenever possible.

Callie grabbed a hairbrush from her white shoulder bag and quickly ran the brush through her hair. Then she marched up to the door that bore her father's name on a polished brass plate near the top and, hoping that he just might take her to dinner at the Club, threw the door open.

To find her father embracing his secretary in the center of the huge, luxurious office.

Callie froze. A sound somewhere between a gasp and a cry left her mouth, startling the pair and causing them to draw apart and turn toward the door. Lindsay had obviously been crying.

"Dad!" Callie accused.

Her father, reading the expression on her face, took a step forward, saying, "Now, wait just a minute, Callie . . ."

Without waiting to hear the rest of what he had to say, Callie whirled and tore out of the room, blonde hair flying out behind her as she ran.

Her father's voice called after her, but she kept going. Instead of heading for the elevators, where she would have to wait and he might catch up with her, she ran to the stairway door and yanked it open. Then she raced down the stairs. When she reached the eighth floor, she left the staircase and emerged into the hall, where she picked up an elevator.

The whole time she was running, Callie had to fight back tears. She would *not* cry, she would *not!* Let that witch Lindsay cry if she wanted to, but not Callie Matthews. Crying was for babies. She wasn't a baby. Hadn't been for a long, long time.

Riding down in the elevator with four student nurses in uniforms, two doctors, and a maintenance man carrying a tool kit, Callie decided angrily that Lindsay had probably only been pretending to cry. Her pathetic attempt at making Caleb Matthews feel sorry for her, just so she could snare him, was disgusting. She'd probably wanted to get her hooks into him ever since the first day she'd come to work at Med Center. She knew he was rich and powerful. And she had to know he had a sick wife. Probably thought that made him an easy target.

And it looked like she'd been right!

At that moment, Callie hated the student nurses, whispering and giggling alongside of her. And she hated the two doctors, with their stupid white jackets and their stupid stethoscopes hanging around their stupid necks. Why did they wear them all the time, anyway? They weren't treating patients in the elevators. Show-offs!

She even hated the maintenance man, because he worked at Med Center. How could she ever have been proud that her father ran this horrible place? If it weren't for Med Center, he'd be home more and he'd have time to take her to dinner once in a while and he wouldn't be hugging Lindsay Cutler. There wouldn't *be* any Lindsay Cutler, at least not in her father's life, if it weren't for Med Center.

She especially hated every single one of the Grants, past, present, and future, because if it weren't for them, there would be no Med Center in the first place. This was all their fault.

If it crossed Callie's mind as she hurried from the elevator that the medical complex she suddenly hated with a fierce rage was also keeping her mother alive, she pushed the thought away. She was too full of shock and fury to think about that now.

As she emerged from the elevator and ran from the building, the pink lady at the reception desk called out cheerfully, "You have a nice day now, Miss Matthews!"

I don't *think* so, Callie thought bitterly as she pushed her way through the glass revolving door.

Tina. She needed Tina. Tina would understand. Tina's father, who worked for Samuel Grant himself at Grant Pharmaceuticals, traveled a lot, so Tina would know better than anyone exactly how Callie was feeling. Maybe that was why they were best friends.

Yeah, right, Callie thought, almost laughing as she emerged, blinking against the bright sunshine. *That's* not why we're best friends. We're best friends because we like the same things.

49

Nice clothes. Brand-new, expensive sports cars. Tina's canary yellow, mine robin's-egg blue. Even our cars are birds of a feather, so to speak. We like being pretty and well dressed and having money and living in the nicest houses in town and belonging to the country club. What we *don't* like is how hard our fathers have to work to make those things possible.

Tina would definitely understand.

In her robin's-egg blue convertible, Callie drove, very fast, to Tina's house, an enormous red brick colonial nestled in the foothills far below the Grant mansion.

No one answered her ring. Callie frowned in annoyance, as if Tina had deliberately made it a point not to be home when Callie needed her.

Maybe Tina and her mother had gone to the Club. If they had, she'd wangle a dinner invitation with them. Then she wouldn't have to eat alone. Her own mother's dialysis treatment that morning had left her drained. She wouldn't be eating much more than a bowl of soup for dinner, if she ate at all.

And her father was clearly out of the question now as a dinner companion. Probably still comforting Miss Tear-Ducts.

Callie turned around and was about to run down the steps, back to her car, when an elderly man working in his garden across the street called out to her, "You looking for the Montgomery girl?"

She nodded and continued on down the steps.

He walked across the road to meet her at her car. "You haven't heard?"

"Heard what?" Callie pulled her car keys out of her purse.

"Your friend's at the hospital, Miss. My wife heard about it at the Club. Seems your friend collapsed at that day camp over at Med Center. Some kind of flu or something. Her mother came down these steps a little bit ago and tore off in her car. Must have been going to the hospital."

"Hospital?" Callie asked, her mouth suddenly gone dry. "No, that can't be right! Tina can't be in the hospital. She was fine last night. Coughing a little bit, but . . . how sick is she?"

The man shook his head. "Don't know, Miss. The wife and I have been waiting for the girl's parents to get home, so we could ask. Wouldn't want them to think we weren't concerned. But no one's come back yet. Are you one of the girl's friends?"

"I'm her *best* friend," Callie said emphatically. "But I didn't know she was in the hospital."

"You might want to call over there, see how she is, since there's no one here to ask."

"Call? I'm not going to *call*! I'm going over there!" Forgetting to thank him for the information, Callie got back into her car and drove to Med Center, wondering as the car raced along the broad, tree-lined boulevard if anything more could possibly go wrong with this beautiful, sunny, but perfectly horrible June day.

chapter
6

In treatment room number five, where doctors continued to work over Jenkins Rue, Susannah said to a nurse passing by with a syringe, "There's another patient in ER with a high fever."

The nurse stopped in her tracks. "What did you say?"

In spite of the high noise level in the room, the doctors at the table overheard. Heads swiveled to stare at Susannah.

She flushed self-consciously. "I wasn't sure if you knew. They brought in a girl from my school a little while ago. She's really sick. The flu, I guess. Anyway, her temp was 104." She waved a hand toward the table.

"Check it out!" one of the doctors ordered the nurse.

She nodded and handed the syringe to another nurse. "You come with me," she told Susannah. "Show me where the girl is."

They left the room and hurried down the hall to where Susannah had last seen Tina.

The room had been cleared. The table was

bare. A nurse was replacing medical supplies in a wall cabinet. She looked up as Susannah and the nurse opened the door and stood just over the threshold.

Susannah frowned. "What happened to the girl who was in here?"

"Upstairs. ICU."

The Intensive Care Unit. "She's that sick?"

"No diagnosis yet?" the nurse with Susannah asked.

"Flu, maybe. She should have seen a doctor days ago, from the look of things. Dr. Izbecki ordered every culture known to man, and a ton of blood work, but no lab results yet. Too soon. Why?"

"We've got another one, down the hall. Accident victim, but he's burning up with fever. I thought there might be a connection."

"Maybe there is. I know the flu's been going around. We've had quite a few cases in here. None as bad as this girl, though. We got her temp down some, but I wouldn't be surprised if it shot right back up again. Anyway, she's up in ICU. Dr. Izbecki's in the cafeteria having lunch if you need to talk to him."

"Thanks."

As they left the room, the nurse said to Susannah, "I'd better go find Dr. Izbecki. I need more info to take back with me. Why don't you go have lunch? There's nothing more you can do for that boy. You've been a big help. None of us knew there was another patient. Thanks."

Susannah felt a warm glow of satisfaction as the nurse hurried away. She had actually done something to help.

"Hey, Sooz, what's up? Ready for lunch?"

Susannah turned. The only person who ever called her "Sooz" was Abby O'Connor, her best friend. "A *lot* is up," she answered as she faced Abby, who was shorter, darker, and rounder than Susannah, and dressed in khaki pants and a camouflage jacket. "I'll tell you over pasta salad. Have you seen Will? I need to ask him something."

Abby grinned, her dark eyes sparkling. "He's right behind you," she said. "So is Kate." Abby was the only person who knew how much Susannah admired Will Jackson. But she had been sworn to secrecy. She wouldn't tell anyone. Abby wasn't like that. She was loyal to the bone. Susannah would have trusted Abby O'Connor with her life.

When Susannah turned around again, tall, lanky Will was smiling down at her. "What did you want to ask me?"

But before she could ask her question, a door swung open and Callie Matthews burst through it, eyes narrowed, hair flying out around her shoulders. "*Where* is Tina?" she demanded of the quartet gathered near the watercooler. "Someone told me she was here. What's wrong with her? Why didn't somebody tell me?"

"You just said someone *did*," Kate answered coolly. If there was one person who could ruin her day, it was Callie Matthews, tanned a glowing bronze and all dressed up in white like Malibu Barbie.

"I mean, someone from *here*!" Callie snapped. "From Med Center. I had to find out from one of Tina's neighbors that she was sick."

"Well, you're not a relative," Susannah said patiently. "Only relatives are notified when a patient's brought in, Callie." Callie's eyes were slightly pink. Had she been crying because of Tina? Did Callie's feelings go that deep? Hard to believe.

"But I'm her best friend!" Callie glanced up and down the busy corridor. A young man on crutches eyed her appreciatively as he passed, narrowly avoiding crashing into a linen cart. "Where is she, anyway? Can I see her?"

"I don't think so," Will said slowly. "She's up in ICU. No one's allowed in there but family." He pointed toward the alcove. "Her parents are over there, though, if you want to wait with them. They can't go upstairs to see Tina until Dr. Izbecki gives them the go-ahead. Maybe they can give you more information."

Callie hesitated, frowning. "What's wrong with Tina?" Then her pretty, tanned face paled slightly as she added nervously, "It's not catching, is it? What she has?"

Kate let out a scornful half-laugh. "Your concern is so touching, Callie. Don't worry, if it was catching, they'd have put your best friend in Isolation, and they haven't done that. So relax. Anyway, she's probably just got a bad case of the flu."

The boy who came around a corner just then and called out Callie's name was of average height, with wide shoulders and short, blonde hair. He would have been good-looking if a look of discontentment hadn't shadowed his features. He hurried over to the group. "I just heard about Tina," he said as he arrived. "What's the matter with her?"

Jeremy Barlow went to the same private day school that Callie, Tina, and Susannah attended. His father was Emsee's famous, highly respected Chief of Cardiology. Jeremy, whose mother had left her family several years earlier to pursue a writing career in California, spent as much time as possible at Med Center in hopes of catching a few moments with the only parent left to him. Susannah suspected that he and Callie were friends because their family situations were similar. With one major difference: Callie's mother was sick, while Jeremy's had simply walked out of the house one day with two suitcases and a laptop computer. And without her son.

As far as Susannah was concerned, that explained why Jeremy seemed moody. Wouldn't anyone be who had been abandoned by his own mother?

"They said Tina might have the flu," Callie told him. "I don't see how the flu could put someone in Intensive Care. That sounds very weird to me." She shrugged. "But that's what they're saying." She glanced at Kate with obvious disdain as she spoke. "Of course," she added, taking Jeremy's arm and beginning to lead him over to the alcove, "they're not doctors or nurses. We should probably talk to someone who is. But first, we'll see what Tina's parents have to say, right?"

Jeremy allowed himself to be led along the hallway.

"Why do I feel like I've just been stepped on?" Kate asked, her eyes on the pair as they arrived in the alcove. Tina's parents stood up to greet them.

"She's not the most tactful person in the world," Susannah said sympathetically. "She and Jeremy make a good pair. Neither one of them is exactly a ray of sunshine."

"Yeah, but Jeremy has a good excuse." Abby's usually cheerful face was somber. "I can't imagine how it must feel to have your mother take off like Mrs. Barlow did. And leave you behind."

"Well, Callie's mother is sick," Susannah said, "so in a way, Callie's been abandoned, too. At least, she probably feels like she has."

"That's no excuse for acting like a queen addressing the peasants," Kate said. "If she thinks I'm going to curtsy when she shows up just because her father runs this place, she is crazy."

Leaving Callie and Jeremy to Tina's parents, the four took an elevator downstairs to the cafeteria.

"Now," Abby said firmly when they were all seated in the large, noisy room surrounded by tables filled with doctors and nurses in white or surgical green, "tell me what's been going on. Does Tina really have the flu?"

Susannah, with some help from Will, filled her in on the hectic arrivals of Tina and Jenkins.

Abby was shocked by the news about Jenkins. "He's not going to die, is he? I mean, it's not *that* serious, is it?" She liked Jenkins. She had talked with him a couple of times when he was doing the windows at Rehab and liked his dry sense of humor.

"He fell two and a half stories, Ab," Susannah pointed out. "His leg is a mess. The weird thing is, I think the doctors were a lot more worried about his fever than the injuries from his fall. I guess because they needed to stabilize him for surgery and his temp was getting in the way. And the other weird thing is, Callie was right about ICU almost never having flu patients. Unless they're really old or have other problems."

"If you go back to Jenkins Rue's treatment room," Kate said, "maybe you should put on a mask, so you won't get sick, too. I think I'm going to."

Susannah found that suggestion sobering. A mask? For the flu? Still, she didn't want to get sick, so maybe Kate was right.

"Anyone feel like hitting The Music Room tonight?" Abby asked as they were getting ready to leave. "Steam Engine is still there. The best band they've had in town in ages." She grinned at Susannah. "And all four of the guys are really cute. Sooz and I are going."

Susannah sighed. "Wrong. I can't go, and neither can you. I forgot, there's a fashion show rehearsal tonight. My mother's expecting us." She thought for a minute, then added, "Listen, Kate, if Tina is still too sick and can't model, would you take her place?" Kate would make a gorgeous model. With those long legs? Perfect! "The clothes are going to be gorgeous, I promise, and we each get a free outfit."

"Model? Me?" Kate envisioned the clothes she would have to wear. Probably all ruffles and lace and pastels. Or maybe those boring classic styles that Susannah's mother wore when she came to the hospital. "I don't think so."

"Oh, come on," Susannah begged. "You'd be perfect, and you know it. There's a sportswear collection you'd look fantastic in. Please?"

Abby and Will joined in then, and the three of them, to Susannah's relief, managed to convince Kate that the fund-raising event could be fun.

"And we'll go to The Music Room tomorrow night, okay? I promise." Susannah jumped up. "Thanks, Kate. My mother will be thrilled."

"Can I have a ride home, Sooz?" Abby asked. "My mom dropped me off this morning. And can you stay over tonight?"

"Sure." Susannah had no desire to spend the evening alone in the house on the hill. Her parents had a concert to attend, and Sam wouldn't be home. Sam was never home.

"Well, I'm going back up to see how Jenkins is doing," Kate said. "Meet you up there, okay?"

"Yep." Susannah hurried off to call her mother, who would be upset to learn that Tina Montgomery was in Intensive Care, but delighted with the news that Kate had agreed to model.

On a side street in downtown Grant, an eighteen-year-old girl and her twelve-year-old brother were racing each other on Rollerblades. The boy laughed triumphantly as he easily pulled ahead of his older sister, not noticing in his glee that she had slowed considerably. She was still moving, but her gait was unsteady and her gloved hands moved up to touch her temples beneath the silver-and-black helmet she was wearing. Even if he had glanced over his shoulder, he wouldn't have been concerned by the scarlet flush on her face, thinking it had been caused by the exertion of their race.

Because he kept going, determined to stay ahead of her, he was almost a full block away when she began staggering on her skates, her hands still at her temples. Seized by a sudden coughing bout, she cried out weakly. She reached out with her hands as if to grasp something, but found nothing to grasp. Reeling dizzily, she staggered backward and fell out into the street, directly in front of an old red Ford pickup truck occupied by an elderly couple looking for the flea market. Because they weren't sure exactly where they were going, the truck was moving slowly. But the girl hit it hard, slamming backward into the passenger's door with a sharp, thwacking sound and bouncing off. She fell to the rough pavement, her hands flying out in front of her in an effort to break her fall.

The truck screeched to a halt.

The sound of its brakes brought the boy up sharply at the corner. His head whipped around. When he saw his sister's helmet lying in the street, his face drained of all color. He whirled sharply and flew back up the street on his skates to drop to his knees beside her, calling out her name.

She didn't answer.

chapter
7

Susannah and Kate arrived in Jenkins's treatment room to find the patient in the throes of a violent seizure. His body bucked wildly. His arms flailed at the air around him, and his legs, including the injured limb, kicked out frantically. The doctors and nurses at his side struggled to restrain him. A nurse who rushed to the table, hypodermic needle in hand, found it impossible to administer the sedative.

"Don't just stand there!" one of the doctors called to the pair standing openmouthed in the doorway, "get over here and help!"

Susannah got there first, and was immediately sideswiped by a flailing foot, which sent her staggering backward. Kate took her place at the table, grabbing for an ankle, seizing it, helping to hold that leg down. Susannah quickly regained her balance and pushed between two nurses who were trying valiantly to hold Jenkins's arm steady long enough for the hypo to find its target. With her help, they were able to do just that. When the medication took hold and the seizure ended, Jenkins's body finally went limp on the table.

"Take him up to X ray," one of the doctors ordered, standing back and stripping off his rubber gloves. "I want a CAT scan, stat! I've got another patient in six to look at, but I'll be up when I'm done."

As the patient was rushed from the room, Susannah looked at Kate quizzically. A brain scan? But it was Jenkins's leg that was most seriously injured.

One of the nurses noticed the look and said abruptly, "Could be the fever that caused the seizure. Maybe. But he could also have a serious head injury. We don't know how hard he hit his skull when he fell. His brain could be mush. Dr. Stiles just wants to make sure it isn't, that's all."

Susannah winced at the language. She still wasn't used to it. Kate's mother had explained to both girls that the only way some doctors and nurses could survive what they saw every day in ER was by talking and acting tough. Pretending it didn't touch them. "But it does," she had added softly. "You'd have to have a heart of stone not to be touched by it, and people with hearts of stone don't go into medicine in the first place."

"Some do," Kate had disagreed.

"If they do, they don't last," Astrid Thompson

insisted. "You have to *care* to do this every day of your life. It's essential."

With Tina already up in ICU and Jenkins on his way to Radiology, Susannah and Kate left to return to their earlier tasks, Susannah sorting insurance forms, Kate filling cabinet shelves with fresh linens.

"You didn't put a mask on before you went into that room," Kate said as they approached the nurses' station.

"Neither did you. None of the staff had them on, either, so I guess there's nothing to worry about. They're pretty careful about that kind of thing."

Kate looked dubious. "How would we know that? There hasn't been anything contagious in ER since we came on the scene. A few head colds and some flu cases, that's all."

That was true. But Susannah trusted the staff, and was positive they *would* be careful if something serious and contagious came along. No one wanted to get sick. They all saw too much of what illness could do. If masks were needed, the staff would wear them. Quickly.

Susannah and Kate had been working at their respective tasks for no more than three or four minutes when a siren died outside again, and then, almost simultaneously, another. Dropping what they were doing, they ran to the entrance to help with incoming, along with several nurses and orderlies.

The first case was a terminally ill cancer patient. He was so emaciated and unaware, Susannah could tell just by looking at him that he probably would never leave the hospital alive again. Knowing she wouldn't be needed and a little reluctant to be involved with a case that allowed no hope, she let Kate go with that stretcher to help with the paperwork, and she waited for the second incoming.

She knew the minute she saw the face that this was another case like Tina and Jenkins. The flushed skin, the eyes rolled back in the head, the coughing, all were unmistakable signs by now.

Will was on the second ambulance. He filled Susannah in as they ran down the corridor alongside of the wheeled cart carrying the patient. "Rollerblading accident," he said quickly. "Female, eighteen years old, hit a truck. No visible injuries from the collision, but whatever Tina has, this one's got it, too. Younger brother, with her at the time, said she wasn't feeling well, but he talked her into a race anyway. He's feeling guilty. Maybe you could talk to him?"

Susannah glanced behind her. A young boy, his face filled with remorse, his feet still encased in black in-line skates, sat on a chair in the hallway, his eyes never leaving the departing gurney carrying his sister. Two helmets — one silver and black, one yellow — dangled from his hands.

She was about to go to him when a third gurney burst through the doors. More nurses and orderlies ran to greet it. Medical information flew, rapid fire, from the mouths of the paramedics. Susannah didn't catch the BP or the heart rates they shouted, but she did hear, "Fifty-three-year-old male, collapsed on the job, foreman of a cleaning crew on duty in the Psych building," and then she heard, "temp, 103," and her heart sank. Another one? What was going *on*?

Susannah moved to comfort the brother of the Rollerblading accident victim.

By midafternoon, with four patients admitted who were suffering from a fever of "unexplained origin," the order had come down from above. All staff members in Emergency were to put on masks, gown, and rubber gloves before treating any patient with a fever above 101 degrees.

"We still believe it's the flu," Astrid Thompson told Susannah, Kate, and Will when she had summoned them into her office. "No lab test results yet, but they're very busy up there. I was here in 1992 when a new, vicious strain of flu hit. We weren't careful enough, and I can tell you that it's almost impossible to run a hospital with half the staff out sick. The administration isn't taking any chances this time. So masks, gloves, and gowns it is, even if you don't expect to have any physical contact with the patients. The order has come down for ICU to isolate the cases we have now, so that's being done. We're blocking off the eighth floor and sending other ICU patients to other hospitals in the complex until we know more about this fever. And if it gets too bad here," she added, looking directly at the three, "I'll have to make the treatment rooms off-limits to you girls. I can't order Will away, because he's a paramedic and has to deliver incoming. But I'd have to answer to your parents if you fell ill, Susannah." Her mouth tightened. "And I'm sure I don't have to remind you that your father is not all that happy about your volunteer work here in the first place."

Susannah nodded. She needed no reminding. Samuel Grant had had a fit when she told him what she intended to do. He thought she should be out partying, like her twin, enjoying what he called her "privileged youth" instead of "ministering to the sick" and, he had actually said, "downtrodden." Downtrodden? She had almost laughed. The richest people in the world came to Med Center. Kings, queens. Political leaders. Artists, authors, film stars, rock stars, people who had been born to wealth and could pay for the very best of everything—all flocked to Med

Center seeking a cure for one ailment or another. Downtrodden? She didn't *think* so.

Nurse Thompson stood up. "I wouldn't want to make an enemy of the most powerful man in town," she told Susannah, and it seemed to the embarrassed girl that the nurse's tone was unusually cool. Kate probably felt the same way. Didn't want to be a really good friend to any daughter of Samuel Grant's. Did Will feel that way, too? Was he afraid of her father? Afraid of who she was? Was that why, although he was nice enough to her, she felt this . . . this wall between them?

She had wondered if it was because she was white. Maybe that didn't have anything to do with it. Maybe instead it was who she was, where she lived, what she had, and especially, who her father was. He didn't run the hospital, but he could certainly see to it that Astrid Thompson lost her job if his only daughter fell seriously ill while working in ER. He could do that. And, Susannah had to admit reluctantly, he probably would.

"One more thing," they were told before they left, "you were instructed in your training that no information about any patient leaves this hospital with you. I realize that rule is broken so often as to be almost useless, but in this case, I have been told to reiterate it for you. You are not to discuss these four new cases with anyone, is that clear?"

All three nodded silently. Susannah remembered with a pang of guilt their discussion at lunch. All of them had discussed Tina and Jenkins with Abby. Abby would have to be warned not to repeat anything she'd heard.

"I mean this!" the head nurse stressed. "Kate, no mention of this to anyone! Do I have your promise?"

They promised.

"Good! And remember, masks, gowns, and gloves tomorrow when you come in. Although by then we'll probably have the lab results. We'll know definitely that it's the flu and we can proceed with the proper treatment. You may go now."

Abby was waiting when Susannah emerged alone into late-afternoon sunshine. Kate was still inside, waiting for the end of her mother's shift. They would go home together. Susannah felt a pang of envy. When did her family ever do anything together? Her parents went to parties and concerts and the opera; Sam attended countless parties that Susannah wasn't invited to; and she did things with her friends. But as a family, they did very little together.

Kate would stare at her in disbelief if Susannah ever said she envied Kate anything, anything at all. She who had everything.

Yeah, right.

She waited until they were in the car before repeating Nurse Thompson's warning to Abby.

"If it's just the flu," Abby said, glancing over at Susannah from the passenger's seat, "why the hush-hush? That doesn't make any sense."

"Sometimes flu becomes an epidemic. People die, sometimes," Susannah explained as she steered the Jeep carefully along the curving lanes of the ten-story parking garage. "If that's what's happening, telling people could cause a mild panic. We'd be inundated with people demanding flu shots. That wouldn't be good. I'm not even sure that ER has stocked up on a flu vaccine. Kate's mother didn't say."

"Well, they could get some fast enough. Wouldn't Grant Pharmaceuticals have it? This all sounds kind of weird to me, Susannah. Are Tina and Jenkins really that sick?"

"Yes. They wouldn't be in ICU Isolation if it wasn't serious, you know that. They took Jenkins up there right after they operated on his leg. And we've had two more cases, Abby. A girl who was Rollerblading, and an older man. They're all in ICU now. They've had practically every test and culture there is. X rays, too. And as far as I know, nobody has a clue about what's wrong with them." Susannah hadn't meant to mention the other two cases, but once the words were out of her mouth, she decided it was the right thing to say. If Abby understood that something unusual was going on, she'd understand why Emsee's administration didn't want it talked about outside of the hospital.

On a tree-lined street not far from Med Center, Susannah pulled up in front of a low, sprawling, brick ranch house.

A tall, tanned woman in bare feet, shorts, and a white T-shirt stood on the front porch, where she was watering hanging baskets of red and white flowers. Waving the brown plastic watering can toward the Jeep in greeting, she kept her other arm wrapped tightly around the dark-haired toddler she was carrying on one hip. "Hey, there!" she called. "C'mon up!" and she disappeared inside the house.

Susannah smiled as she jumped from the Jeep. Abby's mother never seemed to care if there were one or two or even six more people in her house at any given time. With six kids, a husband, and a father-in-law in residence, her attitude seemed to be, What's one or two or six more?

Inside, the O'Connor house was, as always, neat. A miracle, it seemed to Susannah, considering the crowd that occupied the bright, sunny space. The furniture might be a little worn and mismatched, the drapes a little faded, but the house was always in order. Susannah knew that everyone who lived there, including the smallest children, helped maintain that order. Even

Toothless, not quite two years old, was learning to put her toys away.

There it was again, Susannah thought with a pang, that family thing. Doing stuff together. The Grant family didn't clean house together because the Grant family didn't *clean* house. Other people were paid to do it for them.

In spite of the organized household, most mornings when Susannah arrived to pick up Abby for school or Med Center duty, her best friend was inevitably racing around the house, short, curly, dark hair like her mother's bobbing around her face as she called out, "Anybody seen my other sneaker?" (notebook, keys, purse . . .)

She was unquestionably adorable, with wide dark eyes, smooth skin, and full lips that always seemed turned up at the corners as if she were about to smile at any moment. As for the slight extra weight Abby had, it looked good on her. No sharp edges to Abby, just as there was nothing sharp-edged about her personality.

Susannah felt more at home in the O'Connor house than she ever did in her own house. Saying that aloud would have been a knife in her mother's heart, so she kept the thought to herself. Sam knew. He didn't like it, possibly because Abby was one of maybe three girls in the entire city whose heart didn't beat faster at the sight of Samuel Grant III and who didn't try to use Susannah to get to him. But he never commented at home about Susannah's preference for the O'Connor household over her own. Not while their mother was around.

They'd been in the house less than a minute when the phone rang. A boy . . . for Abby.

Knowing she'd be on the telephone at least ten minutes, Susannah took a seat on a high stool at the breakfast bar in the kitchen. With the baby in her arms and four-year-old Matthew, the only male child in the family clinging to her shorts, Mrs. O'Connor still managed to pour Susannah a glass of orange juice and set it in front of her.

"What's wrong with Mattie?" Susannah asked. "He doesn't usually trail around attached to you like that." On the contrary, the little boy was ordinarily out of the house, playing in the tree house out back or visiting a friend or frolicking in the community pool with one of his sisters.

"I think he might be coming down with a cold," Mrs. O'Connor said worriedly. "He's not himself today, are you, Mattie?" She patted his dark head.

"Don't!" he complained, rubbing his scalp. "That hurts."

His mother handed the baby to Susannah and crouched beside her small son. "Your head hurts?" She placed a hand on his forehead. It was clear from her expression that he was warmer than normal.

He nodded. "And my tummy hurts, too. Nap-time, Mommy."

Susannah's stomach lurched. The thought of sweet, adorable Matthew lying on a gurney at the hospital as ill as Tina and Jenkins made her sick.

His mother stood up, sending Susannah a worried look. "He *never* asks to go to bed. And he just got up from his nap a little while ago. I think it's time to call our doctor. I'll get this one tucked into bed first. Could you watch Toothless for a minute?"

Susannah nodded and reached for the baby, whose real name was Emma, and who finally had plenty of teeth. "You go ahead. We'll be fine."

Abby came into the kitchen a few minutes later, a pleased smile on her face. "That was Cory McGill. Wanted to know if he'd see me at The Music Room tonight. He is *so* cute. Don't you think he looks just a little bit like . . . what's wrong? You have a really weird expression on your face. And where's Mom? Wasn't she here a minute ago?"

"Nothing's wrong," Susannah answered quickly. "I mean, not really. Mattie wasn't feeling very well, so she took him up to bed, that's all."

Abby stood very still, her eyes on Susannah's face. "Sick? Mattie? Mattie is never sick. What's wrong with him?"

Susannah didn't answer. She lowered her head, pretending to be playing with the baby.

"Susannah! What's wrong with my brother?"

Susannah lifted her head. "I don't" — the words came reluctantly from Susannah's mouth — "I guess he has . . . he has a fever. But," she added hastily, "your mom thinks it's just a summer cold. I'm sure she's . . ."

But Abby was already running from the room.

chapter
8

When Abby had informed her mother about the new, puzzling cases at Med Center, Mrs. O'Connor didn't hesitate. Holding the feverish little boy by the hand, she asked Susannah and Abby to keep an eye on the other children and hurried out of the house to the family's doctor.

There was no discussion between the two girls about Nurse Thompson's order not to share with anyone the day's events at Med Center. Susannah knew Abby hadn't had a choice. If there was any chance that Mattie had something similar to what Tina and Jenkins had, the sooner he was treated, the better. Hadn't Dr. Izbecki announced in Tina's treatment room that one of the reasons she was so seriously ill was her delay in seeking treatment? Abby shouldn't take that chance with her own little brother.

Mattie and his mother were home within the hour, a relieved smile on Mrs. O'Connor's face. "Just a mild case of the flu," she told the anxious girls. "Aspirin, liquids, bed rest, and he'll be up and driving us all crazy in a day or two."

Susannah's first reaction was relief. It wasn't until she and Abby were in the car on their way to the fashion show rehearsal that she felt a new twinge of anxiety. What if the doctor was wrong? He might not know yet about Tina and Jenkins, and about the cleaning-crew foreman and the Rollerblading girl. Maybe he hadn't done all of the necessary tests on Mattie. Maybe . . .

"I know what you're thinking," Abby interrupted Susannah's thoughts as the Jeep took a sharp corner. "But Doc Alexander has been taking care of all of us since Geneva was born. That's twelve years, and he's never made a mistake yet. Sometimes all he has to do is take a look at us and he knows exactly what's wrong. Don't forget, the flu may not be what the new patients have, but it *is* going around. And that's what Mattie has, so quit worrying."

Susannah relaxed. Abby had to be right. She knew the doctor who had seen Mattie knew him well, and the O'Connors trusted him. That would have to be enough. For now.

But if Mattie wasn't better in a day or two . . .

Telling herself he *would* be, Susannah put the little boy out of her mind and drove back to Med Center.

The fashion show was being held in the Public Affairs auditorium in the Rehabilitation Hospital where Abby did much of her volunteering. One of the newer buildings, it was eight stories of rose-colored brick, with wide verandas on three sides for patients to enjoy on balmy days.

"Maybe rehearsal won't last that long," Abby said with hope as they climbed out of the Jeep, "and we can stop at The Music Room on the way home."

Susannah laughed. "You know my mother. We won't be leaving here until she's satisfied that every last detail is absolutely perfect. I have a feeling The Music Room is going to have to wait until tomorrow night. If we're lucky. If Mother doesn't like what she sees tonight, she could call rehearsals for every night this week."

To Susannah's relief and Mrs. Grant's delight, Kate showed up, ready to model. "I guess I can use a free outfit," she told Susannah with a faint grin. "And I want to do my part for Emsee. If it went out of business due to lack of funds, where would I work when I graduate from med school?"

As they went through their paces for Caroline's inspection, Susannah found herself carefully scrutinizing the faces of the other models, male and female, for any signs of illness. She saw none. A few people were coughing, but no one looked really ill. But then, Tina hadn't looked sick on Sunday night, either, and now she was in ICU.

Callie was modeling, too, but she refused to speak to Susannah and Abby.

"What's with her, anyway?" Susannah complained to Kate and Abby as they watched Callie move confidently down the runway Caroline had ordered for the show. It stretched from the stage out into the front of the auditorium. "It's like she blames us for Tina being sick. Or hasn't forgiven us for not calling her the minute Tina was brought into Emsee."

"You're disappointed that she's not speaking to you?" Kate asked, mock disbelief in her voice. "You should be ecstatic. One of the things I love most about living in Eastridge is that I don't ever, *ever* have to talk to someone like Callie Matthews. She doesn't even know I exist, and that suits me fine." Her eyes on Callie, Kate added, "How does she *do* that? Walk that way without dislocating a hip? Isn't that physiologically impossible?"

Abbie laughed. "Not for Callie. She's been walking that way since preschool. Callie and I are really too short to make good models, but you and Kate are naturals. You look perfect out there on the runway. Magazine covers, both of you. I suppose I'm not going to grow any more," Abby finished wistfully.

"No," Kate said, "you're not. And we like you just the way you are, so live with it."

Abby laughed ruefully and asked, "I don't suppose we're going to get out of here in time to stop in at The Music Room, are we?"

"Doesn't look like it. Didn't I tell you?" Susannah sighed wearily. "I'm not as disappointed as I thought I'd be. It's been a really long and pretty horrible day. I'm not sure I'd have the energy to dance."

"Sure, you would. When are you too tired to dance? But I'm beat, too. How about you, Kate? Going to go hear some music tonight?"

"Not me. I'm going to do my Naomi Campbell thing here and then I'm going home to beddy-bye, just in case tomorrow at Emsee is even worse than today was." Kate's eyes darkened. "My mom was really out of it at dinner. She only gets like that when she's worried. I know she's afraid more of that nasty stuff is going to turn up tomorrow. So," she said to Susannah, "exactly how long do you think your mother is going to keep us here?"

"I'll ask." When Susannah had pleaded their case to her mother, she agreed to let them leave, but insisted on rehearsals the following two nights.

Susannah spent Monday night at Abby's. But she didn't sleep well. Ordinarily, the cozy warmth of the O'Connor house, so different from the vast spaces of her own lavishly decorated suite at the top of Linden Hall, lulled her to sleep instantly. But after the house had stilled for the night, her mind refused to follow suit. Concern over the strange new cases at Emsee and her fears that Mattie was coming down with the same thing, in spite of what the doctor had said, kept her tossing and turning.

Abby had fallen asleep promptly, her clothes in a discarded heap on the hardwood floor, her head buried in her pillow.

Susannah finally succeeded in doing the same by reminding herself sternly that she wasn't a doctor yet, so what did *she* know? If the O'Connor family doctor, with his years of education, training, and experience, said Mattie had a simple case of the flu, then that was what he had.

In the foothills below the Grant mansion, Callie Matthews fumed. Her father had just left her room, after trying in vain to explain what his secretary Lindsay had been doing in his arms. "Perfectly innocent," he had said, sitting on Callie's bed while she paced back and forth angrily on the lush pink carpet. Her arms were folded against her chest like a shield, as if she were determined that his words would bounce off her. "Nothing happened, Callie. I love your mother, and I would never do anything to hurt her. Lindsay's sister is very sick. She's coming to Med Center for treatment, as a matter of fact. Tomorrow. I was simply trying to comfort a friend in need."

Callie wasn't listening. Her response was to toss her head stubbornly and think, Tell it to someone who cares. He could talk until his lips were purple, but she knew what she'd seen. How stupid did he think she was? He was probably just afraid she'd tell her mother. "I would appreciate it," she said icily, "if you would leave my room. I'd like to be alone."

When he left, his shoulders braced as if he expected her to throw something at his back, she still hated Med Center and she still hated every single past, present, and future Grant.

Jeremy Barlow sat alone in the dimly lit kitchen at his home and thought about how quiet the house had become since his mother left. His father called her "unconventional, undisciplined, and immature," and he said it with undisguised contempt. Maybe it was true. But his mother was *fun*. Not quiet and aloof like his father, so lost in his Very Important Work as a world-renowned cardiac surgeon. People came from all over the world to see Dr. Thomas Barlow, while his son and, for a long time, his wife, waited for him at home.

His mother hadn't been quiet. Always making some kind of noise. Laughing or talking or singing at the top of her lungs even though she wasn't very good at it, or yelling at his father or the housekeeper or the gardener or, on the phone, her mother. Some kind of noise. The house was like a tomb since she'd left.

He could have gone with her. She had asked

him to. But he'd lived in Grant all his life. What did he know about California? His friends were here, his life was here, his home . . .

And then there was the money. No small thing, his father's fortune. It paid for cars and camps and stereos and computers and clothes and parties and all those not-so-insignificant things that made life pleasant. Very pleasant. His mother was hoping to eke out a writing career in California. Everyone knew writers didn't make any money.

Jeremy didn't want to be poor. He didn't think he'd be very good at it.

So he hadn't gone. He'd stayed in Grant. But he'd never thought about how quiet the house would be without his noisy, unconventional, *fun* mother in it.

She'd done okay out there in la-la land. She'd actually sold a couple of books. She wasn't going to be poor, after all. Every once in a while she called and said, "Come on out, Jeremy, I miss you." And sounded like she meant it.

He was tempted. But the thought of leaving Grant terrified him. He wasn't good at making friends. One of his few friends was really sick. Tina. When you didn't have all that many friends, even losing one of them temporarily to sickness was depressing. What was wrong with Tina, anyway? She hadn't looked very well at The Music Room the other night. He remembered asking her if she was okay, and recalled her retorting, "Your father's the doctor, not you, Jeremy, remember?"

He hadn't been offended. Tina got like that sometimes. Her life wasn't so perfect, either. Maybe his mother was right. Maybe having money wasn't the answer to everything.

On Tuesday, there were no new cases of the nasty "flu." Every test result came back negative, leaving the illness undiagnosed.

On Wednesday, there were two new cases, one, a friend of Sam's, whose vigilant mother caught her son's fever before it went above 100 and drove him to the hospital. He was given medication and, although he wasn't seriously ill yet, dispatched quickly to Isolation on the eighth floor.

The second patient arrived by ambulance. Kate, wearing the requisite long-sleeved, pale blue coverall, plastic gloves, hood, mask, and goggles, was waiting at the door with other staff members when Will came running in with two other paramedics, pushing a wildly delirious patient on a gurney. She knew who the new patient was the minute she saw the curly, dark brown hair and the thin, silver identification bracelet on one of the flailing wrists. Damon Lawrence.

"I just saw him on Monday," Kate told Will as they ran along the corridor. "He offered me a ride. He didn't look sick."

Alarmed, Will asked, "You didn't accept, did you?"

She knew why he'd asked. The illness, whatever it was, was clearly contagious. No one knew yet exactly what the incubation period was, but it didn't take a medical genius to figure out that being in close quarters, such as the cab of a truck, with Damon on Monday would have been risky.

"No. I took the bus instead."

"Good girl."

Damon Lawrence's temperature was 104. There was an argument in the treatment room about the wisdom of dosing him with a strong antibiotic "cocktail," one of the residents arguing that it could hamper a diagnosis later, if it killed off the bacteria plaguing him before they could identify that bacteria.

"This kid can't afford to wait for cultures to come back!" Dr. Izbecki snapped. "He's on fire here. We'll worry about the consequences later. Besides, we've had no luck culturing the other cases."

The antibiotic "cocktail" was administered.

Kate knew why Damon was so sick. Because he was macho and stubborn and wouldn't have admitted he was sick until his legs would no longer carry him. With *this* sickness, that was a definite mistake.

There were other emergencies all day Tuesday

and Wednesday, but most of the staff, careful to wear the awkward, annoying, protective clothing at all times, was focused on the illness plaguing the ICU. They sutured minor and major lacerations, did X rays on victims of falls and car accidents and brawls, took blood from people with vaguer complaints such as abdominal pain and back pain and headaches, but all the while they were subconsciously awaiting another fever victim to arrive by ambulance.

At rehearsal on Tuesday and Wednesday nights, Susannah listened again for any sounds of a harsh, racking cough, and surreptitiously scanned faces for signs of a feverish flush or unusually bright eyes.

On Thursday morning, Tina Montgomery slipped into a coma.

The news circulated quickly in ER.

Susannah was horrified. Comatose? Tina was comatose? She was that close to . . . dying?

Tina Montgomery was only seventeen years old.

chapter
9

On Thursday, Susannah spent the night at Abby's again. But first, they went to The Music Room.

They said they were going because they wanted to hear Steam Engine play again. They said they were going because they wanted to dance, to be with friends, to have a good time. Hadn't they been waiting all week for this chance?

But they both knew the real reason for their need to have fun was Tina Montgomery's coma. That was too scary. Sitting around the house doing nothing would have given them too much time to think about the fact that someone their own age had suddenly been stricken by an illness so serious that she was hovering near death. That was one part of it. The other part of it was, they needed to reassure themselves that they were still healthy and very much alive and not hovering anywhere *near* death.

But what they told each other aloud was that they were going because they couldn't wait to hear the band again.

At least Mattie was getting better, Susannah told herself as she drove the Benz along the wide, tree-lined boulevards of downtown Grant. He really did have the flu, after all. And Jenkins and the Rollerblader and the cleaning-crew foreman were holding their own, although that friend of Sam's was worse, his fever spiking last night, she'd heard, to 103, and Damon Lawrence had been put on the critical list. But Mattie was okay. Something good to think about. To keep from thinking about Tina's coma.

All of the medical personnel at Memorial had been tested for any sign of the fever. They had all tested negative. So far. No one knew how long it took for the illness to develop. They would all have to be tested again. Soon.

Susannah pulled into the crowded parking lot at The Music Room, a low, sprawling, stone building situated on the far edge of a newly revitalized warehouse district. The club was distant enough from popular restaurants in that area to keep loud music from disturbing patrons.

A cavernous space that easily could have been cold, dark, and forbidding, The Music Room had been made welcoming by the clever use of soft lighting, the warm glow of burnished hardwood flooring, and round, wooden tables covered with yellow-striped cloths that fell to the floor. Candles settled in black, wrought iron candleholders, each the metal silhouette of a musician playing an instrument, were centered on each table, their flickering flames adding to the warmth.

Although the club served no meals, their specialty in snack foods was a generous selection of tiny pizzas in varying combinations of sauces, meats, and cheeses.

Susannah breathed in the spicy smell with anticipation as she and Abby entered to loud music, laughter, and chatter. Too depressed over the news about Tina to eat before they dressed at Abby's house, they'd had nothing to eat since lunch, and she was starving.

The first person she spotted out on the dance floor as they entered was her twin, Sam, as expert at dancing as he was at every other athletic feat. He was with Callie Matthews, who was wearing a sexy, slinky red dress, her hair piled on top of her head with a few undisciplined ringlets curling around her ears and on the nape of her neck. Sam laughed at something Callie said, then bent his head to give her a long, slow kiss. Callie put her arms around his neck and moved as close to him as she could.

Abby looked at the two in disgust. "Could they possibly get any closer? I see she's really devastated by her best friend's illness," Abby said with disgust. "Maybe we should go over there and console her, what do you think?"

"Can we eat first? My stomach feels like it has a hole in it. And," Susannah added sardonically, "I hope Callie realized that kiss meant nothing. I don't care how sexy it was. All Sam was saying was, I'm having a good time and I feel like kissing you. But don't call me tomorrow, I'll call you . . . maybe. If Callie is looking for commitment, she's draping herself around the wrong guy."

They took seats at one of the tables surrounding the dance floor, glancing around the softly lit, noisy room as they waited for their tray of snacks and their drinks. Susannah spotted Kate, sitting at a far table with friends. Will was there, too, talking to a pretty, dark-haired girl. In one split second, Susannah's feelings went from joy that Will was there to disappointment that he seemed unaware of her presence to jealousy of the girl he was talking to.

"He looks great in that blue shirt, doesn't he?" Abby teased, her own eyes traveling through the crowded room in search of friends. "You could ask him to dance, you know. This is the nineties, Sooz."

"I just wanted to wave to Kate," Susannah replied defensively. "And I don't *want* to dance right now. If I don't eat something, I'm going to faint. Besides," she said, glancing disconsolately once more at Kate's table, "he's busy."

Before Abby could reply, Jeremy Barlow appeared at the table. Without waiting for an invitation, he reversed a chair and plopped down in it, resting his chin on the back. "So, how's Tina doing? You guys know what's wrong with her yet? Give! No point in having friends who slave all day at Med Center if you're not going to tell all."

Susannah realized immediately that he didn't know about the coma. His mood would have been very different if he'd been told. He must not have talked to Tina's parents yet.

"Ask your father." Abby's tone was light, but her eyes showed her discomfort. Susannah knew she felt guilty about not telling Jeremy the truth. But that wasn't for them to do. "He probably knows more about Tina's case than we do."

Jeremy shook his head. "Not true. He spends most of his time up there in his ivory tower in Cardiac/Pulmonary, away from ER. Anyway," he added more seriously, "Tina's a friend of mine. Callie and I are worried about her."

"Yeah, right," Abby said dryly. "We noticed." She stared pointedly at Callie and Sam, still dancing to a loud, fast beat from the band onstage at the front of the room. "Paralyzed with grief, that girl."

"We came here to take our minds off it, that's all," Jeremy retorted, offended. "Can't just sit around waiting to hear something. Everyone's talking about how sick Tina is, but no one *knows* anything. I figured you guys would."

"Well, we don't," Abby said, and then the waitress arrived with their snacks and drinks. Abby plucked from the tray four miniature pizzas with a Coke, and a folded yellow-and-white-striped paper napkin. "Anyway, I was at Rehab all day."

Jeremy turned his attention to Susannah, just as she had known he would. Dreaded he would. She didn't like lying. And Jeremy *was* a good friend of Tina's. But Nurse Thompson had been very explicit in her instructions. "You know about hospital rumors, Jeremy," she said. "Your father's a doctor. You must hear stuff all the time. That doesn't mean it's true."

"Doesn't mean it's not, either. Come on, Susannah, I'll find out sooner or later, anyway. Is Tina going to be okay?"

"I'm just an uneducated volunteer. What do I know?"

Jeremy might have continued to argue, but a friend of Susannah's came to ask her to dance. Although she was still hungry, she would have danced with Count Dracula himself at that point to get away from Jeremy's questions. She accepted the invitation and left the table.

She could feel Jeremy's puzzled eyes on her back as she moved away.

She waved at Sam as they passed him on the dance floor. He nodded, his face flushed with exertion. He was dancing with a different girl now, a tall redhead, which didn't surprise Susannah. His eyes seemed unusually bright, but she told herself that was from the exercise. Sam threw himself into his dancing, the same way he did everything else. And he *was* good.

Her partner, a stocky boy named Paul, commented on the band as they passed the stage. "They're really great, aren't they?"

Nodding enthusiastically, Susannah glanced at the four onstage. The boy on lead guitar, standing directly behind the microphone, caught her eye. He grinned, a lazy, confident smile that lit up his eyes and sent an unmistakable message to Susannah. It said very clearly, I like what I'm looking at.

Susannah didn't look away. Instead, she smiled back. Why not? Will Jackson certainly hadn't acknowledged her existence tonight, and this guy was *very* cute. Tall and thin, his jeans slung low on his hips, a white T-shirt on slightly stooped shoulders.

He had the kind of lean, bony looks she liked. His hair was long, to his shoulders, and dark and wavy, but very clean, shining under the stage lights. Susannah was an "eye person." She really believed that you could tell a lot about a person if you just checked out their eyes. His were incredible. Warm and intelligent, dark brown like Will's, but with glints of gold and amber in them. Or maybe that was just the reflection of the stage lights.

Still, they were great eyes. It wasn't easy to look away from that boldly interested gaze, and she didn't. Not until she could no longer see him without craning her neck.

She said hi to Will and Kate as she passed their table and added casually, "Come over and say hi to us when you get a minute."

But she knew they wouldn't. Kate had an unspoken rule about socializing. She had never mentioned it aloud, but Susannah wasn't stupid. When Kate went places with Susannah and Abby, she never asked to bring along any of her school or neighborhood friends. And when she was with *those* friends, someplace where Susannah and Abby happened to be, Kate acted like they hardly knew each other.

Susannah had never said anything about it. She knew it was harder for Kate, who had to go back home to Eastridge after she'd been out socializing with white kids. Maybe Will felt the same way, since he'd never once asked her to dance or to a movie or a party. Abby kept saying he wanted to, she could tell, but that he was afraid, because of who she was. "Your father would have a stroke if he saw you with Will and you know it. So does Will," had been her explanation.

It was all very confusing to Susannah. Sometimes when Will looked at her, she thought she saw interest in his eyes. But nothing ever happened. So maybe, although she was usually good at reading eyes, this time she was reading them wrong. Which meant that Abby was misreading the signs, too, and Will just wasn't interested.

Abby would have laughed and said, "Me? Wrong? Never happen!"

But Will Jackson wasn't approaching the table to ask Susannah Grant to dance, was he?

No, he wasn't.

And that guitar player, who still had his eyes on her, she noticed when she glanced toward the bandstand, was obviously interested.

To Susannah's immense relief, Jeremy had left their table. She saw him sitting with Callie Matthews and two other girls from Tina's crowd. They were all talking earnestly, and she saw Callie glance over her shoulder toward Susannah and Abby with venom in her eyes.

She's mad because we won't tell her anything about Tina, Susannah thought. But we can't tell her, because we don't know anything except that she's in a coma. And *that* we can't tell her. That terrible news has to come from Callie's parents.

Abby and two of her friends took advantage of

the band break to go to the rest room. Susannah was sitting at the table alone, plucking absentmindedly at the music staff candleholder, when the tall, thin guitarist with the amber eyes appeared in front of her.

"Mind if I join you?" he asked, and didn't sit down until Susannah, who wasn't the least bit surprised to see him there, said, "No, I don't mind."

His name was Zack Ballou. The band, Steam Engine, had been his idea, and he really liked Grant, Massachusetts. "What I've seen of it, anyway," he added quickly. "We don't leave here until around two A.M. usually, so we all sleep late, and then we rehearse afternoons. Doesn't leave a lot of time for sightseeing. Pretty town, though. Sort of Beaver Cleaverish. Big trees, nice houses, wide streets. People seem friendly. We sneaked in a quick tour of Med Center. My aunt's a nurse. When she heard I was coming here, she made me promise I'd take a look at it. It's pretty impressive."

"I work there," Susannah said with pride. Deciding that had sounded a little smug, she quickly added, "I mean, I volunteer. In ER."

"Must be exciting. The place is enormous. So many different hospitals. If I ever get sick, I'll know where to come. So," he said, leaning forward and edging his chair a little closer to Susannah's, "going to be a doctor someday, are you?" He smiled. "You're going to be really busy. Every guy in the city will be pounding on your door. They'll quit working out, quit eating right, hoping they'll get sick just so they can see you."

If it was a line, it worked. Susannah smiled back. Most guys would have asked her if she planned to be a nurse, not a doctor. "I haven't decided. Maybe." Abby danced past, grinned, gave her the thumbs-up sign. Susannah hoped Zack hadn't seen.

While the band took its break, a disc jockey took over. The current tune was a slow one. Zack stood up and held out his hand to Susannah. She took it and let him lead her to the dance floor, hoping Will Jackson was watching from his table.

"And your name is?" Zack Ballou asked, which answered one question that had been on Susannah's mind: Whether or not he knew who she was. So far, her dating experiences had involved two kinds of guys: the ones who were terrified of her father and treated her like something breakable, which she hated, and the guys who thought that getting in good with Samuel Grant's daughter might be a smart move.

But Zack didn't even know her name. Probably had never even heard of Samuel Grant II. Just in case he had, she gave him her first name only. Then she gave him a brief history of Grant and Emsee.

"I've been hearing rumors all night about that place," he said. "Something about a new flu. Know anything about that?" Before she could think of how to avoid answering the question, he added, "I don't want to sound like a wimp, but we can't afford to get sick. After we're done here, we're on our way to Vegas. One of our better gigs. Our agent promised us the hotel room would actually have hot water and room service. So if there's something catching going around, we should probably know about it."

"It's nothing to worry about," she said with more conviction than she felt. "I really don't know much about it myself." Except that one of the victims is now in a coma, she thought, and felt a twinge of guilt about not warning him. But she had her orders.

"No problem. I was just curious. If you find out anything more, let me know, okay?"

They talked then about his travels and what it was like to be on the road so much. He said it was hectic, but fun. "Sometimes. We've traveled out of the country once in a while. Those gigs are hard, lugging all of our gear and not having a clue about where anything is. But they're the most interesting, too. I've learned more on those trips than I ever learned in geography in school.

Problem is, we haven't hit it big with an album yet, so some of the places we've played have been pretty sleazy." He smiled down at Susannah. "Grant's one of the best, by the way. At least here, we can drink the water. Can't do that in B.Y.O.B.W. places."

Susannah glanced up inquiringly. "B.Y.O. B.W.?"

He laughed. "Bring your own bottled water. We've been sick a couple of times. In other countries, mostly. Had to cancel some gigs, which we all hate to do, because we were laid out in the hotel room with what the local doctors called 'stomach distress.' Distress is right. The last time was the worst. Man, were we laid low! Now we carry our own water with us."

Abby danced by again, this time in the arms of Cory McGill, the boy who had telephoned her on Monday. Then Sam passed, dancing with an unsmiling Kate. Susannah was surprised. She knew Kate didn't think much of Sam. She'd made remarks from time to time, calling him, among other things, "a party animal." Susannah had retorted once, "That doesn't mean he's not a nice guy."

"Doesn't mean he is, either," Kate had replied.

It struck Susannah now that Sam's face was beet red. Probably from dancing too hard. But his eyes seemed unusually bright, too.

It's all those cases of the flu or whatever we've been seeing, she told herself, returning her attention to Zack. I'm starting to see that same illness in everyone. First Mattie, who only had the flu after all, and now my own brother, who is as healthy as Schwarzenegger. I'm being silly.

But the following morning, she changed her mind.

chapter

10

In an inexpensive motel on the outskirts of Grant, Zack Ballou lay on the thin plaid bedspread thinking about the quiet, pretty girl with the brilliant smile.

"You know who that girl was? The one you danced with?" Skeet, the keyboard player, had asked Zack on the way home.

"Yeah. Her name's Susannah."

"Susannah *Grant*, man. That name ring a bell? Think a minute, Zack. Where *are* we?"

"We're in Grant, Massachusetts." Zack, driving the rental car, had turned his head toward Skeet. "So? Are you telling me that girl has an entire city named after her?"

"That's what I'm sayin', man. Her ancestors founded this place. Her old man practically owns the whole town. Remember that big white house we saw at the top of the hill when we were checking out Med Center? You said it looked like one of those mansions we saw in Beverly Hills when we were meeting with our agent in L.A., remember? We thought it might be a resort."

Zack nodded.

"Well, that's where your Susannah *lives*, Zack. While you, my friend," Skeet added with a grin, "live on the road. You got no home. Well, I mean, you got a family in Sacramento, but you're never there, am I right? You're a vagabond with luggage and guitar, making music, eating in fast-food joints, and sleeping in cheap motels in places where we can't even drink the water. My pitiful little brain tells me that's not what this girl's parents have in mind for her."

I didn't *ask* her to marry me, Zack thought, rolling over restlessly on the bed. She's nice, she's friendly, smart and pretty, and that smile could light up this entire city. But no entanglements, that's the rule. *My* rule. The band's rule. We haven't worked as hard as we have to ruin the whole thing by letting some female come along and carry one of us off, leaving the others in the lurch. Susannah Grant's parents could quit worrying.

Besides, there was something a lot more important to think about. That new sickness rumored to be plaguing Med Center could do a lot more damage to the band than Zack Ballou losing his heart to Susannah Grant. He'd heard there were only six cases. Six was too many, as far as he was concerned. Six meant it was probably contagious. Getting sick was *not* in Steam Engine's master plan. On their last trip out of the country, Skeet had fallen ill only an hour or two before stage time. Too late to try and find a replacement, even if they had spoken the language, which they hadn't.

Their performance wasn't the same without Skeet. Fortunately, the audience hadn't seemed to notice. Too busy yakking. He hated audiences like that. It had been one of those nights he hated, when no one was paying attention. So Skeet's absence hadn't ruined their careers. But another time, in a better club . . . maybe in someplace like Grant, Massachusetts, with a more attentive audience, the absence of one musician could wreck everything.

And there just might be something floating around this city that could strike them all down if they weren't careful. Or lucky.

That girl . . . Susannah . . . she was someone important? Rich? Someone whose parents would lock her in her room forever if they caught her with an itinerant musician? Too bad.

Still, he just might call her or try to see her again. She worked at Med Center. Maybe she could keep him up-to-date on whatever was going around, making people sick.

Well, of course that's why you want to see her again, a sarcastic inner voice scoffed. It has nothing to do with the fact that she's one of the prettiest, nicest females on the planet, right?

Zack closed his eyes. But for just a few more

seconds before he fell asleep, he silently played in his head the last tune he and Susannah had danced to.

At Med Center, on the eighth floor of Grant Memorial in a small room with an Isolation sign on the door, Damon Lawrence, the newest patient to arrive at ICU, went into cardiac arrest.

The green jagged line continuously zigzagging across the screen on a monitor behind the patient's head became instead a steady, flat line.

An alarm sounded at the ICU nurses' station.

Two of the nurses on the floor were already wearing gowns, with masks hanging around their necks. They were on their feet and inside the room in seconds, while other nurses hurriedly donned the proper gear before entering.

The first nurse to reach the patient, snatched up a wrist and quickly called out to the nurses who arrived a second later, "No pulse! Get a crash cart in here, stat! It's right outside! And call Cardiology! Get Barlow. If he's not in the hospital, call his service!"

Feet ran to obey. The nurse was administering CPR to no avail when a white-jacketed resident, looking decidedly weary, arrived alongside the red wheeled crash cart. Quickly realizing that the CPR wasn't doing the trick, he began shouting orders for medication to be injected into the already established IV lines, simultaneously smearing the cart's electrical paddles with gel. The nurses obeyed his orders smoothly, efficiently, as if they'd been choreographed. One inserted the requested amount of medication into an IV line, then quickly stepped away from the bed as the doctor shouted, "Clear! Give me one-fifty!"

The paddles smacked down upon Damon's bare chest.

All eyes went to the monitor.

Nothing. No response.

"I'm gonna hit him again!" the resident said tersely. "Give me two hundred!"

The nurse tending the crash cart moved a dial.

"Clear!"

The paddles smacked downward a second time.

Again, there was no response.

"This kid shouldn't be *dying*!" the resident, a very young man, exclaimed. "He's what . . . sixteen, seventeen?"

"But we don't know what he's *got*!" a young nurse said unnecessarily.

"Two-fifty!" the doctor ordered. "Where the hell is Barlow, anyway?"

"Couldn't raise him. Left a message with his service. If he's in town, he'll call. I put out a call for anyone from Cardiology. Someone's probably on the way."

"Well, they'd better hurry. One more time. Give me three hundred! Clear!"

This time, Damon responded. "I've got a pulse," one of the nurses declared, relief heavy in her voice. "BP one hundred over fifty. He's with us again."

The green line returned to its zigzag pattern again.

There was a palpable easing of tension in the room.

The doctor returned the paddles to the crash cart. "Even if Barlow approved of cracking open chests for open-heart massage, which he doesn't," he said, looking down at the patient, whose chest rose and fell evenly now, "I wouldn't have done it. Whatever he's got, I wouldn't want to be the one to let it loose. Better it stays inside him, where it belongs. Besides," he added wryly with typical hospital humor, "I've never even cracked a walnut without crushing the thing to smithereens."

As the resident and all but one of the nurses left the room, he asked more seriously, "Any luck getting his fever down?"

"Oh, we can get it down. That's no problem. It's *keeping* it down that's got us stumped. It goes right back up again. We're still dosing all of them with antibiotics, but if you ask me, they need a different course of treatment. Just don't ask me what."

Frowning, the young resident left to continue the nap interrupted by the emergency.

When Dr. Barlow, Chief of Cardiology at ER, finally called from the country club where he'd been having dinner, he was told he wasn't needed, after all, and that the patient was stable and resting as comfortably as could be expected.

Susannah stayed at Abby's house again. When she arrived home on Friday morning to change her clothes, her family was gathered in the sunny breakfast room. Her first reaction as she waved casually in her twin's direction was that he looked really terrible. His face was flushed, and his hand shook noticeably as he reached for a pitcher of juice. Instead of responding to her wave, he began to cough.

"What's the matter with you?" she asked abruptly, moving over to stand behind his chair. "I thought you looked weird last night at The Music Room." She glanced at Caroline. "Mother? Sam's sick."

"I am not!" he protested between coughs. "Mind your own business." The coughing stopped. Clearing his throat, he added, "Like you were really paying attention to *me* last night. How many times did you dance with that musician? Three? Four?"

Caroline glanced up in alarm. "Musician? What musician? Good heavens, Susannah, you're not dating a musician, are you?" The tone of her voice made it clear that the word "musician" could easily have been synonymous with "ax murderer."

"Never mind, Mother. Did you hear what I said? Look at Sam! He's sick, isn't that obvious?"

"Sick?" Caroline shook her head. "Don't be silly, darling, your brother is never ill. Neither are you. Nettie Montgomery tells me I have the healthiest children in the world. You know," she added in a confidential tone, as if she were sharing a secret, "her Tina is quite ill."

"I know, Mother. I work in ER, remember? I was there when they brought her in."

"You volunteer, dear." Caroline paused, then added anxiously, "You wouldn't want people thinking we've sent you out to *work*."

"Damn nuisance," Samuel Grant said, "that Montgomery girl getting sick just now. Leonard was supposed to return to South America on Friday, finish up the business with that promising new herb our field people have discovered. Could be a new miracle drug, from the early reports we've received. I can't very well send him when his daughter is in the hospital."

"That was very thoughtless of Tina," Susannah said, annoyed that all attention had shifted away from the physical condition of her twin. "She should have consulted with you before she developed a fever of one hundred and three."

"Susannah!" Caroline said quickly. "You're being rude."

"And *he's* ignoring me as usual! So are you, Mother!" Susannah slapped a hand across Sam's brow before he could stop her. He pushed the hand away immediately, but Susannah had already felt the heat from his skin. "Mother, he's burning up! I told you he was sick."

Smoothly, calmly, Caroline stood up and walked over to her son. She repeated the touch on the brow, and when she pulled her hand away, said slowly, "Why, Sam, you do seem to be warm."

"I just got out of the sauna," he said impatiently, tossing his napkin aside and jumping to his feet. Susannah was sure he was lying. Beginning to cough again, her brother brushed past her and hurried from the room, calling over his shoulder as he left, "Quit treating me like a baby, okay? I am *not* sick!"

"He is *so!*" Susannah insisted, staring at her mother as if to say, What are you going to do about this? "Look, the reason Tina is so sick now is, she didn't get herself to a doctor soon enough. That's what Izbecki said. You don't want Sam to end up in Emergency, too, do you?"

"Izbecki?" her mother asked, frowning. "You don't have any friends named Izbecki, do you, dear? Is that the musician Sam mentioned?"

"He's a doctor, Mother."

"I'll handle this," Samuel said, rising. "No need for you girls to worry your pretty heads about it."

"Mother isn't a girl," Susannah said in exasperation. An overwhelming need to scream in frustration was sweeping over her. "She's a woman."

She might as well have saved her breath. "Well, she's right about one thing," her father continued as he turned to leave the room. "Sam is never sick. Healthy as a horse."

"Why do people always say that?" Susannah cried. "Even horses get sick!"

Ignoring her, her father continued, "I'm sure he's just been overdoing it a little, the way boys his age tend to do. I did it myself, I must admit. I'll have a talk with him."

"Make him see a doctor!" Susannah insisted, thinking of Tina lying on that gurney, her body consumed by fever.

Her father's face reddened slightly. He stared at her coolly, remarking, "Surely your volunteer duties at Med Center haven't equipped you to make medical diagnoses, have they, Susannah? Perhaps you should leave that to the proper professionals for the time being." He managed a small, tolerant smile. "At least until you've graduated from high school."

"Ooh!" Susannah cried, furious, and whirled on her heel to run out of the room and stomp upstairs. She didn't stop at Sam's room to see how he was. What was the point? Even if she decided he was at death's door, no one would listen to her.

She changed into white jeans and a white silk blouse, rolled the sleeves up to the elbow, thrust her pale hair up into a thick, bouncy ponytail, and left the house without saying another word to anyone.

In his own suite of rooms, Sam Grant lay on an upholstered sofa near the window, which was wide open. He was hoping the fresh morning air would clear his head, cool his body, which felt like he *was* in the sauna.

He was *never* sick. Never. Everyone else got colds and the flu, never him.

He hated *this*, whatever it was. It sure felt rotten. He couldn't stop coughing, and his head was about to explode.

He knew how to handle it, though, even if he didn't know what it was. Tough it out. Like the old man was always telling him, "You give in to adversity, son, that makes you a loser. There is nothing you can't overcome, as long as you don't knuckle under."

He wasn't going to knuckle under. But he sure did feel like he was bending a little.

With a great deal of effort, Sam pulled himself upright on the sofa and breathed deeply of the morning air. The result was a coughing spell that doubled him in half. When it had finally passed, he stood up, swiped at his watering eyes with the back of a hand, and moved unsteadily to the medicine cabinet in his bathroom. There, he withdrew a bottle of aspirin and downed two with a glass of water.

An hour later, he decided he felt better, just as he'd expected, and left the house to drive down into Grant in his van to see who was having the most fun. That group was the one he would join.

Another challenge won, he thought with satisfaction. Now, if he could just stop this stupid coughing. . . .

At the O'Connor house, Susannah was delighted to see that Mattie was feeling much better.

"I heard there are more cases at Emsee," Mrs. O'Connor commented quietly when Susannah moved on into the kitchen to wait for Abby to gather all of her things together. "How many?"

Susannah remembered Nurse Thompson's warning. "I . . . I'm not sure."

Abby's mother smiled. "Yeah, you are. Abby wouldn't tell me, either. You're not supposed to, right? And as long as I know Mattie's going to be okay, I guess I should quit worrying." She turned away to pile breakfast remains into the refrigerator, then turned back to Susannah. "But I do have other kids, you know. If there's something nasty going around, parents in Grant should be informed."

"I'm sure if it was anything nasty, you'd be told," Susannah said with more confidence than she felt. Seeing once again Tina's flushed face and wild eyes on the gurney, she suffered a pang of guilt. But orders were orders.

Abby came in then, wearing a Boston Red Sox sweatshirt, baggy white shorts, and work boots with thick white socks. Her face was flushed, her curly, dark hair askew. But she was always flushed after her mad rush around the house gathering her things together, so Susannah knew the high color had nothing to do with illness.

On the way to Med Center, she told Abby about Sam.

"I noticed last night, when he was dancing with Kate, that he looked a little weird," Abby agreed. "Like he was feverish or something. But then I figured it was just that I was worried about Mattie. So I forgot about him and concentrated on you and that guitarist instead. He really is pretty cute, Sooz. I planned to grill you about him last night, but the minute I hit that bed, I was out like a light. Are you going to see him again?"

"Maybe." Susannah smiled slyly, thinking of Zack's eyes on hers. "I do so appreciate good music, don't you?"

Abby laughed. "Oh, I do! I do!"

chapter
11

Callie Matthews arrived at Med Center early Friday morning.

She almost turned around and left when she glimpsed two nurses on their way into a treatment room. They looked like astronauts in weird blue coveralls, hoods, gloves, and goggles! She knew what that clothing was. It was protective gear, protection against contamination of some kind. Against contamination from *Tina*, she'd bet. And the others who had what Tina had. Was it really that dangerous?

She wasn't supposed to have seen the nurses, she knew that, too. She'd bet her sports car that no one outside of the hospital was supposed to see them. They probably didn't put on their space gear until just before they entered a treatment room, and then only if the patient was sick like Tina. They certainly weren't hanging around near any entrances dressed like that. If they were, the whole town would know that someone at Med Center was contagious. And the whole town *didn't*. Not yet.

The protective clothing scared Callie. No one had told her Tina was sick with something that *dangerous*. No one would even tell her how Tina *was*, and she hadn't been allowed near ICU. Tina's parents were so vague. They just kept saying, "She's holding her own, she's holding her own." What did *that* mean?

If Tina had something dangerous and contagious, Callie wondered as she slipped inside an elevator, why hasn't Dad told me about it? Isn't he worried that I'll get it, too? I'm Tina's best friend!

Her father hadn't said a word to her about any dangerous illness at Med Center. He came home very late from the hospital every night, ate a quiet dinner with his wife in their bedroom, and went to bed. Every morning, he left the house earlier than he had the day before. This morning, she had noticed dark circles under his eyes. Her mother had them, too, but that was because of her illness. Her father wasn't ill.

She wasn't on her way up to the tenth floor to apologize for the way she'd acted when he tried to explain about Lindsay. Pigs would fly first. She was there because she'd gone over the limit on one of the credit cards and she wanted him to fix it. There was this divine black dress at a little shop near Med Center. She had to have it. He owed her that much, at least.

That snake Lindsay wasn't at her desk again.

But her jacket wasn't hanging on the coatrack, either, and something about the desk looked different. It was so clean. As if . . . hope rose in Callie's chest . . . as if no one worked there. Maybe, just maybe, her father had actually fired the woman. If he had, maybe she'd think about forgiving him. Not right away, of course. But sometime.

She went straight to the door of her father's office, but her hand on the knob was stopped by the sound of voices from inside. A voice she didn't recognize sounded angry, while her father's was calm, perfectly rational, and very determined.

"We have the finest lab in the world on these premises," he was saying in response to an angry remark that Callie hadn't grasped. "They'll get to the bottom of this. You're overreacting, Doctor Davis. I'm sure this is nothing more than the flu. A new strain of it, maybe, but still, just the flu. I understand there's a lot of it going around. I have also been told that several of the patients took their own sweet time seeking treatment, which is probably why they're so ill."

"The preliminary lab tests on two of the patients came back negative for influenza," the angry voice retorted. "It is *not* the flu, Matthews. We've got six cases now. The Montgomery girl, Jenkins Rue, the girl who was Rollerblading, the cleaning-crew foreman, Damon Lawrence, who is critically ill, and another boy his age. We could have more at any second. We don't even know what those six have in common. Five of them are young. But one of them is fifty-three years old."

Callie pictured her father leaning back in the huge, brown leather chair that she loved to sit in and twirl around. He probably had a look of satisfaction on his face, knowing he was far more important than the doctor standing in front of him. "Send your cultures over to the lab at Grant Pharmaceuticals. It's better equipped than ours. When you have those results, we'll talk again."

But the doctor wasn't so easily dismissed. "Matthews, I'm telling you, we're going to have more cases. This stuff is clearly contagious, and if it turns out to be influenza, I'll turn in my stethoscope. Med Center has a couple of social events scheduled on the grounds. Gathering a lot of people together here now is not a good idea. And we should be getting the word out that there's something nasty going around. May I just remind you that the Lawrence boy arrested last night, and the Montgomery girl is comatose?"

Alone in the hallway, her ear pressed to the heavy wooden door, Callie gasped in shock. Comatose? Tina? Tina was in a coma? "At death's door," that's what her father had called a coma, more than once. Tina was at death's door, and no one had told her? Her father *knew*? He knew, and he hadn't said a word?

Her father's voice was louder, clearer. He must have risen from his chair in anger. "Get the word out?" She knew *that* tone of voice. It meant he was taking her car keys, she was grounded, her allowance was being cut in half, and she'd damn well better get her grades up or she wouldn't leave the house for a year. He didn't use that tone often, but when he did, there was no budging him. Who knew that better than she?

"Get the word out?" he repeated, his voice rising steadily. "You're talking publicity, Doctor Davis? Is that what you're suggesting?"

"I'm suggesting that we warn this community that a nasty illness is making the rounds in Grant and that we don't yet know what it is or how dangerous."

"Well, now, there's a productive suggestion. Let's panic the entire city. Let's spread the word, far and wide, that Med Center is not a safe place to be just now. The resulting bad publicity ought to be an enormous help in getting us the funds we need for the new burn unit wing. Get the word out? If we do that, Doctor, this entire facility, all eighteen buildings, will empty out faster than a movie theater after someone has shouted 'fire.' "

He *knew* Tina was in a coma, Callie thought, sickened.

"Funds?" There was astonishment in the doctor's voice. "You're making this about money?"

"Everything is about money. Where do you think this medical complex would be without money, Doctor? Where would your salary come from? And the expensive equipment you doctors think of as medical toys? However, just in case you find me callous and uncaring, after your telephone call to me, I *did* speak with the Chief of Staff on this matter. I don't mind telling you, the consensus is that you're an alarmist."

"I'm alarmed. I admit that. You should be, too," Dr. Davis said.

"It wasn't wise of you to go over the Chief's head and come to me, Doctor. You would never have had access to this office if my secretary wasn't out on personal business today. A family illness. Now, if you'll excuse me . . ."

Callie's heart twisted bitterly. He hadn't fired Lindsay, after all. She just wasn't in today. She'd be back at her desk on Monday.

"There *will* be more cases," the doctor responded angrily. "And this is an illness that needs immediate treatment if more serious complications like the ones we have in ICU are to be avoided." His angry words were moving dangerously close to where Callie was huddled in hurt and anger outside the door. The doctor was leaving.

She darted sideways, hiding behind a tall, potted plant.

When the doctor, his stride furious, had disappeared inside the elevator, she left, too. The last person in the world she felt like talking to now was her treacherous, traitorous father, who could have, *should* have, warned her that her best friend was ill with something so dangerous, people had to put on protective clothing before they went near her. And how could he not have told her that Tina was in a coma?

She had nothing to say to him.

Fuming, Callie went straight home and talked her mother into giving her a different credit card. Then she went shopping.

She would wear the black dress to The Music Room that night. If she was going to catch what Tina had and maybe become comatose, too, she might as well have as much fun as she could first.

It did occur to Callie, as she drove home with the sexy black dress lying in a large pink box on the bucket seat beside her, that if she hadn't caught the disease or whatever it was from Tina by now, maybe she wasn't *going* to. Maybe she was immune or something. She put the back of her right hand to her forehead. No fever there.

No, she probably wasn't going to get it.

But she still might as well have as much fun as she could.

On Friday morning, Zack called Susannah at ER to ask if she was coming to The Music Room that night. She was surprised and pleased to get the call. But as she talked on the phone in the hall, she was painfully aware of Will standing off to one side. She knew she was being silly. He couldn't possibly know who she was talking to. Besides, why would Will care? She told herself that she was keeping her voice low only because this was, after all, a hospital.

And she told Zack that yes, she was planning on coming to hear them play that night, that she would have come back sooner but she'd been too busy.

"Great!" he said, sounding really pleased. "See you tonight. Save me a dance, okay?"

"Absolutely."

Watching Susannah, Will sensed, with a sharp pang of envy in his chest, that Susannah was talking to a guy. Probably that guitarist from The Music Room. He'd seen her dancing with the musician. Had come very close to jumping from his chair and walking over to ask her to dance himself. But he couldn't do it. He wasn't sure why. It wasn't because she was white. He had plenty of white friends, some of them girls, many of whom he wouldn't have hesitated to ask to dance.

But Susannah was different. And it wasn't her money, or the fact that her father practically owned the entire town. She wasn't a snob, and he was convinced she didn't have a prejudiced bone in her body. It was something else. Maybe it was because he sensed that any relationship between the two of them wouldn't be just a casual, friendly thing. He had a strong, gut feeling that it would go deeper than that. And even if he *could* ever get past her parents, there wasn't any room in his life for that kind of relationship right now. Wouldn't be for a long time. He had plans.

They were friends. And until he'd seen her dancing with that musician, he'd told himself that would be enough. Lying, of course, but it had worked pretty much.

Maybe tonight he would ask her to dance. One dance did not a relationship make. Besides, it would drive him nuts if she danced with that musician all night long.

But that night at The Music Room, just as Will was working up his courage to leave his chair and move swiftly to the table where Susannah, looking very pretty in a bright blue sundress that matched her eyes, sat with Abby and Jeremy Barlow and a few other friends, something happened to stop him.

What stopped him was the way Susannah was watching her twin brother Sam, out on the dance floor with Callie Matthews. The number was a fast one, and they were dancing so well together, other dancers had moved off to the sidelines to watch them. Susannah should have been smiling, as everyone else was. But she wasn't smiling, Will noticed. Her eyes on Sam were concerned, and there was a worried frown on her face.

Picking up on her expression, Will stayed in his chair and switched his attention to Sam. He understood, then, why Susannah looked worried. Sam looked terrible. His face was too flushed, his eyes too bright, and several times during the dance his hand went to his mouth to cover a cough.

While other people watching saw nothing but some awesome dancing, Will had enough experience in his work as a paramedic to recognize illness when he saw it.

They hadn't had any new cases of the fever for the past two days. Will thought, with a stab of sympathy for Susannah, that that was about to change. Because something was very wrong with Samuel Grant III.

Sam, missing a step, stumbled, and was more startled by the misstep than his audience was. Oh, man, his overheated brain thought, *this is not good. This is not good at all.* He continued to dance, his arms and legs moving automatically to the upbeat music. But the coughing was getting worse, and his head felt like he was dancing on *it*, instead of on his feet.

Will stood up. Susannah did the same.

Seized by a sudden, violent coughing spasm, Sam stopped dancing, putting both hands to his mouth.

Callie, her feet still moving, regarded him with a mixture of concern and annoyance. "What's wrong?"

Susannah began to move forward from one side of the room, Will from the other, both heading for the dance floor.

Sam's hands reached out blindly for something to grasp. He turned his head, his fever-bright eyes meeting Susannah's. She thought she saw him shrug helplessly. Then his knees buckled and he slid slowly, still coughing, to the floor. He landed first on his knees, remaining that way for several seconds.

Callie stopped dancing.

Susannah ran to her brother's side. Will arrived at the same moment.

But they weren't in time to stop Sam from toppling forward, landing face first on the burnished hardwood floor.

His eyes were open. But he wasn't moving.

chapter
12

~~~~~~~~~~~~~~~~~~~~~~~~~~~~~~~~

Susannah fell to her knees beside Sam, calling his name.

Shouting for someone to call 911, Will, too, knelt. Gently, carefully, he rolled Sam over onto his back, loosened the collar of his light blue shirt, and took his pulse. "Get a wet cloth!" he ordered.

Kate, hurrying over to join them, turned instead and ran for the rest room.

"Somebody get me a big glass of water!" was Will's second order.

Callie obeyed, but she was so stunned, she didn't move as quickly as Kate had. How could Sam be sick? She'd known Sam Grant all of her life and she couldn't remember one single time, except for the chicken pox that they all had, when he'd been anything less than physically perfect. They'd been having such a great time, with everyone standing around watching them dance. Although now that she thought about it, Sam hadn't looked that great. She'd thought he was just flushed from dancing. Where was her brain these days? How could she not have picked up on the fact that he was getting sick, like Tina? Stupid, stupid! And because she hadn't been paying attention, she'd been breathing in his germs the whole time they were dancing!

But . . . she hadn't caught it from Tina. So maybe she wouldn't catch it from Sam, either.

Susannah leaned over her brother and patted his flushed, scarlet face with the cold cloth Kate had brought her. Fighting tears, she murmured a stready stream of words, "Sam, you idiot, why didn't you listen . . . I told you something was wrong . . . you're not stupid, you had to know you were sick . . . what is the *matter* with you, anyway? . . . oh, God, I've got to call Mother, she's going to be so upset, but I've got to tell them . . . *where* is that ambulance?"

Abby had borrowed a jacket from someone to fold and place beneath Sam's head. She racked her brain to think of something comforting to say to Susannah, but all she could think was, Thank God Mattie doesn't have this. This awful thing.

Will, too, wanted desperately to reassure Susannah. He tried, speaking in his customary calm, quiet voice. But he knew she wasn't hearing him.

When the paramedics arrived, he hurried over to them to say grimly, "We've got another fever case here. You'll want masks and gloves on. But let me clear the place first, okay?" He was remembering his mother's firm instructions about not alarming the public. The crowd gathered around Sam shouldn't see the masks and gloves. And hadn't he seen a music reporter from the local paper at a table earlier tonight? Was she still here?

"Well, clear it fast," one of Will's coworkers said abruptly. "Should have been done before we got here."

The rebuke stung, but Will knew the guy was right. He'd been so concerned about Susannah that he hadn't been thinking clearly, or he would have ushered the crowd out of the club immediately after Sam collapsed.

With the help of Abby, the band members, Jeremy, and Kate, Will managed to quickly clear The Music Room. No one wanted to leave, and most of them, Will knew, would hang around out front out of curiosity. But the ambulance had parked out back, so there was a slim possibility that the stretcher could be removed without anyone spotting it.

Will was just beginning to realize how important that was. The sight of paramedics wearing masks was sure to set off a spate of rumors that no explanation from the hospital, no matter how carefully phrased, would defuse.

When the paramedics inserted an IV line into Sam's arm and placed an oxygen mask on his face, Susannah turned so pale, her skin seemed almost translucent. Will ached to comfort her. But she had seen Tina on her stretcher, knew the girl was now in ICU and comatose, had seen the other patients, too. There was nothing he could say to ease her fears.

Zack didn't say anything, either. But he did move closer to Susannah and put a comforting arm around her shoulders as the paramedics lifted the stretcher. She didn't seem to notice.

Will noticed, however, and wished he'd done it first.

Kate, standing beside Will in the now nearly empty club, was astonished by how shocked she was at Sam's collapse. Why did she feel so shaken? He wasn't a close, personal friend of hers. Besides, she was accustomed to illness. Especially lately. So why were her hands shaking, why was her stomach churning so violently, why did she suddenly feel so icy cold?

Because, the answer came, like everyone else in Grant, you saw Samuel Grant III as invincible. Everyone thinks of him as the Golden Boy, the Grant scion and heir who has everything: good looks, good health, piles and piles of money, plenty of friends, a brilliant, safe, secure future without hardship or tragedy. And there he lies on the floor, struck down like any other mortal. As sick as Jenkins Rue, who had nothing.

And if Sam, so protected, so fortunate, could

get this horrible thing, *anyone* could. Anyone at all. Kate thought of her brother Aaron. She thought of her married sister, the husband who loved her, and the little six-year-old boy both of them adored. And she thought of her mother working so closely with the patients in the initial phases of their treatment.

It was bad enough that Damon Lawrence had been brought into the hospital on a stretcher, seriously ill. That had been a real shock. Damon was tall and strong. Like Sam, he'd looked like nothing could hurt him. But it had. And he wasn't any better today, either. She'd checked before she left for the day. A young nurse had told her he'd arrested during the night, but they'd brought him back. "Technically speaking," she had confided in a low voice, "he *died*. But he's hanging in there."

Kate had been thoroughly shaken by the news that Damon had come so close to not making it.

If her family got this horrible thing, too . . .

Her stomach felt hollow.

Susannah rode in the back of the ambulance with Sam, who was conscious and babbling nonsensically. Even when Susannah held one of his hands, he continued to thrash restlessly on the stretcher. The paramedics were in constant touch with ER by radio. Their only instructions had been to make sure Sam had a clear airway and to begin supplying fluids immediately to battle dehydration. The IVs already swung above Sam's head. His vital signs were repeatedly relayed to the hospital.

Will drove Abby and Kate. They sat silently in the front seat, leaning forward slightly in their anxiety, as if that would somehow make the car go faster. Kate knew why Will was rushing to Med Center behind the ambulance. Because of Susannah. He wanted to be there for her. The same went for Abby, because she was Susannah's best friend. What Kate *wasn't* sure of was why *she* was in the car, instead of heading home to Eastridge with her friends.

She'd been so careful not to let herself think of Susannah as a close friend. Not much future in that. Why get to know someone really well when you'll probably never see them again after graduation? Susannah kept insisting she was going to Grant University just like Kate and Abby, but Kate was sure she wasn't being realistic. Susannah's parents would never let her go to Grant. They'd insist on a top Ivy League college for their daughter. The best in the country, probably.

Kate felt a sharp pang of regret. It would have been fun to have Susannah at Grant U. But that would never happen. Which was why she'd guarded so carefully against anything more than a good working relationship with her at ER and an occasional movie or shopping trip to the mall.

But if that had worked the way she intended, then why did she feel like crying, something she hardly ever did, when she thought of how scared Susannah had looked when she climbed into the back of that ambulance? Why was she hurting for Susannah? That hadn't been part of the plan.

In the low-slung, sleek, black sports car directly behind Will's truck, Jeremy drove as fast as he dared, with Callie and Zack urging him on. The tall, glowing buildings of the enormous medical complex loomed directly ahead of them.

Jeremy wondered if his father would be called in to consult on Sam's case. Probably not, unless Sam got so sick his heart became involved.

Zack wondered just how contagious Sam's illness really was.

Callie wondered if her father was in his office, and if Lindsay had come in to work that day, after all.

And Susannah, sitting in the back of the ambulance holding Sam's dry, hot hand, wondered how she was going to tell her parents just how ill their son really was.

chapter
13

The phone call to her parents was the worst Susannah had ever had to make. She waited until Sam had been rushed into a treatment room. There, medical personnel, wearing protective gear as instructed, began pumping him full of cooling fluids and doing the basic groundwork for intensive blood work and specimen cultures. Susannah hated to leave, but her parents had to be notified, and she didn't want someone else doing it.

Nurse Thompson, on night duty, let her use the desk telephone. Susannah's hand was shaking as she punched the number for an outside line, then dialed Linden Hall.

"Oh, hello, dear," her mother said when she recognized Susannah's voice.

"Mother," Susannah interrupted, "I'm at Emsee. Sam is here. He collapsed at The Music Room. We had to call an ambulance. You and Father need to come here right away."

"Sam? Sick? An ambulance?"

"Mother, put Father on the phone, okay?"

"No. No, I'll tell him. We'll be right there. But . . . Sam's not *very* ill, is he, dear? Not like . . . not like Nettie's Tina?" Caroline began speaking very quickly, sudden anxiety forcing words from her mouth on top of one another. "What is it, the flu? Yes, that must be it, Sam has the flu, that's all, you were right this morning, Susannah, I must apologize for not listening. . . ."

"Mother, just come to ER, okay? I'll be waiting for you." Susannah hung up.

Kate, in the treatment room watching Susannah through the glass window, had to admire the way Sam's sister was holding up. No panic there. They were twins, so it wouldn't have been so surprising if Susannah had fallen apart when Sam collapsed. But she hadn't.

In spite of the fact that every single gowned and masked staff member in that room knew exactly who Sam was, she had to admit they hadn't altered their routine one bit. Hadn't called in the Chief of Staff, hadn't taken all personnel off the floors and dragged them into this room, ignoring other emergency cases. Like the man with the metal object imbedded in his left hand, or the baby with croup, or the truck driver stricken by a sudden asthma attack. They were being treated in other rooms. That was one thing Kate liked about Med Center. All patients were treated the same, no matter where they lived or how much money they had. She wasn't sure that was true of all hospitals. But it was true here.

In minutes, plastic bags of intravenous fluids dangled over Sam's head. Throat cultures were taken and blood was siphoned from his arm in hopes of finding a clue to the illness that had felled him. Two of the doctors held a brief argument over the wisdom of doing a spinal tap.

"He's too sick," one said, "and besides, we've done them on the other six. Negative. Every one was negative. Why put him through that if it's not going to tell us anything?"

Susannah stood as close to the table, near Kate and Will, as she was permitted. She didn't like the way Sam looked. Hard to believe that anyone could look worse than Tina when she'd been brought in, but Sam did. The paramedic had taken his temperature in the ambulance. He hadn't announced it, but he'd jotted it down and Susannah had watched the way his fingers looped the zero and then angled a four. One hundred and four degrees! Her heart had lurched sickeningly.

The doctor on call wasn't Izbecki. The woman tending Sam was identified by the name tag on her white jacket as "Margaret Mulgrew, M.D." Susannah had never seen her before. Where was

Dr. Izbecki? He was familiar with these cases. Dr. Mulgrew was wasting precious time asking questions that they already knew had no answers.

"He's got the same thing the others in ICU have," Susannah finally burst out impatiently, startling the team working on her brother. "Take him up there! They'll know what to do. And call Dr. Izbecki. He knows what's going on."

"Wow," Kate breathed from behind her. She nudged Will with her elbow. "I didn't know she had it in her."

"Well, she's right," he said quietly. "We're wasting time here. We can't do anything for Sam down here. He belongs upstairs."

Instead of reprimanding Susannah and sending her from the room in disgrace, Dr. Mulgrew lifted her head and nodded. "The girl is right," she said crisply. "Take him up to ICU. I want all cultures back *yesterday*. If they come back positive for influenza, page me. But," she added heavily, "they won't."

Susannah watched the gurney hurry away, her heart in her throat. The wheels had just disappeared inside the elevator when her parents hurried up the steps outside the wide glass doors. Nervously straightening the collar of her pink smock and smoothing pale tendrils of hair that had escaped her braid, she ran to meet them.

She could tell immediately that her mother

hadn't absorbed the fact of Sam's illness yet, and probably wouldn't until she had actually seen him lying in Isolation hooked up to tubes and wires like a scientific experiment.

Her father seemed more angry than worried. "I just found out," he said tersely as they joined Susannah, "that the Montgomery girl is comatose. Comatose! When did that happen? Why wasn't I told? No one on the Board of Directors was notified. I found out quite accidently when I called Montgomery to ask how soon he thought he could get back to Brazil to finish up that business down there. He told me about his daughter. He also told me that the other cases are every bit as critical." But when he looked at Susannah, she saw anxiety in his eyes. "Your brother doesn't have the same thing, does he?"

She wanted desperately, more than she had ever wanted anything in her life, to say, "No, of course not." She wanted to lie.

She was spared both the truth and a lie when Dr. Mulgrew arrived. "Mr. and Mrs. Grant? Could we sit down over there, please?" she invited, pointing toward the alcove. "You come, too," she said to Susannah. "The patient is your brother, I believe?"

Susannah nodded and moved with them through the corridor.

She glanced once over her shoulder to the quiet corner where a group of people from The Music Room had gathered to await word on Sam's condition. She caught Abby's eyes, shrugged helplessly, then followed her parents and the doctor to the alcove, where she took a seat on a blue padded bench.

When Dr. Mulgrew had finished outlining the harsh truth for the Grants, Caroline sat perfectly still in shocked disbelief, her hands in the lap of her lemon yellow sheath.

Samuel asked exactly what Susannah had expected him to ask. "What are you doing for my son?"

"Everything possible," Dr. Mulgrew answered calmly. "We've closed off our ICU and have moved our other critical patients to other hospitals in the complex. And we've been trying to talk Matthews into calling in outside help, but . . ."

"What kind of help?" Samuel asked sharply.

"Outside virologists. A team, if necessary. Our team here, and it's a good one, hasn't been able to come up with anything except that it's not influenza. Not a known one, anyway. We need people who know more about this stuff than we do. But Matthews is afraid the word will get out. Bad for business, he says."

Susannah's father nodded reluctantly. "He's right. Bad for the lab, too. Grant Pharmaceuticals is on the edge of a major breakthrough in medical research. A new herb has been found in the Brazilian rain forest that may pave the way for a cure for several major cancers. An outbreak at Med Center now could seriously jeopardize our research."

Dr. Mulgrew barely hid her disgust. Biting off her words, she said, "We now have *seven* cases of this thing. It is very clearly contagious, and to my mind, if it *is* an influenza, it is not an ordinary one, not a known one, and not easily curable. It can't be treated with aspirin and bed rest and fluids. Antibiotics and antibacterials have been unsuccessful so far." Her steely gaze on Samuel Grant never wavered. "I would like you to pay particular attention to the word *contagious*, please."

Caroline stood up, smoothing her skirt nervously. "All I care about," she said clearly, "is my son. He *is* going to be all right, isn't he? I want to see him." Her voice sank then, and she murmured, "It's my fault. I should have . . ."

"Never mind that now," her husband interjected sharply. He inquired of the doctor, "May I assume that my son is getting the best treatment possible?"

Dr. Mulgrew shrugged. "I can't very well tell you that, can I, Mr. Grant, when I don't even know the nature or origin of the illness yet. Your concern for your son is understandable, but may

I respectfully suggest that you take it upstairs to Matthews? We don't even know what we're looking for here." That said, she turned and hurried away.

Susannah's father turned to her, his eyes accusing. "You *knew* about all of this. You knew Tina was comatose, you knew this thing was contagious . . ."

"And I tried to tell you, didn't I? At least, I tried to tell you that Sam was sick. But you weren't listening, as usual." He was being grossly unfair, but she didn't want to fight with him now. All she cared about was Sam. "I think Dr. Mulgrew's right. You have to talk Mr. Matthews into calling in specialists."

For once, he looked as if he were actually listening. But his expression quickly turned to doubt. "I have to agree with Matthews on one point. If a team of medical investigators comes trooping into Grant, the press will find out. It will be all over the papers that we've got some unknown, contagious disease here."

"Why can't you just tell the press that they're here for a conference or something? Medical people come here from all over the world all the time for meetings and conferences and seminars."

His eyebrows arched. "You're suggesting that we lie?"

Susannah stood up, glancing into the hallway

to find Will's eyes on her. She knew how *he* would answer her father. So she did it for him. "That's a better lie than pretending there's nothing wrong here when there is. It's a safer lie. You say your new drug could save lives. That's great. But what about the lives here, now, up in ICU? Don't they count for anything? One of them is your son, Dad."

She hadn't actually been thinking in terms of death, of course. No one had died. She was just being dramatic to make a point, she told herself. Then she saw Sam's face as he lay on the gurney, and wondered just how far off the mark her statement was.

"Samuel," Caroline said quietly but more firmly than Susannah had ever heard her speak, "if you don't do everything within your power to see to it that our son gets the help he needs, I will never forgive you. Never."

Her husband nodded. "I'll go see Matthews right now. You go on up to ICU. I'll meet you there shortly."

"You might not be allowed to see Sam," Susannah was forced to tell her parents as they all moved upward in the elevator. "He'll be quarantined. You can look at him through the door window, but I don't think they'll let you in. Unless you wear protective gear, and I don't know if they'll okay that."

"They'll let us in," Samuel said confidently.

Susannah supposed they would. He was, after all, Samuel Grant II.

Downstairs, Kate joined Will, standing with Callie, Jeremy, and Zack near the watercooler. Callie made some inane remark about absolutely adoring the purple turtleneck Kate was wearing, which Kate ignored. "I only have a sec," she said quickly. "Things have been piling up, so I decided to lend a hand. We've got a boating accident victim in Two, a nasty case of the croup in Five, and a hand that's lucky to still be attached to an arm in Three." She had barely finished speaking when the wail of an ambulance died directly outside. Although he wasn't on duty, Will ran to help.

To Jeremy, Callie, and Zack, Kate said abruptly, "You might as well go home. Susannah probably won't come back down for a while. And all I can tell you about Sam is that he's got a fever and he's being taken care of. The flu, maybe. You can call ICU later if you want. Maybe they can tell you something." But she knew that wasn't true. How could anyone tell them anything when no one *knew* anything?

Will rushed past them then with a gurney flanked by two paramedics. Callie sucked in her breath, fearful of another case of illness whose germs might be floating around in the air. She tugged on Jeremy's arm. "C'mon, let's get out of here. I need air."

"Caucasian male, forties, unconscious, second- and third-degree burns to portions of his upper torso, arms, neck, and face," they heard then, but Callie didn't stop walking. She heard the words, "Car wreck, trapped inside, gasoline spilled, caught fire," but still she kept going. There was far too much sickness in this place, germs everywhere, even if the new patient didn't have the fever. Since she wasn't allowed to see Tina or Sam, why hang around?

Outside, on the steps, a tall, heavyset, blonde woman walked up to Callie and Jeremy. Callie had the feeling she'd been lying in wait for them. Without introducing herself, the woman asked, "You were at The Music Room tonight, am I right?"

Callie nodded, but Jeremy looked at the woman suspiciously and asked, "Who are you?"

A small white card was extended toward them. They didn't take it. "Sheila Dane, music critic for the *Grant Gazette*. I was at the club, too. I saw what happened. I was wondering what you could tell me about your friend. The one who was taken away in the ambulance."

Jeremy tugged on Callie's arm. "C'mon," he urged, "let's go." To the woman, he said politely, "You'll have to talk to someone inside about that."

"But you were with him. And we've been hearing rumors at the paper that there's some kind of sickness going around. Is that true? Is that what your friend has? What kind of sickness is it?"

Zack came out just then. He paused before passing the trio. "I know you," he said to the woman. "You're the music critic from the paper. So what do we get, a thumbs-up or thumbs-down?"

"To tell you the truth," she said apologetically, "I'd just arrived when that boy collapsed, so I haven't really had a chance to hear you yet. Maybe tomorrow night. That is," she added slyly, with a coy smile, "if you can talk your friends here into giving me the dope on that boy who's sick."

Zack laughed. "Oh, I get it. We tell you what we know, and the band gets a good review? Okay. Never underestimate the power of the press, I always say. So here's what I know about the kid who got sick tonight: nothing." He smiled at the woman. "Now we get a good review, right? Wasn't that the deal?" Laughing again, he ran lightly down the steps and hailed a cab waiting at the curb.

Jeremy began to walk down the steps, too, but Callie stayed where she was, looking at the woman with interest. "You're the press?" She was thinking of the conversation she'd overheard outside her father's office. And she was seeing him again in the arms of his secretary, whom he hadn't fired, after all. And she was thinking, very rapidly, as if her brain had suddenly gone on double time, that if the people in Grant found out that the hospital had been keeping secret news of a terrible, contagious disease, they'd be furious. Then Med Center would be in trouble and so would her father, because he ran the place. He might even lose his job. No problem. Her father was very, very smart and capable. He could get a job anywhere. Lots of people would want to hire him. Maybe he'd get a job where he had lots of time off. A nicer job, where he didn't have to hide important information from people just because of money. Maybe a job with an old, ugly secretary.

"Callie!" Jeremy insisted, reaching out to tug on her arm.

"Jeremy, be careful, you'll tear my new dress." Then, she said sweetly, "You run along now. This nice lady will take me home."

Jeremy took a hesitant step backward. "Callie, what are you doing?"

"Go *on*, Jeremy." Callie waved him away. "See you later."

Jeremy had known Callie a long time. He hesitated another moment or two, then sighed in defeat, turned, and loped on down the steps, turning only once to direct a disapproving glance in her direction.

When he was gone, Callie extended one hand toward the woman and said, "My name is Callie Matthews. My father runs this place. Now, what exactly did you want to know?"

chapter
14

"**I** don't know how you stand it, working here," Abby said to Susannah the following morning. They were in the hospital's basement cafeteria with Jeremy and Will, sitting at a long, narrow table in a dim corner. The only other people in the stark, white-walled room were residents with weary faces, a few orderlies, and several worried-looking relatives of patients. Conversation had to battle the constant sound of the PA system summoning staff members or announcing a new emergency. Every few minutes, someone in white or surgical green would get up and hurry from the room. The smell of alcohol and antiseptic lingered, overpowering the rich, more pleasant aroma of fresh coffee.

Susannah had spent the night up on the eighth floor, trying to sleep on a sticky, fake-leather couch in the nurses' lounge. Lavender half-moons had appeared under her eyes, and her face was tense with anxiety over Sam. Abby had brought her a change of clothing. She had slipped into the clean white trousers and a peach knit top in the nurses' lounge, not bothering with her smock. She leaned back against the plastic chair, sipping hot coffee. Her pale, wavy hair, which she had brushed thoroughly and left hanging loose, draped itself over the back of the chair, as Abby added, "It's so hectic here, so noisy. And so gruesome. There are so many nicer places to work at Emsee. We don't get any critical-care patients at Rehab. No blood or broken bones or convulsions from fever. That's what makes it nicer."

Susannah, lost in worry over Sam, shrugged absentmindedly. "I like it here," was all she said.

"Callie talked to a reporter last night," Jeremy announced suddenly.

The remark snapped Susannah to attention. But it was Will who cried, "Say that again?"

Jeremy's handsome face flushed an uneasy red. "I said, Callie talked to the music critic from the *Gazette* last night. I haven't seen this morning's paper, so I don't know if they printed anything." He shook his head. "I tried to talk her out of it, but she wouldn't listen."

"A music critic isn't really a reporter." Abby glanced around the table for confirmation. No one nodded in agreement. But Abby persisted. "She doesn't get to write news, does she? All she writes is music reviews."

"Even if that's true," Will said darkly, "she could tell someone else. Her editor, for instance.

He'd never sit on a story like this one. It could be all over the front page this morning." He jumped to his feet. "I'm going to go dig up a paper. Be right back."

"Why would Callie do something like that?" Abby ran a hand through her dark, curly hair. "I can't believe she didn't know better."

Jeremy laughed, a brittle, humorless sound. "Oh, she knew better. Last night when we were following the ambulance here, I told her my dad warned me to keep quiet about the fever, and Callie said, 'Yeah, mine too.' She sounded mad when she said it, though." Jeremy's thick, light-colored brows drew together in a puzzled frown. "I saw the look on her face when she made up her mind to talk to that woman. No way was she innocent. She was doing it deliberately. What I can't figure is why."

"Because she's mean and thoughtless and self-ish, that's why," Abby said firmly.

Jeremy shook his head. "That's not it. I know Callie is spoiled and selfish. My mother always called her 'Bertha Brat.'" His face darkened when he mentioned his mother. "But then, my mother didn't like very many people in Grant. The thing is, Callie doesn't do anything without a reason. Trust me, she's got a reason for talking to that newspaper woman. I just don't know what it is."

"If the *Gazette* prints what's going on here,"

Susannah said, pushing her chair back and standing up, "the phones in every hospital in this complex will be ringing off the hook. We've got every kind of patient there is, people from all over the world. Cardiac patients. Cancer patients. Burn patients. Victims of horrible accidents. Chronically ill people who can't find the right treatment anywhere else. Med Center is the only hope for a lot of these people. If the word gets out that we have something contagious here, relatives of those patients will pull them out of here. Where will those patients go?" Susannah shook her head. "I can't think about that now. All I can think about is Sam. Maybe if it does come out in the paper, my father and the Board will be forced to call in outside help. I still haven't heard if he and Matthews agreed to do that last night. I haven't seen my parents this morning."

"Doesn't anyone know what it is yet?" Jeremy asked. "What they've got? How sick they really are?"

"No."

Jeremy felt a sharp stab of anger. He had come to the hospital first thing this morning to find out how Tina and Sam were, and no one would tell him. Maybe Callie had done them all a favor. Maybe the only way to find out anything was to go to the press, tell the story, and force the hospital to tell them something.

"Is Kate here?" Susannah asked Abby. "I haven't seen her."

"She's upstairs already. Said she wanted to see how the ICU patients were doing. Are you going up there now?"

Susannah nodded. "I want to talk to my father. Maybe now that he's seen how sick Sam and the others are, he's realized we need help here. Outside help."

Telling her friends she'd see them later, she left the cafeteria.

Upstairs in ICU, one of the alarms at the nurses' desk went off.

The two nurses sitting at the station got up and ran, summoning other nurses from other rooms as they went.

So there was no one at the desk when Kate stepped out of the elevator. And no one in the wide hallway. She decided to wander on her own until she found a nurse. There seemed to be some sort of commotion going on in one of the small rooms fronting the hallway. She hadn't heard a "Code Blue," the signal that meant a patient was in serious trouble and all personnel must respond. But the code could have sounded before she arrived on the floor. She ignored that room and moved along the wide corridor to peer in the door windows of other rooms. Every door bore a large placard reading ISOLATION. DO NOT ENTER.

Jenkins Rue, his head turned away from Kate, his injured leg held in traction, lay very still, his eyes closed. Several IVs were running steadily, their needles taped into one arm and the top of a hand, the containers suspended above his head like makeshift mobiles. His chest was bare and dotted with round, white EKG monitors hooked up to a machine beside his bed. She had heard that his CAT scan had revealed no serious head injury. That was good news. Still, the sight of him reminded Kate of the broken toys she used to "doctor" when she was little, lining them up on the back porch and ministering to them with an inexpensive doctor's kit her grandmother had given her.

There was no nurse in the room, which Kate found odd. Weren't all ICU patients supposed to have twenty-four-hour supervision? Maybe that didn't apply when Isolation was involved. Maybe in contagious cases, they were watched mostly by monitors from the nurses' station. But there was no one at the nurses' station. Weird.

In another room, Damon Lawrence lay among a sea of white. Not only did he have electrodes attached to his chest, he also had a breathing tube taped to his face, the tube attached to a ventilator. It was a shocking sight.

Feeling increasingly uneasy, Kate moved slowly along the corridor. The third room contained the middle-aged cleaning-crew foreman, who was hooked up to the same multitude of wires and tubing as the others. But while the others had been lying still, he seemed to be moving restlessly. Did that mean he was getting better? Or worse?

Kate was about to move along the hallway in search of Sam, when a young nurse, masked, capped, and gowned, burst out of a doorway, raced down the hall to the desk, and snatched up the telephone. Kate couldn't hear what she said, but the call only lasted a second. Then the young nurse flew back down the hall to disappear into the same room.

Curious, Kate moved forward, toward that room. She didn't want to interfere. A mere volunteer would never be allowed to help with an intensive care case. The best thing she could do for the patient in that room was stay out of the way.

But then it occurred to her that the patient might be Sam. If something was going terribly wrong in that room, she had to know.

She took a few more steps and found herself standing directly in front of the door. It was closed, but the voices of the half dozen or so nurses and doctors working on the patient were loud, commanding, and she was able to make out some of what they were saying. Shouting, actually. She couldn't see who the patient was, and there was no chart hanging on the wall outside the room. It could be Sam. Or it could be Tina, or the Rollerblading accident victim.

Her own heart began pounding in her chest as she heard someone shout, "The patient is ventilating, damn it!" Then, "Don't you dare die on me, you hear me?"

Kate's blood chilled. Die? She pressed her face up against the glass, straining to hear, trying to see beyond the furiously active medical staff blocking her view of the patient. They were all bent over the bed. She saw paddles, saw a nurse applying gel, saw her hand the paddles to a tall figure in white, saw the paddles descend, saw feet jerk.

Kate pulled back to glance again at the sign on the door. There it was, ISOLATION. DO NOT ENTER. According to that sign, the patient in this room suffered from the mysterious flu of unknown origin. Not heart disease.

But there in front of her was the crash cart, there were the paddles, set aside for the moment while someone in a blue coverall worked strenuously at closed-chest heart massage.

It must not have worked, because the paddles were handed over again. When they had been slapped down upon the chest, the feet sticking out from beneath the sheet jerked once again. Kate knew that wasn't necessarily a sign of life. Just a reflex from the electrical current.

She waited, holding her breath, straining to

see the monitor beside the bed. But it was turned slightly away from her, and she couldn't tell if the line was flat.

"What's up?" a voice asked in her ear.

Kate gasped and jumped.

"Sorry," Susannah said quietly, peering into the door window. "Didn't mean to scare you. What's going on?"

Kate still didn't know who the patient was. It could be Sam. "I . . . I'm not sure. I guess someone's in trouble."

"Who?"

"I don't know."

Susannah glanced around the hallway. "Are my parents up here?"

"Haven't seen them. Maybe they went downstairs for coffee."

"That isn't Sam in there, is it? Kate?"

"I don't know," Kate said again.

Then they both heard, as clearly as if they'd been standing in the room, an emotionless voice stating, "No pulse."

And both shuddered as a long, wicked-looking needle appeared, poised to plunge directly into the heart. If that didn't work . . .

It didn't.

"Clear!" they heard, and the paddles smacked down again. This time, the lurching motion was more violent.

Because of the masks and caps, Kate and Susannah could see no facial expressions on any of the medical staff. But they could tell from the body language that their attempts at reviving the patient were fruitless.

They tried valiantly for another very long five minutes. Kate had stayed calm up until the very last minute or two. She stayed calm because she fully expected success. She had been lucky so far in her volunteer work. No one had died in ER while she was on duty. Even patients who had suffered full cardiac arrest had been resuscitated every single time. She expected that to happen this time, too, right up until the last minute or two.

"Who do you think it is?" Susannah asked breathlessly. Her face, too, was pressed up against the glass. She was trembling, and her face was chalky.

"It's not Sam, Susannah. I'm sure it isn't." Kate wasn't sure of any such thing, but it killed her to see Susannah so scared.

They had every intention of remaining in front of the door until they knew who was in that bed. But a nurse looked up, saw them, and angrily waved them away.

They left reluctantly, but they didn't go very far. If they waited in the hall long enough, someone would have to tell them something.

Leaning against the wall opposite the room where the frenzied activity was taking place, they talked quietly to hide their anxiety. Susannah told Kate about Callie's interview with the newspaper woman.

Kate's response was, "What could Callie talk to her about? Callie doesn't know anything. She doesn't work here. Wouldn't be caught dead working here. There's no way she could know how sick Tina really is. So what could she have told the woman?"

"Maybe her father told her that Tina's comatose."

"He wouldn't have. He'd be too worried that she'd tell everyone. He's her father, he must know what a big mouth she has."

They stopped talking when a nurse came out of the room and sank into a wooden, straight-backed chair against one wall. When she reached up and pulled off her mask, they saw that she was young. Her face was as white as the stacks of clean linens they often carried from one cubicle to another in ER. And they saw that she was crying. Quietly. Not even bothering to wipe the tears away. They dripped down her cheeks and onto the blue coverall she was wearing over her uniform.

Kate and Susannah exchanged a glance of dread. The nurse had left the door to the room slightly ajar. The sounds coming from inside had changed. The shouting had ended. Footsteps had stopped rushing from bed to machine to supply cabinet. They moved slowly now, heavily. The earlier sharp, staccato commands had been replaced by a dull murmur of voices.

The crisis was over.

Slowly, Kate and Susannah moved to stand next to the nurse's chair. Susannah, her eyes dark blue with fear, was the first to speak. "What's wrong?" She glanced at the plastic name tag on the coverall. "Nurse Fielding? What's happened?"

Mary Fielding lifted her head. "I know I'm supposed to be objective," she said, her voice choked with tears. "But I can't help how I feel. That girl was only seventeen years old. Just two years younger than me."

Kate saw the undisguised relief in Susannah's face at the word "girl." The patient wasn't Sam. There were two girls in ICU. Tina Montgomery, and the victim of the Rollerblading accident. When that thought registered, something else registered as well, and the relief in Susannah's eyes was instantly replaced by new anxiety.

Because the nurse had used the word "was." She hadn't said, "That girl is only seventeen years old." She had said, "That girl was only seventeen years old."

"Which girl?" Kate asked hoarsely.

"That Montgomery girl. She was so young!"

"Was?" Susannah breathed.

Mary Fielding regarded them with moist blue eyes. "That girl died," she answered slowly, as if she wasn't quite ready to believe it herself yet. "They tried everything. They really did. But she died a few minutes ago."

chapter
15

—∿�∿—

Lost in shock, Kate and Susannah didn't hear the elevator arriving at the eighth floor. When Abby suddenly appeared in front of them waving a newspaper, they stared at her blankly.

"There is an article in the paper . . ." she began, but broke off to say, "Hey, you guys look like you just lost your best friend." Then she noticed the nurse, who was still crying quietly. "Uh-oh, what's going on?" Round, dark eyes moved to Susannah's face. "It's not Sam, is it?"

"No," Kate said then, standing up straighter, her eyes losing the blank look of shock.

Susannah's eyes met Abby's. She cleared her throat. "Tina Montgomery just died."

Abby gasped. "Died? Tina? Are you sure?"

The young nurse wiped her eyes and got to her feet. "I've got to get back in there." To Abby, she said, "Like I told your friends here, we tried everything to keep that girl alive. She was just too sick."

"With what?" Kate asked quickly. "Do they know?"

The question caught Mary Fielding off guard. "Oh." She thought for a minute, her lips pursed. "No, I don't think they do." Slowly, reluctantly, as if she were going to her own doom, she walked back to Tina's room and disappeared inside.

"I want to see Sam!" Susannah said urgently. "I need to see my brother, *now*!"

Nodding, Kate moved swiftly to a cart beside the nurses station. She flipped quickly through the medical charts until she found the one she wanted. When her eyes had scanned it, she announced, "Room F. Sam's in Room F." She dropped the chart back into place and the three girls moved down the hall to a room with a large red *F* over the doorway.

They couldn't see much through the door window. Sam was there, attached to the usual network of wires and snaking tubing, but his head was turned away from the door, his body covered to the waist. They could, however, see that his chest was rising and falling evenly, which was all Susannah cared about. Sam might be very, very sick, but he was still alive. Unlike Tina Montgomery.

They had just turned away from the door when Susannah's parents stepped out of an elevator. When they saw the trio gathered in front of Sam's room, Caroline hurried her steps. "Susannah, what's wrong?" she cried when she was still some distance away.

Susannah waited to answer until they were close enough to allow her to speak quietly. When she had told them about Tina, Caroline's eyes filled with tears.

Samuel's reaction was one of anger. "Damn! Last night I let Matthews talk me into holding off on a call to outside experts. His arguments made sense: We have good people here, there have only been seven cases, there'd be no way to keep it quiet, the resulting publicity would be bad for the entire complex, and no one had died . . . and now this!"

"If this . . . this *thing* can kill," his wife said heatedly, "you have no business keeping it quiet. People should be told! They should be *warned*!"

"They know now," Abby said, holding up the newspaper in her hand. "There's an article in this morning's *Gazette*. Front page."

"Let me see that!" Susannah's father reached for the paper.

"Everyone's going to find out now, anyway," Kate pointed out coldly. "Even Matthews can't keep Tina's obituary out of the newspaper, right?"

Samuel winced. But he said as his eyes scanned the newspaper article, "All they will learn from that is that a seventeen-year-old girl is dead. They won't learn what she died of, because no one seems to know. But," he added as he handed the newspaper back to Abby, "we're going to find out. Caroline, you stay here with Sam. I'm going to see Matthews and I'm not leaving that office until he's made a call for outside help."

Susannah stayed with her mother, who was visibly shaken by the news of Tina's death.

Kate and Abby went back downstairs. In the elevator, Abby said, "Well, it's awful about Tina, but at least Mr. Grant is going to find out what this horrible thing is."

An unforgiving Kate said, "Yeah. Too bad he didn't do it before someone died."

"Kate!"

"Well, it's true, isn't it? I wasn't a member of Tina Montgomery's fan club, and I guess you weren't either. But she didn't deserve to die, did she? If they'd brought outside help in faster, maybe she'd still be alive. And do you really think Samuel Grant II would be moving his butt now if his own son weren't sick? I don't think so."

Abby didn't like to hear Med Center criticized. "He probably thought the people here could figure it out, Kate. The best research people in the country are here. Who knew how bad this thing could get?"

"If they're the best people in the country," Kate responded tartly as the elevator doors slid open, "why didn't they know it would get this bad?"

"Because it's something new," Abby persisted.

"Something different. That's why none of the tests they did showed anything. And I don't know about you, Kate, but I'm scared. What if Matthews agrees to call in outside help and they can't figure out what it is? How many more people are going to die like Tina before someone comes up with an answer?"

"Maybe none," Kate said, changing her tactics. No point in arguing with Abby about Med Center. She had the same blind spot as Susannah. Yes, Med Center was wonderful, yes, some brilliant work was being done here, and no, there wasn't any place else in the world where Kate would feel safer if she fell ill. But that didn't mean it was perfect. "Maybe it was one of those bugs that attack really fast and then disappear. No one ever knows where they come from or what caused them. We've read about them, remember?"

An ambulance's wail outside forced Abby to raise her voice slightly. "I remember. But the diseases I read about came from rain forests and jungles, Kate. The last time I looked, Grant didn't have a rain forest or a jungle."

"People travel, Abby. And sometimes when they leave the country, they come back with more than presents for their relatives. Anyway," Kate added as they separated in the hall, "let's just hope Sam's was the last case."

And for a few peaceful days, it looked that

way. There were no new cases. The prominent virologist Dr. John Beck, whom Matthews had finally agreed to summon, flew in from Germany and settled in a large but airless, fully-equipped room at Grant Pharmaceuticals to study all of the cultures and specimens sent over. The news of his arrival somewhat placated the people of Grant, inflamed by Callie's newspaper interview. The truth had been kept from them, and that made them angry. But something was being done now. They would hold off on action against the medical complex until this doctor with all the initials after his name gave them some answers.

Tina's funeral was held on a Tuesday marred by a thick, humid fog that coated the mourners, the hearse, and the green canvas canopy with a damp, glistening film. Susannah and her mother wept for Tina and for Tina's parents, who had lost their only child.

The other six patients held their own, not getting better, but becoming no worse. Only Damon Lawrence required the aid of a machine to help him breathe.

Dr. Beck insisted that all medical personnel be retested, also all of the relatives of the seven patients to date. The wait to hear the results was excruciating, and tempers flared more than once in ER. The strain was showing.

When the residents of Grant heard about the

testing, they showed up in hordes at ER, demanding to be tested as well. Eventually, the lab at Grant Pharmaceuticals took over that job, testing anyone who insisted upon it.

All of the results were negative.

"It is absolutely viral, not bacterial," the virologist, a short, white-haired man, told Samuel Grant at the dinner table in Linden Hall on Friday night. "A fever of unknown origin. I must tell you that my fear is, it could be one we haven't seen before. That would not be good. However, it is clearly not a hemorrhagic fever. You may be grateful for that, Mr. Grant. That is a blessing, I promise you."

"So, what do we do?"

"There is more testing to be done. Then if what I suspect is true, you will need to contact your Centers for Disease Control. In the state of Georgia, is it not?"

Samuel bristled. "We were hoping to avoid that, Dr. Beck. This is why we contacted you instead of calling the CDC. We want some answers here, but we would like to avoid the publicity associated with bringing in their field people. The word always gets out, no matter how careful you are. Bad public relations. What can the people in Atlanta do that you can't?"

"Many things. I am a researcher of disease, Herr Grant. That is what I do. But if what I suspect is true, we will need to find someone who was infected with the illness but fought it successfully. Perhaps he or she became mildly symptomatic, but quickly recovered. Or never became ill at all, which would, of course, make our search that much more difficult, since that patient would not even be aware that he had *been* ill. Might have believed that he had a touch of the flu. If we *could* find him, however, we could use the antibodies in that person's blood to come up with a vaccine. We could do that quickly, with the marvelous equipment you have in your laboratory. But first the person must be located, and that I cannot do for you. Your CDC will be better able to help you there."

Susannah didn't see how they could find that person when they had no idea *where* the illness had originated. Many people in Grant traveled internationally. The task of poring over every airline manifest for the past month or longer seemed to her overwhelming, even with the help of computers. Some people took ships across the ocean because they feared or disliked flying. Those people would have to be considered, too.

"Tina's father traveled," she volunteered as Marcella served chocolate mousse. "Remember, Father? You said he was checking out a new drug. In South America?"

Her father nodded. "I've already talked to him. He stayed in a five-star hotel in Brazil, never left the room except to go to meetings, and even those were held in the hotel. He didn't go wandering around any jungles or rain forests. He was so busy he even took most of his meals in his hotel. And other than becoming airsick, which is normal for him, he wasn't sick. So . . ."

"Still," Dr. Beck said, "I would like to talk to this man. Could you perhaps set up such a meeting?"

Samuel shook his head. "That would be difficult just now. It was his daughter who died. He's taking it hard. I've given him some time off and the key to our cabin in the Berkshires. He and his wife have, I believe, already left town. There is no telephone up there. We go for peace and quiet." He settled back in his chair and lifted his coffee cup. "Isn't it a good sign that there have been no new cases these past few days?"

The doctor shrugged. "Perhaps. But as you do not yet have an epidemic here, it becomes clear that this particular disease is not easily spread. Or perhaps many people have an inborn immunity to it. There may be others who, while not immune, are able to resist it for longer periods of time than those who have already fallen ill. I was told, for example, that the girl who died had had an influenza a short while ago. That would have weakened her immune system. I was also told in answer to my questions that the boy on the ventilator kept late hours and took very poor care of his health. Your own son, I believe," he said, waving his spoon toward Samuel, "was extremely active and might have been fatigued."

Susannah saw her father's lips tighten. He didn't like the suggestion that Sam was actually capable of becoming overtired. How silly. Sam was human, wasn't he? Anyone on his hectic social schedule would become tired. Some people might even admit it.

"In each of those cases," the doctor continued, "the immune system could have been functioning poorly, making them easy targets for our fever. You could have people in your community who actually have the disease now, but are resisting it better because they take excellent care of themselves. They might think they have a summer 'bug,' as you call it, or believe they are simply overtired or suffering from allergies. Unless they have an inborn immunity, they will eventually show up at your hospital. In other words, the fever could still be spreading. Quietly. Taking its time. Another reason why I would suggest you call your CDC in Georgia."

Susannah's heart sank. They might have more cases in town, even now?

Caroline had been listening quietly to the doctor's words. Now, she said to Susannah, "Perhaps we should think about canceling the fashion show. If what Dr. Beck says is true . . . and I'm sure it is," she added hastily, sending a quick smile the doctor's way, "gathering so many people together at one time in one place would be foolish. If we have no way of knowing who is sick and who isn't. I would hate to be responsible for . . ."

"We are not canceling any events scheduled for Med Center!" her husband interrupted, slamming his hand down on the lace tablecloth. When they all stared at him, he lowered his voice to add more calmly, "We will let Dr. Beck finish his tests. If he doesn't come up with anything, I'll talk to Matthews about contacting the CDC. But for right now, life goes on as usual, is that clear?"

Susannah regarded him with incredulity. "But it *isn't*!" She carefully folded her white linen napkin and placed it beside her plate, her dinner only half eaten. "How can you say that? Life *isn't* going on as usual! Look around this table, Father. Do you see Sam sitting here anywhere? You don't, because he's not here! He's lying in a hospital bed in Intensive Care at Emsee." She stood up, left her chair, pushed it back into place. "So please don't talk about life going on as usual." She turned to her mother. "Yes," she said clearly, "I think you *should* cancel the fashion show. And I think if the people in this town knew the whole truth about this horrible disease, they wouldn't step one foot outside their houses until someone comes up with some answers. May I be excused? I want to go see Sam."

Caroline nodded. Susannah told the doctor politely that it had been nice meeting him, and without saying a word to her father, left the room.

Five minutes later, at 8:10 P.M. at a pool party held not far from the foot of Linden Hill, two members of the Grant High School football team advanced upon seventeen-year-old Sally Kent, who was lying listlessly on a chaise lounge in her pink bikini, holding a wet paper towel to her forehead. It was clear to the crowd around the pool that the boys had every intention of tossing pretty, popular Sally into the deep blue water.

"Leave me alone!" she warned as they continued to advance. "I don't want to swim! I don't feel good. My head is splitting. Go away!"

"Nope," the larger of the two boys said, grinning. "This is a *pool* party, Sally, and you haven't gone near the water. We can't have that. C'mon, be a sport."

Sally Kent had never felt so sick in her life. And that scared her, because a girl she hardly knew, a girl who supposedly had been a very healthy athlete, just like herself, had *died* after being in the hospital just a few days. She knew she should be in bed. She knew she shouldn't have come to this stupid party. But she had hoped it would make her feel better. Only it hadn't. She felt worse. Much worse.

"I am *not* going in that water!" she insisted as the boys reached her. They ignored her. One picked up her legs, the other her arms, and as she screamed a protest, they began swinging her.

"Hey, guys," the hostess, a girl named Pinky Dwyer, shouted from the open glass patio door, "you gotta see this! Bill Conti is actually swinging from the dining room chandelier! Come see!"

Laughing, everyone but the two football players and Sally Kent jumped up and ran into the house.

"I gotta see that," the larger of the two boys said. "Let's dump her." They tossed a still-screaming Sally out into the middle of the pool. She landed with a splash and sank immediately.

Then, laughing, the two boys ran into the house to watch their teammate make a total fool of himself. They knew Sally Kent was an excellent swimmer. So they didn't wait to make sure she came back up to the surface.

She didn't.

chapter
16

~~⌇⌇⌇⌇⌇⌇~~

Will didn't mind working nights. The night ambulance runs were usually more interesting.

The call came into the hospital shortly after eight-thirty from a 911 operator at the police station. "Respond to a possible drowning, 11856 Arrowroot Drive, intersection Arrowroot and Linden Hill Boulevard, facing north. Victim young female. See homeowner name of Dwyer."

Will's heart jumped. Linden Hill? Susannah's road. But the address wasn't on Linden Hill, he told himself as he climbed into the ambulance. The young female victim was at a house below the hill, just off the boulevard. Could be someone Susannah knew, but it couldn't be her, he thought as the siren came on and the vehicle raced from the garage, out of the complex, and north on Grant Avenue.

Susannah came around the final curve at the foot of Linden Hill, prepared to increase her speed as she hit the long, straight, tree-lined boulevard. She was anxious to get to Emsee and find out how Sam was doing. But what she saw ahead of her as she braked for the stop sign kept her feet from moving to the accelerator.

Cars lined Arrowroot on both sides of the street, which spelled "party" to Susannah. Nothing unusual there. The corner house facing Susannah was Pinky Dwyer's house. Pinky had a lot of parties. But there were also two police cars and a fire truck in front of the house, a large split-level, brightly lit. No smoke or flames were visible, but it occurred to Susannah as she hesitated at the stop sign that what looked like bright lights inside the house could actually be flames. A fire?

Pinky Dwyer wasn't a close friend of Susannah's. Susannah knew she was popular at Grant High. Thus the parties. Sometimes they were pretty wild, or so she'd heard. She'd never been invited to one. If someone had accidentally set the house on fire, this party must have been even wilder than usual.

Susannah set the Benz in motion. Her intention was to drive by. Whatever the emergency, it was being handled by police and firemen and she'd only be in the way. A siren and the red roof light of an ambulance approaching from the other direction changed her mind. Maybe she could be of some help. Deciding quickly, she pulled the Benz over to the curb and parked behind the two police cars.

When she left the car, she could see immediately that there was no fire in or around the house. Excited voices from the rear of the house carried easily through the quiet evening. Whatever the emergency, it was going on back there, behind the high privacy fence.

Susannah waited on the curb for the paramedics. If they couldn't use her, she would leave, get out of their hair. After she found out what was going on back there.

The ambulance screeched to a halt and Will jumped from the back, along with his partner and, a moment later, the driver. Will was carrying a resuscitator and a cardiac monitor, his partner toted the radio and drug box.

"What's going on?" Susannah asked as they began to run toward the back gate. "Can I come?"

He nodded. "Possible drowning."

Of course. Pinky liked to boast about the pool. "Is it Pinky?"

"Don't know yet. Come on. You can help."

Susannah felt a rush of warmth for Will. She was given so few chances to be of help at the hospital. Maybe she could actually do some good here.

As they yanked the back gate open, she said quickly, "You're not wearing masks, Will."

"It's a drowning, Susannah, not a fever patient."

"You don't know that. Kate's mom said you

guys are supposed to wear masks on all calls until you know for sure that fever isn't involved, remember?"

"You're right." He ran back to the ambulance, returning a minute later to pass out masks. He handed Susannah one, and she put it on, lifting the hair that hung loose around her shoulders.

"Thanks for reminding me," Will said. "Completely forgot."

So she had already helped. It felt good.

The pool area was crowded, a sea of figures in bathing suits, all silent. The only sound was the soft hum of the pool's filter. Moonlight shone on the dark blue water in the pool, empty now except for a lone white rubber float bumping up against the tiled sides.

A limp figure, wet hair splayed out beneath its head, lay on the sea-blue tile on its back while a fireman in uniform administered mouth-to-mouth resuscitation. He stopped just long enough to inform the paramedics that the patient was unconscious and not breathing. Will asked him to continue his resuscitation efforts, using the valve and mask as Will began giving the patient one hundred percent oxygen.

Susannah heard quiet crying in the group forming a semicircle around the victim. Two boys in swimming trunks, boys she recognized as Grant High School football players, were kneeling beside the unconscious girl. Jeremy, in shorts and a sopping-wet T-shirt, sat on the tile directly behind them. All three faces were tense with shock.

"Move the crowd back, Susannah," Will ordered. In a different tone of voice, he announced, "Pulse fifty and weak," then, "sinus bradycardia."

Susannah knew what that meant. It meant the girl lying on the tile, whom she now recognized as Pinky's friend Sally Kent, was in serious trouble. The girl wasn't suddenly going to begin coughing up pool water and sit up, asking what had happened. That pool water had already left her lungs and was circulating throughout her system. She was acidotic, not a good thing. Not good at all.

Using the radio, Will's partner contacted Emsee directly. "Patient unresponsive," he said. "Pupils dilated and reacting sluggishly. Heart rate 68 with ventilation. Blood pressure 108 over 60. No spontaneous respirations."

He turned from the radio to say to Susannah, "Get that crowd back!"

Without hesitation, she began the thankless task of pushing anxious friends of Sally's backward, toward the patio, under strings of brightly colored plastic lights in the shape of fish. Jeremy and the two football players stayed where they were. They weren't in the way, and something about the expressions on their faces kept Susannah from attempting to move them.

The disembodied voice from the hospital, when given complete information on the victim's current condition, ordered an esophogeal airway.

Susannah saw Will hesitate. Tricky business, opening an airway, especially with a patient as small as Sally.

Sure enough, Will's partner, a tall, thin woman Susannah knew as Rita Black, argued with the hospital. But since Sally was still unconscious and not breathing on her own, the voice on the radio insisted.

It was Rita who put the EOA in, not Will. Susannah was almost as relieved as he must have been. Rita had far more experience dealing with esophogeal airways than Will. It was difficult. But with care and a few tense words muttered under her breath, Rita managed the procedure, effectively opening an airway for the patient. She checked Sally's chest to make sure she had been successful, then informed the hospital.

The hospital voice ordered the necessary drugs, which Will inserted in the IV he had already set up.

"Is she dead?" Pinky Dwyer asked Susannah when the crowd had successfully been pushed back against the patio doors. "Is Sally dead?"

"I don't know. What happened?"

Pinky wasn't crying, but her voice was agitated as she tried to explain. "She said she didn't feel very well. She wasn't even going to come tonight.

I talked her into it. She said she had a really bad headache, but I thought she was just mad because Russ Swanson didn't ask her to the party." Pinky took a breath and added nervously, "So you guys don't need those masks, right? I mean, they're pretty creepy. And no one here is sick."

Sally had had a bad headache? Susannah was very glad she'd remembered the masks.

"You still haven't told me what happened." Susannah watched with the others as Sally was loaded onto the gurney, a rolled-up towel beneath her shoulders to help keep the airway open. The fireman continued to ventilate her as they hurried from the pool area, Will and Rita carrying the equipment. Will waved to Susannah, signaling her to come with them.

Pinky looked uncertain. "Well, I guess she just fell in. Jeremy pulled her out. We were all inside, and then Jeremy came back out here. I heard him yelling, and when I got here, he was pulling her out of the pool and yelling at me to call 911. So I did. Jeremy gave her CPR until the firemen arrived. Is Sally going to be all right?"

"Don't know. You guys should all go home. Looks like the party's over. Call her parents, okay? Tell them to come to the ER."

Pinky burst into tears. "Oh, I can't, I can't! They'll blame me! They'll hate me!"

"Pinky," Susannah's voice was stern. "Call

them. Right *now*!" Then she ran to catch up to Will.

"I'm coming, too!" Jeremy called, and followed, his clothes dripping on the grass. Susannah couldn't quite grasp the image of Jeremy as a hero. But he was. He had probably saved Sally Kent's life. If she lived.

"Is she going to be okay?" Susannah asked when the patient had been loaded into the ambulance.

Will's voice was grim. "Don't know. It's too early to tell. She must have been under for more than a few minutes. Where the hell was everyone, that's what I want to know? How could a girl drown at a crowded party?" He climbed inside the vehicle, then turned back to Susannah. "Want to ride along?" He glanced over at the parked Benz. "I can bring you back to your car later."

"Sure. Thanks."

"I'll meet you at the hospital," Jeremy called, and hurried off to his own car.

As Will helped Susannah climb into the back of the ambulance, she said, "I think you should take her temperature."

The driver slammed the doors shut and hurried around to the front.

Overhearing Susannah's suggestion, Rita looked interested. "Temp? Well, we will, but why?"

"Because the girl who held the party said Sally . . . the patient . . . wasn't feeling well when she arrived. I guess if the pool water was cold, that could have lowered her temp, kind of like a refrigerating blanket. But if she did have a fever, wouldn't it be back up by now? Just check, okay?"

Sally Kent's temperature was only 101 degrees.

"But it shouldn't even be that," Rita said. "I think maybe you were right, Susannah. Thanks for reminding us about the masks."

"If she's sick, that fireman was exposed. Jeremy, too. They both gave Sally mouth-to-mouth."

"Well, I don't know about your friend Jeremy, but Tom's fit as a fiddle. It'd take a lot to make him sick. I heard that all of the fever victims were pretty run down before they got it, so I guess Tom's safe enough," Rita said.

Maybe. But could the same be said for all of those party guests at Pinky's? If Sally Kent had the fever, every single one of those guests had been exposed. And from what she'd heard about Pinky's crowd, they kept pretty late hours and their favorite form of exercise was partying. They could be "run down," as Rita had put it.

There had to have been thirty or forty people at that party. If even half of them got sick . . .

At the hospital, Sally was quickly transferred to a hospital gurney and rushed to a trauma room. Dr. Mulgrew spoke briefly with Will and Rita. Then she got busy. She checked Sally's lung sounds and her pupils. Her eyes above the mask seemed to Susannah full of concern as she ordered blood gases, a portable chest X ray, a CBC, and electrolytes. Then, as the orders were being obeyed, she spent a quick few minutes in a second consultation with Rita and Will before returning to her patient.

"What did she say?" Susannah asked as Will joined her in the doorway. "Is Sally going to be okay?"

"Who knows? Dr. Mulgrew's worried about pulmonary edema developing. But that's not Sally's only problem. They weren't going to send her up to ICU because it's all Isolation now, but when we told her about the temp, she checked for other signs of the fever. And found them. So they're sending her upstairs."

Only then did Susannah remember why she had been on her way to the hospital. "I want to see Sam," she said in the same urgent tone of voice she had used when she learned of Tina's death. She looked up at Will with despair in her face. "I thought it was over. That there weren't going to be any more new cases. Didn't you?"

"No." The certainty in his voice surprised her. "I didn't think that. Because we never found the source. Doesn't seem to me that anyone has tried very hard, either. There is probably a carrier out there in Grant somewhere, Susannah, and no one knows who it is. That person will just keep spreading the disease until he or she is found. Thanks to Med Center's aversion to publicity, for which we can all thank Matthews, whoever the person is probably doesn't have a clue that he or she is dangerous."

"But that article in the newspaper . . ."

Will made a sound of disgust as he pushed the elevator button. "That article didn't give one single decent bit of information. It was all hints and innuendo, typical Callie Matthews garbage. And there hasn't been a word printed since, except for that stupid little piece of public relations after Tina died. Blaming her for not getting help sooner."

Susannah fell silent. She didn't want to argue with Will. Besides, she knew he was right. Emsee *should* be doing more to get the word out. Hiring a virologist from another country and hiding him out in a room at the lab wasn't accomplishing what was really necessary . . . which was getting to the origin of the disease. Where was it *coming* from?

"What do you think should be done?" she asked as she pushed the elevator button. "I mean, if you were running things, what would you do?"

His answer was swift and certain. "Call the CDC."

Exactly what Dr. Beck had suggested to her father, Susannah thought with a pang. And her father had refused.

"I'm going to see if I can cheer up Jeremy," Will said, pointing to a chair in the hallway holding a dejected-looking figure. Someone had given Jeremy a white towel. He had draped it around his shoulders, and his head was down. "He saved that girl's life, and no one's paid any attention to him since we got here. Come back down when you're done upstairs and I'll drive you to your car. I'm due for a break, anyway."

Upstairs, the nurse at the desk didn't want to let Susannah into Sam's room. She pointed toward the door. "You see that sign? It says DO NOT ENTER. It's for your own protection, Miss Grant."

"Oh, for heaven's sake!" Susannah cried, "I've already been exposed in ER, before we knew what anyone had. I am *going* in to see my brother. I'll suit up. I'll even wear goggles. But I *am* going in there."

And she did. The nurse gave in. There *were* advantages to being Samuel Grant's daughter.

Feeling strange in the weird protective gear, Susannah sat beside Sam's bed, holding the hand that hadn't been pierced with an IV needle, talking to him in a low, steady voice. He lay perfectly still, his face ashen, his eyes closed, the monitor at his head reflecting a steady zigzagging line that reassured Susannah. As long as that line wasn't flat. . . .

"I know we don't always get along," she said quietly, tears filling her eyes. "And I know we're not like lots of other twins who can read each other's thoughts practically and finish each other's sentences and have the same tastes and habits. I know you're disappointed sometimes because I'm not as much fun as you are. And sometimes I'm disappointed because you don't like the same books and movies that I do." The tears slid from her eyes and down her cheeks. "But I love you like crazy. I love you because you're like the other side of me, the side I'd like to be but can't because that's just not who I am. I always figured that you need the steadier part of me, and I need the fun part of you, and that together we almost make a perfect person. Right?" Susannah reached up with her gloved hand to wipe the tears sliding into her mask. "So you can't die on me. I need you, and you need me. It would be really rotten of you to desert your own twin. So you just hurry up and get better, okay?"

A light tapping on the door window brought Susannah's head up. Her mother was standing in the hall.

"I mean it, Sam." Susannah began to slip her hand from his and, just for a second, thought she had met resistance, thought that his fingers had refused to let go. But when she looked down at him, he was lying perfectly still, his eyes were still closed, and there was no expression on his face.

She pulled her hand free and stood up. Then she went to the door to let her mother take her place.

chapter
17

"Is she dead?" Jeremy asked as Will took a seat beside him. Jeremy's face was white and drawn, his eyes red-rimmed from diving deep into the pool to pull Sally Kent to safety. "Is Sally dead?"

"No. But she would be if it weren't for you, Barlow." Will draped a dry, thick white towel over Jeremy's shoulders. "You're a hero, kid. What I want to know is, where was everybody while that girl was drowning? Why was she out here all alone?"

Jeremy explained about the chandelier stunt. "Tom and Peak feel rotten about throwing her in. She's a good swimmer. Why didn't she come back up?"

"She was too sick. She's got the fever."

Jeremy's head shot up. "I gave her mouth-to-mouth. Before the firemen got there." His face went even paler. "So I guess I'll get it, too, now, right?"

"Not necessarily. Must not be all that easy to get, or the whole town would have it. I know you haven't been sick lately. Do you know if Sally has?"

Some of Jeremy's color returned. "She had a bad head cold a couple of weeks ago. We went to the movies one night, and she coughed the whole time. Very annoying. People kept giving us dirty looks, but she said she couldn't help it. We left before the movie was over."

"Well, that's it, then," Will said, his voice kind. "Her immune system wasn't up to par because of that cold. But you didn't get it, right?"

"No. I haven't had a cold since I was a kid."

"So you're not run down, and you're feeling fine, and I don't think you should worry. Look, Jeremy, you saved a life tonight. That's no small thing. Why don't you just enjoy feeling good about that? Don't make your life miserable by worrying about something that probably isn't going to happen."

There was a commotion at the door, and a rushing of feet toward them. A man and a woman, the woman armed with a microphone, the man with a video camera, joined the pair seated in the hallway. "Which one of you saved that girl's life?" the woman asked.

Will grinned. "Ah, your fifteen minutes of fame are about to begin, Barlow. Enjoy!" He stood up and bowed dramatically in front of the newspeople, then waved a hand in Jeremy's direction. "Here's your hero. Make him look good, okay?"

Instead of being pleased by the sudden attention, Jeremy shrank back against the chair. "Don't leave me here with them!" he begged Will, his voice low. "I don't trust them. Remember Callie's interview?"

"This is not the same thing at all," Will argued, moving away toward the elevator to wait for Susannah. "You deserve this, Barlow. The whole town should know what you did tonight. Relax! And smile nice for the camera."

Susannah stepped out of the elevator then, to find Will waiting for her.

Although her eyes were slightly pink from crying, she smiled when she saw what was happening in the lobby. "I wonder if Dr. Barlow will cut Jeremy's picture out of the paper tomorrow and post it on the hospital bulletin board?"

"Barlow's a busy man. Maybe he doesn't have time to read the paper."

"Well, Jeremy will just have to make sure his father sees the article, that's all. He can tape it to the bathroom mirror or something. Dr. Barlow should know that he's not the only member of that family who saves lives."

Will had already signed out for his break. As they left the building, he said quietly but firmly, "You know your dad has to call in the CDC, don't you? Mulgrew said Sally has the fever, too. That's another new case. So it isn't over."

That really wasn't what Susannah had been expecting or hoping for in the way of conversation. It caught her off guard and she found herself feeling defensive. "It's really not up to my father. Matthews runs the hospital."

They started down the wide, stone steps. A siren close by forced Will to wait with his reply. When it had died down, he laughed and said, "Come on, Susannah! Matthews may run the hospital, but your father runs Matthews. Everyone knows that. Nothing happens in this city without the approval of Samuel Grant II. It's up to him to see that the CDC is called in. Matthews won't do it on his own."

Susannah stopped and turned to face Will on the bottom step. "You make it sound like my father is a dictator! He's not!"

"I didn't say that." Will smiled. "King, maybe." The smile faded. "You know it's true, Susannah. He could get the CDC here in no time if he wanted. And that's what he needs to do. Can't you talk him into it?"

"He called in Dr. Beck," Susannah argued. "The most famous virologist in the world."

"And has he come up with an answer?"

"Well, no, not yet, but . . ."

Someone called Susannah's name. She turned to see Zack Ballou running out of the darkness, waving at her. "There you are!" When he arrived at the foot of the steps, slightly breathless, he nodded at Will and said to Susannah, "I was hoping you'd show up at the club tonight. I wanted to know how your brother was. He's not worse, is he? Sam, isn't that his name?"

"Zack, what are you doing here? Aren't you playing tonight?"

"We're on break. I called your house, and your housekeeper said you were here. So, is Sam okay?"

"He's hanging in there."

Zack glanced up at Will, who was listening silently. "Where are you two off to?"

Susannah couldn't believe Zack had left the club to come looking for her. "There was an accident, near my house. A girl almost drowned. I rode with Will in the ambulance, so he's taking me back to my car."

"Oh, I'll do that." Zack smiled easily at Will. "No need for you to tear yourself away. I know how busy you guys are these days, what with that fever and everything. I'll take Susannah to her car. You can get back to work."

It almost sounded like an order. Will's eyes narrowed. "Well, gee, thanks," he said lazily, "but I promised Susannah I'd give her a lift, and I don't break promises. If you need to talk to her, why don't you follow us out there in your car?"

Susannah hid a smile. All of a sudden, Will was staking a claim on her? Since when?

Since a very good-looking musician had showed up, looking for her.

If Will was determined, Zack was even more so. "That'd be pretty lame. All of us driving out there in two separate cars." He looked to Susannah for support. "Right? Wouldn't it make more sense for you to come with me?"

She had to admit that it did. Besides, Will had a lot of nerve, paying no attention to her whatsoever until someone else did. And he had blamed her father for not doing more to halt the spread of the fever, when that wasn't even her father's job. That job belonged to Matthews. "Zack is right, Will. I really shouldn't take you away from the hospital. Your break is only fifteen minutes. It would take longer than that to drive all the way out the boulevard and back again. That doesn't make much sense. I'll just go with Zack, okay?"

When she saw the look on Will's lean, handsome face, she willed the words back, but it was too late. He stiffened, and his lips drew together tightly. "Sure. Whatever you say. Let's be sensible, by all means. Let us always be sensible." Then he turned and, without hurrying, walked back up the steps and disappeared inside the hospital.

Zack laughed and reached out for Susannah's hand. She let him take it and they began to walk toward the parking garage. "Looks like your paramedic is suffering from an advanced case of jealousy," he said. "You two have something going?"

"No." And until tonight, Susannah thought, I was pretty sure there wasn't any chance of that ever happening. But Will had definitely been annoyed when Zack showed up. So maybe she'd been wrong. "He's just tired. Tonight was awful. Horrible."

In Zack's rental car, speeding along Linden Hill Boulevard, she told him about the near-drowning and about Dr. Mulgrew's diagnosis of another new case of fever. "We thought we'd seen the last case," she added wearily. "And all those people at the party were exposed. We could have lots more cases now." The thought made her head ache. She wished she hadn't hurt Will's feelings. Zack would be gone soon, but Will wouldn't. She'd be working with him at Emsee. He and Kate had always been there for her when no one else was. Now she'd made him mad.

Zack pulled up beside her car in front of the Dwyer house. The street no longer looked like a parking lot, and the house was dark. Pinky and her parents were probably at the hospital waiting for word on Sally's condition. "Come back to the club with me?" he asked. "I could probably squeeze in a couple of dances."

He really was nice. It would have been fun to

go back to the club with him, relax and listen to music, dance a little. Maybe life would seem a little less grim if she went with him. If Abby shows up there, I could stay with her tonight, Susannah thought, and I wouldn't have to go home. Linden Hall is *not* going to be a happy place tonight, with everyone so worried about Sam.

But if she went back to the club, she'd keep seeing Sam out on that dance floor and the way he'd looked at her just before he fell. She couldn't stand that.

"Thanks, but I think I should go back to the hospital. My parents will probably stay there all night, and I might, too. I want Sam to know we're all pulling for him. I know he probably won't even know we're there, but . . ."

"But *you* know it," Zack finished for her in a sympathetic voice. "That's what counts, right?" He reached across her to open the car door. Instead of pushing down on the handle, he reached up, turned her face toward his, and kissed her. It was not a hasty kiss, and he didn't seem to be in a hurry to let her go. Susannah realized she didn't *want* him to let her go. Was it attraction? Fear? When he did release her, he gave her a quick smile and said, "Maybe by tomorrow night, your brother will be sitting up and eating a Quarter Pounder. Then you can come to the club, okay? I'll be waiting."

Still feeling the kiss, Susannah nodded, thanked him for the ride, and left the car.

"I'll be pulling for Sam, too, Susannah," Zack promised as she closed the door and stepped up to the curb. She was touched to the point of tears by his kindness. He was being so nice, and he hardly knew her or Sam. Well . . . that kiss hadn't felt like he hardly knew her. She found herself hoping that she would have time to see more of Zack again before he left town.

But right now, all she wanted to do was go home and take a shower and race back to the hospital. She knew it wasn't just because of Sam. It was partly that. Mostly that. But there was something else. If she didn't make things right with Will, she wouldn't get a wink of sleep. And the way things were going in Grant, anyone who worked at Emsee was going to need all the sleep they could get.

chapter
18

Callie Matthews never watched the news. Too depressing. But her mother, who seldom left the house in the evening, watched it faithfully, wanting to know what was going on in the outside world. Callie was in her room, carefully painting her long fingernails with two coats of Pink Abandon, when her mother's voice called over the intercom, "Callie! Jeremy's on television. Channel three!"

On Callie's set, plainclothes detectives were engaged in a high-speed chase across the city of Chicago. Waving one hand in the air to dry the new polish, Callie reached out with her other hand to switch channels. And there he was. Jeremy. On television! A small banner on the bottom right of the screen announced that the picture of Jeremy was "live," from Med Center's Grant Memorial. Something about him saving somebody's life.

Callie's mouth hung open. Jeremy? Had saved somebody's life? How? He wasn't a paramedic like that Jackson boy, the one who was every bit as gorgeous as Denzel Washington. Besides, Jeremy Barlow wasn't the "hero" type. That paramedic probably was. And Sam Grant was. Even Jenkins Rue, who somebody had said lived in a fishing shack but was, nevertheless, really cute and a great football player, was a better candidate for "hero" than Jeremy was. When Rue wasn't lying flat on his back in a hospital bed, of course.

Must be a mistake. The only thing Jeremy Barlow had ever saved was his stupid coin collection.

Callie turned up the volume.

"In other words," a skinny, red-haired television reporter gushed as she pushed a microphone into Jeremy's face, "if you hadn't come along when you did and noticed the girl floating unconscious in your friend's pool, she would have died."

Callie burned with envy as Jeremy nodded. She couldn't tell if he was embarrassed or thrilled to pieces to be on television. Maybe both. Jeremy was one of those people who was never sure exactly how he felt about anything. Like her own family, the Barlows never talked about feelings. Jeremy had told her that was one of his mother's most frequent complaints. "Not talking about feelings doesn't make them disintegrate," she had shouted at his father many times, according to Jeremy. "Those feelings are still *in* there, turning sour like spoiled milk. And the longer they *stay* in there, the more rancid they get, Thomas, until they become positively poisonous."

Jeremy looked very much as if he were having trouble now figuring out how he felt. He kept trying to avoid the microphone, twisting his head this way and that, but when he looked straight into the camera, Callie saw pride in his eyes.

Callie herself was having *no* trouble identifying her feelings. Jealousy, pure and simple. There was Jeremy on her television set, live, and he was a hero! He was on the news, and tomorrow morning there'd be a big story about his heroism in the newspaper. Probably a picture, too.

Her picture hadn't been in the paper along with her interview. She had asked that stupid music critic if she wanted a picture, had even offered to run home and get one. She knew exactly which one she'd get. The one from last Christmas. She'd been having an exceptionally good hair day, and she looked like a model in that green velvet dress, everyone said so. But the woman had said no, no picture. And the story in the paper had only been a few crummy lines.

Jeremy would get a bigger story. And a picture.

"We have also learned," the reporter continued, swinging the microphone away from Jeremy and meeting the camera head on, "that the nearly drowned girl is the latest victim of the mysterious, unidentified fever plaguing this city. When asked what new measures were being taken to protect the public from this scourge, hospital officials refused to comment beyond assuring this reporter that due to the complete quarantine of every case, the public is not in danger at this time. This is Andrea Gray, reporting for KMXS, channel three."

The reporter was unable to restrain a look of skepticism on her face when she said, "the public is not in danger at this time." It was that look that stirred Callie into action.

Twice this week, she had overheard her father on the telephone, arguing with Samuel Grant. It hadn't been hard to figure out why they were arguing. Ever since Sam got sick, his father had pushed for outside help. Her father refused. Bad publicity and all that. He'd only agreed to call in that guy from Germany to get Samuel Grant off his back. And she'd heard him insisting that the doctor's arrival in town be kept quiet.

Well, it hadn't been. Lots of people knew he was in town. Okay, so maybe she had mentioned it to a few people. But they would have found out anyway.

She knew her mother agreed with Sam's father. She had said, straight out, two mornings ago, that the CDC in Atlanta should be called in. Caleb Matthews, usually so gentle with his ailing wife, had snapped at her. Practically told her to mind her own business, and stormed out of the house without saying good-bye to his wife or daughter.

Even that silly reporter who'd interviewed Jeremy knew that Med Center should be doing more to stop that horrible disease from spreading.

Callie turned off the television.

"Did you see him?" Her mother's voice on the intercom. "He looked so handsome, didn't he? Even with his hair wet like that. His father must be so proud."

"Yeah, he looked great," Callie called back, but her mouth twisted in disgust. If Jeremy could get his picture in the paper, so could she. And she knew exactly how.

Her father hadn't been home to dinner one single night this week. Maybe he was working, and maybe he wasn't. All she knew was, he lived at Med Center, more than he did his own home, and that had to stop. Maybe she could kill two birds with one stone here. Get her picture in the paper and get her father back home where he belonged. He'd find another job. A better job. And in a way, she'd be as much a hero as Jeremy, because she just might be responsible for ending the awful sickness everyone was so worried about. She'd be a heroine to the whole city.

Checking to make sure her new polish job was dry, Callie picked up the telephone book on her nightstand, looked up a number, and dialed. "I'd like to leave a message for Andrea Gray, please," she said when someone answered. "My name is Callie Matthews. My father runs Med Center. Could you ask her to call me, please, when she gets back to the station? It's very important."

Satisfied, she hung up, put the phone book back, surveyed her nails, and lay down on her bed, smiling up at the ceiling. The people of Grant had a right to be protected from that awful fever. What kind of a citizen would she be if she didn't help?

Where had she put that Christmas picture?

When Susannah, her hair windblown, her face flushed from hurrying, arrived in ER, she was surprised to see Abby leaning against a wall near the nurses' station, talking to Will. They were deep in conversation, and he was looking down at her with interest.

As if she's the most fascinating conversationalist Will Jackson has ever met, Susannah thought with a sharp stab of jealousy that took her breath away. And Abby, looking perfectly adorable in denim overall shorts, a white T-shirt, and work boots with thick white socks, was smiling up at Will exactly the same way she smiled up at boys she was dancing with.

She is flirting with him! Susannah thought. Then she almost laughed. You can't possibly be shocked, she scolded mentally. Flirting is as normal for Abby as breathing is for most people. She doesn't mean it.

But it still rankled. Because this time the target of those big dark eyes and that I-really-think-you're-wonderful look was Will Jackson.

Abby looked up and saw her, hesitating in the doorway. "Oh, hi, Sooz," she called, "c'mon over! We were just talking about you." She added as Susannah arrived, "Well, we were really talking about Sam. But that's *almost* like talking about you, right? Will's mom said Sam doesn't seem to be getting any worse. That's good news, right?"

"What are you doing here so late?" Susannah asked abruptly.

"I came to get *you*. Your parents will probably stay here all night, right? Mom didn't want you spending the night in that big old mansion all by yourself. Me, either. I figured this was where you'd be, so I hopped one of the Emsee shuttles. But when I got here, Will said you'd gone off somewhere with Zack."

Susannah flushed with anger. Off somewhere with Zack? Will had made it sound like a *date*? He really must be mad at her. Well, look who was talking. Hadn't he just been enjoying every single minute of Abby's flirting? She refused to look at him, although she was acutely conscious of his presence beside her. She was also remembering the heartfelt kiss. "I didn't *go* somewhere with Zack. He just took me back to my car at the Dwyers'. You heard about Sally Kent?"

Abby nodded somberly. "Isn't it awful? But at least she's still alive, thanks to Jeremy. And Will here, of course." She beamed a smile at Will.

Susannah's teeth clamped down on her tongue. When she felt it was safe to let it go, she glanced around and asked, "Where's Jeremy?"

"He went home." Will's voice was smooth, cool. No hint of anger. But when Susannah looked up at him, she saw no sign of warmth in his eyes. "I think he wanted to make sure his dad saw him on the news. Unfortunately, Barlow's still here. We've had three cardiacs in the last hour, and he was called in on consults. I guess Jeremy went home to an empty house." He smiled at Abby. "You should have rescued him along with Susannah, Abby."

"I don't need rescuing," Susannah snapped.

Will's smile vanished. "I meant, from going home to an empty house."

"I knew what you meant." To Abby, Susannah said, "I'm just going to run up and check on Sam and my parents one more time. I'll meet you outside in ten minutes, okay?" She wanted to add, Is it safe to leave you two alone down here? but she clamped her teeth tightly together and hurried off to the elevator. They could run off and get married, for all she cared! It was *none* of her business. She and Will Jackson had never even had a date! Probably never would, either.

Her father looked tired. He was pacing back and forth in the ICU hallway, hands clasped behind his back. His tie was crooked, the red handkerchief in the breast pocket of his navy blue blazer limp. But her mother, in pale blue linen, looked as perfectly put-together as she always did. What would it take, Susannah wondered, for her to lose it, just totally lose it? And realized that she already knew the answer. Something bad happening to Sam, that's what it would take. Her mother could never handle that.

"How is he?"

Samuel shrugged. "It's this waiting. Enough to drive a person crazy. Beck hasn't come up with anything except what we already knew, which is 'a fever of undiagnosed origin.' He might as well have stayed in Germany. But he's still trying."

"He needs help," Caroline announced firmly, surprising Susannah. "You know he does, Samuel."

"If he doesn't come up with something by tomorrow morning, I'll talk to Matthews again."

"You know there's a new case," Susannah said flatly as she peered in Sam's window. He wasn't moving. She reminded herself that he was, at least, still breathing. "You must have seen them bringing Sally Kent's gurney up here."

Her mother nodded. "The Kent girl. Yes. She's in a room down the hall. The doctors aren't optimistic, but that seems to be due to her accident, not the fever itself. Her parents are frightened half out of their minds. I tried my best to console Ethel, but it was hopeless."

"They shouldn't have had a party without adult supervision," Samuel said angrily.

"Oh, for heaven's sake, Samuel, even if there'd been adults there, they wouldn't have been out by the pool. We never are when our children have a pool party." To take the sting out of her words, Caroline got up and went over to put an arm around her husband. "You're just trying to find someone to blame for all of this. But the fever isn't Ethel and David's fault, now, is it?"

"No. It isn't."

Husband and wife sat down together, holding hands.

Susannah felt a pang of envy. It would be nice to have someone to share her anxiety over Sam with, too, someone who cared about her more than anything else in the world. Zack? How could someone who traveled all the time be there for her? Will? Will cared. But as a friend. Right now, she needed more than that.

She told her parents she was staying at Abby's, and left.

On the way home, although she hadn't meant to, she heard herself saying to Abby, "I can't believe you were flirting with Will!" At first she wished she hadn't said it, and then she thought, oh, what's the difference. She was tired and upset and worried about Sam, and Abby *had* been flirting with Will.

"I wasn't! What are you talking about?"

"You were so, Abigail. I know flirting when I see it, just like I know an expert at it when I see one. You're an expert, and you were batting those big dark eyes of yours."

Abby laughed. "Susannah, you're right, I was! I *was*! I'm sorry. Honestly, I didn't mean to. It just sort of . . . happened. It's like I go on automatic pilot. Don't be mad. He *is* gorgeous, is he not? And I *am* female, am I not?" She laughed again. "You can smack me if you want to. I guess I deserve it."

Susannah laughed then, and felt some of the tension slide away. "Abby, you are hopeless. Totally. Okay, I forgive you. But if it ever happens again, we're finished."

"That's not fair! *You* refuse to make a play for him. He doesn't even know how you feel. So you can't blame anyone else for thinking of him as fair game."

Susannah pulled the Benz up in front of Abby's house and parked. "Listen to yourself! Make a play for? Fair game? That language is practically medieval. Whatever happened to 'I am woman, hear me roar'?"

Laughing, Abby jumped out of the car and waited for Susannah. "Well, *roar* then," she said when they were both walking up the lighted driveway. "Do *something* to let Will know you're interested, before some other girl snaps him up. And," she added hastily, "I'm not talking about me."

"You'd better not be."

"Actually, I was pretty disappointed when Will said you'd gone somewhere with Zack. Because I happen to think *he's* really cute, too."

"I was right," Susannah said, laughing as they entered the O'Connor house, "you are positively hopeless."

"I know." Then, cheerfully, Abby said, "Keep me in mind if you decide you'd rather have Will than Zack, okay? I'll be standing by to pick up the pieces of Zack's broken heart."

They stopped laughing when Mrs. O'Connor appeared in a white terry robe to ask them what they knew about the drowning incident at the Dwyer house.

Ten minutes away, in a house far emptier than the O'Connors', Jeremy Barlow sat alone at the breakfast bar in the kitchen, drinking a glass of orange juice and wondering why he didn't feel like the hero he was supposed to be. He had called his father's office before the reporter started their interview, to tell him to switch on channel three, but there was no answer.

Finally, he'd given up and gone home, hoping

Dr. Thomas Barlow would be waiting for him.

But there was no one there. He picked up the telephone that sat at his elbow and dialed his mother's number in San Francisco.

There was no answer.

He let it ring seventeen times.

chapter
19

—∿⌒∿⌒∿⌒∿⌒∿⌒∿—

When Susannah arrived home from Abby's on Saturday morning, her father was striding furiously back and forth in the living room, waving a newspaper in the air and shouting about "irresponsible journalism." She stood in the doorway, wondering *What now?* as he continued his tirade.

"If Caleb Matthews doesn't have any more control than this over his own daughter," he shouted as his wife sat patiently in a velvet chair beside the fireplace, "maybe he shouldn't be running a first-class medical facility! Every member of the board has called me this morning about this article, and they're all furious with Matthews. His own daughter!"

Susannah realized that her mother wasn't listening. Caroline's eyes had a glazed look, as if she were somewhere else. Probably in Sam's hospital room.

"What's Callie done?" Susannah moved across the thick white carpeting to take a seat on the brick fireplace hearth. "Or should I say, what's Callie done *now*? Did she talk to a reporter again?"

Another wave of the newspaper. "She certainly did! The whole city's going to be up in arms now, in spite of the fact that half of what was printed is pure fabrication."

"That means the other half is true," Susannah couldn't refrain from saying.

Her father sent her a reproving look. "We had our reasons for not calling in the CDC. We had the community's best interests at heart." He tossed the paper at Susannah. She caught it and spread it across her lap, reading rapidly. "Now we have no choice," Samuel said angrily. "We have to call Atlanta. I've already put in a call. What this will do to Med Center, I can't imagine. I don't *want* to imagine."

"Emsee can't be the only hospital in the world that's had to deal with a contagious disease," Caroline pointed out gently. "The people from the CDC will discover what the problem is, and they'll fix it, dear. Isn't that what they're for? And" — a wash of relief flooded her face — "they'll cure Sam. They'll cure all of the patients. Isn't that the most important thing?"

Susannah wasn't listening. She was reading. Callie had laid it on pretty thick. She'd used words like "secrecy" and "plot" and "injustice" when discussing Med Center's reluctance to call in outside help. She had described the eminent virologist Dr. Beck as "some kind of specialist from out of the country, not even an American." She had hinted that the disease was wildly contagious (That's a lie! Susannah thought angrily) and that the entire population was in imminent danger of being wiped out.

Still, she was telling the truth about Emsee not contacting the CDC, and she was right about the reason. Bad publicity. Meaning money. How had Callie known that? Her father wouldn't have admitted it openly, would he? That would be a pretty stupid thing to do if Callie was anywhere within earshot.

"People are going to panic," she said grimly when she had finished reading. "The phones are going to be ringing off the hook at every hospital in the complex. I'd better get down there. One thing I can do is answer phones." Addressing her father, she asked, "So, can I tell people you are calling in the CDC? It might make them feel better. Is that a done deal?"

"Yes. You can tell them. If it will calm their fears, that might be best. The last thing we need right now is a mass panic. Tell them."

Susannah ran to change her clothes and drive to Emsee.

* * *

Saturday was another nightmare for all medical complex personnel. The phones in every hospital, including Rehab and Psych, rang incessantly. While Susannah and every other volunteer answered phones, nurses and doctors were forced to waste valuable time dissuading frightened relatives from yanking patients out of the hospitals. At the same time, Grant residents began pouring into ER, convinced their temperatures had suddenly skyrocketed and absolutely certain that they were coming down with the dreaded fever. Meanwhile, there were the usual number of valid emergencies: broken bones, heart attacks, deep lacerations requiring sutures, near-drownings in summer pools, heat stroke, highway accident victims, and accidental poisonings. ER was filled to overflowing. Doctors, nurses, orderlies, and aides raced around like marathon runners. People began shouting angrily when their needs weren't immediately met. Personnel from Social Services and Public Relations were called on to help quell the crowd's anger, but for the most part, their voices fell on deaf ears. Inflamed by Callie's printed quotes about "secrecy" and "dreaded plague," the citizens of Grant were in no mood to be placated.

It got worse. By two o'clock that afternoon, there were several dozen people marching up and down outside in the center of the complex, bearing placards and signs that read, among other things, LIFE IS MORE IMPORTANT THAN MONEY and GREEDY MED CENTER. The worst sign Susannah saw read: MED CENTER DOESN'T CARE ABOUT LIFE.

When Susannah went looking for Kate, Will told her brusquely, "She's upstairs, on five." She could tell he hadn't thawed yet. He was still ticked about Zack. She was tempted briefly to explain, then decided against it. What exactly was she supposed to explain? She wasn't about to say to him, "It's really you I care about, not Zack," when Will had never said he was interested. What did he think she was, a mind reader?

The crowd had thinned some. But every treatment room was occupied, and people still milling about in the waiting room complained loudly that they'd been waiting "hours" to have their temperatures taken. The phone on the reception desk in the lobby began jiggling shrilly. The nurse stationed there threw up her hands in despair.

Susannah turned her back on Will and wove her way through the crowded hallway to begin answering phone calls again.

Upstairs in ICU, Kate stood outside Damon Lawrence's room. He was still on a respirator and he had no visitors. A nurse wearing protective garb was adjusting an IV. There was no one else in the room. No mother sitting in a wooden chair beside the bed or leaning against the wall praying that her son would get better. Damon's mother was dead. Which was maybe one reason he'd always spent so much time at the Thompson house when he was growing up. Kate had no idea where his father was. He had once worked at the lab, but she vaguely remembered that he'd been fired for missing too many days. A drinking problem, she thought. Hadn't Will told her that a long time ago? Maybe Mr. Lawrence wasn't even around anymore.

Was Damon on his own? How awful. To be so sick and not have anyone around who cared.

Impulsively, Kate whirled around and went to the nurses' station. "I'd like to see Damon Lawrence, please."

"Sorry. No visitors."

"I'm his sister."

The nurse, busy doing paperwork, glanced up. "Oh, you are not," she said blithely. "I know you. You're Astrid Thompson's daughter, Kate, and you are *not* related to Damon Lawrence. So forget it."

"He's my half brother," Kate persisted. "My mother was married twice."

"No, she wasn't. I went to school with her, right here in Grant, and to the University with her after that. Astrid Thompson never had eyes for anyone but your father. So cut it out, okay?" Then, relenting, she added, "You're obviously a friend of the Lawrence boy. But you know the drill. Family only, and then only in protective gear and for only two minutes at a time."

"That's just it. I *do* know the drill. I know exactly what to wear and exactly how far away to stand and I know better than to touch anything. So I'm really a better visitor than family members might be, right?" Kate leaned over the desk. "Look, he's all alone in there. Has he had any visitors at all? Any?"

The nurse consulted the log. "No. Not one. But you're *not* related, Kate. If anyone found out I let you in, I'd be in big trouble."

"We're *all* in big trouble, thanks to this awful disease, whatever it is." Kate stood up straight again. "Hasn't Tina's death made you stop and think about what's important and what isn't? I mean, really, what's so great about a rule that says a boy has to lie dying all alone? That's not right, is it?"

The nurse thought about that for a minute. "He's not even going to know you're in there," she said then.

"Right. But *I'll* know. And you'll know. Won't that make you feel good, knowing he's not in there all by himself, just for a few minutes?"

If the nurse had been older, more experienced, and possibly more cynical, the approach might not have worked. But Kate could see that the idea of doing something that might make her feel good appealed to her. She'd probably had a horrible week. "Please?" Kate pleaded.

"Oh, all right. But you suit up, and don't forget your goggles. We still don't know how this thing spreads. Two minutes, Kate, no more!"

"I promise."

As she donned the awkward gear, Kate had no idea why she'd been so persistent about seeing Damon. He'd been a great kid when he was little, but then he'd changed. They weren't close friends anymore. She didn't even know who his friends were these days. Probably people she didn't want to know. Tough kids, probably, maybe even mean.

But when she got inside and stood beside Damon's bed, he looked anything but tough or mean. There is, she thought, gazing down at him, something so helpless and innocent about a critically ill person. The illness takes over, swallowing up every last trace of who they really are, until all you see is the illness itself. With his eyes closed and his features relaxed, Damon looked so much like the little boy she'd known a long time ago that she felt a lump in her throat.

Tentatively, Kate reached out and touched his

hand with her gloved one. "What happened to you, Damon?" she asked softly. "Before the fever, I mean. Where did you go?"

She was still standing there, still touching his hand, when the nurse opened the door and stuck her head in. "Kate," she said quietly, "time's up. Come on out."

Reluctantly, Kate turned and left the room.

chapter
20

Upstairs in his office, Caleb Matthews, a news-paper lying open on his desk, tried once again to reach his daughter by telephone. The chaos downstairs in ER was her fault, all her fault. This outrageous article in the paper . . . what had got into her? How could she betray her own father like that? If he held on to his job, it would be a miracle. His teeth clenched as the phone went unanswered. He slammed down the receiver. "If I get my hands on that girl . . ."

In her bedroom at home, his daughter lay on her back on the pink carpet, holding an open newspaper above her head. She smiled as she turned the newspaper this way and that, examin-ing from every angle the photograph of herself in the green velvet dress. Pleased with what she saw, she then read the article again, her lips moving as if she were actually saying the words aloud.

Two floors above Caleb Matthews's office in the Emergency Services building, a short blonde secretary entered a large, lavish office. The huge picture window behind an enormous mahogany desk provided a clear view of one half of Med Center. A tall, youthful-looking man with prematurely graying hair sat at the desk, reading. The secretary smiled as she entered, carrying the day's mail, and approached the desk. She placed the packet of mail on the desk and said, "Congratulations, Dr. Barlow! You must be so proud. Having a hero for a son!"

The doctor lifted his head, keeping an index finger on his place in the medical journal article. "Excuse me? What's this about a hero?"

"Oh, Dr. Barlow, don't be modest. I'm talking about Jeremy, of course. Saving that girl's life. My goodness, I would think you'd be bursting your buttons with pride. I would be, if it were my son."

Confusion filled the doctor's face. "Saved a life? Jeremy?"

The secretary looked surprised, then just as confused as the doctor. "You didn't hear about it? But it was on the news and in the paper this morning. With a wonderful picture of Jeremy. Such a nice-looking boy. I wouldn't be surprised if one of those news magazine shows got hold of the story and decided to go national with it. People do so like to hear good news. Especially these days."

When the doctor continued to look blank, the woman went on talking, slowly, one sentence at a time, as if she expected him to say at any moment, "Oh, yes, now I remember!" But he didn't say that. "The Kent girl," she told him, "almost drowned at a party last night. Your son jumped in and pulled her out. He gave her CPR until Fire and Rescue arrived." Still, the doctor said nothing. He was listening, she could tell, but he didn't seem to be taking in what she was saying. He looked blank. "Everyone in the hospital's talking about it. I can't believe he didn't tell you."

"Last night, you say? I got home late. I had a late dinner at the Club with some friends. I assumed my son was already in bed. I had early surgery this morning, so I was out of the house before he woke up. I haven't actually seen him since . . . well, it's been a day or two. Busy, you know, with everything's that's been going on. This place has been a zoo." The doctor leaned back in his expensive leather chair, folded his hands in his lap, and, still looking confused, murmured, "Jeremy? *My* Jeremy?"

"So, has your mom canceled the fashion show?" Abby asked Susannah when they met after work. "You said you thought she should."

Susannah was exhausted, and for the first time since she'd begun volunteering, thankful to be leaving Emsee. "I don't know. I guess so." The marchers with picket signs had gone. The grass where they'd walked, and then tusseled, looked bruised. "This was the worst day I've had since I started here. All those people. Everyone in town is scared to death. No one would come here for the fashion show even if we did have it."

"Tons of people called to cancel surgery at Memorial that they'd had scheduled for weeks. I told every single one of them that all of the fever patients were off in Isolation in your building, but they wouldn't change their minds. At least a dozen patients were yanked out of Psych this afternoon, taken somewhere else by relatives. All of the routine tests that were supposed to be done at the lab have been canceled, too."

"I guess my father was right," Susannah said gloomily. "He said this would happen if the word got out, and now it's happening." She hated the thought of Med Center's image being tarnished in this way. It was easy enough to accuse people of panicking needlessly, but could she really blame them? She understood why they were so frightened. She'd read the article, too. "Why do *you* think Callie did it? I mean, the language she used was so scary. 'Deadly plague,' for instance. Eight cases do not make a plague, and she knows that. It's like she was deliberately trying to scare people. That's so mean."

"How are the others?" Abby wanted to know. "How's Jenkins? And I heard Damon was on a respirator. That's a bad sign, right? Sam isn't that bad, is he? Did you see him today?"

"No, he isn't any worse. They're all hanging in there. It's kind of weird, when you think about it." They reached the Benz and climbed in. "I mean, I couldn't be happier that they're all still alive. But after Tina died, I guess we all thought everyone who got it would die, too. But they're all still with us. Damon is the sickest, but even he is still hanging on. So whatever this thing is, it isn't necessarily fatal, the way we thought at first. Callie had no business hinting that it was. Scaring people like that."

"And making it sound like the most treacherous, uncaring, perfidious people in the world work at Med Center," Abby agreed. "That's hard to forgive."

"Especially when it was mostly her own father who refused to call the CDC."

"And yours," Abby reminded gently.

Susannah sighed. "Yeah, I know. But at least he's doing something constructive now. I hope," she added fervently.

He had. When Susannah arrived home, so tired she walked up the wide, stone steps to Linden Hall slowly, like one of the arthritic patients at Rehab, she found a guest in the library with her father.

He called out to her as she passed the open doorway, "Susannah, I'm glad you're home! I want you to meet someone." The look he gave her as she entered the room clearly said, See? I've done what you've asked. "This is Dr. Leora Cicero from the Centers for Disease Control in Atlanta. This is my daughter, Susannah. We've already talked about her twin, you remember."

Susannah smiled at the tall, thin woman in the navy blue suit, and extended her hand. "I can't tell you how glad I am that you're here." A small, tired laugh escaped her. "And I can't tell you how much I mean that." She noticed then that Dr. Beck was also in the room, and sent him a wave in greeting.

The woman smiled. "I know you've all been very worried. We don't know yet what this is you've been dealing with, but we intend to find out."

We? Susannah quickly glanced around the room. Was she referring to herself and Dr. Beck?

Seeing the glance, Dr. Cicero said, "I have a partner, Dr. Link. He's on a tour of your mother's rose garden." She smiled. "I'm allergic, or I would have gone, too." Then she added with concern, "You look exhausted. You're feeling all right?"

"Oh, sure," Susannah said hastily, seeing the fear that sprang into her father's eyes at the question. "I'm fine. I'm just . . . it was pretty hairy today at ER, because of that article in the paper this morning. I'm a little tired, that's all. Will you be staying here with us?"

"Of course they will, Susannah," her father

answered for the doctor. "Now, if you'll excuse us, we'd like to continue our discussion."

Susannah had been looking forward to a long, hot shower and maybe a quick nap before returning to the hospital to visit Sam. But she hadn't anticipated being in the company of a medical investigator from the CDC. It was such a wonderful opportunity to learn. "Could I stay, please? I'd like to know what's going on."

Her father shook his head no, but Dr. Cicero said, "Of course. The illness has struck down a member of your family, so naturally you're interested." She smiled again. Susannah realized that the doctor was only a plain woman until she smiled. Then she was very pretty. "And I'm told you work at Med Center, Susannah, so you're practically a colleague. I think you should stay."

When Dr. Cicero's partner had returned from the rose garden, Susannah had no trouble staying awake to listen to the conversation. She was eager to hear what, if anything, Dr. Beck had discovered.

Not much, apparently. It wasn't hemorrhagic fever, that was clear, he said, because there were no signs of bleeding. Nor was it any known type of influenza. Although, he added, it could still be an entirely new strain.

When he had told them all of the things that the fever wasn't, Dr. Cicero asked, "So, what's your best guess so far?"

Susannah leaned forward to catch Dr. Beck's answer. "My best guess," he said in his very formal English, "is that what we are dealing with is a brand-new virus, one that has never surfaced before in this country."

chapter
21

"**T**ests show that it isn't typhoid, dengue, malaria, or influenza," Dr. Beck continued, "nor is it any other known arboviral, enteroviral, or adenoviral infection. I believe there is every reason to suspect something new and unknown."

Susannah expected Dr. Cicero to look disheartened by the news. Instead, she seemed intrigued. "None of the current patients have recently traveled out of the country?"

Dr. Beck shook his head no.

"Then we'll begin," the CDC investigator said briskly, "with a massive media campaign."

Samuel Grant audibly drew in his breath. Susannah could almost feel shock waves coming from him. "Media?"

"Yes, of course. The disease originated out of this country, that much I'm sure of. What we probably have on our hands is one of the new viruses that seem to be popping up more frequently as we move into more remote corners of the world. Since none of the patients had traveled recently, we must use the media to ask that people from this area who have been out of the country come forward to be tested for the virus. And then we must hope there will be a survivor who is a native of this country, rather than someone who was just visiting and might already have returned home."

When no one said anything, the doctor continued, "We will, of course, use our computers to inquire about recent, unexplained fever deaths in other countries. But if the source of this disease came from some remote village, that information may not be available to us. So, what we need is someone who survived the fever and is available to us. A resident of this area, preferably. He probably didn't even realize what he had. And we must hope that he will respond to our media request to come forward and be tested."

"That's a lot of if's," Samuel said grudgingly.

Dr. Cicero stood up, signaling to her partner, Dr. Link, a young man with thinning hair and very thick glasses, to do the same. "Yes, it is," she admitted. "But there are always a lot of questions in a situation like this. Our job is to find the answers. We will do that, Mr. Grant, if there is an answer to be found."

"Another if."

"Yes. Possibly the most important one. Meanwhile, I want everyone at Med Center tested, right down to the least important delivery person."

"All of the medical personnel have been tested," Dr. Beck said as he stood up.

"Test them again. Also administration, clerical, maintenance, delivery people, everyone. And everyone at the University, as well. We have no idea what the incubation period of this disease is. These people who tested negative last week could be positive now. What we are primarily interested in just now is anyone who might have been out of the country recently."

Susannah had been listening quietly. Now she said slowly, "I think I might know some people who've been out of the country." Zack Ballou had told her the band occasionally traveled internationally. "I don't know how recently. And they were sick on their last trip. But I don't know when that was. They thought it was the water."

Dr. Cicero nodded. "It probably was. Still, we must check." Susannah gave him Zack's name. He wrote it down on a yellow pad.

Dr. Cicero nodded and made notes, too.

"Well, there's Montgomery, too," Samuel reluctantly said then. "Leonard Montgomery. My man from the lab. Recently returned from a trip to South America. It was his daughter who died. But," he added quickly, "he wasn't sick."

Dr. Cicero and Dr. Link looked interested. "Where in South America?" Link asked.

"Brazil. Although. . . ." Samuel paused.

Susannah knew how much her father did *not* want one of his employees to be responsible for the fever. Because that would almost make *him* responsible.

"Yes?" Dr. Cicero prompted.

"Although *he* stayed in the city, the people he contacted while he was there were from a small village in a remote area, a place called Esperanza. I know that it took them a long time to make the trip to meet with Montgomery. But," he added quickly, "he would have told me if any of them were sick."

"He has been tested?"

"No, not yet. He's Administration. We tested the medical personnel."

More note-taking. It seemed to Susannah, watching carefully, that all three doctors looked optimistic. But that could be, she told herself, because it's how I want them to look. Optimistic. Like they're going to get to the bottom of this very quickly. And fix it.

When Samuel had agreed to take the doctors to the lab at Grant Pharmaceuticals and led them from the room, Caroline turned to Susannah. There were new worry lines around her eyes and mouth. "I have postponed the fashion show. Would you mind calling your friends who were modeling and telling them? I have so many other calls to make, and I really want to get back to the hospital. Tell them I had no choice but to postpone. The musicians I had hired canceled, as did the florist. No one wants to come near Med Center just now. I don't blame them." Then, in the same tone of voice, Caroline added, "And, of course, you're not to go near there, either, Susannah. Except to visit Sam. No volunteering, not now. It's simply too dangerous."

Susannah stared at her. "You're kidding!"

Her mother returned the stare. "Kidding? Why would I be kidding? I'm quite serious." She reached up to adjust her gold necklace absent-mindedly. "I have one child in the hospital already, Susannah. Isn't that enough?"

"Mother, I'm not staying away from Emsee. Not now. They need all the help they can get. We've had a lot of people from Grant volunteering, but we've also had staff and maintenance workers calling in sick. They're not really sick. They're scared. So we're understaffed, and the phones ring constantly. I can't stay home."

Caroline drew herself up to her full height, two inches taller than her daughter. "Yes. You can. And you will. I don't want to discuss this now, Susannah. I must go say good-bye to our guests." She turned and began striding from the room.

"Mother!" When was the last time her mother had given her an order? Susannah couldn't remember that far back. Caroline turned only halfway around, glancing over her shoulder at her daughter, indicating that she wasn't prepared to stop and talk. "Mother, I know you're scared. We all are. I promise I'll be careful, but I am going back down there."

"No. You are not." Then she was gone, leaving Susannah standing in the center of the room in front of the fireplace with her mouth open.

She stood there for several minutes, feeling as shocked as her father must have felt when Dr. Cicero had mentioned a media campaign. Not go back to Emsee? Now? When she was so needed? When she was actually being allowed to be of some use?

Recovering from the shock of her mother's order, she turned and walked swiftly to the telephone. "Abby?" she began when her ring was answered. "Abby, I'm coming over there. Can I stay all night? And maybe tomorrow night and the next night, in fact, maybe forever, because I might not ever be allowed to come home again. Can I come?"

She quickly changed into a black miniskirt and a black-and-white-striped crop top and black flats, piled her hair carelessly on top of her head, and began packing an overnight bag. She hastily stuffed the black bag with T-shirts and a clean pair of jeans and four pairs of white socks and a heavy sweater in case the nights got cold, her alarm clock, and a blue denim skirt and two white blouses in case she really did have to stay at

Abby's forever. She was crying tears of fury and frustration as she moved into the bathroom to angrily snatch up her toothbrush and toothpaste, makeup and a can of mousse. "I know she's worried," she muttered to herself as she traveled back and forth across the rose-colored carpet fetching and carrying, "but I'm not a child. I can take care of myself! Since when does she give me orders? Anyway, I'm not a coward, and she shouldn't want me to be one. I'm not afraid of that disease. If *everyone* was, who would take care of the patients at Emsee? Who would take care of Sam?"

She would have asked that of Caroline if she'd run into her on her way out of the house, but she didn't. And she didn't want to go hunting for her. Neither one of them was in any shape for a real battle. It could wait.

She scribbled a note on the pad beside the telephone in the front hall and left the house, wishing she had the Jeep instead of the Benz. Who ever heard of someone running away from home in a Mercedes-Benz? It seemed almost as ludicrous as being driven away in a chauffered limousine.

At the O'Connor house, Abby was waiting for her, sitting on the lawn at the edge of the driveway in the deepening twilight, one red-sweatshirted arm around her brother Mattie, the other around the old dog, Lazybones. She climbed to her feet as Susannah got out of the car, toting the overnight bag.

"Hey, what's up? You and your dad have a fight?"

"Guess again. Me and my mother."

"You're kidding!" Abby knew how lax Caroline was about discipline. "What about?"

Susannah told her as they walked up to the house.

"She's scared about Sam, Sooz."

"I know. I'm not mad at her anymore. But I'm not staying away from Emsee, either. In fact" — she glanced at Abby as they entered the house — "I was thinking of going over there tonight. Interested?"

"I thought you were beat."

"I was. But I feel better now that the CDC is in town, and I know how short-staffed they are in ER. Want to come along?"

"You know how I feel about ER." They hurried down the hall to Abby and Moira's room, where Susannah deposited her bag and flopped down on one of the twin beds. Abby sat on the hardwood floor. "Besides, I was hoping I could talk you into going to The Music Room tonight."

"You're kidding! Dancing? How can you dance when the whole town has turned against the hospital? When everyone in Grant is scared to death of getting sick?"

Abby looked genuinely puzzled. "What's that

got to do with anything? People aren't mad at us. And we're not sick." She lay down on her back, propping her legs, in black leggings, up on the edge of her bed. "Don't you care about Zack at all? With people hiding in their houses to avoid the fever, hardly anyone will be at The Music Room. He'll feel bad. He'll think people don't like his band. Maybe the manager will think the same thing, and fire them." Smiling shyly, Abby added, "Will's going. So is Kate. They like the band, they don't think it's fair that the fever is ruining business for Zack, and they want to show their support."

"Are you sure?"

"I promise. Kate called earlier, wanted to know if we were going. She said all of the ER night shift people showed up for work, so they're not understaffed tonight. Come on, Susannah, you worked over there all day long. So did I. We deserve a break."

Susannah was tempted. It could be the perfect opportunity to make things right with Will. Unless . . . unless Zack got in the way again.

That thought surprised her. Zack was in the way? Cute, talented Zack, who had been so understanding? In the way of what?

But she knew of what. Of any chance for her to have a relationship with Will. And that was what she wanted. What she didn't know was if he wanted that, too.

"Okay, I'll go." Susannah stood up, picking up her overnight bag and slinging it over her shoulder. "But I need a shower first. My hair feels like straw. And I want to stop at Emsee on the way and check on Sam." In the doorway, she stopped and said over her shoulder, "Abby, remember you told me that if I wasn't interested in Zack to let you know? Well, I say go for it!"

Abby grinned with delight. "Really?"

"Really." Susannah felt compelled to add, "I have to warn you, though, there's a chance that the band might be responsible for the fever." At the look of alarm on Abby's face, Susannah added hastily, "I mean, maybe not. But the doctors from the CDC think this is a new virus, something that probably came in from another country. And Zack said they sometimes travel internationally. He even said the band had been sick on one of those trips. They could have had the virus without knowing it and brought it here. I guess the CDC is looking into it. I thought you should know."

Abby thought about that for a minute or two. "You danced with him, and you don't have it."

"True. But no one knows how long it takes to get it after you've been exposed." She had danced with Zack over a week ago. And . . . he had kissed her. If he really was spreading the fever, wouldn't she have some sign of the disease by now?

236

Abby thought again. Then, grinning, her dark eyes sparkling with mischief, she said, "Tell you what. I won't kiss him, okay? Not tonight."

Susannah remained uncertain. "You could wait and see what the CDC finds out when they test him and the other band members. Before you make a move on him, I mean."

Abby's grin widened. "Right. The guy is only going to be here another week and you expect me to wait. I've already wasted most of this week because of your mother's fashion show and because I thought *you* wanted him for yourself. I say, seize the moment, that's what *I* say."

"Okay, okay. But don't say I didn't warn you."

"I won't say you didn't warn me. Go take your shower."

Although the shower was relaxing in spite of various O'Connor offspring knocking on the bathroom door every few minutes, Susannah felt her neck muscles tensing again as she dried her hair. Maybe she shouldn't have agreed to go to The Music Room. If she'd refused, Abby would have stayed home, too. She wouldn't go without Susannah.

Here I am, Susannah thought, angry with herself, encouraging my best friend to get friendly with someone I *know* was out of the country, and even got sick while he was there. That doesn't mean he had the virus, or that he brought it into Grant, but it *could*. Why don't I just give her a bomb to play with?

An hour later, as they drove first to Emsee and then, when Susannah had learned that there was no change in Sam's condition, to The Music Room, they found the streets of Grant eerily quiet and deserted. As if, Susannah thought nervously, the fever had already stripped the city of life.

It wasn't going to *do* that, was it?

chapter
22

The Music Room, when Susannah and Abby arrived, was as empty as a store at closing time. But it wasn't closing time. It was only nine o'clock, and on a Saturday evening at that hour, the club should have been noisy and lively.

Kate and Will were seated, by themselves, at a table close to the bandstand. At another table on the opposite side of the room, Jeremy sat with, to Susannah's dismay, Callie Matthews, vibrant in a black strapless dress very different from the casual clothes Abby and Susannah were wearing. The pair didn't look like they were having a good time. Susannah said as much to Abby.

"How could anyone have a good time with *her*?" Abby replied, casting a look of scorn Callie's way. "Jeremy shouldn't even be speaking to her, after that horrible interview she gave to the paper. His father's a doctor. Didn't he ever warn his son to stay away from poison?"

There were a few other tables occupied, but not many. Susannah knew why. The crowd usually in this club, dancing and having fun, was, on average, the same age as all but one of the fever victims now in Intensive Care Isolation. They were scared. If they hadn't been at first, the collapse of a formerly healthy specimen like Samuel Grant III right in front of their very eyes, in this same club, must have erased the last bit of doubt that they were at risk.

They weren't taking any chances.

Abby and Susannah joined Kate and Will at their table.

Susannah felt sorry for Zack, who looked very dejected up there on stage. He didn't look sick, though. She wondered if anyone else in the room, besides Abby, knew that he was going to be interviewed and tested by the CDC tomorrow, and quickly decided no one did.

Though she felt sorry for him, she danced with him only once, and when he asked her to a movie on Sunday night when the club was closed, she said no.

He was surprised, she could tell. "You're busy?" he asked.

"No . . . yes . . . I . . ." Her eyes went to Will, deep in conversation with Kate and Abby at the table.

Zack followed her glance. "Oh. Gotcha. That explains the other night." He laughed, a not unfriendly sound. "He sure was ticked! I couldn't figure out why. Now I know."

Afraid Zack would say something to Will, she

said quickly, "Well, we're not . . . I mean, nothing's . . . we're not dating or anything. He's never even asked me to dance."

"But he didn't say no when you asked him to dance, did he?"

"Oh, I've never asked . . ." Susannah flushed as Zack grinned at her. She nodded and echoed his, "Gotcha! But I think he's mad at me now."

"So, ask him to dance and maybe he'll get over it. I can tell you for a fact that I'd get over my mad pretty fast for a chance to dance with you."

"Abby's a better dancer than I am," Susannah said quickly as he led her back to the table.

"Abby? The one with the eyes?"

Susannah laughed. "We all have eyes, Zack."

"You know what I mean. Big brown eyes. I had a springer spaniel with eyes like that when I was a kid." He smiled down at Susannah as she took a seat beside Kate. Then he turned to Abby. "Feel like making a fool of yourself by dancing when there's no one else out on the dance floor?"

"I hate crowds," she said, and got up to follow him out onto the floor.

Susannah felt Will's eyes on her as Zack and Abby left the table. But he continued his conversation with Kate. "It's worse than that," he was saying. "We had a cardiac arrest today, downtown, right in front of Sturgess's department store. When we got there, the guy was lying in the middle of the sidewalk, with a dozen or more people standing around. But no one had loosened his collar or put anything under his head, and no one was attempting CPR. They were all scared he had the fever. Man, it chilled my blood. The guy could have died. He didn't, but no thanks to all those people."

"They're not the only ones who are scared," Kate replied. "Look at this place! It's practically deserted. It's rough at home, too. My brother Aaron didn't speak to anyone at dinner tonight, he's so furious with my mother and me for continuing to work at Emsee. He's terrified we'll bring the fever home. Mom said she was going to talk to him, but I don't think it'll do any good."

"The investigators from the CDC are here," Susannah announced, optimism in her voice. "They seem to know what they're doing. Maybe we'll have an answer soon . . . and a vaccine. Will, would you like to dance?"

Will and Kate stared at her. Susannah couldn't tell which had surprised them more, her announcement about the CDC people arriving, or her invitation to Will. She was betting it was the invitation.

When Will didn't respond immediately, Kate said dryly, "Will, I think someone just asked you to dance."

"Someone did," Susannah said boldly. "Me. And I'm still waiting for a yes or no."

"Yes," Will said then, getting up and coming over to stand beside her chair.

Susannah left her chair and led the way to the dance floor. "I thought you were going to say no," she said when she was in his arms in a slow dance. "You took long enough answering me."

"That's what I always thought about you," he said, his chin on the top of her head. "That you'd say no. That's why I never asked."

"I wouldn't have said no."

"I didn't know that. And even if I'd thought you would say yes, there's always your father."

"Oh, he'd definitely say no if you asked him to dance," Susannah said seriously, but she was smiling, her cheek against Will's blue denim shirt.

He laughed. "You know what I mean. If your father has a list of requirements for the perfect guy for his daughter, and I'll bet he does, 'white' is probably at the very top."

"Doesn't matter. I ran away from home tonight. I'm staying at Abby's."

He reached down with one hand and lifted her chin so that she was looking straight into his eyes. "Are you serious?"

"Sort of. My mother and I had an argument. She ordered me to stay away from Emsee, and I can't do that. So I'm staying at Abby's."

"Your mother? Not your father?"

"Nope. It was my mother this time. Big surprise. It's *so* unlike her, giving orders. She's scared about Sam, that's all. But I'm staying out of her way until this is over. I'll have to visit Sam when my parents are taking a coffee break downstairs."

"I'm sorry you're having a rough time," he said quietly.

He was *so* nice. "Thanks," she said quietly. This was what she had wished for, after all. Someone to understand what she was feeling, how scared she was. She moved closer, lay her cheek against his shoulder. It felt warm and solid. She was dancing with Will, something she'd dreamed of for a long time. They were good together, she could feel it. They moved across the floor almost like one person.

She lifted her head, looked up at him. "You didn't ask me to dance before this because you thought I'd say no?"

"That's exactly what I thought," he said firmly.

"Well, don't ever use that as an excuse again, okay?"

"Gotcha. Now quit looking at me like that. It makes me want to kiss you, and I don't think that's a good idea. Not here. Not now."

Smiling, Susannah lay her head back against his shoulder.

They were just returning to the table when Caleb Matthews, looking flushed and anxious, appeared in the doorway. Susannah saw him come in. She watched as he strode quickly across the room to Callie and Jeremy's table.

The room was so empty and quiet, everyone could hear clearly as Matthews said to his daughter. "You were grounded! Because of the mess you've made of things with that newspaper article. I thought you were home with your mother! You have to come, now! She's sick. She's very sick."

Callie looked up at him with cool eyes. "She's sick? She was asleep when I left the house. She seemed okay." She thought for a minute, twirling the glass in her hand. Then she looked up at her father and asked, "You can handle it, right?" Sarcasm coated her words. "You're so good at handling things. Of course, you don't know the routine when she has one of these attacks as well as I do, because you're never around when she has them. But it's not that complicated, really. Take her to the ER. They'll know what to do."

"She's already at the ER." Callie's father's voice was cold. "I took her there. But it's not an attack." He reached down and grabbed Callie's left arm, yanking her out of the chair and upright. "You're coming with me. Your mother is very ill. You should be there."

Callie glared at him. "What's wrong with her?"

Susannah, listening, knew what he was going to say even before the words slid from his mouth. Her heart stopped and her breath caught in her throat. No, please, she thought, please don't let him say it! Please let me be wrong.

She wasn't wrong.

"Your mother has the same fever that killed Tina," Caleb Matthews told his daughter, his voice harsh. "She's one of three new cases that were brought into the ER tonight."

Then he threw Callie's black-sequined sweater around her shoulders and hurried her out of the nearly deserted club.

chapter
23

At the words "three new cases," The Music Room emptied out fast. Susannah, Will, Kate, Abby, and Jeremy all followed the Matthews car to Med Center. If things had gone from bad to worse at ER, the three volunteers and the paramedic wanted to be there to help. Jeremy went hoping to provide moral support for Callie.

ER was chaotic. Word had already spread of the three new cases. People who had been placated earlier that day by the news that CDC investigators had arrived had panicked anew, descending upon Med Center en masse. They filled the waiting rooms and the hallways, making it difficult for orderlies and paramedics pushing gurneyed patients to get through to treatment rooms.

"Why haven't they *done* anything?" a tall, husky friend of Jenkins Rue shouted, waving a fist in the air. "How come it's still spreading?"

A woman with pink foam rollers poking out from beneath her red print head scarf cried, "My kids aren't safe! I thought you said this afternoon that my kids would be safe! But now we've got these new cases."

The young boy at her side echoed, "Yeah, and I don't wanta get it!"

"What a mess!" Susannah murmured as she stood in the doorway with Will, surveying the scene in dismay. Kate, Abby, and Jeremy were behind them, commenting on the chaos.

Off to one side of the packed hallway, Callie Matthews stood, arguing with her father. In spite of the buzz of anger coming from the crowd, the voices of father and daughter rang clearly throughout the hall.

"That's why you gave that hateful interview?" Mr. Matthews, his face lined with weariness and worry, asked his daughter in a loud voice. "But I told you, you were wrong about that! I explained. I was telling the truth, Callie. Your mother is the most important person in the world to me."

People became aware that something was happening, and the crowd gradually fell silent, listening.

"Then why aren't you ever home?" Callie shouted. A diminutive figure dressed in sophisticated black, her fair hair hanging down her back, she looked ready for battle. Her voice rang out in the corridor. Nurses frantically trying to field phone calls held the receivers away from them, tilting their heads, their interest piqued. "Why would you rather be here than there, with us?" Her voice lowered slightly. "I can't do it all by myself. It's hard, when she's sick half the time. . . ."

"That's the girl who let us know what was going on," someone in the crowd said loudly. "I recognize her from her picture. She's the only one who would tell us the truth."

It *wasn't* the truth, Susannah wanted to shout. But she couldn't, because *half* of it *was* the truth.

"You tell 'im, Callie!" someone shouted, and there was sporadic applause from the crowd. Other voices shouted support, urging her on.

Callie paid no attention. She was completely caught up in the confrontation with her father. She hated him. This was all his fault. His and Med Center's and the Grants'. "If you'd told the truth about this from the start," she cried, looking up at him, "if you'd called in outside help immediately, maybe Mom wouldn't have the fever now!"

Her father's face drained completely of color. "Callie, don't say that! Don't *say* that!" he cried.

"She could *die*, Dad," Callie pressed on relentlessly. "She's not strong like the other people who have it. You know she's not."

"I've been keeping a very close watch on her, Callie. I was worried about the fever, too. And I brought her in the very second she felt the least bit warm. Dr. Mulgrew said she couldn't have had a temperature for more than a few hours. Look, we have to be there for your mother, both of us."

Watching, Susannah felt a pang of sympathy for the man. Abby must have, too, because she murmured, "Oh, damn it, Callie, give him a hug!" Even the angry crowd, who knew now that the big man in the light blue sweater, standing against the wall with his head down, was one of the targets of their anger, had hushed and seemed to be holding its breath. Powerful though the man might be, he, too, was now a victim of the indiscriminating fever, and it was clear to all that he was in great pain. Maybe that was punishment enough.

"I know she's spoiled," Jeremy said softly as he watched and waited with everyone else to see what Callie would do, "but she's not heartless."

Callie had never felt so torn. She was still so angry with her father. But his face was twisted in pain, and there were tears in his eyes. "You really love Mom?" she asked, her voice softening just a little.

He nodded. "And you, too, Callie."

"You care about us?"

"I do. Very much."

Callie nodded. She didn't hug him. But she nodded again and said, "Okay. Then let's go up and see how she is."

Abby, watching, knew Callie's softening was

only temporary. Callie, after all, was Callie. Caleb Matthews appeared to be satisfied, however, as if he hadn't dared hope for even that much from his daughter.

The elevator doors slid open. Father and daughter disappeared inside.

Jeremy made his way through the crowd to follow them upstairs.

The drama over, people returned to their own concerns. They remembered why they were there and why they were angry. Voices began clamoring once again to have temperatures taken, to be taken directly to the CDC investigators, to be given a hospital bed immediately because they were feeling "very, very sick."

It was, finally, Susannah's father who cleared the waiting rooms and corridors. An orderly had gone upstairs to tell him of the latest public relations crisis. Samuel had chosen to act on it immediately. His voice over the PA system promised, "We will have answers for you very soon. You make our task more difficult by being here. If you go home, we can finish our work that much more quickly."

It worked. People were used to listening to Samuel Grant II. And obeying. Once the crowd had gone, muttering among themselves, a huge sigh of relief seemed to sweep the ER.

"You can all go home now, too," Astrid Thompson told the volunteers. "You were here all day. Not a good idea to become overtired just now, right? And the crisis has passed for now, although that crowd will be back if your father doesn't deliver on his promise, Susannah."

Tired and upset about the new cases of fever, Susannah, Will, and Abby headed for the exit. Kate had announced that she was going upstairs to see how Damon was, maybe sit with him awhile.

"They won't let you in," Will told her.

"Yeah," she said with a grin, "they will."

Susannah regretted not having had more time to talk with Will. But even if he had asked to take her home, which he hadn't, she had her own car. He seemed more distant now than he had at the club, and she wondered if she'd made a mistake, asking him to dance. Maybe he was regretting having accepted.

She was too tired to think about that now. Maybe next week when, if her father delivered on his promise, they had some answers. She'd think about Will then. Right now, the fever was taking up so much space, there wasn't room for Will.

Susannah stayed at Abby's. No point in going home to argue with her mother. After the three new cases, Caroline couldn't possibly have changed her mind. Before she visited her brother, Susannah checked at the ICU reception desk to make sure her parents weren't in Sam's room.

The protests died down, as people awaited word from the CDC, as promised by Samuel Grant. The streets of the city remained deserted, and all Med Center or University social events scheduled for the week were canceled.

Driving to Abby's from the hospital on Monday evening, after one of the worst weekends she had ever endured, Susannah thought that it was as if the city of Grant, Massachusetts, had been evacuated. Yet all of the people were still there. They were hiding inside their homes, hoping the fever wouldn't find them there.

Zack called to tell her he and all the band members had been tested. "Haven't heard yet whether we passed or not," he said lightly, but she heard anxiety in his voice. She couldn't blame him. I'd be nervous, too, she thought. Who would want to be responsible for this awful disease?

Everyone was tense, waiting for answers from the CDC investigators, who were working around the clock at the Grant Pharmaceutical's massive lab.

At work, Will remained cool. Confused, Susannah avoided him. She was sure he regretted dancing with her. There were times when she wished she had never asked him, and vowed never to make the same mistake again. Other times, she blamed his attitude on the tension at

Emsee. No one was acting normally. Why should Will be the exception?

Late on Monday night, Susannah answered the telephone in Abby's room while Abby was taking a shower, and heard her father's voice.

"Susannah." His voice was low, urgent. "Your brother has taken a turn for the worse. Your mother needs you. You'll come right away." It wasn't a question.

"I'll be right there," she said, and hung up the phone.

chapter
24

Although the day had been clear, with a beautiful, cloudless blue sky, it was beginning to rain as Susannah, with Abby in the front seat beside her, sped to Med Center.

"If your mom is still mad at you, you'll need a friend there," Abby had insisted. Susannah hadn't argued. Even if her mother wasn't mad at her, she'd still need a friend at Emsee if Sam was . . . if Sam was . . . her mind refused to finish the thought.

By the time they ran from the parking garage, the rain was coming down steadily, pelting the ground and slapping against windows and roofs all over the complex.

Many of Sam's friends had gathered in the ER waiting room. They jumped to their feet when Susannah came rushing in. She had to tell them she knew nothing, that she hadn't even seen Sam yet. "How did you find out he was worse?" she asked Tom Cooper, one of Sam's soccer teammates.

"Callie called me. She's here, somewhere. Upstairs with her mother, I guess. She knows I call the hospital every night to see how Sam is, since we're not allowed in to see him. I was just about to call when the phone rang. Callie was really upset. She said there were all kinds of doctors and nurses rushing into Sam's room and that your parents looked really scared. So I called everyone together and we came over here. Don't you know anything?" he finished in a pleading voice.

"No. I'm sorry. I'll go up, and then I'll come back down and tell you, okay? If they tell me anything."

What she found out when she went upstairs was that Sam had stopped breathing. He had been resuscitated, but was now on life supports, like Damon. When Susannah looked in through the door window and saw her twin hooked up to even more machinery, her own heart nearly stopped. "Oh, God," she breathed to Abby, "he doesn't even look alive!"

"But he is, Susannah. He still is. You hold on to that."

Everything that could be done had been, Susannah was told. If Sam's vital organs didn't fail, they could "maintain" him, a word that made Susannah flinch, until a vaccine was made available, if that happened very quickly.

It didn't happen for the next two days. All the Grant family could do was wait. The only time they left the complex was for a quick shower and change of clothes. The rest of the time, they sat in the ICU waiting room, and what they did there was wait.

They weren't alone. Caleb and Callie Matthews were there, as well as relatives of the other patients who had family.

Kate took turns visiting Jenkins Rue and Damon Lawerence. The nurses in ICU no longer questioned her visits, since no one else ever showed up and asked to see the two.

On Thursday, the two CDC investigators, accompanied by Dr. Beck, called a meeting in Caleb Matthews's office. Susannah was allowed to attend.

"We know it isn't any of the musicians who played at the club," Dr. Cicero said when they were all seated. Caleb Matthews, looking physically drained, sat at his desk, clearly impatient for an answer that would save his wife. "They've all tested negative. And although they were ill on their last trip out of the country, we're fairly certain that was simply a reaction to the change in environment. One band member may have had a touch of the flu when they played in South America, but that's it."

Dr. Cicero repeatedly consulted her yellow-pad notes as she spoke. "With our computers and the help of our Atlanta staff, we've contacted every resident in the area who has traveled internationally within the past month. There weren't that many. By early this afternoon, we were able to narrow the possibilities down to only the four band members and one other person. Now that we've eliminated the band, that leaves only one more possibility." Dr. Cicero raised her eyes from the notepad in her lap. She looked at Samuel Grant. "I'm sorry, Mr. Grant. I know you were hoping otherwise, but we believe the person we're seeking may be your employee, Mr. Montgomery. The dead girl's father. We must get in touch with him immediately."

Susannah and Abby exchanged a horrified glance. Tina's father might be told that he had, however innocently, brought back from his South American trip an illness that had taken the life of his only child?

"What we've learned from his coworkers," Dr. Link interjected, "is, while Mr. Montgomery himself stayed pretty close to his city hotel, the people who came to him, bringing the new herb he was after, were indeed from a remote village, the place called Esperanza, deep in the rain forest, just as you told us, Mr. Grant. They came by boat. We believe this is a virus that is transmitted through animal or insect bite. One of the bearers could have been bitten on the trip by a mosquito, or perhaps a river rat. Or he might have been bitten by a monkey or bat before he began the trip. He couldn't have been symptomatic yet, or someone would have noticed. He wouldn't even have known that he was ill. I understand that two of the bearers failed to return to the village, that they quit their positions and disappeared. They may have returned to their own villages, and are probably dead. We've had no reports of any outbreaks similar to this one elsewhere, but we probably will, sooner or later. News doesn't travel as quickly in other parts of the world as it does here."

"And I was right," Dr. Beck added. "It is a new virus. For now, the CDC is simply calling it 'Esperanza fever.' They have begun a file and will add to it as new information comes in."

"Then," Samuel said heavily, "there is no cure. No vaccine."

"Not yet," Dr. Link said. "That's why we need Montgomery. He brought it back here. He had it. It just didn't affect him to any degree. You did say he had a touch of travel sickness?"

Samuel nodded.

"That probably was the fever. And he may have been sicker than he was willing to admit. The man has a strong immune system, I'll say that. At any rate, if we're right, if he did have it and recovered quickly, we can use his antibodies to create a vaccine."

"How long will that take?" Samuel's eyes were anxious.

"Not long. Your lab is beautifully set up for

what we need to do. In the meantime, if any of the current patients worsen, we'll put them on life supports until the vaccine is ready, and do everything we can to protect their vital organs from serious damage."

"Montgomery isn't here," Samuel said. "I told you, he's in the Berkshires, at our lodge. There is no telephone."

"Someone will have to take one of us up there to get him," Dr. Cicero said matter-of-factly. "Now."

Susannah stood up. "I'll go."

"No!" Caroline stood up, too. "Not you." Her eyes were not cold with anger. They were warm and pleading. "Please, Susannah, I need you here. Someone else can go."

"Mother, I know how to get to the lodge."

"I'll hire a driver," Samuel said.

"No, I'll go," Abby volunteered. "I've been there. I remember where it is. We shouldn't waste time hiring someone."

Susannah hesitated. She wanted Abby with her. But she could see that Abby was determined to be helpful. "Take the Benz. It'd take too long to go home and get your station wagon. Besides, those roads curve like snakes, and the Benz can turn on a dime."

Abby nodded. "Thanks."

"I'll go with you," Dr. Link volunteered. "Cicero and Beck have work to do here, at the lab."

Susannah was torn. It was raining again, had been since late that afternoon. She didn't really want Abby driving all the way up to the Berkshires on such a nasty night. But Sam was just barely hanging on. Time was crucial. They couldn't afford to wait until tomorrow for someone to fetch Mr. Montgomery.

She let out a deep breath. "Okay, Abby. We owe you."

"Don't mention it. C'mon, Dr. Link," Abby said cheerfully, "let's go bring the man back alive. Keys, Sooz?"

Susannah handed her the keys.

But when they'd gone, she had to fight an impulse to run after Abby and the young doctor. Telling herself that she was probably just upset about Sam's worsening condition, and telling herself that if anyone she knew could take care of herself, it was Abby, Susannah turned to join her parents in Sam's room.

chapter
25

Abby wasn't willing to admit aloud to Dr. Link that although the Benz *was* handling like a dream in spite of the slick roads, she was having trouble seeing the road that snaked up the hill, flanked by thick, dark woods on both sides. If she'd remembered correctly, they'd be at the lodge in four or five minutes. Why give the doctor something new to worry about?

It was almost dawn, although since the rain hadn't lessened at all, there was no sign of a rising sun off to the east. The horizon was heavy only with dark, gray clouds. They'd be driving back in pouring rain, too.

The Montgomerys would be asleep. There hadn't been any way to warn them that someone was coming to drag them out of bed and give them more bad news. Horrible news.

"You have to tell them," she said as the lodge appeared in view at the top of a hill ahead of them. "I got us here. You be the bearer of bad tidings, okay? I can't do it."

"I'm not planning on telling them that

much," Dr. Link said. "Only that Mr. Montgomery is needed back at Med Center. He won't be surprised. He knows there's a crisis there."

"His daughter died last week," Abby said soberly as she pulled up the long, narrow driveway curving up the hill. "Won't he think it's pretty callous of us to be dragging him back to work?"

"It *is* pretty callous. But absolutely necessary. And remember, this man, if Cicero is right, will be saving many lives. I don't think he'll give us a hard time."

He didn't. Although he and his wife were clearly upset at being disturbed, Montgomery was used to being called to duty at odd times, on an emergency basis. Abby even had a feeling as they all left the house and the Montgomerys climbed into their Cadillac, that, in a way, the man was relieved to be going back to work.

She felt bad for him. Any other time, work might have been the best cure for his grief. If Dr. Cicero weren't awaiting him at Med Center with some awful news.

"Poor guy," Dr. Link said as Abby, in the lead car, carefully steered the Benz back down the steep hill. "I wouldn't want to be in his shoes."

"Well," she said as they arrived on the main road, "maybe Dr. Cicero will think to tell Tina's father what you said before, that he'll be saving lives. It won't bring Tina back, but it's still a good thing. And it wasn't his fault that she got sick, right?"

"No. Definitely not his fault. There are going to be more of these fevers hitting the populace from time to time," Dr. Link told her, "as people dig deeper into unknown territory. And there's the other side of the coin, too, which is that every time we plunge into these remote areas, we bring disease with *us*, threatening the lives of the natives already living there. So we're not the only victims, just in case you thought we were."

"Until this disgusting fever came along," Abby replied, peering into the thick sheet of rain pelting the car, "I hadn't thought about it at all, Dr. Link. But I will now. I promise you that."

By the time they were on the outskirts of Grant, she was exhausted. Every bone and muscle in her body ached. Her eyes felt gritty. Her head ached. But she had stayed awake! All night long. Something to be proud of. She'd done something good. Maybe not for Mr. Montgomery, who was about to get his second major shock in two weeks. But for the others in ICU. Like Sam.

She could only hope they were in time.

She glanced in the rearview mirror. The Montgomerys were still right behind them, the Caddy hugging the road every bit as snugly as the Benz.

Her eyes went back to the road only a fraction of a second too late. Weather conditions being what they were, even a moment's distraction was too much. The right side of the car swerved off the road and onto the rain-soaked soft shoulder. Too late, Abby realized her mistake. Gasping, she struggled with the steering wheel, whipping it to the left to force the car back on track. But the right wheels had sunk into the wet, muddy berm and refused to leave it. She slammed on the brake, her second mistake. The small, silver car spun around in a semicircle, then left the road completely, slamming into the guardrail now on Abby's side, where it shouldn't have been. The guardrail gave, and the car, totally out of control, flew through the broken rail and careened down the slippery, sodden hill, gathering speed as it went.

When Abby saw the huge, gnarled old tree, thick and forbidding, looming up out of the rain suddenly at midpoint on the hill, she knew they were going to hit it. Her hands frozen to the steering wheel, she tried with all her strength to wrest it left or right, didn't matter which, any direction at all if it meant missing that enormous tree. But the car refused to obey any of her commands and it was going faster and faster, though she'd long since taken her shaking foot off the accelerator.

There was no way they could miss that tree, which looked like a stone barricade in the middle of the hill. And might as well have been.

"Get down!" Dr. Link shouted frantically, and an arm shot out to shove Abby's head down into her lap.

Her last thought before they hit was, Now we're not going to get there in time to help Sam.

She would have screamed in terror then. If there had been time. But there wasn't.

chapter
26

~~~∿∿∿∿∿~~~

On Friday morning, Will was on the ambulance dispatched to a rainy slope on the outskirts of Grant.

"Oh, my God," he whispered as he helped pull an injured girl from the crumpled heap of silver metal lying at the base of an enormous tree. In spite of the blood streaking her face and hair, in spite of the thick cervical collar already applied to her neck inside the car before she was gently placed on the backboard, Will knew her instantly. "It's Abby! Oh, man, how can I tell Susannah about this? First Sam, now Abby?"

Abby opened her eyes. "Oh, relax, Will, I'll tell her myself," she said weakly. Will's knees went limp with relief as he laughed aloud. "Don't ever scare me like that again!"

"Okay, I won't. I promise."

Will and his partner carried Abby to the ambulance. She had a deep laceration on her forehead, a shallow but wider one on her chin, and a third, the most serious, on her right shoulder. But miraculously, she seemed to have no other injuries and her vital signs indicated no internal injuries. Will couldn't believe it. Susannah's car looked like it had been processed through a compactor. "You're going to be fine, Abby. Just lie still, okay? But," Will said, smiling, "you're a real mess. Can't you do something with your hair?"

She smiled back. "Nope, never could. How's Dr. Link?"

The doctor hadn't fared as well as Abby. "My chest . . ." he had gasped as they gently placed him on a stretcher. "Hurts . . ." When Will checked, his abdomen was tender, his breathing was labored, and the young doctor was fading from consciousness quickly.

"Pulse 140, respirations 36 and shallow, BP 70/50," Will's partner said. "Breath sounds diminished on right side. I think we'd better phone in, fast. Let's get him inside."

In the ambulance, they obeyed the orders from the hospital, setting up the IVs and, when the rapid infusion of fluids failed to affect the blood pressure, applying antishock trousers and inflating them.

"What's wrong with him?" Abby asked from her gurney.

"I don't know for sure," Will told her. "Chest injury, maybe something internal, too."

"He's not going to die, is he? I think he saved my life. Made me put my head down right before we hit."

"He won't die," Will said confidently. "But he'll be on his way to surgery as soon as they put a chest tube into him in ER and take X rays to see what's going on inside."

"Good." Abby closed her eyes.

Susannah had just come downstairs to get coffee for everyone in the ICU waiting room when the ambulance pulled up outside. She automatically turned around, one hand still on the coffeepot's faucet, watching the doors to see how bad the damage was as the gurney came racing by.

She would have known that dark curly hair anywhere, even rain-soaked and streaked with blood. And she knew, she knew with sickening certainty, why she hadn't felt right about letting her best friend drive all the way up to the Berkshires on such an awful night. Because she'd known something terrible would happen. And it had.

"Abby?" Susannah asked hoarsely. "Abby?" The Styrofoam cup filled with hot coffee dropped from her hand and landed on the white tile with a plopping sound and a thick spray of dark brown. The hallway began spinning crazily. She saw Will's dark eyes glancing over at her as he passed, she saw the blood on Abby's cheek, forehead, and chin. Her stomach mimicked the hallway's crazy spinning.

She would have fallen then if she hadn't heard

Astrid Thompson's voice saying inside her dizzily spinning mind, "Being allowed in the treatment rooms without any formal medical training is an honor, Susannah. It's being given you because the consensus is that you can handle it. It will be rough at times, sometimes very rough. But we believe you're strong enough."

She couldn't pass out. She was exhausted from the strain of the past weeks and would have liked nothing more at that moment than to slide to the floor and wait for someone to pick her up, put her on a gurney, and take her away to a peaceful, quiet, treatment room to sleep for days.

But Abby needed her.

Susannah jerked upright, stiffening her spine. And noticed instantly that Abby's eyes were open . . . they were open! . . . she was *alive* . . . she hadn't died.

Abby's mouth opened as well, and although she was shaking with cold and shock, which made her voice unsteady, it was clear enough. "You look like you're staring at a ghost, Susannah. Stop that. I might think I actually *am* one."

Susannah managed a weak laugh. "Well, you're not. You are very much alive. Now shut up and let the doctors be nice to you."

While Abby's lacerations, only one of which required stitches, were being tended to, Dr. Link was sent upstairs to surgery for a lacerated liver. Susannah was assured he would be fine.

"We're going to keep Abby here overnight," Susannah was told when Abby had been treated. "I'm sure she's fine, but she took quite a ride down that hill according to Will, and we'd like to keep an eye on her. You can go up and see her when she's settled."

On her way back to Sam's room, Susannah saw Mr. Montgomery emerging from an office in the company of Dr. Cicero. He was wiping tears from his face with a white handkerchief. Susannah's heart ached for him.

But in the next minute, she saw him straighten his shoulders, take a deep breath, and let it out. Then he headed in the direction of the lab with the doctor for the blood tests. He looked like a man with a purpose.

Susannah had no idea why Mr. Montgomery hadn't been ravaged by the fever. He was strong and healthy, but so were her brother Sam and Jenkins Rue. It was rare, but Montgomery must have had an inborn immunity to the disease. He hadn't even known he had it. Now the antibodies in his blood would save others from getting it.

He's going to save them, she thought with certainty. He's going to save all of them. The ones who have the fever now, and the others who might have had it if it weren't for Tina Montgomery's father. Dr. Cicero and the other doctors will use his antibodies to create a vaccine. They'll do it quickly, thanks to my father's lab, and after a while, ICU will no longer be under quarantine. Sam and his friend will be out playing soccer and baseball and dating every girl in town. Jenkins Rue will be fishing off the riverbank. That girl will be back on Rollerblades, and Damon Lawrence will be racing around town in that old truck of his. The other people up in ICU will be back home where they belong, back at work or school, back to normal. I will have my brother back, and Callie will have her mother back.

But no one in this town, Susannah told herself with conviction, will ever forget that this happened.

It wasn't over yet, she knew that. They would have to keep all of the victims alive until the vaccine was ready. That would take every bit of medical knowledge available. It would take diligence, vigilance, and a whole lot of caring.

But then, there wasn't any place in the world with more of those things than Med Center.

Callie, upstairs visiting her mother, heard about the accident and came downstairs to find out how Abby was. She had just rounded the corner into the ER waiting room when Jeremy came in through the front door. "My father's going to go to breakfast with me," he told Callie with determination, "or I'm going to California to live with my mother. That's the deal. He can take it or leave it. No more sitting on the sidelines, waiting for him."

He expected Callie to say, "Good for you, Jeremy!" Instead, she said, "I thought you were here because you heard about Abby's accident."

Jeremy's face paled. "Abby? What accident?"

When Susannah had explained to them that Abby was in no serious danger, she was quick to add the news about Mr. Montgomery.

Callie's face flooded with relief. "Oh, God, I've got to go tell my mother! Oh, Susannah, thank you, thanks for telling me!" She whirled and ran.

"Does Kate know?" Jeremy asked Susannah.

"Does Kate know what?" Kate asked as she came up behind them. She tossed her shoulder bag into a cupboard, and grabbed her smock off a peg and slipped it on over a pink-and-purple tie-dyed T-shirt. "What's happening that I don't know about?"

Susannah explained about the accident, and added the news about Mr. Montgomery. "So," she finished with a smile, "looks like you're going to have to model in my mother's fashion show, after all, Kate. It's not going to be canceled."

Kate ran a pick through her bangs, then slipped the pick into her jeans pocket. "Well, at least Abby's okay," she said. "We all owe her for driving all the way up there to bring Montgomery back, right?"

Susannah and Jeremy nodded.

"And," Kate added with a grin, "it just so happens I *like* the idea of modeling. Maybe an editor from a fashion magazine will spot me up there on that runway and offer me big bucks to grace her cover. I'll become as world-famous as Med Center, make zillions of dollars, date rock stars and professional football players, and you can all say you knew me when."

Jeremy looked at her with concern, but Susannah laughed. "Relax, Jeremy! She'd last about two seconds in the modeling business. People telling her where to sit, where to stand, how to smile? I think half the reason Kate is going to become a doctor is so she can tell people what to do. I can't see her sitting on some beach in February, freezing to death in a bikini."

Jeremy did relax. He grinned. "I can see her in a bikini."

"Quit leering," Kate said with mock disapproval. "If you're on your way upstairs, I'll go with you. I want to see how Damon is. If he's awake, I'll give him the good news about Montgomery."

"You going up to see Sam?" Will's voice asked suddenly from over Susannah's shoulder.

She turned around. "Yes. Want to come? You can't go in to see him. But . . ." she hesitated, wondering if this was the right time. Maybe not. He had pulled away from her again after that one dance at The Music Room.

But the past two weeks had taught her that maybe it wasn't such a hot idea to wait for "the right time." Something could come along and knock "the right time" right off the clock.

Deciding, Susannah said, "I'm on my way up to tell my parents that Abby brought Mr. Montgomery back, and that a vaccine is on the way. You could come up and say hello to them."

Susannah almost smiled then at the look of uncertainty that spread across Will's face. Will, who was always so confident. "I've never even met them," he said.

"I know." She did smile then. "I'm asking you if you want to. Now."

It was his turn to hesitate.

It doesn't mean a commitment, Susannah wanted to say. Meeting my parents doesn't mean I'm asking you for anything. It just means that I want you to meet them. And that you're ready to. That's all it means.

Although she didn't say any of that aloud, he might have seen it in her eyes, because he said then, "Yeah. Sure. I guess I can say hello to them. Anyway," he added quickly, "I wanted to see how Damon and Jenkins are doing. I'll check that out while I'm up there."

"Right," Susannah said, still smiling as she pushed the elevator button.

While they waited for the cage to arrive, she glanced around ER, at the staff moving quickly from room to room, the orderlies pushing gurneys or wheelchairs along the hallway, other volunteers her age in pink smocks marching along armed with magazines and hospital menus. When school began again in September, she would have to cut back on her volunteer time. They all would. But for now, she thought with satisfaction, this is where I want to be.

Then, as the elevator doors began to slide closed upon her and Will, she caught a glimpse of a white-faced young man, a red-stained, pale yellow towel wrapped around his left hand, as he rushed in through the doorway, calling, "I need help here!"

As two nurses and a resident ran to his aid, Susannah sent a mental message to the injured boy. You have come to the right place, she told him silently. Just. Like. Me.

The elevator doors slid shut.

An exciting excerpt from *Flood*, Med Center #2, coming next.

It began raining in Grant, Massachusetts, at 11:23 on a Tuesday night in mid-September. It rained lightly at first, a pleasant, refreshing, early autumn shower. Gardeners all over the city welcomed it, after ten straight days with no moisture for their fall gardens and the last of their roses.

During that night and most of the next day, the parched ground eagerly soaked up the falling rain.

But by the following evening, as commuters were making their way home, the pleasant shower turned nasty, throwing a temper tantrum. The wind rose, tearing at limbs of the huge old trees lining both sides of Linden Hill Boulevard, the main artery between the east and west sides of town. The skies turned an ominous black and, seconds later, opened, dumping thick torrents of rain, flooding streets with deep washes of water, and snarling traffic throughout the city. The already saturated ground refused to accept this additional drink of water and spilled it out into the streets. Stubborn drivers intent on making it home drove through rushing pockets of water at low-lying intersections, a mistake that resulted in wet, ineffective brakes, which in turn caused a series of "fender-bender" accidents throughout the city.

The Revere River, a narrow body of water normally ambling its way peacefully through Grant, began to swell, edging up the riverbanks on both sides like water filling a bathtub.

On the west side of the river, nestled on a knoll in the heart of the city, the world-famous medical complex known as Med Center stood staunchly against the onslaught of rain and wind. At Grant Memorial Hospital, the tallest of eighteen red brick buildings in varying shapes and sizes, Astrid Thompson, head nurse in Emergency Services, peered out a rain-streaked window and exclaimed, "Oh, great! A storm during rush hour. Just what we need. Step lively, everyone, it's going to be an interesting night!"

It was.

The water rose higher . . . and higher.

It was the sound of the water lapping nearby that awakened Kate. Still seated in the librarian's chair, she had fallen asleep. It took her several moments to realize where she was. The library was so still and silent, she could hear her own breath. The only other sound was the smacking of the encroaching water upon the wooden stairs, and it was that sound that caught her attention. It was too close. Much closer than it should have been.

If only she could see. She would have given anything for a candle, a flashlight, a lantern. Anything to break this thick black curtain and take away her feeling of helplessness. How could she do anything useful if she couldn't *see*?

It wasn't the darkness she was frightened of. It was the water, so stubborn, so persistent, climbing ever higher. Without a light, how could she tell how close it was getting?

MED CENTER

CENTER

FLOOD

prologue

It began raining in Grant, Massachusetts, at 11:23 on a Tuesday night in mid-September. It rained lightly at first — a pleasant, refreshing, early autumn shower. Gardeners all over the city welcomed it, after ten straight days with no moisture for their fall gardens and the last of their roses.

During that night and most of the next day, the parched ground eagerly soaked up the falling rain.

But by the following evening, as commuters were making their way home, the pleasant shower turned nasty, throwing a temper tantrum. The wind rose, tearing at limbs of the huge old trees lining both sides of Linden Hill Boulevard, the main artery between the east and west sides of town. The skies turned an ominous black and, seconds later, opened, dumping thick torrents of rain on the city, flooding streets with deep washes of water, and snarling traffic throughout the city. Already-saturated ground refused to accept this additional drink of water, and spit it back up, spilling it out into the streets. Stubborn drivers intent on making it home drove through rushing pockets of water at low-lying intersections, a mistake that resulted in wet, ineffective brakes, causing a series of "fender bender" accidents throughout the city.

The Revere River began to swell, edging up the riverbanks on both sides like water filling a bathtub.

On the west side of the river, nestled on a knoll in the heart of the city, the world-famous medical complex known as Med Center stood staunchly against the onslaught of rain and wind. At Grant Memorial Hospital, Astrid Thompson, head nurse in Emergency Services, peered out a rain-streaked window and exclaimed, "Oh, great! A storm during rush hour. Just what we need. *Step lively*, everyone, it's going to be an interesting night!"

It was.

chapter

1

The medical complex known as Med Center, eighteen red brick buildings of varying shapes and sizes, sat up on a knoll in the very heart of the city — a jewel in the center of a crown. On the lush, meticulously landscaped grounds, seventeen of the buildings encircled the tallest and busiest of the hospitals, Grant Memorial, creating a giant wheel whose spokes were the glass-enclosed passageways leading from one building to another.

There was not a medical need that couldn't be addressed at Med Center. People from all over the world came to the Oncology building for its state-of-the-art cancer treatments. They came to the Llewelyn T. Grant Psychiatric Hospital, to the Hannah Rose Grant Women's and Children's Hospital, to the Dorcas Peterson Rehabilitation Center to seek treatment, cures, and advice. They came to all of the hospitals in the facility because they wanted, needed, the best. And the best was what they got. Because only the best were allowed the privilege of working at world-famous Med Center in Grant, Massachusetts.

Aside from the expertise offered there, it was a beautiful place. Lush woods bordered the vast acreage, and beyond the woods the Revere River ambled peacefully through the city, sparkling on sunny days like freshly polished silver.

Some days, however, were not sunny. There was no sun during the storm that hit the city on a Wednesday evening in September, when the charcoal skies opened and thick sheets of rain began falling on the complex and the shops, churches, schools, and residential areas surrounding it. The Revere River stopped sparkling and turned a muddy brown. It swelled rapidly and instead of ambling, it began to rush through the city as if late for an appointment.

"Hey, look, it's pouring! Now I won't be able to go dancing tonight. Life is just full of disappointments, right, Abby?"

Abby O'Connor, wearing a pink volunteer's smock over jeans and a pink turtleneck sweater, her dark, curly hair piled casually on top of her head, was standing at one of the big, wide picture windows in the Rehabilitation Hospital, looking out in dismay at the thick curtain of rain slapping against the glass. She jumped, startled, when the voice sounded at her elbow. Sid Costello had pulled up alongside her so quietly, she hadn't heard a sound. She whirled to face him. "Sid! Give me some warning, okay? That wheelchair isn't called Quiet-Ride for nothing. You'd make a great spy—no one would ever hear you coming."

"Oh, you bet. Must be all kinds of government agencies searching worldwide for an operative in a wheelchair." His voice was bitter. "I'll have to give that some thought. The best part would be, no one would ever notice me skulking around in doorways, listening at keyholes. You become invisible when you live in a wheelchair. People see a wheelchair and immediately look away. Perfect for a spy, if you ask me." He glanced up at Abby, his thick, dark eyebrows lifted skeptically. "Right? From now on, just think of me as Agent Costello. Have to have a code name, though. Something catchy." His eyes boring into hers, he said, "How does 'Useless' strike you?"

Her own eyes, round and dark and thickly lashed, held a mixture of compassion and exasperation as she returned his gaze. He was wrapped in a white terry cloth robe with his initials embroidered in navy blue on the chest pocket. The feet he had referred to as "useless" were encased in maroon hospital slippers. Whenever Abby saw those feet, her heart twisted in pain for Sid. Until a couple of months ago, he'd been one of Grant High School's star football players. And a great dancer. "You're not useless. You could even dance if you wanted to, Sid. I've been to some of the dances they hold right here in Rehab. Lots of people in chairs get out there on the floor. Sometimes by themselves, sometimes with a partner either pushing the chair or sitting on the patient's lap. They always look like they're having fun."

Sid turned his head toward the rain-streaked window, regarding with a morose stare the moisture shrouding the glass. "Right. And I'll bet it'd be even *more* fun at one of the dances at Grant High, where I'd be the *only* person in a wheelchair. Wouldn't *that* be a blast? Think of the attention I'd get. Probably be almost as good as scoring a touchdown, right?"

Abby stood her ground under his cold gaze. She was finally getting used to Sid's moods. "I wasn't talking about when you get out of here and go back to school. I was talking about *now!*"

"There isn't any *now!*" he said angrily. "That's what you people just don't get. All you do-gooding volunteers. You're as bad as my sadistic physical therapists with their master's degrees in Pain and Torture. None of you get it! 'Now' is about what someone is *doing*. People say 'I'm going to the store now' or 'I'm playing football now' or 'I'm dancing now.' If you can't *do* anything, there isn't any now. Get it?"

"Oh, that's ridiculous! People also say 'I'm reading now' and 'I'm eating now' and 'I'm writing a letter now!' You can do all of those things.

So you *do* have a now. If you were a quad, some-one else would have to do those things for you." Abby was referring to a quadriplegic. Unlike Sid, who had been paralyzed from the waist down following a fall, quadriplegics were paralyzed from the neck down. "At least you can still use your arms."

Rumor had it that he'd been using those arms to spray-paint the water tower just before he fell. He and two other Grant football players had been signing their names on the white metal, there had been some horsing around, and Sid had gone over the side.

He answered her sarcastically. "You're abso-lutely right, O'Connor. What's wrong with me, anyway, being so ungrateful? I keep forgetting how really lucky I am. Good thing I have you to remind me, Little Miss Sunshine."

Abby's cheeks flamed. A couple of the older doctors called her that, but with a smile and in a completely different tone of voice. Sid meant it as an insult. He was saying that she didn't under-stand how he felt. That hurt.

She did understand. Maybe not completely, because she'd never been paralyzed. Hadn't ever been sick, really. But she had an imagination, didn't she? Did he really think she couldn't guess how awful it was for him? One minute he'd been a popular, gorgeous, dark-haired god of a foot-ball player, in fantastic physical condition. The girls at Grant High called him "Sid the Bod." Then, in one tiny, horrible little second, Sid Costello had tumbled over the side of the tall, old water tower. And this time, Sid hadn't rolled over and jumped to his feet, the way he always did when he'd been tackled on the football field. He wouldn't *ever* jump to his feet again. At least, it looked that way now.

He was still gorgeous. Nothing had happened to his face, or the thick, curly hair on his head. But his legs no longer worked.

She *did* understand. She could feel the shock, when he'd first awakened and found himself in an ambulance racing for Med Center. Then another shock when he awakened again later, in a hospital bed, with a tube down his throat to help him breathe, and no feeling in his lower body. She could feel the horror when he had realized that he couldn't move his legs, couldn't walk, couldn't run or jog or play football or dance. He must have been terrified.

No one seemed to know yet whether or not the condition was permanent. The wheelchair that Sid Costello was sitting in could be his for life.

Just thinking about it now brought tears to her eyes. She swiped at them quickly. He mustn't see them. Although Sid regularly indulged in self-pity, he detested sympathy from others.

His girlfriend, a pretty, popular girl who, in

Abby's opinion, had all the depth and compassion of a fingernail clipping, had dumped Sid the very second she found out his wheelchair wasn't just a convenient mode of transportation.

Abby felt bad about that. But what made her mad was, Sid wasn't even trying. The therapeutic regimen at Rehab, like everything else at Emsee (her best friend Susannah Grant's nickname for the complex), was the best. People with injuries similar to Sid's came from all over the world to take advantage of the rehabilitative expertise. But Sid wasn't interested. He seemed to have given up already.

It bothered her that she couldn't seem to reach him. It made her feel stupid and inadequate, and when she felt that way, she wasn't her normal, patient self. Their encounters regularly ended with the two of them snapping at each other. And she often went home now feeling drained and frustrated. After a really bad day with Sid, she sometimes wondered if she should quit her volunteer work.

She took him back to his room. The tray she had brought him earlier sat on his table, untouched. "Are you going to eat your dinner or not?"

"Not. Get it out of here."

He wouldn't let her help him into bed, insisting instead on parking his wheelchair at the window. He was still staring out into the night when, her back stiff with anger and frustration, she left with the tray.

The blackening sky had turned the city of Grant as dark as night. The rain cut visibility down to zero, making driving extremely hazardous. The fender bender accident victims began arriving at Grant Memorial's ER on the grounds of Med Center shortly after four o'clock, as people began leaving school and work in large numbers.

Two patients quickly became four, then seven, then ten. After that, there was a steady stream of incoming traffic. Gurneys raced back and forth from ambulances to the hallway outside the trauma rooms, where critical patients were first seen, and to treatment rooms, where less serious injuries were dealt with. As soon as a patient had been removed to an examination table, that empty gurney was wheeled away again, ready for its next load.

Most of the injuries were minor. A broken wrist, shallow lacerations on foreheads and chins, a sprained ankle. A recent safety campaign had made Grant residents more aware of the benefits of seat belts, and most people were using them.

But not all. Kate Thompson, one of only two high school students who, as volunteers, had been given access to the treatment rooms in Emergency, glanced down at the woman lying on the wheeled stretcher. Her nose was obviously broken, and both eyes were already beginning to blacken. There was a deep laceration on her chin, another slashed across her forehead. Kate had seen many accident victims since she'd begun volunteering and she guessed correctly that this woman, whose car had slid on the slick road and skidded into a utility pole, had been picked up by the force of the collision and tossed across the front seat, her head slamming into the passenger's window. Her carelessness in ignoring the seat belt had nearly cost her her life.

I am not here to judge, Kate told herself sternly. I am *not* here to judge. I'm here to help. She held the woman's medical chart, just begun, in her hands and stood off to one side recording vital statistics as the doctors and nurses checked for chest trauma. When one of the doctors called for a portable X ray, it was Kate who ran to get it. Tall and lean, her dark skin contrasting with the pale pink of her smock, her hair neatly cornrowed, she moved swiftly and efficiently. She never argued with an order from medical personnel. Her mother, head nurse Astrid Thompson, had said more than once, "Med Center is the *only* place you don't question an order, Kate. I only wish you were that cooperative at home." But she usually smiled as she said it.

Kate didn't question orders from ER's staff because she knew it was a privilege for a high school student to be allowed into trauma and treatment rooms. She wasn't about to throw that away by pretending to know more than her training had taught her.

The process of applying for access to the treatment rooms had been a grueling one. So many questions, so many classes, so many tests. She had passed them all. So had Susannah Grant. Big surprise there. The last person Kate had expected to show up on that first day of volunteering was the daughter of the richest, most powerful man in town. Samuel Grant II practically owned the entire city. His ancestors had founded it, had established the world-famous medical center, the University, and Grant Pharmaceuticals, a mammoth research and development facility on the grounds of Med Center. Susannah Grant could have anything in the world that she wanted. It was hard to believe that what she wanted was to volunteer in ER.

But truth be told, she was good at it. Another surprise. And she was nice. Never once had Susannah been stupid enough to say to Kate, as some white girls had on occasion, "I just *love* the color of your skin. Me, I don't even tan well." Comments like that still made her sick. They were so condescending. If they liked the color of her skin so much, why was it they never invited her to their parties? Not that she'd go, of course.

When the woman had been sedated and a

doctor had begun sewing up the lacerations with neat, precise sutures, Kate left the treatment room, wondering which room Susannah was in. She hadn't seen her in a while. It had been so hectic the last hour or so, it was hard to keep track of the rest of the staff.

Will Jackson, a paramedic and a classmate of Kate's at Grant High, passed her then, with two of his fellow paramedics. Their navy blue windbreakers dripped water on the white tile as they ran, rushing a gurney along the noisy hallway through a crowd of people waiting to be treated for minor sprains, and cuts and bumps on the head. As he went, Will rattled off vital statistics to the doctor and nurse who met them at the door.

"Auto wreck," Will told the team, his words rushing together without pause, "thirty-year-old male . . . no seat belt . . . blunt trauma to the chest . . . some chest pain . . . tenderness in abdomen, upper left quadrant." The gurney rounded a corner, aiming for treatment room four. "Pulse one thirty-six," one of Will's partners said. "Respiration thirty-six and labored, BP one-twenty over ninety."

Kate fingered one of the heavy wooden earrings she was wearing, which she had made herself. She held the door open so the gurney could slide inside the small, white room. Other doctors arrived, and the team began working in earnest on the patient, the fourth to arrive in similar condition in the past hour. Susannah was already inside, performing the minor but helpful tasks the two were usually assigned, so Kate left.

Will followed. He joined her at the coffee machine in the cluttered staff lounge. The white tile floor was muddy with footprints. Open bags of cookies and chips dotted the counter, and half-empty Styrofoam coffee cups stretched across the white counter near the sink. Kate bit back a comment about "the laziness of some people!" because she knew how busy they'd been this afternoon. There had hardly been a free moment to grab a sip of hot coffee, let alone find the time to dispose of the cup properly.

With every staff member working in one treatment room or another, Kate and Will had the room to themselves. "I've only been here for an hour," she said, "but in that time we've had more car wreck injuries than we usually get in an entire weekend. And rush hour isn't even over yet. It's only five-twenty." She poured herself a cup of coffee, adding sugar and creamer, keeping her senses alert for another ambulance wail. "You're drenched, Will. You look like you took a shower with your clothes on."

Will, taller than Kate by a head, poured his own coffee. He leaned against the counter, absentmindedly stirring the steaming brown liquid with a white plastic spoon. "It's nasty out there.

Coming down in buckets. River's already rising. We were skidding all over the road. Rush hour's going to be a nightmare." He handed her his coffee cup to hold while he slipped out of his sodden jacket and draped it over a chair. "I might pull a double shift tonight. If the rain doesn't let up, this place is going to be jumping. And some people won't be able to get here for their shift. How long are you going to hang around? Eastridge floods first. You should go home while you still can."

Both Will and Kate lived on the east side of town, north of the curve where the Revere took a sharp turn and headed south. "I'm not going home," she answered. "But I am leaving. I hate to when we're so busy, but I've got to hang out at the library tonight. Heavy-duty research on a science paper." Kate's sharply angled face softened with a smile. "Susannah's still here, Will, in case you didn't see her. Maybe she needs a ride home."

Before he could answer, a tall, very pretty girl, with shoulder-length pale hair brushed away from her face and fastened behind her ears, emerged from one of the rooms and walked gracefully toward them. Her eyes on Will, she smiled as she approached. "Talking about me? My ears are burning. I didn't know you were here, Will. I thought you'd left." Dressed in jeans and a white silk shirt, sleeves rolled to the elbow, she moved to the counter, where she pulled a tea bag from a canister and dropped it into a cup before adding hot water. The tea in hand, she turned to Kate and Will. Her face was oval, her skin peach-toned and smooth, her eyes a brilliant blue. "Will, you look like a drowned rat. Is it that bad out there?"

"Worse." As Will went on to describe for Susannah the deplorable weather conditions, Kate sipped her coffee, watching them silently. They made a striking pair. Will with his dark skin, hair, and eyes, Susannah Grant so blonde, her hair almost white. Two of the best-looking people in Grant, Kate decided. Susannah's twin, Samuel Grant III, known to one and all as Sam, was technically better-looking than Will, who had one slightly crooked eyetooth. Sam Grant didn't have a crooked anything. His face was perfect. But Kate liked Will better, so her vote went to him. And it wasn't just because they were both African-American. Will was smart, funny, and kind. She trusted him. Everyone did.

While Susannah's eyes clearly reflected her feelings as they settled on Will's face, his were veiled. It drove Kate nuts that he was so dead-set on keeping the girl at a distance just because she was a Grant and he was plain old Will Jackson from the east side of town where, Will liked to joke, "No white man has ever gone before. Except the tax collector." Then he would add harshly, "At least, no white person named *Grant*."

Maybe not. But there was always a first time. And Susannah didn't act like the rich white girl that she was, anyway. What also annoyed Kate was the way the rest of the staff kept Susannah at a distance, just like Will. They were nervous about a Grant hanging around. Afraid if they screwed up, she'd run home to tell Daddy. Which, of course, Susannah would never do.

"I was just wondering," Kate said slyly when Will had finished his weather report, "if you needed a ride home, Susannah. It's such a nasty night to be driving." She smiled innocently at Will, who was glaring at her. "I'm sure Will here would be happy to give you a lift."

But Susannah had seen the look on his face. Her cheeks deepened in color as she said hastily, "Oh, I wasn't planning on leaving. Not now, when things are so hectic. Anyway, I have my Be . . . car."

Kate knew she'd started to say "Benz," and then must have decided it would sound like she was showing off. It wouldn't have. Everyone in town knew Samuel Grant II had bought his daughter a gorgeous silver Mercedes-Benz convertible for her sixteenth birthday. Few people, however, knew that Susannah didn't like it. Kate and Abby O'Connor were aware that Susannah preferred the Jeep her father had purchased for the Grants' gardener, Paolo. She borrowed it every chance she got. It had more room, and Susannah said it was "more fun."

"When we do leave," Susannah asked Will, "do you think we'll have any trouble getting home?"

Will resisted the urge to point out to Susannah that he couldn't possibly answer that question, since they wouldn't be going in the same direction. Susannah would be going back to the west side of Grant, where she lived at the very top of Linden Hill, in a mansion that actually had a name — Linden Hall — while Will would be heading east, to a small white house that suited him fine but wasn't much larger than Linden Hall's six-car garage. Not the same thing at all.

Before Will could throttle Kate for offering his services as a chauffeur to Susannah Grant, Susannah's twin burst in through the door, his handsome face and blonde hair wet with rain. Spotting the trio gathered around the coffee machine, he called out, "Hey, who's up for a flood party?"

chapter
2

Kate, Will, and Susannah all stared at Sam. Susannah was the first to speak. "A party? In this weather? Sam, that's crazy. The river's already rising. Will said so."

Sam laughed. He reached over and took Susannah's cup from her, taking a sip and then making a face when he realized the cup held tea, not coffee. "Ugh! How can you drink that stuff?" While he helped himself to coffee, he said, "It wouldn't be a flood party if there wasn't a flood, would it? And if there's going to be one, what better place to view the festivities from than the fishing cabin?"

Susannah's jaw dropped. "The fishing cabin? Sam, you're not going down there, are you? That's on the South Side. It's right on the riverbank!"

"The cabin sits up high, Susannah. If the river rises, we can fish right off the verandas." He laughed again. "Quit worrying. Jeez, if everyone was like you, it wouldn't be much of a party. Fortunately, everyone isn't. A whole bunch of people said they'd come. Will, Kate, how about you two? Should be a blast."

He's only asking us, Will thought, because we're standing right here. Sam Grant gives more parties than anyone else in town. He has never invited a Thompson or a Jackson before. "No, thanks. I'm hanging out here. Going to be a pretty hairy night." He regarded Sam coolly. "You're really headed for the South Side? Ever heard the expression 'inviting trouble'?"

"Man, you guys really are a bunch of deadheads," Sam declared, finishing his coffee in one hearty swallow and crumpling the Styrofoam cup.

Kate noticed he didn't toss it into a nearby trash can. He simply dropped it onto the counter. Of course. Servants probably followed him around at Linden Hall for the sole purpose of picking up after him. "There's a trash can right there by your left elbow," she said tartly. "And since you're going south, how about dropping me off at the library on your way?"

"You're picking the dull old library over a Sam Grant party?" Sam asked, placing a hand over his heart as if he were mortally wounded, simultaneously gifting Kate with a grin. Susannah recognized it as the grin that melted young female hearts all across the city. She almost laughed aloud. A wasted effort. Kate wouldn't fall for that grin in a million years. She was too smart.

"Yes, I *am* picking the dull old library over your party," Kate said briskly. "Now, are you going to give me a ride, or do I have to hike through the wind and rain and dark of night?"

Sam tossed the cup into the trash can and sighed heavily. "I guess I'm going to give you a ride. Never let it be said that Samuel Grant III wasn't willing to rescue a maiden in need. Come on." Waving carelessly at Susannah and Will, he grabbed Kate's hand and strode away, taking her with him. She barely managed to grab her sweatshirt as she passed the pegs on the alcove wall.

"What am I supposed to tell Mother when she asks where you are?" Susannah called after him. "I can't say you went to the cabin. She'll worry herself sick."

"Don't worry about it. I'll call her. I'll take care of it. Relax!"

Susannah didn't look relaxed as she watched them leave the building. Rain and wind invaded the lobby as the door opened. "He's crazy," she muttered, "absolutely crazy."

"He said the cabin is on high ground," Will said. "Is it?"

"Not *that* high."

Then an ambulance arrived with two more accident victims. A house code sounded over the PA system, and staff members began running past the open door of the lounge toward trauma room six.

This was no minor emergency, Susannah knew. Her nerves began to tingle as they always did when a life-threatening injury arrived at ER.

"Don't get addicted to it," Kate's mother, Astrid Thompson, had warned Susannah and Kate on their first day of volunteer work. "The excitement, I mean. Some people thrive on the adrenaline that flows every time the doors open and you don't know what kind of incoming you're getting. We're not here to get that kind of rush. We're here to help. Remember that."

So far, Susannah's "rush" had come *after* a patient had been treated and she knew the volunteers had done some good, not before. Still, she couldn't deny that her adrenaline did get itself in an uproar when the crisis was obviously serious, as this new one seemed to be.

Two policeman, black slickers on over their uniforms, were filling out forms at the reception desk. One of them saw Susannah and Will heading for the trauma room and shook his head. "You don't want to go in there," he said emphatically. "Car hit a puddle, skidded, slammed into a utility pole, and caught on fire. There were two people trapped inside. Both your age. I'd steer clear if I were you. Let the doctors and nurses handle it."

Susannah hesitated. She had seen only two burn patients since she'd begun volunteering. A woman who had fallen against a space heater, and a little boy who had pulled a pot of cocoa off the stove on top of himself. Those burns had been serious, but not life threatening. The policeman's tone of voice told her that was not the case this time.

"He's right," Will said. "You stay here. I'll check it out. Maybe they don't need you."

Susannah bristled, although she knew he meant well. But he was implying that he could take it and she couldn't. She was hypersensitive about that kind of attitude. So much of the staff seemed to think that because she was wealthy, she had to have a weak stomach. Ridiculous.

"Kate's gone," she reminded Will. "I'm the only volunteer float left. I'm going in." She matched his stride as they hurried to trauma room six.

The patient on the table, surrounded by eight doctors and nurses, was conscious and talking. She was also coughing, in spite of the oxygen mask on her face. But she was not screaming in agony, as Susannah had feared. It was impossible to recognize her, her face was so black with smoke. Her hair had been singed, and her clothes had been either burned from her body or ripped away by the staff. She was partially covered by a sterile sheet, but the burn damage was clearly visible on her arms, legs, and upper torso.

Susannah swallowed a gasp of horror. Whoever that was on the table, she was never going to be the same from this moment on.

"Pete?" the girl asked repeatedly, her voice hoarse. "Is Pete okay? Where is he?"

"Why isn't she screaming?" Susannah asked Will, her voice low.

He lowered his to a whisper. "Her burns are too severe. I can tell from here. When you're burned that seriously, nerve endings that would be sending pain messages to your brain have probably been destroyed. Anyway, she's still in shock. It'll hit her later, if she survives."

Susannah moved to the table to take the chart from a nurse. Glancing down at the name, she gasped. Toni Scott. The severely burned girl was a student at Grant High. Susannah had met her through Abby. Incredibly bright. President of the debating team at Grant, a team that had defeated Susannah's private day school team twice. Toni Scott?

"Don't look," a nurse advised, pulling gently on Susannah's elbow to move her away from the table. "No need. You'll just give yourself nightmares. Believe me, I'm doing you a favor. The girl's in a bad way. Of course, she *is* still alive, which is more than I can say for the boy driving the car." After a moment, she added, "Maybe he's better off. If this one lives, she's going to go through hell recovering."

Susannah swallowed hard. And she forced herself to look at the patient. She had to. What kind of doctor would she make if she couldn't stand to look at a burn victim?

Although it was hard to be sure, with all that black smoke dusting Toni's face, it looked to Susannah as though her facial skin was only singed. But her arms and upper torso and legs were bad. Very, *very* bad.

When the respiratory technician who had been summoned stepped into the room, he balked for a second at the sight of the patient. Then he got a grip and hurried to the table, where he set up suction and prepared instruments that would maintain an airway for the patient. Her lungs were probably in horrible shape.

Susannah helped a nurse soak gauze strips in a sterile saline solution. When an airway had been cleared and the patient had been sedated with morphine, her burned limbs and upper body were carefully wrapped with the sterile gauze strips. She was covered with blankets and prepared for a hasty move from Memorial through an enclosed passageway to the Walter E. Miller Burn Unit on the grounds.

When she had departed in the care of two nurses and an orderly, Susannah returned to Will. "Do you think she'll make it?" she asked quietly.

He shook his head. "Maybe. I heard one of

the doctors say she was fifty percent third degree. But she's young and healthy, so if she's willing to fight, she has a chance, I guess. Pete Dawes was with her. He didn't make it."

Susannah didn't know Pete Dawes. And never would, now. "I thought," she said slowly as they left the room, "that most of the injuries we would have tonight would be connected to the storm. People swept off the road in their cars by high water, some near drownings, maybe, if the river really got high. Minor injuries from fender benders, things like that. I never once thought of fire."

"This *was* storm-related. That cop said they skidded because of a puddle."

"I know. But I still never thought I'd see a burn patient tonight. Not one like that, anyway." Susannah shuddered. "Sometimes I wonder if I'm really cut out for this kind of work."

"Well, stop wondering." Will put a comforting arm around her shoulders and held her eyes with his. "Because you *are*. There wasn't a person in that room who wasn't affected by what they saw just now, and one of those doctors has been practicing medicine for over twenty-five years. Maybe the time to worry is when you're *not* affected by something like that. But"—he stood back and looked at her for a moment—"somehow, I don't think that's ever going to happen to you. You're not the tough-as-nails type."

"A few minutes ago, I wished I were," Susannah said ruefully. "But I guess you're right. I wouldn't really want to be like that. I don't like the doctors who are. Nothing seems to get to them. It's like they're wearing full-body shields that keep anything from touching them."

"Yeah, I know what you mean." Will smiled down at her. "We'll make a pact, okay? When we're doctors, if I see you taking up a shield, I'll call you on it, and you do the same for me. Promise?"

Susannah laughed. "Promise."

Will reached out to brush a few stray strands of blonde hair from Susannah's forehead. As he brought his hand back down, she captured it in one of hers and held it for a brief moment.

Then three ambulances arrived at the same time, and they were off and running again.

chapter
3

"**A**re you really going to celebrate this atrocious weather with a party?" Kate asked Sam as he steered his sleek, silver van along the dark, wet streets of Grant. Traffic had thinned, and shoppers had abandoned the streets for their warm, dry homes. "The South Side always floods faster than anywhere in town except Eastridge. You could get stranded down there, Sam."

He laughed. "Sounds like fun."

"I don't think so. People died in that last flood. I was only eleven, but I remember. There wasn't anything fun about it." But Kate knew Sam had made up his mind. According to his sister, trying to change it would be as futile a task as trying to empty out the Revere River with a teaspoon. He was going to party, and he was going to do it on the South Side, where the riverbanks were too low to hold back rapidly rising water.

Kate gave up, falling silent. Her eyes followed the windshield wipers racing back and forth in a vain attempt to defeat the rain.

"You should come with me," Sam said lightly. "You work too hard. The library's probably closed anyway on a night like this."

It was Kate's turn to laugh. "Oh, right, it's a great night for partying, but not for studying? And they say women are illogical! I'll be *safe* in the library, Sam. I can't say the same for you, down there on the South Side. Anyway, I've got to get this chem paper done. But thanks for the invite." Like you really meant it, she thought cynically.

She had been to Linden Hall only once, delivering a jacket Susannah had forgotten at ER. Sam had been there. He had barely acknowledged her existence, sending a nod her way as he tore out of the house for soccer practice. Now he suddenly wanted her to party with him and his west Grant friends? Right. And the moon was made of chocolate chip cookie dough.

"You realize you're battering my ego," he said. "Choosing chemistry over one of my parties. Don't tell anyone, okay? It's too humiliating."

Kate didn't reply. She really didn't want to go to the library. What she wanted to do was head for home, make sure her family was okay. But chemistry was proving to be more of a challenge than she had anticipated. One of the conditions of her admittance into ER's treatment rooms was to keep her grades way up there. She'd need the grades for medical school, too. Even if partying *had* been on her agenda, which it wasn't right now, she couldn't afford it.

"You're crazy, Sam," she said, softening the comment with a smile. Sam was okay. Maybe not as compassionate as his twin, but not a jerk, either. A little spoiled, but then, most of the kids from the Linden Hill area were spoiled. They all had everything money could buy, and then some. Sam was no exception. Fifty-dollar haircuts and two hundred-dollar sneakers were Sam's way of life. He took all of it — the mansion at the top of Linden Hill, the silver van, the haircuts and clothes and swimming pool and sauna and boats and computers — for granted, Kate knew that. And the possibility of not doing as he pleased when he pleased (if such a thought ever occurred to him, which she doubted) would probably send him into a catatonic state.

At the library, she added one final warning about keeping an eye on the river as she jumped from the van. Sam grinned, waved, and took off, his wheels spinning on the wet pavement.

Well, I tried, Kate told herself. Yanking the hood of her maroon sweatshirt up over her head, she ran up the puddled walkway and disappeared inside the low, white frame and red brick building.

At ER, during a momentary lull in activity, most of the staff had gathered in one of the lounges to check out the weather channel. Will,

Susannah, and Abby were in the group clustered beneath the television set suspended high on one wall. The map was heavily green, which indicated areas of rain, and advancing rapidly toward the city were large splotches of yellow and red, which meant very heavy rain, probably including thunderstorms.

Someone pushed a button on the remote. A local news commentator stared out over their heads. "Police and rescue personnel are urging all citizens to remain indoors unless absolutely necessary. Many low-lying areas of the city are already flooded, and there are reports that the river is rising rapidly in the east and south. With more rain on the way, sandbag crews have been dispatched to those areas. Police are asking for volunteers. Do not call 911 to offer your help. Those lines must be kept clear for emergency calls. If you wish to volunteer, please call the number you see on your screen."

Abby thought the blonde woman in the red suit gazing out over their heads looked anxious as she spoke, and wondered if she had family in east or south Grant.

No one in the group jotted down the number appearing on the screen. They had their hands full where they were. And as long as ambulances were screeching to a halt outside of Grant Memorial every three to five minutes, no one was going anywhere.

Susannah could see that Will was torn. He lived in Eastridge. His family was there. That area flooded quickly, she knew. Helping to construct barriers against the river had to be something he wanted to do. But he was needed here at ER, too.

"Lots of people will volunteer," she assured him as they left the lounge. "I remember six years ago, when we had that terrible flood, they kept showing Eastridge on television. Everyone in the area was helping on the sandbag line, even little kids. Other people were taking boats out to collect people who hadn't evacuated in time. Some people volunteered at the evacuee center over at the Psych building. Everyone was helping."

Will nodded, and his frown eased a little. Before he could respond, he was called to ambulance duty.

Susannah decided to stay at ER until she was sure she was no longer needed. Abby wanted to stay, too. She wanted to go back to Rehab to see how Sid was. She didn't like the way he'd been acting lately. Even moodier than usual. But she knew she was needed at home. Her mother had recently gone back to work part-time, writing ad copy for Grant Pharmaceuticals, and Wednesday was the one day a week she worked late. There were five younger O'Connors at home. Moira was twelve and smart enough, Abby told herself, to come in out of the rain. But Moira would have her hands full with ten-year-old Geneva and eight-year-old Carmel, plus Mattie, who was only four, and Emma, still affectionately known as Toothless, though at two years and two months old, she no longer was.

"And it's raining!" Abby finished explaining to Susannah, who hadn't asked for an explanation. "The kids can't even go outside and play. Moira will be tearing every last red hair out of her scalp. I'd better go, Sooz."

"You didn't drive. I picked you up after school, remember?" Although the two were best friends, Abby attended Grant High, where she was a cheerleader and treasurer of her class, while Susannah attended one of two private day schools in the city. Sam attended the other. "Can you take a University shuttle, or would you rather I drive you? I can drop you off and come right back here."

"Don't be silly." Abby slipped into a copper-colored rain cape and yanked its hood up over her curly hair. She hoisted a huge brown leather shoulder bag. "Why should both of us get soaked? I'll hop the University shuttle. It stops right outside for the nursing students, and it'll take me straight to my house. Call me later, okay?"

Susannah was about to suggest they call the University, adjacent to Med Center, to make sure the shuttle was running in spite of the weather, when one of the short, squat, blue buses pulled up at the curb outside, its lights glowing eerily through the veil of rain.

Abby raced to catch it. Another chill, damp gust of wind rushed into the room as she left.

Susannah hated to see her go. Will was on an ambulance run, and Kate had gone to the library and wouldn't be back tonight. Kate's mother had left at three when her shift was over. While most of the staff was cautiously civil around Samuel Grant's daughter, Will and Kate were friendly and helpful, and Nurse Thompson tried very hard to see that Susannah was included in some of the more serious cases. With all three of them absent, it would have been nice to have Abby around for moral support. Now she, too, was gone.

But Susannah's brief lapse into loneliness ended quickly as Will, along with a young intern Susannah knew only as "Jonesy," and three other paramedics arrived. Two other ambulances, each with a seriously injured patient, arrived right behind them.

"Car swept off Bunker Road near Eastridge," Will said as Susannah ran with them to a treatment room. "Family in it. Mother, father, little boy. We've got the mother. Chest injury. Father and kid right behind us."

Medical personnel had been alerted to more

incoming by radio and were waiting in trauma rooms five, seven, and eight.

Although Will's voice was, as always, outwardly calm, this run had left him shaken. The station wagon with the family in it had been pulled over a steep incline by the rushing water. When the ambulance arrived, the car lay on its side far below them in a pool of water at the edge of a deep ravine. Will and his partners had had to tie ropes to the back of their vehicles and toss them down the hill to use as guides down the treacherously slippery slope. Donning harnesses, they'd clipped them onto the ropes before beginning the hazardous trip downhill, taking with them a Stokes stretcher, a resuscitator, drug box, cervical collars, the radio, and monitors.

The rain continued to batter them. Their navy slickers kept their clothing dry, but what they really needed was better footgear. "Should have worn my football cleats," Will remarked halfway down the hill.

Over the annoying, smacking sound of the rain as it hit the ground, they heard moaning from the car as they approached. Someone inside was still alive. Hadn't been killed on impact, hadn't been crushed when the car rolled over on its side, hadn't drowned in the deep puddle of water.

The first thing they had to do when they reached the vehicle was make sure it was secure.

If it had been in danger of being swept into the ravine, more ropes would have been necessary to secure it, wasting precious moments. As soon as they were positive that the overturned station wagon would stay put, Will squeezed in through the open passenger's window.

The driver, still in her seat belt, was a woman in her early thirties, lying on her side, unconscious, behind the steering wheel, her head resting on the windowsill. The sill had kept her head out of the pool of water, saving her from drowning. When Will checked, he found the breathing sounds clear in her left lung, but diminished in the lower right. Her skin felt moist and cool. He called for the resuscitator, which his partner passed though the window, and Will put an oxygen mask on the woman.

The car shifted slightly. Will held his breath. They'd been so sure it was secure. Had they been wrong? Were they about to slide off the road into the ravine?

The slight movement stopped. Will exhaled.

When he glanced into the backseat, he found a man, conscious and complaining of pain in his left leg. Lying on top of him was a small boy, fully awake but so dazed, he didn't answer when Will spoke to him. He was holding one hand over his left eye, but there was no blood on his face. A good sign?

The woman was obviously the most critically

injured, and required immediate attention. While Will slipped a collar around her neck as a precaution, his partners had carefully jimmied open the back door, which was now on the top of the car, and climbed in to examine the boy and his father.

"Eye injury here," one said about the boy. The father murmured, "Lollipop. He had a lollipop in his hand when we hit. Maybe the stick went into his eye. Is he okay?"

Using his penlight, the paramedic checked the eye injury. "I don't see a laceration. But just to be on the safe side, I'm going to bandage both eyes," he told the worried father. "That way, his injured eye won't move sympathetically with his good one."

Although the child complained that his eye burned, he was quiet while his eyes were bandaged. He had no other injuries, which Will considered a miracle.

After a sterile dressing had been applied to the father's open leg fracture, Will's partners immobilized the leg with a ladder splint.

Their actions took no more than seven or eight minutes. They worked quickly, as careful as possible to avoid sudden, sharp movements that might dislodge the vehicle from its spot.

Will knew the real difficulty would come when it was time to transport the three patients back up the dangerously muddy slope. The ropes would help, but both the woman and the man were unable to walk, and the boy couldn't see.

A call went out over the radio for more help, but they all knew there was a good chance no other ambulances would be available.

The climb back up the hill proved to be the most difficult task Will had yet faced as a paramedic. It took them, with the help of two men who had stopped along the highway above them, and later the crews from two additional ambulances, twenty-five minutes to get all three patients onboard. By that time, the woman's condition had worsened, showing increased breathing difficulty. There wasn't much they could do for her, and Will hated that. She needed surgery, and she needed it quickly, but the driver didn't dare go too fast. The vehicle skidded three times on the slick roads. Each time, the little boy screamed in terror, clearly afraid that his terrible ordeal in the station wagon was about to be repeated.

Although they remained constantly in touch with the hospital during their trip, the radio line was cluttered with static due to the weather, and they had great difficulty interpreting the messages from Med Center.

It was a harrowing ride. Will had never been so glad to see the tall, brick buildings appearing out of the darkness.

The woman was sent immediately to surgery.

The father was treated in ER by an orthopedic surgeon who then ordered him to another operating room. The terrified child was handed over to a social worker who would stay with him to await the arrival of the ophthalmologist treating him for the eye injury.

When the three had been dispatched to proper care, Will walked on shaky legs to the staff lounge and sank gratefully into a chair.

chapter
4

In the basement cubicle at the library where Kate sat at a small table poring over chemistry textbooks for her report, she could hear the rain slapping against the building. The library, usually busy in the evening, was nearly deserted. Kate had seen only two people upstairs when she came in, and one of them was the librarian. He had asked as she passed the circulation desk, "Not flooding out there yet, is it?"

"Not over here," she answered, referring to the middle of town where the library was, "but it probably is in Eastridge, and on the South Side."

"They'll have to evacuate," he said knowingly. "If the river rises."

Kate went on down the stairs, knowing he was right, and wondering if her family would be at the house when she got there or if they would already have gone to the shelter at Med Center. She could remember very clearly the spring when she was eleven. The Revere had risen so quickly during a deluge that many Eastridge residents, including her family, had had to be taken out by boat. At the medical complex, the Psych building, located a safe distance from the riverbank, had been turned into a makeshift refuge for people threatened by high water. They'd had food and hot chocolate and coffee, they'd been warm and dry and safe, and there had been a lot of jokes about getting free psychiatric care while they were there. But on the whole, the experience had been terrifying. They'd had to leave their home in the middle of the night, when it was dark, climbing out of bedroom windows into a torrent of cold rain and blowing wind. And as they left their small yellow house, there was no way of knowing if it would still be there when they returned.

The worst part had been when the water had finally gone down and they'd been able to go back home. Her mother had cried when they walked into the house, and Astrid Thompson did not cry easily. Their furniture, their rugs, the curtains, even the kitchen appliances, had all been covered with a thick layer of smelly, oozing mud.

They had all helped with the cleanup, a truly disgusting job. It had been three weeks before they could sleep in their own house. The musty smell lingered for months.

There had been heavy rains since, and some minor flooding. Every year in the spring and fall, they had storms. But until now, they'd been lucky. Except for basements, where all Eastridge residents had learned not to store anything valuable, houses had remained untouched.

Kate could only hope their luck would hold out. She couldn't study for a chem test in a shelter. Too noisy. And she didn't want to see that look on her mother's face again when she had to step inside a flood-ravaged home.

Pushing her worry from her mind, she immersed herself thoroughly in her studying.

An hour later, the librarian called down the stairs, "Anyone there? I'm closing early so I won't have to swim home. I'll be locking up now."

Kate didn't answer. She wasn't finished with her research yet. And if the weather didn't improve, the library might not be open the next day. There was a side door at the end of the hallway. She'd used it many times after a study session. She'd go out that way. One more hour should do it.

The light in the hallway snapped off, and a few minutes later, Kate heard the front door upstairs slam shut. She had the whole building to herself. With so much quiet, maybe she could finish in less than an hour. She'd catch a shuttle in front of the building, be home in forty-five minutes, nice and dry and cozy. Maybe she'd make hot chocolate. It was that kind of night.

She got up, moved to the stacks, put one book

away and took out another. Then, legs curled up underneath her, she settled back in her chair, content with the peace and quiet, undisturbed by the continued smacking of the rain against the pavement outside.

At Med Center, on the fifth floor of Rehab, Sid Costello, his wheelchair still parked beside the window in his room, reached out to slide the glass open. Wind-driven rain slapped at him and tore at his hair. Uncaring, he reached out to grip the sill, pulling his chair closer to the window. His upper body was still an athlete's. It took little effort on his part to maneuver the chair close enough to the opening for him to thrust his head out and look down. "Five floors," he murmured while rain soaked through his terry-cloth robe, "that's pretty high up."

"Mr. Costello?" a voice behind him asked abruptly. "What do you think you're doing?"

Damn those rubber-soled shoes! The staff probably wore them just so they could sneak up on people. "Just checking out the storm," Sid said in the same calm, even tone of voice he'd used in the past to make people think he was totally in control of a situation. It always worked. He'd learned long ago that if you spoke with certainty, people thought you knew what you were doing. Of course, he knew differently, but he wasn't telling. "Pretty rough out there, right? Glad I'm in here." Liar. He would never, *never* be glad he was in here.

"Look at you!" Nurse Plummer bustled over to his side. She reached out and slammed the window shut, carefully locking it. "You're soaked! Now we're going to have to get you into dry clothing, and I've got a bandage to change in 506, and back rubs in eight and ten." She frowned down at him. "We really don't have time for this, Mr. Costello. Not on a night like this."

Sid almost said, "What do you mean, *we*? I have all the time in the world. For now, anyway." But he didn't. Remarks like that got him nothing but disapproving looks. Everyone, including Abby O'Connor, wanted, no, make that *demanded*, a positive, upbeat attitude from him. But then, they weren't in wheelchairs, were they? Anyway, Abby had enough positive attitude for ten people, why did she need his?

He didn't have any to give her.

The nurse had locked the window. There was no way he could reach that lock from a sitting position. Not that he'd planned to keep it open on a night like this. Still, the fresh air had felt good. Why did hospitals have to be so stuffy? And with all of the windows closed up tighter than a bank vault, there wasn't any way for the smells of disinfectant and rubbing alcohol, and overcooked meat loaf from the kitchen, to escape the building. The stale odors were prisoners, just like him.

Nurse Plummer glared down at him suspiciously. "Is that really what you were doing with the window open? Just checking out the storm? You weren't thinking of doing anything stupid, were you, Mr. Costello? Because if we thought for one minute that you were, we'd have to transfer you to Psych."

Talking the whole time, she helped him out of his wet robe and into bed. This was the part he hated the most. Feeling so helpless. It wasn't the pain. They gave him medicine for that. Besides, he'd had all kinds of football injuries. He wasn't any stranger to pain. No big deal. But having to have things done for him, God, how he hated that! He would *never* get used to that. Never.

The phrase "transfer you to Psych" jolted him. She thought he'd been thinking about jumping? That made him mad. He was no coward! She could ask anyone. They'd all say that Sid Costello was no coward.

"We know that depression is common in cases like yours." The nurse pulled the blanket up over his legs. "You've had a rotten break, and that's the truth. That's why we feel it's important that you see one of the psychiatrists regularly." When he was safely tucked in, she handed him a clean white towel, gesturing at him to dry his hair. Her tone of voice changed as she added, "It'll pass, you know. The depression."

If she tells me how lucky I am, Sid resolved as he unenthusiastically rubbed at his hair with the towel, I'm going to throw my water pitcher at her.

"Everyone here is rooting for you," the nurse said. "You were an athlete. You're strong and healthy. There is every reason to believe you'll walk again. Why don't you just wait and see before you decide your life is over? That's always a good way to handle things." She smiled. "No jumping to conclusions."

"Actually," Sid said in a deliberately friendly voice, "I'm not doing much jumping of any kind these days, Nurse Plummer."

The smile disappeared. Two bright spots of red appeared on her cheeks. She plopped the buzzer in his lap. "If you need anything, just buzz." Then she was gone.

He was alone again, with the window closed and locked. A feeling of isolation swept over Sid. He was used to having hordes of people around at games, at practices, at school, at parties and dances. Now, here he was all alone, shut up in this coffin of a room. So much white. Why couldn't they paint the walls green or red or orange?

When the storm ended, maybe he could complain about the room being stuffy, and talk some sweet, innocent, young nurse into opening the window for him.

Sid was suddenly very, very tired. He might as well give it up for tonight and get some sleep. It was only seven o'clock. But it wasn't like he had plans. He wasn't going anywhere.

He fell asleep chuckling bitterly to himself over the nurse's choice of words. "Jumping to conclusions." If he ever did what she was worried about, the conclusion he'd be jumping to would be his *own*. Dumb idea. Really dumb.

He had just wanted some fresh air, that was all.

O'Connor should have stayed, Sid thought angrily as he drifted off to the sound of rain pounding incessantly against the windows. If she'd been here, I wouldn't have opened the window, and the nurse wouldn't have written down on my chart what she's probably writing at this moment. That I need to be watched.

Abby shouldn't have left.

He fell asleep and, as he often did, dreamed of the accident that had sent him to Med Center in a shrieking ambulance on a hot, sticky night in July.

They were bored, he and Rick and Santos. Too broke for a movie, too broke even to rent one. But Sid had enough gas in his car to drive out to the water tower. Rick's idea. "We're going to be seniors," he said. "Seniors always sign the tower. Why wait until school starts? Why not do it right now, get a head start on the other guys?"

Sid and Santos didn't argue with him, mostly because they couldn't think of any better way to spend a summer night.

It was easy climbing up the ladder leading to the top of the fat, white water tower on the outskirts of town. A three-quarter moon lit the fields surrounding the tower, and Santos had brought a flashlight. They stood at the very top for a few minutes, laughing triumphantly, giddy with the headiness of being so high up.

They wrote their names. Rick's was, of course, larger than Sid's or Santos's.

Then (and Sid could never remember this part very well), Santos made a crack about Rick being an egomaniac, taking up practically half the tower with his name, leaving very little room for anyone else. Rick laughed and swept an arm sideways in a gesture that meant "Get outa here." Santos knocked the arm away, Rick swept it back again, and they began wrestling in earnest. Sid was leaning against the railing, facing the tower, studying his name in black paint and feeling satisfied with the way it looked against all that white, when Rick's linebacking arm slammed into the side of his chest, lifting Sid's feet off the ground and knocking him off-balance.

He knew he was going to fall. Knew it even before he toppled over the railing, knew it before he felt the loss of a solid surface beneath his feet, knew it before the rush of air around him made him dizzy. His head filled with blood as he spiraled downward; his arms flew out as if he could suddenly, magically, create wings and save himself from the cold, hard ground.

No wings sprouted.

The next thing Sid was aware of was the calm, reassuring voice of Will Jackson, a football teammate of his. There seemed to be a red, spinning light behind Will's head, and Will was telling Sid not to move.

No problem there. Sid had already tried, when he first regained consciousness and realized slowly that he was lying flat on his back on the ground, to get back on his feet. Had tried really hard. Felt stupid lying there on the ground with Santos and Rick, weird looks on their faces, staring down at him. But his efforts had failed. He had used all of the strength he had, expecting to rise without a problem, just as he did on the football field. He'd get up, dust himself off, and stay away from water towers from now on.

It hadn't happened. In his dazed state, it had taken him a while to realize what the problem was, but it had finally hit him. The problem was, he couldn't jump to his feet because he couldn't *feel* his feet, or his legs. They were still there, he could see them clearly. But . . . it didn't *feel* like they were still there.

That terrified him.

But Santos and Rick were staring down at him, and Will was asking him questions, and, just like on the football field, he had to pretend it didn't hurt and he wasn't scared.

Will and two other guys wearing paramedic jackets were talking to each other, saying things Sid didn't understand. But what he did understand, very clearly, was the urgency in their words. And Will was frowning, looking as worried as Sid felt.

They opened his shirt and attached round rubber things to his chest, then hooked him up to a small machine. Then, although he had said very loudly and clearly that he wasn't in any pain, couldn't feel a thing, they stuck a needle in his arm and started an IV. He knew that's what it was because his grandfather had had a whole bunch of them when he had pneumonia the year before.

"What's that for?" Sid asked. "It's not medication, is it? I told you, I'm not in any pain."

"This isn't for pain," Will said quietly. "This is to keep you stable. You might have internal injuries."

He might be bleeding inside? That was almost as scary as not being able to feel his legs.

The ride in the ambulance was more frightening than Sid had ever thought it would be, if he'd ever thought about it at all. It was cold, and the light was odd, not quite yellow, not quite white. Like the inside of a lemon, he thought as he lay very, very still, hoping he wasn't shaking. He couldn't tell. His whole body seemed out of kilter, as if his brain had decided to stop sending messages to the rest of him.

The hospital was even worse than the ambulance. Besides the weird lighting and the cold, white walls and the cold itself, there were all these strangers bending over him, asking him questions he couldn't answer, and poking and prodding at him. Sometimes the only way he knew someone had poked him with a needle was when they said so. A doctor or nurse said, "Did you feel that?" and that was how Sid knew they had jabbed him. He hadn't felt a thing.

They scared him. He knew they didn't mean to. But there was so much *intensity* in their faces as they worked over him. It was frightening. He was in no pain, and would have allowed himself the luxury of thinking that he was going to be fine if it hadn't been for the expressions on their faces, and the atmosphere in the cubicle. You could *feel* disaster in the air. *He* could feel it.

They hooked him up to so much equipment, he felt like Frankenstein's monster, and they kept hovering over him as if they were waiting for him to rise and jump from the table. He wasn't left alone for a single second during those first few hours, and not much more than that in the following hours. Days. Weeks.

The last scene in his nightmare was always the same: the moment when his parents walked into his hospital room and he saw the looks on their faces. His mother might as well have hung a sign around her neck that read, YOUR LIFE HAS CHANGED FOREVER.

And at that point, Sid always woke up, clammy with cold sweat.

As he did now, on this chilly, rainy night.

They had all tried to sugarcoat it, he remembered in the dark of his room. Everyone did. Even the orderly who put him in a wheelchair the first time had said heartily, "Looks like a good fit."

A good *fit*? He didn't *want* it to fit. Why would *anyone* want a wheelchair to be a good fit? If it fit, didn't that mean you belonged in it? That you might stay in it forever?

No! That couldn't happen. Not to him.

Everyone said Med Center was a great place. It was, it was. Chock-full of cheerful, helpful people. Experts in their fields. The most expensive equipment, the latest in medical breakthroughs.

So why wasn't he walking yet?

Sid glanced over at the closed, locked window. It still ran with silvery rivulets of water.

chapter
5

〜〜〜〜〜〜〜〜〜

When Abby O'Connor arrived home, dripping water on the parquet floor in the entry hall of the one-story, sprawling ranch house, she called out, "Hey, where is everybody? Big sister's here!"

"Alert the media," her sister Moira called from the living room. "I'm in here. Don't ask me where anyone else is, because it's not my mission in life to keep track of everyone."

Slipping out of her rain cape and tossing it haphazardly onto the coatrack near the door, Abby went into the living room. Toothless was playing with Tinkertoys in the middle of the room. Moira, lanky and already, at twelve, a head taller than Abby, was stretched out on the couch, reading. Mattie, four years old and the only O'Connor male child, was engrossed in cartoons on television and didn't even glance up when Abby entered the room. Carmel and Geneva were not anywhere in sight.

"Well, I *am* going to ask you," Abby said, walking over to crouch down beside the toddler, who looked up and beamed a delighted smile at her older sister. "Where are the girls?"

A shrug. "How should I know?"

"Moira, you're supposed to be keeping an eye on them. You agreed. When Mom went back to work, she said you could have the computer you've been screaming for, *if* you did your part around here."

Moira never lifted her eyes off her book. "I put a roast in the oven. I even peeled carrots and potatoes. I hate peeling things. And I've been keeping an eye on Toothless and Mattie, while you were off playing doctor at Med Center. I've done my part. *More* than my part, if you ask me."

"Were the girls here when you got home?"

"Yeah. I think so."

Abby sighed. "You think so? You let them go out in this weather?"

"It's just raining. They won't melt."

Abby got to her feet. "I'd better start calling around. If Mom gets home and they're not here, she's going to be mad at someone, and I don't want it to be me."

No comment from the guilty party.

Abby called every one of Geneva's friends, and then every one of Carmel's. No one had seen them since they got off the school bus at four that afternoon. "They aren't *out* in this weather, are they, Abby?" one of the mothers asked, causing Abby's heart to flutter anxiously. "There are all kinds of warnings on television. They're saying flooding is inevitable. You'd better find those girls."

As she replaced the receiver again, Abby's hand shook. Flooding? Inevitable? Not that their neighborhood was in danger. West Grant never flooded. And the girls wouldn't go out of the area without permission . . . would they?

Geneva would. And she could have talked Carmel into going, too. Carmel loved going places with her older sister. Their dad called Carmel "Geneva's shadow."

Abby returned to the living room and stood in the doorway. "Moira!" she called sharply. Red curly hair turned in her direction. "Are you sure they didn't say where they were going? Mrs. Conte says it's going to flood. They wouldn't have gone down to watch the river rise, would they?"

"Well, if they did, they're dumber than I thought." Moira thought for a minute, then said emphatically, "Geneva would, though. She thinks natural disasters like floods and fires and hurricanes are exciting. And she was only four the last time. She doesn't remember that people died and houses and businesses were totally wrecked." Her eyes widened. "If they wanted to see the river rise, they'd head for the South Side," she added slowly, sitting up straighter on the sofa. Her book slid down into her lap. She didn't notice.

When Abby said nothing, Moira asked in a shaky voice, "Even Geneva wouldn't go all the way down to the riverbank, would she?"

Abby looked straight at her. "You know she would."

"We should call Mom." Moira's voice was subdued, heavy with guilt.

"No, we're not calling Mom. Not yet. She'll freak. I'm going to look for them. You stay here with Toothless and Mattie."

"You shouldn't go out there alone, Abby. It's dark out, and it's pouring. Call one of your boyfriends. Make them go with you."

"There's no time. Keep an eye on the roast, okay? When I do get back with Geneva and Carmel, I'll be hungry. I won't want to eat charred meat, you got that?"

"I've got it." Moira watched as Abby put her rain cape on again. "Aren't you taking an umbrella?"

"In this wind? Waste of time."

"Abby?"

"What?"

"What'll I tell Mom if she gets home before you get back?"

"That's your problem. You'll think of something. You'd better."

"Abby?"

"What?"

"Be careful, okay?"

"Right." Abby hesitated in the doorway. She had hoped to return to Med Center immediately after her mother got home. She was worried about Sid. She didn't like the way he was acting. The spirits of most of the patients at Rehab lifted after they'd been there awhile, learning to do more and more things they'd thought they could no longer do. But not Sid. He seemed to be sinking deeper into depression.

But this was family stuff, and that came first. Glancing over her shoulder, Abby warned Moira, "You're in charge here. Don't forget that, okay?" Then she yanked the door open and plunged out into the downpour.

The phones were ringing constantly in ER. Susannah had taken over the chore of answering them when ambulances began arriving so close together that every staff member was needed to keep up with the flow. She was thankful that they'd only had one critical case since the burn victim. An elderly man from Eastridge had become so agitated upon having to evacuate his house, he'd suffered a heart attack. They'd brought him into ER in full arrest, but Dr. Jonah Izbecki and the staff had started his heart again. His wife and two middle-aged sons were still in the waiting room, sipping coffee, not talking.

While the major emergencies were the most intense, involving a lot of anxious activity, it was actually the minor injuries that took up the most time. Treating "criticals" was hectic and harried, but it went quickly. Those patients were speedily given the emergency care needed to save their lives, and then dispatched to the specialty area they required, either at Memorial or at one of the other hospitals in the complex. They never stayed in ER long.

The less seriously injured were not so quickly dispatched. And they had had a slew of those injuries in the past few hours, many from auto collisions. Because the vehicles had been traveling slowly due to the bad weather, the gurneys that came in one right after the other arrived with no great sense of urgency. Still, the treatments required created a backlog. Deep lacerations required careful suturing. Strains and sprains meant X rays, which took time, then ice packs or heat, depending upon the injury, and wrapping in Ace bandages. Possible concussions meant more X rays and an examination by a neurologist who, on a night like this, might not be readily available.

By eight o'clock, all of the treatment rooms were occupied with patients needing one or more non-life-threatening but time-consuming medical measures, and the waiting room and hallway were crowded with their relatives, waiting to see how the patients were doing, waiting to give them a ride home. The coffeepot in the lounge had been emptied and refilled half a dozen times since late afternoon, faces on staff members were lined with fatigue, and rubber-soled shoes dragged along the white tile as doctors and nurses moved dutifully from one cubicle to another.

Susannah had been doing phone duty for several hours when she answered a call, anticipating a question about a missing relative, and heard instead a very young, quavering voice telling her, "I cut myself. There's an awful lot of blood. I don't know how to stop it."

Susannah jerked upright in her chair, her eyes widening. She hadn't been trained in telephone emergency. Most people called 911. Those operators *were* trained. "You cut yourself? Where is the cut?"

"On my arm. I was letting my dog in the house and he was so glad to come in out of the rain, he jumped up and knocked me into the sliding-glass door, and it broke. Into lots of pieces. One of them stabbed me in the arm. I got it out, but now I can't stop the bleeding."

The glass shouldn't have been removed from the wound. It might have acted as a plug, minimizing blood loss. But a young child wouldn't know that. "Where on your arm is the cut?" Susannah asked.

"Here! Where my watch was. It's broke now, though."

On his wrist? Had he cut an artery?

"There's glass everywhere, all over the place. My dad's going to be really mad. But I had to let Jericho in. My mom says he's not allowed in the house, but the backyard looks like a swimming pool, and I was scared Jericho would drown." The young voice began to tremble. "Why am I bleeding so much? It's getting all over the floor."

The voice sounded male, but it also sounded so young, it was hard to be sure. "What's your name? And how old are you?"

"My name is Gus. And I'm seven. But I'll be eight in October. October eleventh. That's my birthday." The voice was no longer as strong as it had been when Susannah first heard it. It sounded farther away. "We're going to Chuck E. Cheese for my birthday, my friends and me. Eight friends. Because I'll be eight, see?"

Glancing around frantically to try to catch the attention of someone more qualified to deal with the emergency, Susannah saw no one. They were all in treatment rooms, stitching and wrapping and X-raying. "Is anybody with you? Where are your parents?"

"They went to get my brother at karate practice. Nicholas. He's ten. He gets to wear this neat white robe for karate. I didn't want to go, 'cause it's yucky out, so my mom said I could stay home if I just played Nintendo and didn't let anybody into the house. She said they'd be right back."

Susannah had no idea what to do. However serious the wound was, someone should be applying pressure to stop the bleeding. Would he be able to do that if she gave him instructions? Out of the corner of her eye, she spotted a blur of white, and whirled in her chair to see an orderly coming from a treatment room. Waving frantically, she flagged him down. Keeping the telephone pressed against her ear and covering the mouthpiece with one hand, she hissed, "Get an ambulance! Child fell through a glass door. Bleeding. Home alone. Wait'll I get the address. Don't move!" To the boy, she said quickly, "Gus, do you know your street address? I want to send someone to help you." With her free hand, she grabbed a pencil and a piece of paper.

"Thirty-one sixty-two Dean Street," he said. "Our house is red, like a barn." His voice was very weak. Susannah thrust the piece of paper with the address scribbled on it at the orderly. He took it and ran.

"It's raining into the house," the little boy said. " 'Cause the door is broken. My mom's going to be mad. And Jericho got mud all over the floor. My mom just mopped it after dinner, and now there's mud and rain and lots of blood on it. I don't feel very good. The walls look like they're spinning." His tone became frightened, plaintive. "Can you come and get me, please?"

Where were his parents? How could they go off and leave a little seven-year-old boy home alone? "Gus," Susannah said firmly, "I want you to do something for me. Are you in the kitchen?"

"Um-hum."

"Is there a towel anywhere around? A clean towel?"

"In the drawer. Over there." He was probably pointing. She hoped he wasn't doing so with the arm that was bleeding.

"I want you to get one of those clean towels and wrap it around your cut, okay? Nice and tight. And then I want you to push down, hard, on the towel with your good hand and keep it there until the ambulance arrives. Can you do that?"

"Am'blance?" That really scared him. "Can't you come and get me?"

"No, honey, I can't. The ambulance people are very nice. They want to help you. Will you go get the towel? Do it now, okay? But stay on the phone, don't hang up!" she added quickly.

"Okay." Susannah heard padding sounds, then the whisper of a drawer sliding open. How far from Med Center was Dean Street? She had no idea.

"I can't put the towel on," he said, sounding very tired, " 'less I put down the telephone."

Good point. "Okay, put the phone down, Gus. But keep it near you so you can hear my voice, okay?"

"I don't feel good. I got to sit down."

Susannah was shaking. He sounded disoriented. Going into shock? That could kill him. And if the glass had indeed sliced into an artery, he could bleed to death if help didn't arrive soon.

She was clutching the telephone so hard, her fingers ached. Her voice rose sharply. "Gus! Gus, you can sit down. Go ahead, put the phone on the floor and sit down. Just don't hang up, okay? Are you sitting?"

"Um-hum." His voice sounded even farther away.

She thought she heard footsteps behind her, but there was no time to stop to see if help had arrived. "Okay, do the towel thing now, okay? The ambulance will be there in a minute." She hoped, prayed that was true. "But first you need to wrap that towel around your wrist and press down really hard, okay?" Had a chunk of glass sliced into an artery? Was that why there was so much blood? "And keep your ear as close to the telephone as you can, okay?" When she glanced over her shoulder, she saw that a group had gathered around her. Dr. Izbecki, three nurses, and the orderly who had summoned the ambulance.

Susannah immediately handed the telephone to the physician. He shook his head no and said,

347

"You're doing fine. Don't stop now. The ambulance is almost there."

She couldn't believe he wasn't taking over. He was a *doctor*. Wouldn't he know better than she what to say to a terrified child? Why was he making her do this?

"He's used to *your* voice," a nurse named Deborah told Susannah. "We're right here if you need us, but keep talking to him."

Reluctant, but deciding Deborah was probably right, Susannah said into the receiver, "Gus? You still there?"

He didn't answer.

Susannah felt increased anxiety emanating from the group gathered around her chair. "Gus?" she asked again. "Gus, where are you?"

"I'm here," he said in almost a whisper. "And I'm holding on to the towel, like you said. But it hurts. My arm hurts."

At the sound of his voice, an audible sigh of relief swept through the group. "That's a good sign," Dr. Izbecki said quietly. "That it hurts. If the wound was really bad, he probably wouldn't be feeling anything. Keep talking. Let him know you're still with him."

Susannah began talking again. Later, she wouldn't remember what she had said to the child other than reminding him to keep holding the towel tightly against the wound. She didn't hear the wail of the ambulance arriving at the

Dean Street house. But when the little boy spoke again, it was to say, "Somebody's here. I heard a siren, and now they're knocking on the door."

"Is the door locked, Gus?"

"I just remembered I was supposed to lock it, only I forgot. My mom's going to be mad."

Maybe not, Susannah thought, tears of relief gathering in her eyes. Maybe Gus's mother would just be grateful that her son was still alive. "Can you go let the paramedics in, or are you too sick? They'll come in if the door's open."

"I can't get up. My head is dizzy."

A moment later, Susannah heard the wonderful sound of voices, and a second later, Will said into the phone, "Hey, it's okay, we're here. You can hang up."

"No, wait! Is he . . . is he all right? Is he still conscious?"

"He'll be fine. Looks like . . . looks like a bad laceration. No arterial involvement. He was lucky. The place is a mess. It's a miracle he wasn't sliced to ribbons." Will paused, then added, "Talked to Dr. Izbecki a few minutes ago on the radio. He told us what you were doing. Now you know how a 911 operator feels."

"Something I *never* want to be," Susannah said. Her entire body, from her toes to her scalp, felt soupy with relief. She was totally drained. "Are you bringing him right in?"

"Yep. See you then!"

Susannah hung up the phone to an enthusiastic round of applause. With a weak smile, she stood up on liquid knees and left the desk, motioning to one of the nurses to take her place. She headed straight for the lounge, where she sank down on a couch and put her head in her hands until her head cleared.

She was still sitting there, leaning back against the rough tweed, when Will came in, his hair and jacket soaked. He walked over, sat down beside her, and put an arm around her shoulders. In spite of how cold and wet he was, she could feel the warmth of his hand through her smock. It felt reassuring, and it steadied her.

"You done good, kid," he said lightly. "Everyone's talking about you."

"And Gus? He's okay?"

"He's fine. Didn't hit an artery. His parents arrived just as we were loading him up."

"He was afraid his mother would be mad at him."

Will smiled and shook his head. "Trust me, she wasn't mad. Not at him, anyway. Mad at herself, I guess, for leaving him home alone. She thought they'd only be gone a few minutes, but they hit high water and had to take a detour. Anyway," he added, hugging her, "the kid wants to see you. He's all stitched up and a little groggy from the shot they gave him, but he keeps saying, 'I want to talk to the phone girl.'" He laughed. "People will be calling you that for a while, you do realize that?"

"I don't care." Though she was reluctant to leave the safety of Will's arm, Susannah wanted to see Gus before he fell asleep from the medication. "That's better than calling me the daughter of the richest man in town, right?"

"Right." Will stood up, too. There was admiration in his dark eyes as he regarded her seriously. "You're made of pretty strong stuff, you know that?"

She winced at the surprise in his voice. But she focused on the fact that he seemed very sincere. He meant what he was saying. "Thanks. That means a lot, coming from you."

"Yeah? More than it would coming from, say, Callie Matthews?" He was joking. Callie was the daughter of Caleb Matthews, Med Center's administrator. She spent a lot of time at the hospital, hoping to see her father, and both Will and Susannah found her demanding, superior manner annoying.

Susannah laughed. "Oh, please. Callie wouldn't know strong stuff if it walked up and bit her. She cries if she breaks a fingernail."

As they left the lounge, Will warned, "You do know this is going to be the longest night of our lives, right? I mean, you're prepared for that? Just be grateful that we're in here, safe and dry, instead of out there."

"Right." Susannah's stomach knotted as she remembered where Sam was. "I just hope my brother is okay."

"If anyone can take care of himself, it's your brother, Sam." Then someone called Will's name, and saying he'd see her later, he loped off down the hall.

Sam *can* take care of himself, Susannah echoed silently.

Even in a flood? a voice in her head questioned skeptically. He isn't SuperSam, is he, this brother of yours? Seems to me it's not very bright to challenge nature when it's on a rampage. Nature almost always wins.

Silencing the voice in her head, Susannah swallowed hard and went in search of the little boy whose life she had saved.

chapter

6

Not everyone who had eagerly accepted Sam Grant's invitation to his "flood party" showed up. When those who had were gathered in the enormous main room of the two-story log house settled on a slope overlooking the roaring river, several people complained that friends of theirs hadn't been allowed to attend because of the storm.

"Nick's mother actually said that you were crazy, Sam," a pretty girl in a denim jumpsuit said. "She said Nick would go out of the house tonight over her dead body." Laughing, the girl tossed her long, silky dark hair. "Nick was standing right behind her in the doorway when she said that, and I could see that he was seriously considering taking a contract out on her."

Everyone laughed. A short, stocky boy in cutoffs and a gray sweatshirt said, "My dad told me, 'Go ahead if you're stupid enough, but don't call me when you get stranded. I'm not going out on a night like this to rescue someone who's too dumb to come in out of the rain.'" The boy's voice rose indignantly. "Rescue me? Like I can't take care of myself!"

The dark-haired girl glanced around her at the exposed beams overhead, the huge fieldstone fireplace, the black leather furniture. "I thought you said this was a fishing cabin, Sam. You'd better look up the word *cabin* in the dictionary. This ain't it. This place is a *lodge*. You could entertain our entire class in this one room."

Sam shrugged. "We fish from the riverbank and when the water's high, we fish from the verandas. That makes it a fishing cabin, right?"

The girl, whose name was Becka, moved to an expensive stereo system against one wall and inserted a CD. "Personally," she said, turning back to Sam as a slow song began, "if we're going to be stranded in a flood, we couldn't ask for a nicer place. It's gorgeous, it's warm and cozy, there's plenty of food, and stuff to drink, and the music isn't half-bad, either. Dance with me, Sam."

As he took her in his arms and they began to move across the hardwood floor, she added, "And we're perfectly safe up here, right?"

"Right," Sam answered heartily.

But as they danced, he glanced over her shoulder toward a wall of windows and French doors overlooking the river. The floodlights, on tall poles marching down the grassy slope, were on. He had noticed as they arrived and he switched them on that the river was already up to the first of three terraces below the house. He hadn't seen it that high since the bad flood six years ago, and then he'd only seen it on television.

And the water was still rising.

Only then did Sam remember that when the city of Grant had finally dried out that time, his mother had redecorated the entire first floor of the fishing lodge. Had she done that because she'd felt like decorating something, as she often did? Or had she been forced to by flood damage? Could the river possibly have come all the way up the slope and on inside the house?

He should have asked. He should have asked one of his parents if the lodge had ever been flooded, before he invited people here tonight. Why hadn't he thought to do that?

Because then he'd have had to tell them about the party, and they'd have clamped down hard on that idea.

Sam paused as they reached a telephone resting on a small table. He reached out, picked it up, and was about to dial Linden Hall when he realized there was no dial tone.

The phone was dead.

The fender bender accidents began to diminish as many people retreated to their homes to seek refuge from the storm. But the flow of patients into ER remained steady. Stubborn residents of Grant who had ignored the warnings on television and radio and insisted on going out into the night were swept off flooded roads in their vehicles. Some got out. Some of those swam to safety, while others, after being battered by the rushing waters, had to be rescued by crews scouting the city for such emergencies. It was those patients who were brought in with blackening eyes, broken or fractured limbs, perhaps a concussion from an encounter with one of the larger boulders in the river or a floating tree limb.

Those who hadn't made it out of their cars were less battered, with fewer minor injuries. But some of them had come so close to drowning that they had to be transferred through the enclosed passageway to the Elizabeth Grant Ross Cardiopulmonary Hospital. And some were rescued too late.

One of those victims was a young boy who worked as a page at the public library. Susannah recognized him immediately, even though his struggle in a car caught up in torrential floodwaters had drained him of any sign of life.

His name was Curtis Brock, a quiet, unathletic boy who had just turned sixteen. Susannah knew this because he had been so ecstatic the day just weeks earlier when he had received his driver's license in the mail. She had stopped at a local bakery to pick up a German chocolate cake Abby's mother had ordered, and Curtis had been inside, buying doughnuts. He'd been waving the license around, beaming with pride. "Now my mom doesn't have to drive me anymore!" Curtis had cried with glee.

Everyone in the store, including Susannah, had smiled at his unrestrained joy over turning sixteen and owning a driver's license.

Now, he lay on the gurney pale and drained.

That driver's license killed him, she thought angrily. If he hadn't had it, he wouldn't have been out there tonight, and he would still be alive.

The rational part of her mind told her it was the flood that had killed him, not the license.

He hadn't drowned, news that shocked everyone in the trauma room. What had killed him, according to the attending physician, a tall, attractive woman named Dr. Lincoln, was terror. Curtis Brock, she told them, had had a heart problem since birth. Nothing life threatening, and as long as Curtis led a fairly stress-free lifestyle, surgery hadn't been required. But, locked inside the vehicle bobbing and tossing in raging floodwaters, he had become so frightened, so totally panic-stricken, that the strain on his heart had been too much. "It wasn't the water that killed him," she announced, "it was terror, pure and simple."

"I think you're right," one of the nurses agreed. She picked up a hand, surveyed it, placed it back on the white sheet. "Look at his fingernails. Ripped to shreds. The knuckles are bloody. Looks like he put up quite a fight before panic got the best of him. Must have clawed at the windows, trying to get out." She was an older woman in her late fifties, with lines of fatigue etching her face. She shook her head. "New car, one of the rescue workers told me. Electronic windows. Not a way in hell this kid could have opened those windows once that car hit the water. But they said there was a pocket of air at the top, near the ceiling, that would have kept him alive until they got him out. If his heart hadn't stopped."

Susannah stayed in the room after the gurney had been taken away. She helped put away the crash cart, wishing the paddles had been needed, that with the application of electrical stimuli Curtis Brock would have returned to life, as two earlier near-drowning patients had done. But, though he had been rushed straight to Med Center the moment he was pulled out of that river, his heart had already been stopped for too long. Even if they had been able to revive him, it was almost certain that there would have been significant brain damage. He wouldn't have returned to life as the same Curtis Brock that she'd seen in the supermarket. That Curtis was already gone.

It seemed bitterly ironic to Susannah, as she tore off the disposable sheet on the table and replaced it with a fresh one, that Curtis had died of terror at being trapped inside a car, when the last time she had seen him, he'd been so excited about driving one.

When she had done everything she could do to bring order back to the trauma room, she left it, closing the door quietly behind her.

Callie Matthews hadn't intended to go out in such terrible weather. Her hair, which she'd had done that very afternoon because who knew it was going to rain so hard you'd need a canoe just to get downtown, would frizz if she went out. Might as well just stick her finger in an electrical outlet and be done with it.

But her mother, who suffered from chronic kidney disease, needed a prescription, and she needed it tonight. Besides, the truth was, Callie *wanted* to get out of the huge, quiet house on Linden Hill Boulevard. She was lost without her best friend, Tina Montgomery, who had died at Med Center when a deadly virus swept Grant. She hadn't yet found anyone to take Tina's place. No one would ever understand her as well as

Tina had. They'd been two of a kind. "Privileged, pampered, and pretty," Tina had joked, "that's us. What could be better? There *is no* other way to live."

Brushing her hair, Callie winced. It hurt to think about Tina. So mostly, she didn't. But sometimes, it was hard not to. Like on a foul, rainy night when she didn't have anything to do. She'd been invited to Sam Grant's flood party, but her mother had said absolutely not. "You are not going anywhere *near* the South Side in this weather, and that's final!"

Okay, so she'd just run to the drugstore before any flooding took over the city. If it ever did. Probably wouldn't flood at all. People got all excited about things like that because they were bored.

Maybe she'd buy a new fashion magazine to read. And new nail polish. At the hospital the other day, when Susannah had made that stupid remark about how she'd rather drive her gardener's Jeep than that beautiful little silver Benz her father had bought her, Callie, aghast, had cried, "That is too weird, Susannah! You want to ride in a car the hired help uses?" And Kate Thompson, who admittedly always looked as if she'd stepped straight off the cover of a fashion magazine herself, had said coolly, "Callie, someone who wears nail polish in that disgusting shade of putrid purple for the whole world to see has no business calling someone else weird."

Callie's hands had flown behind her back so fast, her fingers had almost fallen off.

If gorgeous Kate Thompson thought Callie's nail polish was weird, maybe it was.

Normally, Callie wouldn't even think of letting someone from Eastridge dictate what she should wear. But Kate always looked so perfect. How did she do that when she wasn't even rich? And that soft, pale pink she'd been wearing on *her* nails was nice.

Maybe I'll look for something like that at the drugstore, Callie thought as she donned a designer hooded raincoat in a vibrant shade of purple. Then, remembering Kate's comment about the purple nail polish, she discarded that coat and slipped instead into a bright red one with a matching wide-brimmed hat that tied under her chin, and a pair of red high-heeled boots to make her feel taller than her five feet.

The outfit was pretty, but impractical. She was already drenched by the time she had run from the house to her robin's-egg blue sports car, which, as usual, she had left out in the driveway to show it off instead of parking it in the garage. She turned on the engine and the wipers. What an awful night! There was sure to be flooding, after all. Especially in Eastridge and on the South

Side, and Sam Grant was absolutely insane to hold a party down there now. Anyone who'd gone was crazy, too.

So why did she wish, as she drove down a dangerously slick Linden Hill Boulevard, that she was there, on that riverbank, in Sam's fishing lodge, instead of taking a nice, safe trip to the drugstore?

At Med Center, motorists stranded in high water, rescued by Emergency crews or fire or police personnel, continued to arrive in a steady stream.

"You're still here?" Will asked a beleaguered Susannah, who was trying to balance a telephone on one shoulder while her other arm struggled to maintain a shaky hold on a handful of patient charts. She was trying valiantly to keep track of each patient upon arrival, jotting down a name given to her by one of the rescue crew, if they had it. Sometimes they didn't. People who had been dragged from the wildly rushing river had, for the most part, been stripped of their identity temporarily. No wallet, no purse, no ID anywhere on their person. If they were conscious and not in deep shock, they were able to give a name, and Susannah quickly jotted it down on a chart. The unconscious ones remained unidentified, unless someone on the crew knew them personally and could identify them.

In response to Will's query, Susannah rolled her eyes heavenward. She glanced pointedly toward the crowded waiting room, filled with patients awaiting treatment, and relatives awaiting word of patients currently being treated. "Yes, I am still here," she said. "And I've decided I'm not leaving. Unless it stops raining. Then maybe I'll think about it."

It did not stop raining.

chapter
7

$$\sim\!\!\!\wedge\!\!\!\wedge\!\!\!\wedge\!\!\!\wedge\!\!\!\wedge\!\!\!\wedge\!\!\!\sim$$

Jeremy Barlow, on his way to Med Center to meet his father for dinner, was glad his father had given him a Chevy Blazer instead of the low-slung black sports car he'd really wanted. The Blazer sat higher off the ground. Jeremy had had no idea the weather was this bad. He hadn't been watching television, and anytime a news program broke in on his radio, he had quickly switched the station or turned it off and put a CD on his stereo. News was depressing.

It was becoming very clear to him that this was one night when he shouldn't have switched the radio station so quickly. The announcer had probably told everyone to stay home. Not a bad idea.

Steering the Blazer away from a deep pool that glistened under the pale yellow streetlights, Jeremy thought about turning around on the deserted road and going back home.

But he and his father had so little time together. Eminent heart surgeons like Thomas Barlow didn't have a lot of evenings free. If he wasn't operating on a life-or-death case, he was attending a committee meeting or a Board meeting or a fund-raiser for Med Center, or traveling out of town to give speeches. Jeremy had learned to make plans with his father weeks in advance. Sometimes that worked. Sometimes it didn't. On this particular night, there hadn't been any phone calls from the hospital canceling the plans they'd made three weeks ago. So why spoil it by worrying about the weather?

He kept going. There was very little traffic on this stormy, windy night. But negotiating the low-lying areas rushing with water took some doing. Jeremy tried to concentrate, but instead he found himself thinking about his mother leaving the way she had. If she hadn't gone away, maybe his father would be home more often.

Ha! Who was he kidding? Had his father been home any more often before his wife packed up a couple of suitcases and her laptop computer and left the house for San Francisco to become a writer? Nosiree, he had *not!* Wasn't that part of the reason his mother had left in the first place?

He hadn't gone with her, although she'd asked, because he hadn't wanted to leave Grant. Besides, his mother was probably going to be poor, and Jeremy knew he wouldn't be good at that.

Because he wasn't concentrating, he neglected

to steer around the next pocket of deep water. When he hit it, thick sheets of water sprayed upward, coating the windshield and splashing against the windows. Jeremy sucked in his breath as for one scary second, the Blazer hydroplaned, its wheels completely off the ground. The sensation was eerie. It was as if he were taking off in an airplane.

But an airplane was *supposed* to take off. A car wasn't.

When the wheels once again hit solid ground, Jeremy exhaled with relief. He focused his mind after that on driving, and made it to the hospital without any more scares.

There was no answer when he knocked on the door of his father's office on the eighth floor of Grant Memorial. Still in surgery? Sighing, Jeremy took a seat on a padded leather bench and waited. And waited. And waited.

He was about to give up when his father, still wearing his surgical greens, his mask hanging around his neck, came striding down the hallway. A tall, impressive figure, he smiled a welcome when he spotted his son.

I wish I were that tall, Jeremy thought as he stood up. He looked like his mother, average height, blonde hair, decent bone structure, nice eyes, but no distinguishing features. If he were taller, like his father, that would have helped make him more interesting-looking. But he wasn't taller. Five ten, tops. His father was six two.

"Sorry, kid," his father said regretfully as he joined Jeremy, "but I've got to get back down there. We've got a real mess on our hands. I told this guy a hundred times to quit smoking and buy a treadmill, but he ignored my advice. Got stranded in high water. Panicked, and had a heart attack. Now he's in serious trouble. Triple bypass, and we've run into some bleeding problems. Dinner's going to have to wait for another night."

Jeremy wasn't surprised. He was used to it. At least his father hadn't forgotten, though that wouldn't have been a surprise, either. "No big deal," he said lightly, hiding his disappointment. "Pretty nasty out there, anyway. I'll probably just go home and watch television. It's okay, Dad."

But it wasn't.

He wasn't going home to watch the stupid boob tube. He'd go down to ER and see if Kate was on duty. Seeing Kate, even if he didn't talk to her, always brightened his mood, no matter how gloomy he was feeling. When he was feeling sorry for himself, no one snapped him out of it faster than Kate, with her caustic sense of humor.

His second disappointment of the evening came when he arrived down in ER and there was no sign of Kate. Will and Susannah told him she'd gone to the library.

"In this?" he asked, waving a hand toward the windows, sheeted with rain. "She didn't walk, did she?"

"Sam took her," Susannah said. "Dropped her off on the way to his flood party. I thought you'd be there."

"Flood party? Your brother is actually celebrating this lousy weather?"

"Yep. At our fishing lodge on the South Side of town."

"You're kidding!"

"No. I wish I were. I just thought you'd be there. You always go to Sam's parties."

"I was supposed to have dinner with my dad. He couldn't make it. I didn't know anything about any party, but I wouldn't have gone, anyway. Not down there, not tonight. Your brother's braver than I am."

"You mean crazier," Susannah said darkly. "And I'll bet he got a whole bunch of people to join him, too. If anything happens . . ."

"Nothing's going to happen," Will interjected, smiling at her. He didn't like seeing her so anxious. It was hard enough that they'd had such a hectic night in ER. She should have gone home hours ago. She looked tired. But she had refused to leave, saying there was too much to do and the staff needed all the help they could get. He had stayed, too, but that was a decision he'd made when the first high-water victims began arriving. It had nothing to do with Susannah. Almost nothing. "Your brother can take care of himself. And anyone who's with him."

"Maybe." She didn't sound convinced, but her face had brightened a little.

"If Sam dropped Kate off, she'll need a ride home, right?" Jeremy asked. His bare head was very wet. His hair, usually neatly parted and combed smooth, had begun waving around his ears and forehead.

Susannah thought it made him look more relaxed. Jeremy was very good-looking, but his face always looked so tense. Will called Jeremy "uptight." Will was right. "She might," Susannah said. "But the library probably closed early. She could already be on her way home."

"Well, it won't hurt to go see," Jeremy said. "If she's not there, fine. But if she is, maybe she'll be glad to have a ride. I'll give it a shot."

When he had gone, Will turned to Susannah, grinning. "Young love?"

"Not in a million years!" Susannah laughed. And even though she knew he wasn't referring to himself and Susannah, because all they'd ever shared was a dance or two and hours of work, Susannah felt her face growing warm.

She was relieved when one of the doctors called to her then, announcing that incoming was arriving and she'd be needed to chart vital statistics. Grateful for the interruption, she hurried away from Will.

Dr. Jonah Izbecki was on call. He was a man Susannah liked and respected. He'd been wary of her at first, just like all the others, but after a while, he'd thawed. Now, he was one of the doctors who tended to give her more responsibility. This time, the moment she hurried into the treatment room, he directed her to one of the supply cabinets, asking for a second bottle of sterile saline solution to irrigate a nasty wound he was suturing. "Floodwaters swept this guy's car into the plate glass window of a store," he was informing the nurse who stood beside him. As if to fortify his argument, Izbecki held a large chunk of glass up to the surgical lamp. "Quit raining yet?" he asked Susannah.

She handed the nurse the bottle and waited for further instructions. "No. Doesn't look like it's going to, either."

Dr. Izbecki groaned audibly. He poised the long surgical tweezers over the chest of the patient. "That means this endless parade of unfortunates is going to continue. I need six more hands. Half the night shift hasn't arrived. Can't get here, or so they say. Why didn't I go into law the way my parents wanted? My eyes are killing me. Some of these glass shards are tiny. Pull that lamp closer."

Susannah reached out to obey. She was so tired, her body yearned for a nap, even a short one. But Izbecki was right. Until the rain stopped, the flow of patients would continue. Eventually, everyone would get the message, and the fender benders would end. People would stop risking death by drowning, and take to the indoors. Most of them, anyway.

But sooner or later, the evacuations would begin. That could mean people falling from ladders and roofs and out of boats as they tried to escape floodwaters. There might be fires as gas lines were split in two by the force of rushing water. People trying to leave their area on foot or in vehicles could be swept up in the flood before rescue crews arrived.

It's going to be a really long night, Susannah thought as she went back to the cabinet for gauze pads and adhesive tape.

Jeremy, on his way to the library, wondered if he was making a mistake. Should he really offer to drive Kate home? She lived in Eastridge. Wouldn't that be flooded by now? It always flooded first, even before the South Side. Did he really want to risk driving into that, even for Kate?

Maybe . . . maybe he wouldn't take her home. He could take her to his house. The west side of town never flooded. She'd be safe there. The housekeeper, Mrs. Lamme, was staying the night. He'd tell Kate that, so she'd know right away that he was just talking friendship, not romance. He wanted her to have a safe, dry place to stay, that was all.

That's not *quite* all, a nasty little voice in the back of his head told him. Be honest, Jeremy. Aren't you picturing the look on your father's face if he came down to breakfast tomorrow morning to find a pretty, African-American girl in his kitchen? *That* would certainly get his attention, wouldn't it, Jeremy? Isn't that what you're thinking about?

"No," he said aloud. "I'm thinking about Kate." Then he added reluctantly, "Mostly." And he continued steering the Blazer through the dark, wet streets toward the library.

Will came out of treatment room five, looking for Susannah. Her face had looked strained and tired the last time he'd seen her. Maybe he could talk her into going home. She could come back in the morning. She'd be needed then, too. If she stayed at the hospital all night, she'd be no good tomorrow.

"You have to go home," he said firmly when she came out into the corridor behind the gurney that was being wheeled up to X Ray by an orderly. "Things are going to be just as busy tomorrow. School will be canceled, so you can work all day if you want. But you need some sleep first."

She glared up at him. "Look who's talking. You've been here longer than I have. Are *you* going home?"

"Yeah, sure," he lied. "Not right now, though. Got a few things I have to do first. And listen, don't take that Benz of yours, okay? Leave it in the parking garage and grab a shuttle. Safer that way."

Glancing up at the big round clock over the nurses' desk, Susannah said, "They're not running. It's too late. But," she added with phony innocence, "since you're leaving any second now, I'll just wait for you and you can drive me home." She knew he had no intention of leaving. She just wanted to see if he'd admit it.

"Oh. Sure. I mean . . . uh, yeah, I can take you home. Why don't we go right now? I guess that other stuff can wait."

Susannah laughed. "Who are you kidding? You'll take me home and then you'll turn right around and come back here. Forget it, Will. I'm staying if you are, and that's that. Live with it."

He fixed his dark eyes on hers. "Man, you're stubborn!"

Susannah was so tired, she had to fight the impulse to lean against him, nestle her head against his shoulder, and close her eyes. She wondered what he would do if she did that, right out here in the hallway with a waiting room full of Grant residents watching. Maybe he'd faint. She'd have to haul him up onto a gurney and wheel him into a treatment room.

The image struck her funny, and she began laughing. Before it could turn into hysterics, she stopped, took a deep breath, and let it out. Then she grinned up at him and said jokingly, "I *beg* your pardon. *I*, sir, am Susannah Grant, a spoiled rich girl from the *very* best part of town. I live in a mansion fully equipped with servants. I do not take orders from mere paramedics. I shall return to the mansion when *I* decide it is time, and not one tiny little moment before."

He laughed and raised his hands in a gesture of defeat. "Okay, okay, I get it! I was just trying to be a little considerate, that's all."

Susannah's grin widened. If she hadn't been so tired, she would have let the remark go without commenting. But her brain was on overdrive and she wasn't herself. "Gee," she said lightly, "I didn't know you cared!"

And although an ambulance wail at the back door drowned out his reply, she could have sworn that what he said then was, "Well, I do."

Before she could mull that over, he was off and running again and one of the nurses was calling to her to bring a bunch of clean towels to trauma room two.

Thinking about what Will's comment meant would have to wait. Like everything else on this wild, stormy night.

Still, Susannah's step was considerably lighter as she hurried to the linen closet.

chapter
8

Abby hesitated at the corner of Fourth Street and Liberty. It was raining so hard, staring ahead of her was like looking through a pair of dirty eyeglasses. But she could see that the side street she was on was deserted. The post office, the parking garages, the little boutiques, all were closed. There was no traffic, and deep, rushing streams ran alongside both curbs. She was still four blocks away from Massachusetts Avenue, the main drag that paralleled the Revere. If the water was this deep here, what would it be like there, where the river had almost certainly overflowed its banks?

And *where* were her sisters?

Head down, Abby forged ahead, battling ferocious gusts of wind until she reached the avenue. The lights were on at the drugstore to her left. She could try there. Maybe someone inside had seen Geneva and Carmel.

The upper half of the wide avenue, where she was standing, hadn't flooded yet. The banks up here were steeper. But farther down the street where the banks were lower, just beyond the arching stone bridge that crossed the river, she could see that the avenue had become a lake. The shops there were closed, but their interior lights, left on for safety's sake, shone out upon a swirling, muddy mess inching ever closer to their doors.

Abby's heart lurched with fear. She had to find her sisters. She whirled and ran up the street to the drugstore. "Please," she murmured as she ran, "please let it be open."

It was. Abby flung herself against the door and pushed, spilling out into a store empty but for three people. The owners, an elderly couple, stood behind the prescription counter talking to a small, thin girl in a bright red raincoat, matching hat, and high-heeled red boots. She turned around when the door burst open.

Abby recognized the girl and groaned silently. Callie Matthews. If she was going to run into anyone, why did it have to be Callie? She'd be about as helpful as an umbrella full of holes.

Still, Callie knew Geneva and Carmel. Maybe she'd seen them tonight.

"You young people!" the woman called cheerfully as Abby approached the counter. "Out on a night like this. Both you girls ought to have your heads examined."

Abby shook rain from her cape and swiped at her face with a tissue. She asked the owners if they had seen her sisters, describing them.

"Hasn't been much of anybody in here tonight," the man said. "We planned to close early, but decided there ought to be at least one drugstore open on a night like this. We live upstairs, so there's no place we have to get to before the flooding hits. Guess we'll be safe enough up there."

Abby turned to Callie. "You haven't seen Geneva and Carmel, have you?"

"I just got here. But no, I haven't. Why? Your mother would never let them out in this weather, would she?"

"My mother's not home. She's working. Moira was supposed to be in charge. I've called all the girls' friends. No one has seen them. I'm scared they might have come down here to watch the river rise."

"Oh, mercy," the woman declared, "I hope not. Won't be any time at all till that river's jumped its banks."

"It already has." Abby gestured with one hand. "Below the bridge, just south of the intersection out there. I could see it from the corner. Looks like a lake. Hasn't crossed the intersection yet, though."

The man thought for a minute, then said, "You'd best find those sisters of yours. Callie, you go with her. You're a good swimmer. Lord knows, you've come in here enough times waving a newspaper picture of yourself with a swimming trophy. I'd come along, too, but I don't swim. Never did learn. Neither did Susan here." He asked Abby then if she wanted them to call Search and Rescue.

The suggestion horrified Abby. She wasn't going to need such extraordinary help, was she? Wasn't she just going to find her sisters watching the river from a safe distance? Wasn't she going to yell at them until her throat was sore, and then take them home? After that, she'd hurry back to Med Center to see how Sid was doing. That was the way the scenario had unfolded in her mind. This man was suggesting something very different. "No," she said sharply, beginning to back away from the counter. "No, thanks. Callie, are you coming?" Having Callie along was better than going back out there all alone.

Callie looked surprised. "Oh. Yeah, I guess so. It's not like I have anything better to do." She glanced down at the small white bag in her hands. "My mother doesn't need this stuff right this very second. Besides, I like Geneva."

"The only reason you like her," Abby said flatly as they left the store, "is, she's always doing things the rest of us don't dare do. Like climbing the water tower, and crossing the trestle on the railroad bridge, and talking back to her teachers.

She's been in more trouble than the other five of us combined. You're getting your kicks vicariously through my sister, Callie."

"I have to get them somewhere," Callie grumbled, reaching up with one hand to restrain the red hat that threatened to blow away in spite of the tie under her chin.

"You Susannah Grant?"

The voice startled Susannah. She was perched on a high stool near the nurses' station, busily scribbling patients' names on a small notepad in her lap. When she glanced up, she recognized the tall, thin boy in front of her, his face and hair wet, as Aaron Thompson, Kate's younger brother. She slid off the stool. "Yes, I am. And you're Kate's brother. I've seen pictures of you." She extended a hand. "Hi. Nice to meet you."

To her chagrin, he ignored her extended hand. "Where's my sister?" he asked abruptly, keeping his eyes focused on a point somewhere above her head.

Flushing, Susannah withdrew her hand. "She . . . she isn't here. She went to the library."

A gurney flew by. Susannah had a vague image of someone who looked as if she'd just been swimming. Sodden, long dark hair hung over the edge of the wheeled stretcher, dripping water onto the floor. Another narrow escape from floodwaters? The gurney disappeared into trauma room three.

"I have to go," she told Kate's brother. She waved a hand. "They might need me in there."

"My sister is supposed to be here," he said brusquely. "Where is she? I have to tell her we're not at the house. That she shouldn't go there. We've already left. They made us evacuate." His eyes flashed darkly, and Susannah sensed that he was angry about having to leave his house. He shrugged toward the door. "We're over there, at the Rehab building. Tell Kate to go there."

A group of nurses and doctors hurried by them. A nurse accidentally brushed against the arm of Aaron's wet jacket and, without turning around, automatically reached out to wipe her own arm dry. "Don't worry," he called softly after her, "the color doesn't rub off."

Oh, Susannah thought, he's like that, is he? Angry at more than just the evacuation. Kate wasn't like that. If she was, she hid it well. Which was a possibility, Susannah supposed. "I told you, Kate isn't here. She left. She had a paper to work on, so she went to the library. As far as I know, she's still there."

His eyes narrowed suspiciously. "How'd she get there? In this weather?"

"My brother took her. He was going . . . somewhere." Susannah felt foolish, being unwilling to admit to this boy she didn't even know that her brother had ventured into the South Side of the city in spite of imminent flooding. "So he gave Kate a lift."

"He's taking her home, too?"

"Oh. No, I . . . he was on his way somewhere. I guess she was going to take the shuttle home." Susannah remembered Jeremy then. "But . . . a friend of ours went looking for her. He'll probably give her a ride home. I wouldn't worry about her."

He looked at her then. "No, I don't guess you would. Why should you?"

Annoyed, Susannah drew herself up to her full height. "Because she's my friend," she said heatedly. "But I'm sure she's okay." She paused, then added, "I'm sorry you had to leave your home. I don't blame you for being upset. I would be, too."

He laughed. There was no humor in the sound. "Like that's something you'd ever have to worry about. I *know* where you live. Way up there on that hill, high and dry, so far above everybody else. What's that feel like, anyway?"

"High and dry," Susannah answered curtly. Without saying that it had been nice meeting him, because it hadn't, she turned on her heel and left.

At the library, Kate slammed a book shut and uncurled her legs from underneath her, stretching them out before lowering her feet to the floor.

They landed in water. Very cold, and very wet. She was wearing black flats. Water spilled over the edges of the shoes and into her knee-highs.

Her eyes flew to the floor. It was covered with half an inch of dark, muddy water.

"Oh, no!" Kate jumped from her chair, wincing as her feet squished. "How . . . ?"

She couldn't believe that water had entered the building and snaked its way down the hall and into her little cubicle without her noticing. But the only light in the room was a small desk lamp on her table. There was no light at all out in the hallway. She'd been engrossed in her research, and the water hadn't made any noise. It wasn't rushing, wasn't bumping into chair or table legs with a loud thumping noise. It had seeped into the building quietly, sneaking up on her.

Kate stood in the middle of the small cubicle, gazing around her with wide, astonished eyes, then looking down again at the pool in which she stood. "This," she said aloud, "is not good. This is not good *at all*."

At the fishing lodge on the South Side, the party was in full swing. The music was loud, the crowd in good spirits in spite of the howling of the wind outside. People were eating and drinking and talking and laughing and dancing, as if it were just an ordinary party on an ordinary night.

But because it wasn't an ordinary night, the party's host wasn't doing any of the things his guests were doing. Because it wasn't an ordinary night, he was standing at one of the wide picture windows overlooking the river, watching silently as the Revere climbed steadily to the second of the three terraces, as if it had every intention of joining the party.

There was only one more terrace to go. Above that was a short but steep slope planted with shrubbery held in place by railroad ties, and then the first-floor veranda. Those were the only obstacles between the rapidly advancing river and the fishing lodge.

At the rate it's rising, Sam told himself grimly, all of that will be swallowed up in no time. Unless it stops raining. If it stops raining, the river will go down quickly.

If it didn't . . .

To keep that grim possibility out of his mind, Sam turned away from the window and rejoined his guests.

During a momentary lull in the steady stream of gurneys arriving at ER, Will and Susannah were sipping hot coffee in the lounge when Kate's mother, Astrid Thompson, poked her head into the room. "Since my family and I have been relocated temporarily to Rehab," she said cheerfully, "I decided to volunteer my services over here." She grinned. "So convenient, being right next door. Don't have to take a bus. Not that I'd want to take up permanent residency at Rehab. Anyway, my husband and my son have left for a sandbag crew, so here I am. What do you need?"

"How many hours do you have to spare?" Will asked dryly.

Nurse Thompson laughed. "I figured. That's why I'm here. I remember the last flood. Wasn't just near-drownings that kept us going. We had just about every injury you could think of. Bumps, bruises, lacerations, heart attacks, concussions, you name it, it was all there. And we were short-staffed at the same time. Not a pleasant experience, I can tell you. Where's Kate? In a treatment room?"

Susannah and Will exchanged a reluctant glance. He was the one to say, "She's not here."

Nurse Thompson had been leaning against the door frame. As Will's answer to her question registered, she stood up straight, her eyes dark with concern. "Not here? She has to be here! She didn't come home for dinner, and she didn't call. When I checked the phones and realized the lines were down in Eastridge, I just figured she'd decided to stay here where she was needed but hadn't been able to call to tell me." Looking at Susannah, she asked, "If she's not here, where is she?"

"She had to go to the library. But," Susannah added hastily, "she left before the roads got too bad. So I'm sure she got there okay. And Jeremy went over there to give her a ride home." She didn't add that she'd been worried ever since Jeremy left that the library might have closed early and he wouldn't find Kate there.

"The library?" Astrid frowned. She was an attractive woman, tall and thin like her daughter. Susannah admired and respected her, and was grateful for the support the nurse had given her from the moment she had first begun volunteering. "The library's in the middle of town, and it's not up on high ground like Med Center. It'll flood, like it did the last time. How long ago did Jeremy go after Kate?"

Susannah and Will said they didn't remember exactly, but she knew they were both thinking the same thing. By the time Jeremy went to get Kate, the library had probably already taken on some water. It was very possible that Kate had left the building.

What troubled Susannah about that possibility was, Kate would have realized almost immediately, when she saw the streets flowing with water, that she wouldn't be able to get back to Eastridge. She would then have changed her mind and returned instead to Med Center.

But she hadn't shown up. Not yet.

So where *was* she?

At the library, Kate slipped out of her wet flats. Carrying them in her hands, she sloshed out of the room and down the hall to the back-door.

It was locked. From the outside.

She remembered, then, reports in the newspaper about recent break-ins. Nothing had been stolen, but there had been some vandalism. The librarian must have decided to take additional safety measures as a result of those incidents.

He'd picked a fine time to get cautious. How was she supposed to get out?

You're not supposed to be *in* here in the first place, she reminded herself. If he'd known you were down here, maybe he would have unlocked the door for you. You should have spoken up when he yelled down the stairs.

Too late now.

Kate peered out through the glass door window into nothing but darkness. The rest of the world had disappeared. Maybe it *floated* away, she thought with an uneasy giggle.

"No problem," she said aloud, turning away from the door. "I'll just go upstairs, find an extra set of keys, and go out the front door."

The water in the hallway was cold, her knee-highs little protection. By the time she reached the stairs and hurried up them, she was feeling chilled. She sat down on the top step to shed the sodden knee-highs and rub her feet dry with the edge of her maroon sweatshirt. Then she jumped up and hurried in her bare feet to the semicircular desk in the center of the main room, where she knew keys were kept on a hook beside one of the computers. She'd seen them when she was checking out books. There were several small lights still burning, probably another security measure. She was grateful she wouldn't have to hunt in the dark.

The keys weren't there.

The only thing hanging on the hook now was a small plastic card bearing the emergency telephone numbers of police, fire, and Search and Rescue.

Might come in handy, Kate thought dryly. I might need those numbers if I can't find the keys.

She moved around behind the desk to begin her search.

In the staff lounge, the conversation between Astrid Thompson and Susannah and Will was abruptly interrupted by a loud, urgent shout from outside the room.

"My boy! Where's my boy!" a deep, anguished voice called out. The shout was followed by

loud, crashing sounds, and then more shouting. *"My boy, my boy, I want to see my boy!"* There was such raw pain in the voice, it was blood-chilling to all who heard it.

Astrid Thompson whirled and ran. Susannah and Will followed, with the two nurses and the orderly dropping their coffee cups and exiting right behind them.

chapter
9

—♒︎⎯⋀⋁⋀⎯⋀⎯⋀⋁⎯⋀⎯⋀⋁⋀⎯—

The group led by Nurse Thompson arrived in the ER lobby to find a huge, burly man with a reddish beard and thick, fierce eyebrows, his beefy face scarlet with rage, in the process of lifting the wheeled steel cart filled with patient charts. The seams of his red-and-black-checked flannel shirt strained as he bodily lifted the cart and tossed it against the wall. Charts flew everywhere. Some landed on the nurses' desk, knocking pens and pencils and a clock to the floor; some hit the walls so hard, they left dents in the pale yellow wallboard. Most fell to the floor and skidded crazily.

The man continued to shout, his words slightly slurred. *"You bring me my son, you hear me? You bring him to me, right now! I'll take care of him, don't you worry about that, I can take care of my own son!"*

The cart disposed of, the bearlike man lumbered toward his next target, a wooden table loaded with magazines, sitting between two blue plastic chairs.

"Has anyone called security?" Astrid Thompson asked of a young, white-faced nurse standing behind the desk now littered with charts.

The girl nodded silently. "They said it might be a few minutes. They're all downstairs checking out the emergency generator." She paused, her wide, frightened eyes never leaving the rampaging man, then added, "He said his name is Brock. I think he's been drinking."

"Oh, God," Susannah cried softly, "his son just died! Curtis. He was trapped in the river in his car. But it wasn't a drowning. Dr. Lincoln thinks he panicked and had a heart attack. He . . . he was only sixteen." She turned to Will and the orderly, standing slightly behind her. "We have to do something! Before he hurts himself or somebody else."

"What have you done to my son?" the man screamed. He lifted the table high above his head, the magazines slipping and sliding off the edge. Then he heaved it. People watching in horror from the wide doorway of the waiting room cried out as the table flew through the air straight toward them. Some dove out of the way, some hid their faces against the wall as if not seeing would protect them, others fell to the floor and covered their heads.

The table crashed to the floor, splintering into a dozen pieces of shattered wood. A thin slice of wood landed in the hair of a woman in a plaid dress standing with her face pressed into the wall. A longer shard penetrated the fleshy upper arm of a man lying on the floor. He cried out in pain and shock. A third chunk hit a teenaged boy just below the left knee, buckling it and sending him to the floor.

"What have you done to my boy?"

Before Susannah could stop him, Will broke away from the group and slowly, carefully, but very deliberately, approached the man, speaking in a calm, quiet voice. "Sir, you don't want to do this. You've hurt some people here, people who didn't have anything to do with what happened to your son, okay? If you'll just calm down, someone will come and talk to you about the boy, explain what happened. Could you just calm down, sir? You don't want anybody else to get hurt."

Susannah held her breath. Will was tall and strong. An athlete. But the man possessed twice Will's bulk, and his rage was an awesome thing to witness. "Will," she breathed, "be careful."

The man glared at Will with reddened eyes. *"You know what they did?"* he cried, his bearded mouth twisting in pain. *"They killed my boy! They said his heart stopped! Then they sent someone to the refinery, a cop, a cop I didn't even know, a stranger, to tell me my boy was dead!"*

Will laid a hand on the man's arm. Susannah froze. If that arm came up and swatted at Will with the full force of the man's unbridled anger . . .

"I am really sorry about your son, sir," Will said. "I know how you must be feeling. How about if we go into the lounge over there and I get you some coffee and we'll talk about your boy? Would that be okay?"

Security arrived at that moment, a man and a woman in Med Center's tan uniforms. They would have moved toward the man, but Astrid Thompson put up a hand, signaling to them to hold off.

"You know about my boy?" the man asked Will. All of the anger seemed to have left him. Susannah saw tears gathering in the red-rimmed eyes. "You knew my Curtis? He was my only kid, you know."

"No, I'm afraid I didn't know him, Mr. Brock. But I would like you to tell me about him. Over here, in the lounge?" Gently, making no sudden moves, Will led the man, docile now, out of the lobby and into the lounge. The two security officers followed.

* * *

Sam knew he should do something.

The road leading from the cabin to the main highway was at the foot of the slope, where the third terrace began. If it didn't stop raining and if the river continued to rise, that road would become impassable. *Soon.* And there was no other road out. He didn't mind spending the night in the cabin if the entire slope flooded. But he had to let everyone else know what was happening.

He turned away from the window and moved through the crowd to the stereo to switch it off. The music ended so abruptly, it startled everyone into silence, making it easier for Sam to make his announcement. He stepped up onto the wide, stone fireplace hearth and addressed his friends in his normal, hearty tone of voice. "Listen up, everyone! Sorry about interrupting the festivities, but I think it's only fair to warn you that if we don't leave soon, we might not be able to leave at all. The old Revere is climbing the walls out there . . . and I mean that literally. It's up to the second terrace. When it reaches the third, we'll need a boat to make it back to town. The road out of here will be an Olympic-sized swimming pool."

"So?" one of Sam's soccer teammates spoke up.

"You've got boats, right, Grant? Didn't I see a boathouse out there?"

"The only way anyone could get to that boathouse now," Sam replied, "would be to swim. The river has it surrounded. Look, I'm staying here, but anyone who'd rather beat a hasty retreat right now won't get any flak from me, okay? It's probably the smart thing to do. All I'm saying is, if you intend to go back to town tonight, you'd better do it right now." When no one said anything, he added, "If you're *not* leaving, and you parked anywhere below that third terrace, you'd better go out and haul your car up here closer to the cabin before it becomes amphibious."

The party guests divided quickly into two groups: those who were staying and those who weren't willing to risk it. Most thought it was wise to leave, although no one really wanted to. Some couples argued, one partner wanting to stay, the other determined to leave. One girl became so incensed, she stomped from the cabin without her date. Sam thought he recovered very quickly, gravitating toward a girl whose date had also left. They consoled each other by calling the deserters "wimps."

Sam didn't agree. There were six people left,

including himself and Becka, and he found himself wishing they had all chosen to leave. This party had been *his* idea, and they were in his cabin. That made him responsible for them on a night when Mother Nature was in charge, not Samuel Grant III.

He was just about to turn to the remaining party guests and try to convince them to leave, when a brilliant streak of lightning lit up the windows, a resounding crack of thunder shook the lodge, and all of the lights went out.

Sid Costello awoke again, this time with a start, his heart pounding in his chest. The room was completely shrouded in a black-velvet darkness. The small half-moon of light that usually shone beneath his door from the hallway was gone. He turned his head toward the window. He was on the fifth floor, too high up to see any light from below. But on every other night since they'd brought him to this room, there had been outside that window the reflected glow of the complex's walkway lamps, a pale but constant illumination that Sid had found reassuring, as if the faint cloud of yellow was telling him, yes, life is still going on out here and we expect you to rejoin us soon.

That glow was gone now. There was nothing

but unbroken darkness outside his window, as if someone had hung a thick, black drape over the glass.

Maybe someone had. Maybe the nurse who had found him with the window open had put it there. To keep him inside.

That wouldn't explain why the hallway outside his room was also pitch-black.

Sid fumbled for the buzzer to summon a nurse. He couldn't find it. He hadn't been taking his nighttime medication, and had been sleeping restlessly. If the cord to the buzzer hadn't been looped tightly over the bed rail, he might have dislodged it in his sleep, maybe even knocked it to the floor.

Well, I'll just jump out of bed and pick it up, he thought giddily. And laughed aloud, a harsh sound in the silent room.

Another clap of thunder sounded as lightning lit up the window.

Sid got it then. No one had hung anything over his window. The electricity was out, that was all. So why bother hunting for the buzzer? Wasn't it electric? It wouldn't work, anyway, not until the emergency generator came on.

The door opened and a nurse with a flashlight hurried over to his bed. It was the same nurse who had found him at the window. "Oh, you're awake," she said when she reached him. "Didn't you take your sleeping pill?" Her face was a disapproving yellow moon above the flashlight. "Not hoarding them, are you? Where are they, under your pillow?"

It annoyed him that she was assuming he was suicidal just because he was paralyzed. Wasn't she also assuming then that his life must no longer be worth living? Who did she think she was to decide that? He'd make that decision himself. When he was ready. He wasn't ready yet.

Before she could begin fishing around under his pillow for the pills, he shook his head and pointed to the drawer on his bedside table. "I'm not hoarding anything. I just don't want them anymore. They make me too groggy in the morning." He didn't add that if he wanted to do something as stupid as take his own life, collecting enough sleeping pills to do the job would take too long. The window was faster and surer. Provided he could figure out how to hoist himself up over the sill from a wheelchair. But he still thought of that as a coward's way out. "What's with the lights?"

"They'll be on in a minute." She opened the drawer, collected the half-dozen pills, and pocketed them. "Dr. Davids will have to hear about this."

Davids. The shrink. So? Why would a shrink care if a patient takes his sleeping pills or not? "Why aren't the lights on now?" Sid asked angrily. "Doesn't your emergency generator come on automatically? This *is* supposed to be a modern facility, isn't it? My parents are paying a small fortune so that I can lie here in the dark?"

"Your parents aren't paying anything. The insurance company is. And I told you, the lights will be on in a sec. There seems to be some little glitch with the emergency equipment."

Some little glitch. She said it so casually, as if it were totally unimportant, because after all, she wasn't lying here in this bed in total darkness, was she? She had a flashlight, and she could turn and walk out of the room and close the door and go back to other people with flashlights. She could go back to the outside world and be normal, but he couldn't. He had to stay here, in this black hole, by himself, knowing that if a real emergency came, he wouldn't be able to save himself. Scary thought. Very scary thought.

"I want O'Connor," he said flatly. "Now! Get that stupid flashlight out of my face and get O'Connor for me."

The nurse stared down at him. "O'Connor? We don't have a Dr. O'Connor on staff."

"She's not a doctor, you dimwit!" He was

shouting now, waving his arms at her. "She's a volunteer! Abby O'Connor! Call her and tell her to come over here!"

The nurse was dumbfounded. The flashlight wavered in her hand. "A volunteer? Now? It's too late . . . it's too nasty out there . . . I can't . . ."

"Yes, you can!" Sid tried, and failed, to sit up straighter, hoping for the appearance of authority. Instead, he slid further down on the pillow. That made him even more furious. He could feel his heart pounding like the drums he played in his rock band, and his hands were shaking with fury. "Call her at home! Tell her it's me, tell her it's an emergency. Just get her over here! Or I'll . . ."

The nurse didn't say, "Or you'll do what?" But Sid himself thought it, and that sickening feeling of total helplessness that he'd been fighting so hard to squelch swept over him. Or what? What was he going to do if the nurse refused to call Abby? Jump out of bed and race for the door? Hike all the way home? Steal a bicycle and pump the pedals until he was at his own front door?

"Please," he said quietly, looking away from her. "Please call Abby."

The nurse hesitated only a moment. She directed the flashlight away from his face, and said just as quietly, "Okay, I will. I'll call her."

She was halfway to the door when she turned, walked back to the bed, and thrust the flashlight at him. "Here. You keep this. I'll get another." Then she left.

Even without the light, he would have been grateful to her. Because she hadn't said, "Or you'll do what?"

The flashlight helped calm him down. He held it tightly in one hand, letting its beam illuminate the doorway so that when Abby came in, he'd see her clearly.

In downtown Grant, Abby and Callie struggled, side by side, along Massachusetts Avenue in water up to their knees. The riverbank, underwater now, was to their left, the darkened stores and restaurants on their right. The avenue itself had disappeared, swallowed up by the swollen Revere.

"This is dangerous!" Callie shouted above the wind. "This water is moving too fast! And there isn't anybody around to help us if we get caught up in the current. I'm barely staying on my feet!"

"That's because you're wearing stupid high-heel boots!" Abby called back. "Who goes on a rescue mission in high-heeled boots?"

"When I left my house, I didn't *know* I was going on a rescue mission, did I?" Callie grabbed at the branches of a semisubmerged shrub for support. "You should have warned me in advance that your sisters were going to do something this dumb."

"Dumb? Dumb? You're the one who said you liked Geneva!"

"That was then. This is now." A sudden gust of wind ripped Callie's wide-brimmed red hat off her head, in spite of the ties beneath her chin. The ties gave, and the hat sailed away, landing upside down in the muddy water and rushing away amid a sea of debris. "Damn! I loved that hat! And my hair . . . look, Abby," Callie shouted, "I am soaked through to the bone, I'm going to drown any minute now, my toes are so wet, they're probably going to have to be amputated at Med Center, so no, I don't like your sister anymore, not one tiny little bit. When we find her, I'll be the one to strangle her, not you. I'm going to do it with my bare hands. If I have any strength left."

Abby clutched the top of a parking meter whose pole had disappeared beneath floodwater. She had to gasp her answer, but she managed to pack a certain amount of smugness into it.

"I knew you'd change your mind about Geneva," she said.

chapter
10

The emergency generator had kicked in quickly, providing adequate light and the use of all electronic medical equipment, to the relief of the staff.

When the patients who had been injured in Mr. Brock's rampage had been treated, Susannah returned to telephone duty. There were fewer calls now, which she realized had to be due to lines being down in other parts of the city. That made her uneasy. If the phones went out at Med Center, too, how would people call for help? Were there, even now, people stranded or injured out there who hadn't been able to get to a working telephone?

There was a phone at the fishing lodge. The library, too, had telephones. But neither Sam nor Kate had called. Were those phones out?

"No, ma'am," she told an anxious mother who called, "I don't see your daughter's name on my list. She's probably at a friend's house, waiting out the storm." She hung up, hoping the daughter hadn't been one of those brought in without identification. There had been quite a few, although the pace had slowed somewhat. People were finally getting the message and staying indoors.

Will was about to join a crew on an ambulance run when Nurse Thompson stopped him.

"No, Will," she said firmly. "You've already put in your hours. You must be exhausted. I want you to rest."

"How can I rest? I haven't heard from anyone in my family, have you, Susannah? My mom and brothers weren't brought in while I was in the lounge with Brock, were they?" His tone was light, but Susannah heard an underlying anxiety.

If I had family in Eastridge, she thought, I'd be worried, too. My family is safe at the top of a very high hill. Except for Sam, of course.

"No. I'd have told you if anyone from your family came in. I'd have interrupted you and Brock, who, by the way, you were brilliant with, Will." Susannah smiled at him. "How did you stay so calm? The rest of us were quaking in our shoes."

He shrugged. "The man wasn't drunk. He was in pain. I guess he wanted someone else to feel it."

"But you're the only one who did."

Another shrug.

"I'm sure your mother and the boys are safe," Nurse Thompson told Will. "You might want to check at Rehab on your way out. See if they're over there yet. Now go on, get out of here. Dr. Lincoln will take care of Mr. Brock, so you can leave. Scoot! That's an order."

"See you later, Will," Susannah said, knowing the nurse was right, but still sorry to see Will go.

"Oh, no, you don't!" Nurse Thompson said. "What I told Will goes for you, too, Susannah. You've been here almost as long as he has. Go home and get your beauty sleep."

"But . . ."

"No buts. I know it's been horrendous here tonight, but we've got staff coming on at eleven. Go home. Your parents must be worried about you."

"No, they're not. I called and told them I was staying here." Her mother hadn't mentioned Sam, and neither had Susannah. She could only assume he'd called home and said that everything was fine. She hoped. Not that her mother would have asked *her* about Sam. Her parents knew that she and her twin led very different social lives. Susannah hardly ever knew exactly which party or dance Sam was attending, or which girl he had chosen to honor with his presence.

When Nurse Thompson had returned to her desk, Susannah said to Will, "I can't go home and sit around doing nothing while the city is flooding. I'd never be able to sleep."

Will nodded. "I'm with you. But orders are

orders." They began walking toward the door. The crowd in the waiting room had thinned some. Those who remained, still shaken by the episode with the angry Brock, sat quietly watching the weather channel on television. As Susannah and Will passed, one man jumped to his feet and approached them.

"I just want to shake your hand," he said to Will, extending his own hand. "If you hadn't calmed that man down, Lord only knows what would have happened. You're a very brave young man. Thanks."

Susannah smiled at Will's obvious discomfort. But he shook the man's hand and made a hasty statement in support of the grieving father.

Outside, they were reluctant to dash out into the steady downpour. They stood on the top step under an overhang. "I feel so guilty about leaving," Susannah said, hugging her arms around her chest against the wind. "The weather hasn't improved at all. The staff is going to be up to its elbows in patients all night long."

"Astrid's right, though. We're burned out, Susannah. People make mistakes when they're tired. We could send a cardiac patient to the Psych ward or vice versa." Will zipped up his navy windbreaker. "You said you brought the Benz?"

Susannah had to raise her voice to be heard above the sound of water smacking against the cement steps. "Yes! Do you need a lift?"

"No, but *you* do. You can't drive that. It sits too close to the ground. I've got my truck. I'll take you home."

Susannah loved the idea of being alone in Will's truck with him. But she knew how tired he was. He should go find his family, and then get some rest. "West Grant won't be flooded. I'll be okay. That car handles like a dream, even on slippery roads."

"Don't argue with me. I know your part of town doesn't flood. But you have to get there from here. You could hit high water almost anywhere. You're coming with me. You'll be as safe as if you were in a tank."

"An amphibious one, I hope." Will took her hand and they ran down the steps and across the spongy grass to the parking garage.

When they were inside the truck and on their way out the long, wide, tree-lined driveway, he said, "Tell you what. Neither one of us wants to leave, right? Maybe all we need is a quick break. Why don't we go somewhere and grab coffee, maybe a doughnut or a piece of pie, see how we feel then? Anyway" — he glanced over at her with a grin — "by the time we get back, maybe Astrid will be back at Rehab. A new night nurse won't know how long we've been there, right? How about it?"

"Great!" The trees along the driveway were bending double under the force of the wind. The truck splashed through deep puddles, sending cascades of water against the windows and windshield. "*If* any of the night staff can get to the hospital."

"Yeah, well, there is that. But it's worth a try." Then he concentrated on steering the truck through the sea of swirling black water. Susannah glanced at his handsome profile and smiled. In spite of the weather, she felt safe with Will at the wheel.

Kate couldn't locate any extra library keys. They weren't on the desk anywhere, and the desk drawers were all locked. Maybe, as another precautionary measure, the librarian had taken all of the keys home with him, so that if someone did break in, they wouldn't have easy access to the drawers.

Like they couldn't break into the drawers the same way they'd broken into the building!

Irritated, her feet cold, her ears attuned to the sound of water lapping hungrily at the basement stairs, Kate lifted the telephone on the desk to call for help. She had her fingers already poised to dial when the unmistakable sound of dead air greeted her.

Kate replaced the receiver. Her irritation was quickly replaced with real disappointment. She had planned to call Med Center, talk to Will, ask him to come and get her in his truck. No problem. She knew he'd do it willingly. And he'd find a way to get a library door open. Will was smart and resourceful. Now she couldn't even call him.

The disappointment was just as quickly replaced by a sensation Kate quickly recognized as uneasiness. She had no key, no way out of the building, and the water in the basement was rising rapidly. This was trouble, no doubt about it.

She stood at the desk in her cold, bare feet, glancing around the room with narrowed eyes. Okay, so she was *not* going to be using the telephone to summon help. The world outside had not only disappeared from sight, it had disappeared from *sound*, too. Her one link to voices in other, safer places was gone.

She was alone. She was more alone than she had ever been before. This was nothing like spending a night alone in the small yellow house when her parents had gone to the Berkshires for a well-deserved minivacation, and Aaron spent the night at a friend's house. Those nights were fun. Pretending that she lived alone in the house, watching whatever she wanted on television, playing her stereo at full blast, eating whenever and whatever she liked, staying up late, spending hours on the phone with friends. She hadn't been lonely for a second. Besides, she'd had Lancelot, the family English springer spaniel, who loved to sit at her feet with his head and long, matted ears in her lap.

Feeling uncertain, a feeling Kate definitely wasn't used to and found almost more frightening than her circumstances, she sank into the desk chair and tucked her feet up underneath her in an effort to warm them. She knew she had to do something. She just wasn't sure what that something was.

The only coffee shop still open in the area was a diner with worn red plastic booths and a pattern of muddy footprints across the black tile floor. The waitress, the sole employee, had scattered short, fat candles across the counter and on the tables, and had substituted an old-fashioned coffeepot on the gas stove for the electric coffeemaker. The candlelight was kind to the worn surroundings. There were no other customers.

The coffee smelled wonderful, and the pecan pie sitting on the counter in a glass case looked delicious.

It was. And the waitress was very friendly. "I live in Eastridge," she said as she poured coffee for Susannah and Will. "They just said on the radio that they're not letting anybody back into that area now. It's being evacuated. Everyone's being taken to the Rehab Center. I think maybe I'll just sleep here tonight. Might even keep the place open. That way, rescue crews and the like can stop in and load up on caffeine if they want."

When she had left them alone, Will looked so bleak, Susannah said, "You should probably go straight to Rehab when we get back. You must want to be with your family."

"It's not that. They'll be okay. My mother will see to that. It's the thought of the cleanup afterward. I remember it from last time. It was really putrid. The mud clings to everything. It gets in the cupboards, the closets, the drawers. All of our family photo albums were wrecked. That hit my mother hard. And all the bleach in the world won't make that smell go away until it's good and ready. Takes forever."

Susannah pictured her beautiful three-room suite at the top of Linden Hall covered with foul-smelling mud, and shuddered. "I guess I'd want to move."

It was an innocent comment, sympathetically delivered, but Will's face tightened. "I guess you would. That wouldn't be a problem for your family, would it? Your parents could just buy another mansion somewhere else in town and fill it with brand-new furniture and rugs and drapes. No one in Eastridge has that luxury."

"I know that," she said quietly. "I didn't mean . . ."

He waved a hand. "Forget it. That wasn't fair. It's just . . . I get a little ticked sometimes because Eastridge always seems to get hit the hardest with floods, the refinery fires, that kind of stuff. Like I said, most of the people there can't afford to live anywhere else in town."

Uncomfortable, Susannah sipped her coffee silently. Outside, the storm continued unabated. There was almost no traffic now, although during their twenty minutes in the diner, three ambulances, two fire trucks, and two police cars raced by.

"I'm not going to live there all my life," Will added emphatically. "But I *am* going to work with the people there. A clinic, I think. Maybe in that big, old red brick building on East Sixth, the one that used to be a theater before it was closed down? That'd make a great clinic. When I'm a practicing physician." His lean, handsome face cleared, and he laughed. "Ever wonder why they call it a practice? Don't doctors ever get it right?"

"You will." Susannah smiled. "You'll get it right. And," she added boldly, "you'll need another doctor working there with you, won't you? In your clinic? Keep me in mind, okay?"

He plunked his coffee cup down on the table. Unlike her smile, his was cynical. "Oh, sure, Susannah. There probably isn't anything in the world your father would rather see you do than work in some shabby little clinic on the east side."

Her own smile widened into an impish grin. "It doesn't have to be shabby. We'll get my mother to decorate. She's an expert, and I can talk her into donating her services."

Will shook his head, but he was laughing. When his laughter died, he said seriously, "You'd really consider it? Working in a clinic with me?"

"I think I'd love it," she said just as seriously.

Impulsively, he reached out and covered her hand with his. "Well, I'd like it, too."

The door opened and Jeremy Barlow burst into the diner. He stopped abruptly, just inside the door, as he took in what he was seeing.

Will's face closed off and he withdrew his hand. "Hey, Barlow," he said casually, leaning back in the booth, "what are you doing out on a night like this?"

"Looking for Kate." Jeremy slid into the booth beside Susannah. "She's supposed to be at the library. But I drove by there, and it was closed. There were a few lights on, but it looked totally deserted. She couldn't have been in there."

"Well, at least the electricity isn't off in that part of the city, like it is here," Susannah said. "Not yet, anyway. But I wonder where Kate went? She wasn't at Med Center. Unless she went straight to Rehab looking for her family."

Jeremy frowned. "I don't see how she could have gone to Med Center from the library on her own. I had a hard time navigating. On foot would have been worse. The streets over there are starting to flood. Looked like there was al-

413

ready water in the library's basement."

"Probably was." Will stood up. "It flooded last time. Lost a lot of books, some of them rare. Kate must have left when the water started coming into the basement. If she was doing research, she'd have been down there. Would have seen it right away."

"Will's right," Susannah added, standing up, too. "But Kate wouldn't have gone home, even if she could get there. She'd know Eastridge was about to be evacuated. I'll bet anything she's at Rehab. We're going back there now, Jeremy. Why don't you come, too, check it out?"

Jeremy nodded. "Right. Let me grab a cup of coffee to go. I'll be along in a sec. But," he added grimly as Susannah and Will left, "she'd better be there."

Kate had just begun her search for the keys when the electricity went out. Every last ray of light disappeared, both inside the building and out. Everything around her had been erased in one swift stroke. She couldn't even see the floor beneath her feet. She stood perfectly still, her mouth open in surprise.

"Well!" she said finally, disgust in her voice, "isn't *this* exactly what I need!"

chapter
11

The temperature began to drop drastically. Neither Abby's nor Callie's raincoat was lined, and both were so thoroughly drenched, they no longer provided even a hint of warmth. Both girls were shivering, their teeth chattering as they continued to slog through the deep water covering Massachusetts Avenue. Although they were not more than a few blocks from the public library, the avenue lights were still on, and they could see the river continuing to rise and swell, spreading out to snake its way under the doors of the closed shops and restaurants on their right.

"Abby, this is totally crazy!" Callie shouted. "This water may only be up to *your* thighs, but I'm shorter than you. It's up to my waist. I can't keep walking through this. The current's too strong. Can't we just go to the police and make them look for your stupid sisters? That's their job!"

"It would take too long," Abby called back through a jaw clenched with cold. "You go if you want. They're not *your* sisters. You can bring the police back with you, or a rescue crew. They must be around somewhere. But I'm going to keep going. I know Geneva and Carmel have to be down here, and I'm going to find them if it kills me."

"It just might," Callie said grimly. But she didn't leave. She wasn't sure why. She knew she was not particularly brave. Privileged and pampered all of her life, there'd been little need for bravery. The closest she'd come until now was the courage it took to drive her chronically ill mother to Med Center three times a week for dialysis, a painful procedure necessary to do the job her mother's kidneys could no longer perform. That took courage on the part of mother and daughter alike. But Callie didn't think of that as bravery. She thought of it as necessity.

Now, she wanted nothing more than to turn around and go home to her nice, dry, warm, luxurious house, completely safe from muddy floodwaters. She would take a long, hot shower and put on her best silk pajamas, the peach pair her father had brought her back from Hong Kong. She would put her newest CD on and crawl into bed to get warm. But first, she'd give her mother the bottle of medication that she had tucked into her blouse chest pocket to keep safe and dry.

Abby had *said* it was okay for her to leave. So why wasn't she leaving?

She knew why. She wanted Abby O'Connor

to *like* her. That's why she wasn't leaving.

What puzzled Callie about Abby was, of all the people Callie knew, Abby seemed the happiest. And Abby had the least. Oh, she had a nice enough house, and her family owned two cars, a station wagon and a van. But they weren't *rich*, like practically every other girl Callie knew. Abby lived in a perfectly ordinary house in a perfectly ordinary neighborhood and went to perfectly ordinary Grant High instead of private day school. Abby had a big, noisy family and tons of friends and she smiled a lot, even though she lived such a perfectly ordinary life. Why was it that Abby smiled so much more often than Callie Matthews? Why did she date more than Callie did? And why did she have so many more friends? When she was so . . . *ordinary*?

And why did Callie want someone so ordinary to like her? So much so that she was risking her very life trying to help Abby O'Connor find her stupid sisters?

Callie didn't have the answer to those questions. All she knew was that she didn't want to turn around and leave Abby out here all alone in the middle of an avenue that had become a tributary of the Revere River.

Gritting her teeth, Callie plunged onward.

Susannah and Will, with Jeremy right behind them, went directly to Rehab when they arrived back at Med Center. Will wanted to check on his family, and Susannah had picked up on Jeremy's anxiety about Kate. What if she wasn't at Rehab? They knew she couldn't still be at the flooding library, and she couldn't have gone home to Eastridge. What if she'd begun to walk home in the storm and had been caught up in heavy floodwater somewhere in the city?

Did Kate swim? Did she swim *well?* Susannah didn't know.

If Kate wasn't at Rehab with her family, they would have to check with the rescue teams to see if her name was on any of the lists of rescued flood victims. Beyond that, Susannah had no idea how they'd go about locating Kate.

There was a large, handmade sign tacked onto the wall beside the entrance to Rehab, a wide, low building some distance behind Grant Memorial. Susannah guessed that when the sign had first been hung, it had read FLOOD SHELTER. But the ink used hadn't been waterproof, and the letters had begun to drip down the sign in black rivulets. It now read F O D ELT R.

Inside, the building looked very different. The main lobby, decorated with leather furniture, expensive leather-topped tables which Susannah knew her mother had picked out, and huge pots of fresh flowers, was mobbed with people receiving name tags and filling out forms. Will, intent on finding his family, and Susannah, equally intent on locating Kate, pushed their way through the crowd and into the main room on the first floor. The huge space, which Abby liked to call "The Ballroom," although as far as Susannah knew, nothing as formal as a ball had ever been held there, was bustling with activity. The floor was a landscape of cots and bedding spread out across its shiny hardwood surface. People sat or lay on the makeshift beds. The few belongings they'd managed to bring with them were piled at their feet. The faces of the adults, most of whom were women, registered confusion or anger or shock, while the older children looked interested in this exciting change in their normal routine. The very young children were perfectly happy anywhere as long as their mothers were with them. Their fathers were out working on the sandbag crews.

There was no sign of Kate.

But her brother, Aaron, was standing in the middle of the room. Susannah spotted the tall, thin boy who had confronted her earlier in ER, and was torn. She didn't want to ask Aaron Thompson about his sister. He'd probably bite her head off. But how else could she find out if Kate's family had heard from her?

She was spared the question when Aaron moved over to her and asked, "Have you seen Kate?"

Susannah shook her head. "No. And I'm worried. Although," she added quickly, "I know she can take care of herself."

"Are you sure?" he asked rudely, and walked off. His face was filled with concern.

Susannah wondered what to do next. She was standing alone, her eyes searching the crowded room for someone else who might have seen Kate, when a deep voice behind her asked, "Aren't you a friend of O'Connor's?"

Susannah turned around. The boy in the wheelchair was almost as good-looking as Will. Same strong face, high cheekbones, and keen, intelligent eyes, although these eyes were not as warm as Will's. And they were blue, not dark brown. The hair was dark brown, and the mouth had an unpleasant downturn to it, which Susannah guessed probably had something to do with the wheelchair. "You mean Abby?"

"Abby, yeah. Abby O'Connor. I think I've seen you here with her."

"She's my best friend. You know Abby?"

He shrugged. "Yeah, I know her. She's my volunteer."

Susannah raised an eyebrow. *His* volunteer? Volunteers weren't supposed to become attached, emotionally or otherwise, to any of the patients. They'd been warned about that. Had Abby disobeyed? Not likely. Besides, she hadn't mentioned anyone special at Rehab. "What's your name?"

"Sid Costello."

The name registered with a shock. Susannah recognized him, then. She remembered the stories and his picture in the newspaper and on television when he'd fallen from the water tower. Everyone in town had been interested because everyone in town knew who Sid Costello was. He looked very different now from those pictures. They had been of a tall, strong, healthy football player in a Grant High uniform. His smile had been a little arrogant, she'd thought at the time. Maybe a *lot* arrogant. This Sid, wearing a bright red V-necked sweater over a white T-shirt, his legs covered with a plaid blanket, wasn't smiling at all, and didn't look as if he would be anytime soon.

"Where is she?" he demanded.

"Abby? She went home."

"I know *that*. But I told the nurse to get her back here. She said she would. That was more than an hour ago. I finally got tired of waiting in my room. Too noisy to sleep, with all the doors slamming down here, and people yelling. I could hear it five floors up." He glanced around the room as Susannah had. "I thought O'Connor might be down here, doing her do-gooder thing. She's still at home?"

"I guess so." Abby had never once mentioned Sid Costello to Susannah. She must not be as interested in this guy as he seemed to be in her. If she wasn't interested, it certainly wouldn't be because of the wheelchair. Not Abby. If she really liked a guy, he could have paws instead of feet and she wouldn't care.

But the guy would have to be really likeable. Sid Costello didn't seem to qualify. "Is there anything I can get you?" Susannah asked politely. "Since Abby's not here, I mean. Did you need her to do something?"

He looked her up and down with thinly disguised contempt. "You mean since I can't do things for myself?"

Susannah's cheeks burned. "No, I . . ."

"I just want to see her, that's all. You know her number?"

"Of course I know her number," she snapped. "I told you, she's my best friend." She'd met lots of people in wheelchairs while volunteering. None of them had been as rude and unpleasant as this boy. Maybe he thought that just because he was in a wheelchair, he deserved special treatment and didn't need to be civil to people. That wasn't what the volunteers had been taught in their training.

"Don't coddle them," Astrid Thompson had warned them. "You will have to make allowances for their physical challenges, of course. But other than that, you must treat them as you would any other human being. They deserve that. They're entitled to it. Getting nothing but sympathy would do them no good at all."

"If Abby's home," Susannah said more matter-of-factly, "she's probably very busy. Taking care of her brothers and sisters. She might not have time to talk on the phone."

"Just give me the number, okay? If she doesn't want to talk, fine. I can deal with that. But that's up to her, not you."

She gave him the number and stalked away. She was going to have a talk with Abby about this Costello boy. Weird that Abby hadn't mentioned him. He wasn't exactly forgettable.

Having made sure that his family was safe, Will was ready to leave with her and return to ER. Jeremy decided to return to the library. His face looked very strained as he left.

"Maybe Astrid won't let us back in," Susannah told Will as they left Rehab. "We were ordered off the premises, remember? For the safety of the patients, I believe we were told."

Will glanced at his watch. "It's after eleven. The new staff's probably on duty by now. And if Astrid got stubborn and didn't leave and won't let down the drawbridge for us, we'll come back over here. They could use help here, too."

It occurred to Susannah as they hurried through the enclosed passageway from Rehab to ER that every hospital on the grounds of Med

Center could probably use extra help tonight, since all of them would almost certainly be short-staffed due to the weather. Will was right. If they weren't allowed back into ER, they wouldn't have any trouble finding somewhere else to volunteer.

But she knew that ER, as always, was where she really wanted to be.

When the lights suddenly went out at the fishing cabin, there were startled cries as the six remaining occupants reacted to the sudden darkness.

But what Sam decided was worse than the darkness inside was the loss of the outside floodlights. With the storm continuing, he would have liked to send everyone back to their own homes. He could have talked them into leaving. He'd talked them into coming down here, hadn't he? But unless he found a couple of flashlights or lanterns, he couldn't let anyone step one foot outside the cabin now, because there was no way to see how high the water had risen.

"Sam?" Becka's voice was shaking. He knew she hated the dark. Still slept with a night-light on, she had told him in a rare moment of openness. Most of the time, it was impossible to figure out what Becka was thinking. No problem figuring out what she was thinking now. She was scared. "Sam, where *are* you?"

He reached out a searching hand. His fingers connected with hers. They were clammy and cold. "Sam, do something!"

"Come with me." His own voice was firm, steady. Deliberately so. "I know where the flashlights are. Don't let go of my hand."

"Don't worry, I won't!"

Leading the frightened girl, Sam cautiously made his way to a cupboard beside the fireplace, pulled a drawer open, and unearthed a large flashlight. He could tell by its feel that it was the black one his father often carried on nighttime visits to the boathouse. Wondering when it last had new batteries. Sam flicked it on. The beam was orange-yellow, and it was very strong.

Beside him, Becka breathed a sigh of relief, and her grip on his hand eased a little. But just a little.

Sam played the flashlight's beam on the other party guests, clustered together now in a tight little group in the center of the room. The sudden darkness had rendered all of them, even Joel Mitchum, the practical joker in the room, silent. No one said, "Hey, Sam, it's okay, no big deal!"

"Sam," Becka said, her voice hushed, "I want to go home. Now. Please."

Sam turned slightly toward her. He didn't know how to tell her there was no way that could happen now. Even if they could somehow get away from the cabin in spite of the water surrounding it, the lights were probably out all across the city, and the Revere was on its worst rampage in years. There would be no highway lights, no working traffic signals, only car headlights to see if the road being traveled was underwater. By the time those headlights illuminated a deep lake spreading out in front of a vehicle, it could be too late to turn back.

Complete darkness and flooding were a lethal combination.

Wishing fervently that he had listened to Susannah hours earlier, Sam began awkwardly, "Listen, Becka, the thing is . . ."

The new night nurse in ER was regaling the staff with tales of her journey through the storm when Will and Susannah returned. Nurse Thompson was absent, although one of the nurses said she was still on duty, but had gone upstairs on an errand. Lost in her story of trees uprooted by the wind, and deep, torrential streams washing the roads she'd traveled to Med Center, the new nurse took no notice when the two arrived.

They hung their jackets on the rack in the staff lounge, signed in, and when Susannah had donned her pink smock, they went out into the lobby. Will moved quickly to the chart cart, restored to order after Brock's attack on it, and casually began leafing through the charts.

"Look at this!" He waved one in the air. "Nine patients while we were gone! Nine!" He glanced over at the staff gathered around the night nurse. "We must be having a lull. Temporary, though, I'll bet." He replaced the chart. "Most of the incoming were people pulled out of the river or low-water crossings. Minor bumps and bruises, that kind of thing. Couple of car wrecks. Nothing critical." He shook his head. "Can you believe there are people out in this?"

Susannah smiled. "Will, we were just out in it."

He laughed. "Yeah, but *I* know what I'm doing. Lived here all my life. I know which roads to take and which ones to avoid during flooding. Anyway, the diner was just up the road."

"Yeah, but you didn't know when we left here that it would be open, did you?"

He donned a look of mock ferocity. "Are you trying to pick a fight with me? If that one hadn't been open, I'd have taken only certain, very safe streets to find another place." He had a very serious expression on his face now. "I would never take any chances with you in the car, Susannah."

She knew that was true. Still, it felt nice to hear him say it aloud.

"Anyway, my point was," Will said, clearly wanting to change the subject, "they've been busy here, Doesn't look like it's going to ease up anytime soon. The storm *or* the inflow of patients. I'm glad we came back."

"Me, too." Almost as an afterthought, Susannah asked, "Do you know Sid Costello?"

Will nodded. "He's a friend of mine. I go to Grant High too, remember? We're . . . we were on the same football team. I stop in to see him whenever I can. Some of the people at Rehab think he's not handling this business very well. But nobody ever says what handling it well means. Is he supposed to smile and say, 'Hey, this isn't so bad after all'?"

"I don't know what handling it well means. Anyway, he seemed awfully anxious to get in touch with Abby. I didn't even know she knew him. I should call her, let her know he wants to talk to her. Just in case he wasn't able to get through."

A voice barked over the PA system. Incoming. A car had hit a telephone pole. The pole had fallen on top of the car. Three patients, all critical. ETA seven minutes.

"If you're going to call her," Will told Susannah, "you'd better get to it. In seven minutes, this place is going to be too noisy to hold a telephone conversation."

Susannah ran to the desk and dialed Abby's number.

"Oh, Susannah," Moira wailed into the phone, "Abby isn't here! She went out looking for Geneva and Carmel, and she never came back!"

chapter
12

It was the sound of the water lapping nearby that awakened Kate. Still seated in the librarian's chair, she had fallen asleep. It took her several moments to realize where she was. The library was so still and silent, she could hear her own breath. The only other sound was the smacking of the encroaching water upon the wooden stairs, and it was that sound that caught her attention. It was too close. Much closer than it should have been.

Kate pulled herself upright in the chair, her eyes searching the darkness. She couldn't believe she had fallen asleep. I must have been more tired than I thought, she decided, peering around her. All that studying . . .

If only she could see. She would have given anything for a candle, a flashlight, a lantern. Anything to break this thick black curtain and take away her feeling of helplessness. How could she do anything useful if she couldn't *see*?

It wasn't the darkness she was frightened of. It was the water, so stubborn, so persistent, climbing ever higher. Without a light, how could she tell how close it was getting?

She remembered, too late, that the library had been flooded more than once in the past. Which made it not the best place to be trapped in on a night like this one.

Kate stood up. She was stiff from sleeping in the chair. Her muscles ached. How could she have forgotten that the library had been flooded previously? If she'd remembered, would she have come here, anyway? Probably. For one thing, she would never have expected the water to rise so quickly. She would have been positive that she could finish her work and beat a hasty retreat while the building was still dry.

Exploring the darkness with her hands and stepping cautiously, Kate made her way slowly to the top of the stairs. Stepped down one step. Dry. Stepped down another. Still dry. But the sound of the water slapping persistently against the steps was louder now. She imagined it calling to her, saying slyly, "Come on in, the water's fine." Down another step. This time, her bare foot landed on wood that felt damp and slick. Not yet fully engulfed, but about to be.

She calculated quickly in her head. There had been, she thought, nine or ten steps leading up from the basement. Only the top two were still dry. The step below them was about to be swallowed up. The basement hallway below was completely lost to her now. Underwater. Her only hope of exit was the front door. If she could get it open.

She tried. She tugged and pulled on the doorknob, kicked the door with her bare feet, pounded on it until her fists felt raw. But it didn't budge. Kate couldn't believe that vandals had ever gained entry to this place. To her, the library seemed locked up tighter than a fortress.

Although there was no full second floor to the building, there was, she knew, a small loft at the top of a set of six wide, wooden steps off to one side behind the librarian's desk. The loft was a small, private, quiet reading area filled with bookshelves and two comfortable old chairs, each with a small lamp table.

And . . . wasn't there a long, narrow window up there looking out over the street? If she could get that window open, she could shout for help.

That would only work, she knew, *if* there was another human being within miles, which, given the weather, there probably wasn't.

But it was worth a try. Kate stifled an ironic laugh. Like she had a choice? Window or not, there was only one place for her to go to escape the rising water, and that was *up*. The loft wasn't very *far* up, but it was all she had.

Searching with her hands again, Kate moved toward the staircase.

* * *

The victims of the car wreck and the utility pole arrived at the ER in a flurry of activity. All were teenagers.

"They probably thought it would be a lark to drive on flooded streets," Dr. Izbecki grumbled as the three gurneys arrived, one after the other. But after that initial complaint, he settled down to begin the business of saving lives.

One patient, a boy Susannah didn't recognize, had no pulse and wasn't breathing. The second patient, a girl whose short, spiked black hair was streaked with blood, had a severe head injury, while the third, a younger girl, had a critical chest injury.

"No seat belts," one of the paramedics announced unnecessarily. It was already obvious to the medical professionals that seat belts had not been used. The injuries were too severe.

Each patient was directed to a different trauma room. Susannah decided she would be of more use in the room with the chest injury. And that girl was so young; if she regained consciousness, she'd be frightened.

The girl with the head injury was wearing a cervical collar and lying on a backboard, measures taken at the accident site to prevent further injury. She, too, was unconscious, but the wound on the back of her skull had stopped bleeding. The paramedic pushing her wheeled cart snapped, "She's in a bad way. Unresponsive.

Pupils unequal. Blood pressure's in the basement, seventy over fifty. There wasn't much we could do for her in the field. She's all yours. Lots of luck!" He sounded depressed.

Susannah, running alongside the second gurney, overheard. Severe head injury. Not good. The patient might not die . . . Dr. Izbecki could probably save her with his initial efforts, and then the neurosurgeons would take over. Med Center surgeons were the best in the world. But sometimes there was only so much they could do. The girl might never again be the person she was when she'd climbed into that car earlier in the evening. Even if there was no permanent brain damage, she would probably have to learn to walk and talk all over again, as if she were an infant. The recuperative period would be long and painful.

Of the chest injury patient, the paramedic said, a bit breathlessly, "We've been pouring fluids into her, but we got nothing. BP was still low. So we applied the antishock trousers."

"I advised against it on the radio," Dr. Izbecki snapped. "The last thing we need in a chest injury is an increase in pressure in the girl's chest. The trousers could have done that. You could have killed her."

The paramedic frowned. "We knew the risks. But giving her fluids did zilch for blood pressure. We thought it was necessary."

His partner added, a bit defensively, "We were watching her. At the first sign of respiratory distress, we would have deflated the trousers."

"Never mind," the doctor said brusquely, "just get her into the trauma room. And somebody get me X Ray, stat!"

Susannah ran to the phone and made the call.

She learned later that the boy who hadn't been breathing when he was brought in was the driver of the vehicle. After what Will described to Susannah as a tense, lengthy period of resuscitation attempts by Dr. Lincoln, he had revived, with no signs of brain damage from a lack of oxygen. Both his legs were broken, one suffering a compound fracture, and he had a serious eye injury.

"He's also facing reckless driving charges," Will added, standing beside Susannah as she finished gathering up towels in the trauma room. "The officer on the scene said they can do that because of the warnings that went out over television and radio. No one's supposed to be out on the roads. And that kid almost killed two other people. They're sisters, those girls. If they'd both died, their parents wouldn't have any daughters left at all."

"They'll live," Susannah said confidently. Both girls had been taken up to surgery and would be transferred to separate hospitals in the complex when they passed the critical period. "Dr. Izbecki was amazing with the chest injury. Fast and efficient, but so gentle. If I were going to work in Emergency Care, I'd want to be exactly like him."

"Well, as long as you don't *look* like him!"

Susannah laughed. Dr. Izbecki was not the most handsome doctor on staff. His face was rugged and weathered, as if he'd spent too many hours in the sun. She knew that wasn't true, because the man hardly ever left the hospital. Someone had told her he'd grown up very poor, in Chicago, and hadn't had it easy. Maybe that was what she saw in his face. Handsome or not, he was still her hero. He had saved a twelve-year-old girl's life, and as the girl had been wheeled off to surgery, one of the other doctors in the room had said in admiration, "Great work, Jonah! I didn't think you'd pull it off. Not this time." And Dr. Izbecki had said only, in his usual gruff tone, "That's what we're here for." Then he'd stripped off his rubber gloves and hurried off to see how the patient was doing.

"I'm going over to Rehab to see if Abby is there yet," Susannah told Will when she had tossed the towels into the laundry bin. "Moira said she went looking for Geneva and Carmel. But I can't believe she's out in this. I don't *want* to believe she's out in this! Maybe she found them and instead of taking them home, decided all three of them could help out at Rehab."

"Carmel's only eight, Susannah," Will said.

"Do you really think Abby would expect her to volunteer? Carmel isn't even big enough to push a wheelchair."

"She could maybe answer phones or something," Susannah said stubbornly. Her eyes pleaded with Will. "I'll be right back."

"We might need you here."

Susannah was exhausted, and her uneasiness about Abby was growing. "Well, it's not like I'm a nurse or doctor," Susannah said testily. She waved a hand toward the staff, some of whom were just emerging from a trauma room. "You've got *plenty* of help. I said I'd be right back. Okay?" Without waiting for a response, she hurried off in the direction of the enclosed passageway leading to Rehab.

"This is Sid Costello," he said into the telephone. "I'd like to speak to Abby, please." He was sitting at a pay telephone in the lobby of Rehab, surrounded by throngs of people waiting to make calls on one of the six phones. They crowded around him, impatient. He found himself wishing for the privacy of a booth, even though he knew a booth would be inaccessible to his wheelchair. Rehab had freestanding phones for wheelchair patients. He had chosen not to use the phone in his room because he'd been afraid a nurse would barge into his room while he was talking, and afterward she'd ask all kinds of stupid questions about "the girl in his life." Gag. He couldn't deal with that.

It was impossible to hear. There was a great deal of static on the line, and the lobby was so noisy with so many people in it. He'd never seen the place this packed. He could barely make out the voice that finally answered. "What did you say? You didn't say she wasn't home, did you?" He'd been so sure that all he had to do was pick up a phone and she'd be there, on the other end of the line. "Are you sure? She left here a long time ago. She was supposed to be going home. Where else would she be?"

Crackle, crackle, snap, on the line. "She's out" . . . crackle, crackle, snap . . . "for . . . sisters . . ." crackle, snap, crackle. It was hopeless. All he could gather from the garbled conversation was that Abby was not home.

Then even the crackling snap disappeared. The line went dead.

"Sorry," Sid said as he handed the telephone to the person behind him, an older man with anxious eyes, "it's not working anymore." The man glared at Sid as if it were his fault.

Sid wheeled himself over to the elevator. He punched the button. But before the doors slid open, the girl with long, blonde hair, the one he'd talked to earlier because she was a close friend of Abby's . . . best friend, she'd said . . . came hurrying down the hall, calling his name.

He couldn't believe how glad he was to see her. She'd know where Abby was.

But she didn't. "Have you seen Abby?" were the first words out of her mouth.

Sid let the elevator doors open and close again without him. He turned his wheelchair so that he was facing Susannah. "I just called her house. I think I was told that she wasn't home, but I can't be sure. The line was a mess, and then it went dead. Why?"

"Because she *isn't* home. Moira, that's her sister, said Abby had gone out looking for her two younger sisters, and hadn't come back yet. I was hoping they were all here. You haven't seen them?"

Sid shook his head.

Susannah surveyed the lobby. Then she moved around behind Sid's chair to begin pushing him toward The Ballroom.

"What are you doing?" he cried over his shoulder. "I don't want to go in there! It's packed with people. I was on my way to my room when you showed up. Take me back to the elevator!"

Susannah continued to push the chair. She leaned over his shoulder. "You were going to go up and hide in your room with all this going on down here? Why aren't you helping?"

"Helping? Me?" His laugh was scornful. "Oh, man, I'd be a big help, wouldn't I? I'll bet all of the other volunteers are wishing like mad that I'd offer my services. Probably bitterly disappointed that I haven't."

"Well, you still can. There are plenty of things you can do to help. You can ride this chariot to the linen closet and bring back towels and blankets. You can answer phones."

"I told you, they're not working."

"Well, you can take names from people here then, and the phone numbers of their relatives. Then, when the phones are working again, you can call them and tell them their family members are here. There's plenty of work here for someone even as cantankerous as you."

Cantankerous? An old-fashioned word. But Sid knew what it meant. It meant cranky, difficult, even rude. He'd thought she was going to say "crippled" or even "physically disadvantaged." Cantankerous wasn't so bad.

Susannah steered the wheelchair into the wide open doorway to The Ballroom, her eyes quickly scanning the crowd. "Darn, she's not here! Oh, God, Sid, do you really think Abby is out in that storm somewhere?"

The look he sent her then was full of suspicion. Instead of pitying him, she was dumping her worry on his shoulders, as if she expected him to know what to do with it. As if he could make *her* feel better. She was talking to him the same way she would to anyone, as if he were an ordinary person. Was this some new form of therapy? Or was she so worried about her best friend that she'd forgotten whom she was talking to?

Still, he sat up straighter in his chair. And he found himself wanting to reassure her. He didn't know what to say. He wasn't used to people asking him for something. All he could come up with was, "I don't know if she's out there. But . . . but I sure hope she isn't."

He knew it wasn't enough. Susannah's face didn't suddenly relax; her eyes, which were a really bright blue, didn't look relieved. He felt like he had let her down. Hating the feeling, he felt compelled to add with fake enthusiasm, "Okay, if you insist, I guess I could go get some blankets or pillows or something. Just until O'Connor shows up, though, okay? Then I'm outa here."

Susannah looked down at him. "You think she'll come here?"

"Oh, yeah, sure." He forced a grin, the cocky grin he'd worn in the pictures in the newspaper. It wasn't easy. He hadn't used it in a long time. But it finally appeared on his face. "How could she stay away, when *I'm* here?"

"Oh, you are *so* full of it!"

But Sid thought, as Susannah began pushing his chair toward the linen closet, that she looked a little less worried.

chapter
13

At the fishing lodge on the South Side, Sam returned to the window overlooking the Revere. Becka had unearthed a bunch of candles from the cupboard beside the fireplace, and the first-floor living room danced with flickering flames. But that didn't help illuminate anything outside. Without the floodlights, it was impossible to see how high the water had risen in the past few hours. They'd been sitting inside, alternately partying halfheartedly and sleeping, for what seemed like days. But it wasn't days. Sam's watch informed him that it was one-thirty in the morning. His parents wouldn't be frantic yet. But soon.

He didn't have to *see* the river to know how high it was. He knew how bad the situation had become. All this time, he deliberately hadn't opened the front or back door to check, because he didn't *want* to see. What difference did it make how high the water had risen? They couldn't leave, anyway. It was better not to know.

Still, his curiosity was getting the better of

him. Anyway, sooner or later, he was going to have to step outside to see if his foot landed on something solid, or floated. Might as well get it over with.

He waited until the other five were engaged in a heated discussion about who really *was* the sexiest man in the movies (Becka taking the position that it definitely wasn't Brad Pitt), before moving quietly to the front door, opening it, and stepping onto the porch.

His foot landed on wet, but not submerged, wood.

This was good.

But when he moved across the porch and stepped down one step, his foot was instantly soaked.

Oh, man! The *top* step?

Everything below that top step was underwater.

At the rate the water was rising, it would be only minutes before the Revere River inched its way into the living room where his friends were arguing.

He had no choice. He would have to move the party upstairs. And he'd better have a really good explanation for insisting they leave the perfectly comfortable living room with the big stone fireplace and the oh-so-excellent stereo system, and move upstairs to a floor that housed only bedrooms.

Sam *knew* what the explanation had to be. He would have to tell them the truth.

Will, standing just inside the ER entrance as a car screeched to a halt in the driveway, found himself wishing Susannah would return. They couldn't possibly need her as much at Rehab as she was needed at ER. Following the three teenagers whose car had been creamed by a telephone pole, there had been two near-drowning victims, rescued from floodwaters, a six-year-old child who had fallen from a ladder while being evacuated from the second story of his house in Eastridge, two cardiac arrests, and two teenaged boys who had thought it would be a blast to take a raft down the raging Revere. They had collided with the stone bridge in the center of town.

Those two cases had been the worst. One critical head injury, similar to the girl in the utility-poled car, and one near drowning. Both victims were still teetering on the edge upstairs in Intensive Care. They were both lucky to be alive. If they weren't in the best ICU facility in the country, they wouldn't stand a chance.

Since the two cardiacs, one of whom, a retired postman, hadn't made it, things had quieted down some. But Will knew it wouldn't last. In the meantime, there were reports to be filled out, supplies to restock, frantic relatives in the waiting room to placate. How many times tonight had a nurse or doctor said (voice rising a little each time the standard quote was repeated), "I assure you, we're doing the best we can"? He'd said it himself when an anxious relative in the waiting room waylaid him as he ran by to greet an ambulance and help rush a patient to a treatment room.

Susannah was better at that than he was. She had what he called The Perfect Patient Touch, and it applied to relatives of patients, as well. A calm, soothing voice, never condescending or impatient, combined with the ability to listen to even the most trivial complaints without losing her temper. She *would* be a valuable asset to his clinic. But her parents would never allow it. Never! Before the ink was even dry on her medical license, Samuel Grant would have Susannah set up in a lucrative private practice somewhere up near Linden Hill.

She *had* sounded interested, though. Probably just being polite. She'd probably never even been *in* Eastridge. Parts of it were nice enough. Other parts weren't. They'd get all kinds of people in his clinic. And while there wasn't a snobbish or intolerant bone in Susannah's body as far as he could tell, was she really prepared for what they might see at the clinic?

The car that had screeched to a halt, an older-model sedan, still had its lights on, glowing eerily through the sheets of rain. A door opened, a woman in shorts and a T-shirt jumped out, ran to the passenger's door, reached in and plucked something from the seat, turned, and ran through the rain up the sidewalk. Will yanked the door open for her.

She was carrying a small child, wrapped in a blanket. The woman was crying hysterically, lines of black mascara streaking her face. "Help me!" she cried when she saw Will. "You have to help me!"

Will signaled to a doctor and nurse in the lounge. They jumped up and hurried toward him. "What happened?" he asked, taking the limp child from its mother's arms. She didn't want to let go, and continued to clutch at one edge of the sodden blanket as Will turned and began moving down the hallway. The child, who looked to be around two or three years old, lay as limp as a rag doll in his arms. Its eyes were closed, the lids bluish, its mouth open.

"I thought he was asleep," she cried. "In his room. But when I went up to check, he wasn't there. I couldn't believe his bed was empty! I don't know how he got by me. I was just sitting in the living room, watching the late movie. He must have come downstairs and slipped right past me. The doorway is behind the couch."

Patiently, Will repeated, "What happened?"

The woman let go of the blanket to swipe at the wet hair hanging in her eyes. "He got out of the house, he does that sometimes if I forget to lock the door after I put him down for the night. He got out!" She clearly still didn't believe it. "I found him" — she choked on her tears, stopped, tried again — "I found him in the drainage ditch in front of our house. Floating. It was overflowing, because of the rain, and I found him *floating*!"

With the doctor and nurse alongside them, they reached a trauma room. Dr. Izbecki was inside, waiting. Although his manner was rough, Will trusted him completely with children. He was always very gentle with them. And he would know what to do for a child this small.

"If a big branch hadn't been blocking the culvert," the woman finished as Will carefully laid the child on the table, "he . . . he would have floated away, the water was rushing so fast. It was trying so hard to push him right through the sewer pipe, but the branch wouldn't let go of him. That's what that scratch on his cheek is from. If it hadn't been for that branch, he would have kept going, just disappeared, yanked off to . . . to the river. I never would have found him in time!" Her voice trembled with terror as she reached out to clutch at the child's limp right hand, hanging over the edge of the table. "I did find him in time, didn't I?" When no one answered her, her voice rose. "*Tell* me I found him in time!"

Instead of answering, the nurse asked quietly, "What's his name?"

"What? Oh. His name is Louis. Louie. For my husband. He's out of town. He was supposed to be back tonight, but the weather got so bad, his flight was canceled." Her voice broke. "Oh, God, how am I going to tell him I forgot to lock the door? He'll blame me, he will! He keeps saying three-year-olds don't go out of the house in the dark alone, but Louie does, he does, I don't know why, he just does. . . ."

The nurse did her best to persuade the young mother away from the table, but to no avail. Will knew Susannah could have done it, and felt a wash of anger. Why wasn't she here, where she belonged, when they needed her? He couldn't even remember what had been important enough to drag her away from ER. Something about Abby.

"Why didn't *my* electricity go out?" the young mother wailed. "Driving over here, I saw lots of houses that were dark, and the streetlights were out. If mine had gone out, too, I wouldn't have been watching the late movie, and maybe I would have checked on Louie sooner!"

"Get her out of here!" Dr. Izbecki snapped as he and his colleagues began working on the child. "Give her a sedative. I'll sign the order. All we need now is for her to go into shock on us. Do it, okay?"

Everyone in ER joked about Dr. Izbecki, "His bark is worse than his bedside manner, but not by much." Will respected the man. He knew what he was doing, and what he was doing right now was trying to save the woman's child. For that, he needed her calm and out of the way.

The mother, whose name was Edie Murphy, refused the sedative until Dr. Izbecki, already beginning resuscitation efforts on her child, told her sternly that without it, she would have to be removed from the room. As he worked, he ordered equipment. One nurse reached for an oxygen mask, another reached for a small needle to take blood, while a third ran for the portable chest X ray standing against a wall.

Taking seriously the threat to have her removed from the room, the toddler's mother submitted to the small blue pill one of the nurses handed her. She calmed down almost immediately and was allowed to stay.

Will knew the pill couldn't have worked that quickly, but for some people, just the idea of having taken a sedative calmed them down instantly, before the medicine could possibly have taken effect. He was grateful that this was evidently the case with Mrs. Murphy.

"No pulse, and he's apneic," Dr. Izbecki announced grimly as he worked on the small, limp form. "Let's get going here! We need to bring this one back."

Easier said than done, Will thought to himself. He knew the baby's chances weren't good. Everyone in the room knew it . . . except maybe Edie Murphy. She might not know that *apneic* meant he wasn't breathing. Small children almost always fall into water with their mouths open, filling their lungs very quickly. The child's chances, if he had any, depended on how long he'd been in that ditch before his mother found him.

If Louie died, this woman would never forgive herself. It would be futile to tell her that she hadn't killed her child, the storm had. She'd never believe that. Her husband might not forgive her, either. Will knew that even strong, healthy marriages were often destroyed by the death of a child, compounding the tragedy.

Will also knew you had to be careful administering CPR to a child as small as this one. The risk of tiny ribs breaking under the pressure of chest compressions was greater than with a full-sized teenager or adult. But for all his gruffness, Dr. Izbecki was incredibly gentle.

There was almost total silence in the room as the effort to save the baby's life continued. Other sirens came and went, but everyone stayed where they were. They had a child to revive.

Two more doctors, whom Will recognized as a pediatrician and a cardiopulmonary specialist, arrived and stood by silently, waiting to see if they would be needed. Word of new emergencies traveled fast at Grant Memorial.

"Please, please, please," Edie Murphy breathed, her clenched fists to her mouth, her eyes never leaving the table, "please don't take him from me!"

Will swallowed hard and silently echoed the word *please*.

"We've got a pulse," the nurse announced excitedly. "It's thready, but it's there."

Will knew that Mrs. Murphy was waiting for something dramatic to happen then, like Louie beginning to cough and then maybe cry, to prove that he was back among the living. It wasn't going to happen that way, if it happened at all. They might get a pulse, and he might even begin to breathe on his own . . . although he probably wouldn't, not right away . . . but he wasn't going to sit up and smile at his mom. No television program with a happy ending in thirty minutes here. When they'd finished emergency treatment, he'd be carted off to Pediatric ICU, probably hooked up to a whole bunch of monitors, more wires and tubes in him than a television set. Even then, they wouldn't know for a couple of days if he was going to be okay.

Then Dr. Izbecki said, "Well, all right!" and, heaving a sigh of relief, stood up straight. "This little one is among the living. Get him upstairs, stat! And tell them up there that I want an hourly update, you got that?"

"Yessir," the nurse said. She was smiling.

"He's okay?" Mrs. Murphy cried, taking a step forward. "He's going to be all right?"

Will couldn't stomach watching her face fall again when Dr. Izbecki bluntly explained the dangers still ahead for Edie Murphy's small son, so he offered to escort the gurney upstairs, along with the nurse. No one argued with him.

Behind him, as he left the room pushing the still-limp form on the white, wheeled table, he heard Dr. Izbecki begin, "Mrs. Murphy, I need you to understand what I'm about to say, so please listen carefully."

But . . . at least the baby was still alive. Everyone in ER would be keeping their fingers crossed for him. That should help.

"That was rough," the nurse said, looking down at the boy with compassion in her eyes. "Think he'll make it?"

The elevator arrived, and Will held the door while she pushed the cart inside. "Yes," he said firmly as the door closed, "I do. I think Louie here is going to grow up just fine and live to hear his mother telling stories about how he wandered around at night like a baby vampire when he was only three. That's what I believe."

That was what he *wanted* to believe.

He was still annoyed with Susannah for not being there, for not going through this with him.

What was she doing all this time over at Rehab, anyway?

What Susannah was doing at Rehab was trying to reassure Jeremy Barlow that Kate Thompson was safe.

"I tried to get back to the library again," he'd said when he located her near the linen closet. "I couldn't get there. That whole area is flooding fast. Some of the streets are blocked off. So if she's not there, where *is* she?"

"Wherever she is, I'm sure she's fine. You know Kate. Who can take care of herself better than Kate can?"

"On a night like this?" Jeremy shook his head. His wavy blonde hair was very wet, and drops of water cascaded to the floor. "*Nobody* can take care of themselves in that storm! I was just over in ER, looking for you. I'll bet all those people they're bringing in by ambulance thought they could take care of themselves, too. Thought they could drive through high water, thought they could raft down the Revere, thought they were better and stronger than any dumb old storm." Jeremy's face was reddening.

"Hey, take it easy, man!" Sid called, turning his wheelchair to face the worried boy. "I know Kate Thompson. She goes to my school. She's vice president of our class, and that's because she's organized and efficient. Our friend here is

452

right," waving a hand toward Susannah, who realized with a jolt that he probably didn't remember her name. "You don't need to worry about Kate Thompson." He astonished Susannah by smiling. "No storm is safe around Kate."

Jeremy didn't look convinced.

chapter
14

Although Kate was slender, she was very strong. She had on occasion pushed gurneys carrying patients who weighed twice what she did, and often hefted heavy loads of clean linen from one part of the hospital to another. Nevertheless, she had a terrible time trying to open the long, narrow, floor-to-ceiling window at the top of the stairs leading to the library's small loft. Unlocking the latch had been no problem. But when she reached down, confident that in another minute she would be able to scream for help, she was dismayed to discover that the window was firmly stuck. It probably hadn't been opened in years, if ever.

"I have got" — she tugged and pulled — "to get" — more tugging, more yanking, on the wooden frame — "this window open!" Using all of her strength, she gave the lower pane of glass an angry tug, and it jerked upward half an inch. "Come on, come on!" she urged, renewing her efforts, "I can't scream for help through that little bit of space." As she pulled, she repeatedly glanced over her shoulder toward the foot of the stairs, not so far below her. Although she could see almost nothing in the flat darkness around her, she thought she sensed motion. The floor was moving? No, the floor couldn't be moving. This was a flood, not an earthquake.

But something *on* it was moving.

And Kate knew what that something had to be. Water. Already! In the space of the ten minutes that it had taken her to climb the stairs and wrestle with the window, the water from the basement had gobbled up the remaining two wooden steps leading from the basement and slid across the first floor like spilled syrup.

The window came up another five inches. Then, with an additional tug, it opened all the way to the upper pane of glass.

There were no new iron burglar bars up here as there were on the first floor. Kate stuck her head through the opening. Rain slapped against her face and hair, but she hardly felt it. She was concentrating instead on finding some sign of life out there in that thoroughly saturated world, some person she could call to for help. Even a dog would be better than nothing, because if she started screaming, maybe the dog would bark, and someone would come to find out what all the racket was about.

She was greeted by nothing but an eerie darkness made complete by the absence of streetlights or any kind of illumination emanating from buildings in the area. When her eyes had become accustomed to the darkness, she could make out below her a swirling, muddy river, completely encompassing the building. She didn't need anyone to tell her that the water surrounding the library was rising steadily. What had happened in the basement was proof enough of that.

"I'm in the middle of the damn Revere River!" she cried out in disbelief. "You're supposed to be blocks away from here!" she shouted angrily. "What are you *doing* in this part of the city?"

Stupid girl, she chided mentally. You know perfectly well what it's doing. It's flooding, that's what! And you're stuck right in the middle of it. Because you had your feet up on a chair and weren't paying attention.

There was no point at all in screaming, she knew that. There was no one out there. Why would anybody in their right mind, which of course excluded *her,* be out on a night like this? All of Grant had probably been warned to stay inside their nice, safe, dry homes, and *they'd* paid attention.

She didn't know how to swim. She had never learned. There was no public pool in Eastridge, and traveling across town to the Y was too much of a hassle. If the building were on fire and flames were nipping at her heels, she'd have to jump to the ground and take her chances. It wasn't that high up. A story and a half. Maybe she'd break an ankle or a wrist when she hit the ground.

But there *was* no ground down there. Only water. Muddy, swirling, angry water. There was a gurgling sound below her. She looked down upon the wide, carpeted steps to her right. She couldn't be sure, but it seemed to her that the bottom step was now awash.

How could the water be rising so quickly?

"Stop *raining*!" she shouted out the window. "Stop it!"

The only answer she got was an angry gust of wind smacking her in the face so hard, she recoiled from the window in shock.

"I have to do something!" Jeremy insisted as he and Susannah walked back to ER.

"Well, just don't worry her family, okay? Her mother's on duty. At least, she was when I left ER. Don't say anything to her. Why don't you try the library again?"

"I told you, I can't *get* there! Besides, I thought we agreed that she couldn't be there. It's been closed since the first time I went over there. Unless she got locked in somehow, she's not there."

"Maybe she did."

The lights in the enclosed corridor, courtesy of the emergency generator, cast a sickly yellow pallor across Jeremy's face as he turned his head to look at Susannah. "Maybe she did what?"

"Maybe she got locked in. You know how she is. I've studied with her once or twice. She disappears, totally, into any book she's reading. That could have happened, Jeremy." They rounded a corner, arriving at the glass door to ER. Susannah pulled it open. "There's a side door in the basement Kate sometimes uses. If she went inside that way, the librarian wouldn't even have known she was down there. And if she was concentrating the way she usually does, she might not have heard him leave. He could have locked her in accidentally."

"Finally!" Will exclaimed when he saw Susannah approaching. "Where have you been?"

"But I went over there," Jeremy argued. "It was pitch-black inside the library."

"The electricity could be out, Jeremy. That doesn't mean Kate's not *in* there! I think you should figure out a way to get over there and double-check." Susannah turned to Will to ask, "Kate's not here, is she? She didn't come in while I was gone?"

He shook his head no.

She turned back to Jeremy. "She's not here, and she's not at Rehab, and I don't know where else she could be. If she's in the library, and the whole area is flooded, she won't be able to get out. Not without help."

Jeremy looked dubious at the idea of *him* being the help Kate needed. So did Will. "I might be able to get through in my truck," Will said. "It rides pretty high off the ground."

Jeremy bristled. "I can do it myself. If I can't drive in, I'll swim in."

Will nodded. "Okay. I just thought I'd offer. I mean, we could go together. Like they say, two heads are better than one."

"I don't need you." To Susannah, Jeremy said, "I'll bring her back here. If I don't find her, I'll come back, anyway, so you'll know."

In spite of Will's obvious skepticism, Susannah believed that Jeremy *would* find Kate and bring her safely to Med Center. He had, after all, recently saved the life of a girl who'd been drowning in a private pool at a party in Susannah's neighborhood. Two football players had tossed the girl who, unknown to the boys, was in the first stages of the virus sweeping the city of Grant, into the pool. Then the boys had gone inside, not realizing that the girl was in trouble. Too weak and ill to save herself, she would have drowned if Jeremy hadn't arrived.

"What'd I say?" Will asked, a bewildered expression on his face when Jeremy, his back stiff, his jaw jutting forward with determination, had left the building.

"Nothing." Silently, Susannah wished Jeremy good luck. If he came back to ER without Kate, they would have to tell Astrid Thompson the bad news and see what she thought should be done to locate her daughter.

She had to admit that until Jeremy came back with Kate, every time a gurney came rushing in, she'd immediately look to see if the patient might be a tall, slender girl with dark, cornrowed hair, heavy wooden earrings dangling from her earlobes.

No, that couldn't happen. Kate would be okay. Kate could take care of herself.

As an ambulance pulled up in front of the entrance and Susannah joined Will in the familiar rush to the door, she hoped fervently that she was right.

Abby had almost no voice left. Although she continued to shout the names of her sisters as she and Callie struggled through the deep water covering Massachusetts Avenue, what came out of her mouth was little more than a hoarse croak. "We need a boat," she called across the water to Callie. The water was at Callie's waist, and Abby knew the girl couldn't go much farther. It was too dangerous. Callie weighed less than a hundred pounds. It was amazing that she'd managed to trek this far, with the current tugging viciously at her. "We need to give this up and go get some help. Maybe we can find a rescue crew somewhere around here."

"Abby! Abby, up here!" Geneva's voice came

not from the riverbed to their left, which Abby had dreaded, knowing it would be impossible to rescue anyone out there without a boat, but from somewhere ahead of them. Up? Geneva had shouted, "Up here!" Up where?

Abby raised her head, peering into the dark night. It was impossible to see. Every last bit of light had disappeared when the electricity blinked off some time ago. "Where are you, Geneva," Abby called.

"We're here, up in this tree!"

"Omigod, they climbed a tree!" Callie shouted. "They actually climbed a tree? Well, I'm not climbing any tree, Abigail O'Connor, I promise you that!"

A floating garbage can, metal and very large, slammed Abby in the small of her back. She would have fallen facedown into the water had there not been a parking meter to her right. She grabbed it and held on. The garbage can continued on its way. "Geneva? Keep shouting, so we can find you. We can't see a thing! Keep making noise. Sing or something."

There was moment or two of silence, then Geneva's deep, strong voice and Carmel's sweet soprano broke into a chorus of "Row, Row, Row Your Boat."

"So, what do we do when we find the tree they're in?" Callie asked, weakness and impatience in her voice.

"I'm going to kill them. We'll get them down out of the tree and then we'll drown them."

"Then what are we going to all this trouble for?" Callie grumbled. She was shaking with cold, her teeth chattering uncontrollably.

"Gently down the stream . . ."

Abby brushed a strand of thoroughly saturated hair from her eyes and glanced over at Callie. Most of the time, Callie was shallow, selfish, and spoiled. But if it weren't for Callie, Abby thought, trying to hurry, I'd be out here all alone. I don't even want to *think* about that. "Callie," she called, "in case I don't get a chance later, thanks. Thanks for . . . for being here."

"Life is but a dream. Row, row, row . . ."

"Right. Let's say you owe me, O'Connor. Let's say maybe you could think about getting me a date with one of those cute Grant High football players, okay?" Callie batted aside a pair of potted plants floating toward her. "You're a cheerleader. They're all your friends. They don't ask me out because I go to private school. See what you can do, okay? And we'll call it even."

Abby laughed, a laugh that got lost in the whistling of the wind, and thought, I should have known she'd want something. That's Callie.

"Gently down the stream . . ."

Then, suddenly, the singing voices were directly over their heads. They looked up. Carmel was on the lowest branch, a thin limb that didn't look strong enough to hold her. Abby could barely make out Geneva's taller, heavier shape on the branch above Carmel.

"I'm going to kill both of you," she called up, trying to steady herself against the rushing water by hugging the tree trunk. "But first, you have to come down."

"I can't," Carmel said tremulously. "I'm too scared. Abby? I can't come down. You have to come up and get me."

Jeremy had driven as far as he dared. The moment he felt the wheels losing their grip on the road, he pulled over and parked on a slope, then set out on foot, flashlight in hand, toward the library. Taking side streets and shortcuts, he managed to avoid the most heavily flooded streets. Until he came to Market Street, two blocks north of the library. It was there that he had to begin wading in earnest.

He stood at the corner, knee-deep in water, looking down toward where the street had been. Now, there was nothing but water, churning and swirling under his flashlight. It had risen so high on the library building, the lower set of windows had disappeared entirely, and they were tall windows.

If Kate is in there, he thought grimly, striking

out from the corner with a look of fierce determination on his square-jawed face, she's in deep trouble.

"But I don't *want* to go upstairs, Sam!" Becka protested. "It's so nice down here, and we've got everything we need, and the stereo isn't portable, so we can't take it up there with us, and we won't have any music, and . . ."

Sam put up a hand, interrupting her. He knew what she was doing. Becka wasn't stupid. She had already guessed why they had to move upstairs, and she didn't want to hear it. If he said it aloud, actually *said* it, that would make it real, and she didn't want that. She was afraid.

And, he realized reluctantly, so was he.

chapter
15

Patients continued to stream into Emergency. Some had cuts and bruises from scrambling to safety as the car in which they were traveling to higher ground began to waver in the rushing waters. Others, not so lucky, were suffering from shock, broken limbs, or deep lacerations after their vehicles had been swept off the road and into a stone wall or another car. People who had waited until the last possible moment to evacuate their homes staggered in thoroughly soaked, shaken, and cold to the bone. There were two more near-drownings within seconds of each other.

Every treatment and trauma room was occupied. Susannah ran from one room to another, restocking supplies, taking information from relatives or friends, carrying hot coffee to the harried medical staff.

The moment there was another lull in activity in ER, Susannah went to the phone to see if it was working yet. The dial tone came and went.

She took a chance, dialing Abby's house, and she got through.

"No," Moira said, her voice cracking slightly. "They're not back yet."

"We should have gone for more help," Callie complained, "like I wanted. We can't get them down out of this tree by ourselves." She was clinging to the trunk of the tree as if it were a life preserver. In a way, it was. The tree was only a few yards from the riverbank, long since submerged, and the water was highest where they stood. Or tried to stand. The current was so strong, Callie was repeatedly swept off her feet, remaining where she was only because she was clutching the tree. "I can't hold on here forever, Abby," she shouted. "What are we going to do? We need help! We've been in this water for hours. It's the middle of the night already. My mother's asleep, but yours must be going crazy!"

Neither the wind nor the rain had lessened even a little bit. Callie's long hair, unrestrained in the absence of her hat, whipped around her face. She didn't dare loosen her grip on the tree to brush the hair out of her eyes.

Abby, her own hair wet, her face ruddy with windburn, hung on to the tree and shouted back, "Where would we get help? Everyone's out rescuing people from flooded houses, and from stranded cars! And we can't wait! The water's going to climb right up into this tree and pluck my sisters out if we don't do something *now*! I'm not leaving without them. Listen, you climb up onto my shoulders, okay? You're shorter than me. And lighter." Stooping to feel beneath the water with one hand, she called, "Here! I found something. There's a big, fat knot on the lower part of the tree. You can use that to push yourself up onto my shoulders. Then you can go up there and grab Carmel." Although Abby's shouts sounded steady enough, she was shaking with fear. The water was up to her waist. Carmel was only eight, and not tall like Moira and Geneva. If they did get her down out of the tree, wouldn't the water be over Carmel's head?

I'll have to carry her, Abby decided, and groaned mentally. In this current? They would probably both drown.

Abby snapped at Callie, "Well, what are you waiting for? We don't have a lot of time here, Callie. We do this kind of stuff in cheerleading all the time. It's easy."

"Yeah, well, you don't do it in the middle of a flood. And *I'm* not a cheerleader, Abby." But Callie knew there wasn't any choice. She sloshed over to grip Abby's strong, round shoulders, took a deep breath and, fumbling around with her booted foot until she found the thick knot on the tree trunk, which she used as a step, she hoisted her own slender body upward. She was so water-laden, she weighed more than usual, so the maneuver that should have been a simple one for someone so lightweight and agile took far more strength than she'd expected. It took her three tries before she succeeded. When she was perched on Abby's shoulders, the boots of her heels digging painfully into Abby's flesh, Callie swayed precariously and almost fell backward into the river below her.

"Be careful!" Abby screamed.

"I can't be careful! Oh, God, this is *so* not a good idea!" But Callie steadied herself by grabbing the upper branch Carmel was lying on and clutching it with a white-knuckled grip, and reached out for Carmel's hand.

Carmel flinched. "No! I'm not moving. You'll drown me! I'm staying here until a rescue boat comes."

"No, you're *not!*" Geneva shouted from the branch above Carmel's head. "You are getting out of this tree right this minute, Carmel O'Connor! Because I can't go down until you do. You're in my way. I need that branch you're hugging. And I am *not* staying up here. Now get going!"

And although Carmel burst into tears of terror, she sat up slowly, carefully. Her sweatshirt and jeans were so wet, they clung to her skin, her short, dark hair dripped like her tears, and her eyes were wide with shock and fear. "Don't drop me, okay? Please don't drop me," she pleaded.

"What I'm going to do," Callie said as patiently as she could manage in view of her own terror, "is hand you down to your sister. She can let go of the tree with one hand and take yours. You stay right there with her now, you hear? The water is really rough, and it will pull on you, but you can't let go of Abby's hand. Promise?"

"I promise," Carmel agreed through her tears.

She weighed more than Callie had expected. A one-handed grip on a water-laden eight-year-old when perched uncertainly on someone else's shoulders high above a raging river would have been completely impossible if Callie hadn't feared for her own life. Her determination to survive allowed her to hand the terrified child down to her sister, who let go of the tree with one hand and grabbed Carmel's arm the very second it was within reach. Carmel's feet never touched the ground. The water picked her legs up and tore at them, in an earnest effort to rip her from Abby's grasp. Abby held on. So did Carmel.

But Abby didn't know how long they could hold on to each other, or how long she could bear the pain of Callie's heels digging into her shoulders, or how long Callie could remain where she was.

And Geneva was still up in the tree.

* * *

Three ambulances arrived at ER at once, carrying victims stranded in an office elevator when the electricity failed. Two were unconscious from lack of air, the third suffering a broken leg as a result of his heroic but disastrous attempt to climb out through the elevator's ceiling. The fourth, a pregnant woman in her third trimester, was experiencing early labor pains.

"Saw it on a movie on television," the failed hero, his words breathy and weak, told Will as the gurney rolled toward a treatment room. "This guy on TV, he saved the lives of eight people, all stranded in an elevator during a fire. Just climbed right up there and opened that little window in the ceiling, climbed out, shinnied down the cable, swung his way across to another floor, and got help. Saved all them people. Me, I couldn't even get the little door in the ceiling open. Fell right back down, clumsy as a ten-ton gorilla. Felt like a fool, I tell you. Landed on a metal cleaning cart the maintenance guy had on the elevator with him. That's how I broke my leg. How is he, anyway?"

"He'll be okay," Will answered. "He's getting oxygen now, they all are. That'll perk them right up." He steered the cart into a room where a doctor he didn't recognize and two nurses were waiting.

"What about the lady with the baby? She told

me while we were sitting there on the floor that she wasn't due for another six weeks. She going to be okay?"

"Can't tell you that. They won't bring her in here, though. They'll take her straight upstairs to OB-GYN. They'll take good care of her. Even if she does have the baby, our Neonatal Intensive Care is one of the best."

The nurses and doctor began checking the man's vital signs, which seemed to be normal. His only injury appeared to be the broken leg. And wounded pride. "Neonatal? What's that?"

"Newborn. Intensive care for preemies and babies born with problems. If that baby decides not to wait, its mother couldn't have come to a better place."

"Wish I could figure out how that guy on TV got out of that elevator," the man said, already drowsy from the medication a nurse had given him for pain.

When he had been taken upstairs to Orthopedics to have the leg set, Will went to the nurses' desk to inquire about the pregnant woman.

"She'll be fine," Nurse Thompson told him. She looked exhausted, with dark circles under her eyes. Will had never seen her looking anything but bright and cheerful. She should have stayed home, after working a double shift. "They took her upstairs. Susannah went along, for moral support. She's very good in situations like that, you know."

Will knew.

"But," Nurse Thompson continued, "I don't think they'll be keeping the woman. That baby's not going to show up tonight."

"Good. How about the other two?"

"Fine. They've already been treated and sent home. If they can get there. I'm surprised we haven't had more cases like theirs. Elevators must have stopped all over the city when the electricity went out."

"Maybe most people left work early," Will suggested. "Because of the storm." He wanted to ask if she'd heard from Kate, but she looked so tired, he couldn't do it. If she'd heard anything, she would have said so. "Aaron working on the sandbag lines?" he asked instead.

"Um-hum. Him and his father. And practically everyone else in Eastridge. They said on TV that it was bad over there." A worried frown creased her brow. "I'd go sandbag, too, if I wasn't needed here. Three of our night nurses didn't make it in." She sipped coffee from a Styrofoam cup, then added, "I wonder if our homes will be there when we return."

Will lived only two blocks from the Thompsons. "They made it through the last time. Six years ago."

Nurse Thompson nodded. "This one might be worse, though. The rain hasn't let up at all. I can't remember how long it rained that last time."

Will didn't remember, either. And he really didn't want to.

Now that Kate had the library's upstairs window wide open, she couldn't see that it had done her any good. She wasn't going to jump into that black, swirling lake beneath her window. All she seemed to have accomplished so far was soaking herself and the rose-colored carpet in the loft.

She had to do *something*. Since she couldn't go down the stairs, she would have to go *up*. Up and away from the water, which was about to swallow up the third of the six steps and was now not that far from where she stood at the top of the stairs.

Kate poked her head and upper body through the open window. She twisted slightly to glance to the side, where she noticed a thick, white drainpipe. Its lower half had disappeared beneath the water below, but the upper half edged its way up the corner of the building to the roof.

I was the first person in my sixth-grade class to climb the rope, Kate thought, studying the drainpipe. The very first.

The drainpipe was not a rope. It wasn't rough,

with fibers to cling to. It was metal and smooth and shiny, and slick with rainwater. But it was all she had.

Kate pulled back from the window, turning to look down upon the steps again. Floodwater was continuing to reach for her at a horrifyingly rapid pace.

She spun around again, facing the window, and put one leg over the low sill.

At the corner, Jeremy tried to plan the best way to get to the library without actually diving into the water and swimming. There was too much debris in the water. A kitchen chair floated by, then a cuckoo clock, and a doghouse.

He aimed his flashlight across the water toward the library. All he saw, beyond the street-sign pole and closed, dark shops, was more water, almost all the way up to the building's upper floor. No sign of life. No lights. It was just him and the rain and the wind. Jeremy raised the light, played it on the library's small, upper-story window, expecting to see nothing.

Instead, he saw movement. Even with the light, he couldn't make out exactly what the movement was, or what it meant. "Kate?" he called automatically.

His voice was swallowed up by the storm. And in the next second, before he could convince himself that he really *had* seen something there in the library's upper-story window, a sudden, powerful gust of wind caught the street-sign pole, which read FIFTH STREET on one side and MARKET STREET on the other, yanked it out of the ground where it had been stationed since before Jeremy was born, and slammed it down upon Jeremy's head and back, knocking him off his feet and into the gushing torrent, face first.

"I've been trying to call the fishing lodge," Susannah told Will as they took a much-needed break. Instead of retreating to the staff lounge, they had taken up a position at the hospital's front double-glass door, where they could look out upon the storm. "I can't get through. The line isn't busy. There's just this weird sound after I dial; you know, that absence of sound you get when there's nothingness?"

"That lodge is on the South Side, right? Those lines are probably down. Ours could go out at any second, and stay out. There's a scary thought. How would anyone call us?"

"They're not calling us now, much. The phones have been quiet for the past hour. Astrid says it's because ours are probably the only working phones left in the city."

They were quiet for a few minutes. Then Will leaned against the door, facing Susannah, and said, his tone casual, "So, did you mean what you said about working in my clinic?"

"Of course I did. I wouldn't have said so if I didn't mean it."

He knew that was true. Susannah wasn't the kind of person to say things she didn't mean. Callie was, and Sam probably was, too. At least with girls. But not Susannah.

Will looked straight at her. "It'd be hard. We'd get all kinds in the kind of clinic I want. You're not really used to all kinds, Susannah. No offense, but you're not. Living up there, on that hill, so far above everybody else? Real life doesn't reach up that high, does it?"

She didn't get mad, as he'd been afraid she would. "No," she answered calmly, "real life doesn't very often intrude on Linden Hill. But," she added, her voice firm, "I work *here*, Will. And we get all kinds here, too." She lifted her chin proudly. "I think I'm pretty good at dealing with all kinds of people."

"I wasn't insulting you, Susannah," he said gently, reaching out to take her hand in his. "I just want you to know that the kind of clinic I have in mind for Eastridge won't be a piece of cake."

"I don't eat cake." Smiling up at him, Susannah curled her fingers tightly around his. "Except on my birthday. Too much cholesterol. What kind of doctor are you going to be if you don't warn people away from something so hazardous to their health?"

He laughed. "I *was* warning you away from something that could be hazardous to your health. My clinic. Is it my fault you refuse to take my warning seriously?"

They stood in the doorway, their hands linked, looking silently into each other's eyes.

chapter
16

"I have to go get one of the boats," Sam told the friend standing at his elbow, a boy named Chad Beck. They were outside, on the lodge's upper veranda. Everyone else was still inside, talking quietly, and dozing. All traces of party atmosphere had left them in the last hour when the seriousness of their situation had finally sunk in.

On the veranda, Sam used the large black flashlight to illuminate the river now surrounding them completely. It had risen to less than two feet below the spot where they stood. He was surprised by how noisy the water was. It churned and it bubbled and boiled and it smacked angrily at the doors and windows, as if it were very angry to find this large, solid obstacle in its path.

"How are you going to get to the boathouse?" Chad asked him.

"Swim." Sam's voice was grim. Swimming in that debris-laden, roiling mess wouldn't be anything like swimming in the river when it was calm, as he'd been doing all of his life. "I'll swim to the boathouse, free one of the smaller boats, and come back to get all of you."

"And how do *we* get into the boat?" Chad asked, staring anxiously down into the churning black river beneath them.

"You jump," Sam answered grimly. "And you hope your aim isn't off. Now go back inside and keep everyone busy so they don't notice I've taken a leap off this veranda."

Chad did as he'd been told.

Sam shed his sneakers, took a deep breath, and dove over the railing into the water.

The ambulance had brought in two children who had been hurled into floodwaters while hiding in a tree house from a father angry because they had neglected their chores. While they were still in their refuge, the tree had been uprooted by the powerfully angry wind and tossed into the river. Rescue crews had rescued the children, who had bravely clung to the tree throughout their long, cold, wet ride.

Their father, quietly contrite now, had arrived twenty minutes after the ambulance. Mr. Samuelson paced anxiously back and forth in the waiting room while the children were being treated for hypothermia from their stay in the cold water, abrasions from floating debris, and a broken wrist on the younger of the two boys.

They were lying on separate gurneys in the same trauma room, covered with warming blankets, their faces turned toward each other. They had stopped shivering. Their countless abrasions were being cleaned and disinfected. Susannah held the five-year-old's hand while Dr. Lincoln applied a soothing salve to the cuts, most of which were on his face, arm, and hands.

"We're really gonna get it now," the older boy told his brother. "If you thought he was mad before, wait'll you see how mad he is when we get outa here! We prob'ly won't be allowed out of the house for a *year*!"

His brother began shivering again. He was in pain because of his fractured wrist and had been given a sedative, but it hadn't taken effect yet. The wrist, still unwrapped, would be tended to upstairs in Orthopedics.

"Your father won't hit you boys, will he?" Dr. Lincoln asked calmly as she daubed antiseptic on one last cut. Susannah knew she wouldn't have asked if the boys hadn't seemed so frightened. Of course that could have been from their brush with death. "Nah." The older boy, who had said his name was Tim, burrowed deeper beneath the warming blanket. "Our dad just yells a lot, that's all. He don't believe in hittin' people smaller than him, and we're smaller than him." He heaved a deep sigh of relief. "Good thing, too."

As they left the treatment room, Dr. Lincoln

said, "You were very good with those boys in there. Calming them down, reassuring them. I saw you holding the older boy's hand when I was disinfecting his wounds. And I've seen you work with children before. You have a gift. Have you thought about a career in pediatrics?"

Susannah was surprised by the praise. Everyone in ER said that if a word of praise ever came from Dr. Lincoln's lips, it would die of shock on the way out of her mouth. She was a stern taskmaster, with very high standards.

Unsure of how to respond, Susannah said slowly, "I think . . . well, I think I might go into family practice."

"Good thinking. You're going to make a fine doctor, Grant. Keep your grades up, stay on here for experience, and apply to every school in the country. The competition is keen, you know that. You'll have to fight to get in."

That pleased Susannah more than the compliment had. She knows who I am, she thought, she knows who my father is. Everyone in the hospital knows that. But instead of taking it for granted that Samuel Grant II could use his considerable influence and equally considerable fortune to guarantee his daughter a place at Harvard or Yale, Dr. Lincoln was implying that Susannah would have to fight for that place on her own. She liked that idea, liked it very much. Besides, she already knew where she wanted to go to college. Right here in Grant. She was going to Grant University, along with Will, Kate, and Abby, no matter what kind of fit her parents threw. "I will fight for it," she promised Dr. Lincoln. "Medicine is the only field I'm interested in. So I'll do whatever I have to."

"Good. Anytime you have any questions, please feel free to come to me."

When the two had separated, Susannah hurried to the telephone again to try Abby's house.

Abby felt as if her back were going to crack in two. With Callie on her shoulders and Carmel's weight dragging on her right arm, her spine ached with a ferocious pain. "Get Geneva down!" she gasped. "Callie, hurry! I'm going to fold!"

"Can she swim?"

"Yes!"

"Geneva!" Callie shouted upward at Geneva. "Jump!"

"From *here*? It's too far! I'm up higher than Carmel was."

"Well, I *know* that, Geneva. But it's not that far to the ground anymore because the ground isn't where it used to be. In fact, it's not there at all. There's only water. The water is much higher than the ground was. So you don't have very far to jump at all. Just be prepared to start swimming the minute you land."

Turning her head to look down at Abby, Callie said, "We should all take my advice and just dive in and start swimming. Look, the water's almost up to your chest now. We can't walk in this. We've *got* to swim."

"I don't think I can," Abby said, her voice hoarse. "I think I'm too tired."

Carmel cried, "You can't be too tired, Abby. You have to take care of *me*." She started crying again. "I'm not a very good swimmer. I try, but I always sink."

"Okay, you guys, watch out below!" There was a splash to their right as Geneva hit the water and immediately began stroking away from them.

"Why didn't she do that before?" Callie complained. "And swim home? Then we wouldn't have had to go through this hell."

"Because she'd never leave Carmel!" Abby snapped. "Now, could you please get down? Before I collapse?"

Abby was never sure what, exactly, happened next. Callie tried to jump down, but something went wrong and in the next second, Callie screamed and began to topple sideways, to the right. But her feet remained firmly planted on Abby's shoulders for another moment, and that pull, plus the tug of Carmel's weight on Abby's right arm, tipped Abby sideways, too. By the time Callie's feet left her shoulders, it was too late. Abby had already lost her balance. Callie hit the water with a startled cry, and then so did Abby. Carmel, still clinging to Abby's right arm, completely disappeared beneath the surface.

Abby, splashing frantically in the deep, rushing water, trying desperately to orient herself to this newest shock, screamed Carmel's name. But the icy, viselike grip on her arm was gone.

Her little sister was gone, too.

"I hear you have magical powers with small people," Will told Susannah. She was sitting at the admissions desk and had just tried again, in vain, to call Abby's house. "Maybe we'll make pediatrics a specialty in our clinic."

She was too worried to respond. "No one answers at the O'Connor house," she said flatly, swiveling in her chair to face him.

At her failure to respond to his praise, his own face fell. And closed against her, as she'd seen it do so often before. Each time she thought they were drawing closer, breaking down the barriers between them, something happened. Sometimes it was something he said or did, sometimes she was responsible. Like now.

"I can't help it!" she cried defensively. "I know Abby would have been back here by now if she could have been. Something is really wrong. And as far as I know, Kate hasn't been heard from, either." She looked up at Will, her eyes dark with anxiety. "I haven't forgotten that sixteen people died in the last flood, Will. Sixteen!"

He relented then, his face easing again. He moved to put a comforting arm around her shoulders. "There isn't anything we can do about Abby or Kate, Susannah."

Before Susannah could respond, a call came over the PA system announcing incoming.

"This is a bad one," Dr. Izbecki called to them as he ran past, headed for the entrance. "Church bus bringing a load of teenagers back from a concert swept off the road, hit a tree, caught on fire. We've got criticals! Get everyone available down here, *now*! Call a house code, do whatever you have to, just *do* it!"

chapter
17

Panicking, Abby began thrashing wildly against the floodwaters, screaming Carmel's name repeatedly.

"Calm down, for pete's sake!" Callie shouted, turning to swim back to Abby. "Where *is* she? Where did she go?"

Abby stopped thrashing. "I don't know! I can't see a thing!" Abby's voice caught on a sob. "Carmel doesn't swim that well, Callie. And this current . . . she's so little. . . ."

"Relax, I'll find her. You go catch up with Geneva." Without waiting for an answer, Callie took a deep breath and dove beneath the rushing water in search of Carmel.

Although Callie Matthews was the last person in the world Abby would normally have trusted to handle an emergency, she knew she had no choice now. Callie stood a much better chance of finding Carmel than Carmel's own sister, who was a competent swimmer in a nice, quiet, peaceful swimming pool but not expert enough to battle the uncontrolled fury of the Revere on its rampage.

Trusting the one person she had never expected to trust, Abby struck out after Geneva.

The victims from the bus accident had thrown ER into chaos that would have been carefully controlled, had they not been understaffed. The more seriously injured arrived by ambulance, the minor injuries by police car. All had been delivered by boat to the vehicles waiting on higher, dry ground.

Susannah and Will ran from room to room, helping wherever they could. Portable X-ray machines needed for immediate diagnosis of broken limbs and chest or head injuries flew back and forth along the busy corridors. They ran out of gauze in one treatment room, sending Susannah upstairs for more. Will temporarily took over patient charts as she ran errands, racing up the stairs because they were quicker than the elevator.

"X ray shows a pneumothorax!" Dr. Lincoln called, reaching for a chest tube. "Let's get air into this child." She was working on a patient from the bus crash whose left leg was so bloody, Susannah couldn't tell if the limb was still inside the jeans. "Chest tube!"

Susannah knew a pneumothorax was medical

terminology for a collapsed lung. Which could be deadly. Lucky for the patient that Dr. Lincoln hadn't missed it. Air would have collected around the lung, the lung would have begun pushing on the heart, shifting it so the heart couldn't fill with blood, it would quit working, and the young patient would go into cardiac arrest.

Inserting a chest tube to suck the air out of the lung so that it could re-expand was a painful procedure for the patient. But Susannah decided this particular patient, who hadn't made a sound since he'd been brought into the room, wouldn't even be aware of the pain.

At least he hadn't been burned, like some of the other patients. All of the burn victims had hastily been transferred to the Burn Unit hospital next door. They had been trapped by flames near the front door of the bus. The side door had been imploded by the collision and wouldn't open. A police officer had told the staff that someone had ripped a metal rail from one of the seats and used it as a battering ram against a bus window, creating an escape route. He was one of those who had been taken to the Burn Unit. Although no one had said so, Susannah suspected that he'd waited to escape himself until everyone else had jumped to safety, and the flames had caught up with him while he waited.

Blood and mud smeared the white tile

floors. Policemen who had accompanied incoming leaned wearily against the walls outside the rooms, drinking hot coffee, not talking. They had reports to file, and were waiting for follow-up news on the victims before going back out into the storm. They were careful to move out of the way of any wheeled or foot traffic.

If we had the burn patients, too, Susannah thought as she opened a fresh package of gauze pads, we'd be going insane. All she knew about those patients was that of the six, three were suspected to have third-degree burns, while the other four were more likely to have mostly second degree. She felt sorry for the three. If they lived, they would suffer terribly.

But she learned a moment later that they wouldn't be suffering after all. "Just got a call," a nurse named Ruby said, poking her head into treatment room three. "The severe burn patients didn't make it. Sorry." Then she disappeared as quickly as she had arrived.

"That brings the total to five," Dr. Lincoln murmured, concentrating on the stitches she was making in a deep leg laceration. "I'm keeping track."

Confused, Susannah asked, "What total?"

Lincoln lifted her head. "Fatalities. From the storm. The flood."

"There'll be more," the doctor said matter-of-factly, finishing her work with a flourish of the needle. She clipped the suture with surgical scissors. "More drownings, especially. We're just getting started, Grant. Even if we got through the night without a single drowning victim, which is as likely as me getting off work anytime soon, they'll be finding more bodies after the mud settles. They always do."

Susannah felt sick. Five people dead! She glanced up at the fat, round clock on the wall. Three twenty-six. Hours yet until dawn. And morning didn't necessarily mean an end to the storm. When Susannah cocked an ear to listen, it sounded just as loud outside as it had earlier. The wind, the rain smacking against the windows. Why did people always say things would look better in the morning? If the storm didn't end, nothing would look better. And nothing would *be* better.

"You look terrible," Astrid Thompson told her flatly when Susannah walked out to the desk. "Go into the lounge and sack out. That's an order! You aren't even supposed to be here. I chased you and Will out hours ago. If you won't lie down, you'll have to go home, and I mean that."

Susannah was too tired to argue. After a quick glance around to see where Will was, and not finding him, she went to the lounge and flopped down on the worn tweed couch.

* * *

Kate settled on the slightly peaked roof of the library, crouching on her hands and knees, rain and wind battering her mercilessly. She wondered how she had managed to climb up the slick, wet drainpipe. She couldn't believe she had made it. There had been moments when her knees, gripping the pipe tightly, had slipped, or the palms of her hands had slid an inch downward, and she had thought for sure she was going to end up in that murky mess below her.

But she hadn't. The distance from the window to the roof had been a short one, and she had been determined. So she had made it. She had no idea what to do now, but at least she had bought herself some time. It would take a while for the water seeping up the steps to climb another half-story. And that *would* happen. She didn't believe for a minute that it wouldn't. This building was lower than many of the houses in Eastridge, and she could clearly remember people there sitting on the roofs of their small homes waiting for rescue, the water nearly as high as the rooflines.

But she was safe for a moment. Wet and cold and in danger of being blown right off her perch by gusting winds that bent the trees opposite her, she was, however, still safe. Comparatively speaking.

When she thought she heard someone call her name, she was sure she was hallucinating. Her first reaction was, it's the shock of climbing up that drainpipe, knowing the whole time that I was risking my stupid life. It did something to my brain. Or my hearing. There is *no* one out there!

She shook her wet head to clear it of the illusion that someone in this dark, empty, silent world was actually speaking to her.

"Kate? Are you in there?"

Carefully, holding on tightly to the roof shingles, Kate peered over the edge. Her eyes had become accustomed now to the unbroken darkness and she was able to make out outlines and shadows. There was definitely an outline down there, something moving near the doorway. Floating? A log, a garbage can, a piece of furniture?

No, those were arms waving. That was a *person* down there?

The object shouted. "Kate! Kate, are you here?"

It *was* a person! Someone had come to get her? Who?

"Kate, answer me if you're in there!"

Kate sagged backward on her heels with relief. But she was so astonished, giddy laughter bubbled up inside her throat. Jeremy Barlow, spoiled and rich and pampered every bit as much as Callie Matthews, had braved this atrocious night to come looking for Kate Thompson?

Will's appearance on the scene wouldn't have

surprised her. He had known she intended to go to the library, and he was a close friend. Or the arrival of Sam Grant wouldn't have been such a shock. He had dropped her off here. He might have come back to offer her a safe ride home.

But Jeremy? Why wasn't he safe in his palatial home on Linden Boulevard, lying on a leather couch in his den, a fire in the fireplace she was sure the den possessed, watching television on what was surely a giant screen? What was he doing down there, swimming around in that cold, filthy water?

You *know* what he's doing down there, Kate told herself, leaning over the edge again. Hasn't he been shouting your name? He's looking for *you*, twit!

"Jeremy!" she called. "I'm up here!"

Sam was amazed at how easy it was to swim into the boathouse and untie a small motorboat. He was going in the right direction, and the current obligingly carried him swiftly to the spot where the boathouse lay underwater. He could no longer even see the roofline of the small structure. But two rowboats and a small motorboat had been yanked out of the boathouse by the current, and though still moored, were accessible to Sam. He grabbed the edge of the motorboat as he reached it.

Getting into it was no small task, given the

current and the maddening bobbing of the boat. But Sam was determined. Using his broad shoulders and considerable upper-body strength, courtesy of hours of intense tennis playing, he managed to climb into the boat. He struggled to light the lantern affixed to the front of the boat, and finally had to give up, the wind huffing out every match he lit. Then he realized it would be essential to bail before he dared pull away into open water. That took many precious minutes. When he felt it was safe to venture forth, he tried again to light the lantern and this time, succeeded. Then he wasted more valuable time fighting with the motor. It balked.

He refused to give up. The wind tugged and pulled at him angrily, the rain slapped his face, but he kept trying to bring the motor to life. He had to get those people out of the cabin.

After many tries, his perseverance was rewarded by a roar from the motor. He was on his way. He untied the boat and, using the garish yellow glow of the lantern, headed for the lodge.

When he finally reached the cabin, Chad was waiting on the upper veranda. He leaned over the railing. "Everyone's rattled!" he shouted. "The water's only got three more steps to go before it pours into the bedrooms. They thought you weren't coming back! Some of them," he added hastily.

Sam tossed him a rope. "Tie this around the

railing until we're loaded up! Then go get everyone, bring them out here! Hurry up!"

Chad did as he'd been told. When he returned, the other four were with him, their tense faces turned a sickly yellow by the light from Sam's boat.

"You'll have to jump!" Sam shouted, struggling to keep the boat as steady as possible. "Jump in, grab the rope, and follow it to the boat. I'll haul you in."

The looks on their faces told him how frightened they were at the thought of jumping into the rough water.

"You have no choice! That whole floor is going to be underwater before long! The water's only a couple of feet below you. Kind of like jumping into a pool from a diving board, right? Come on, hurry up, I can't hold the boat steady much longer!"

He saw them glance behind them, all of them, checking just one more time to see if a miracle had happened and the water behind them had stopped its mad chase.

When they turned around, it was clear that no such miracle had taken place.

Pinky Dwyer went first. She was a good swimmer, had won several awards at the country club her family and Sam's belonged to. She bobbed to the surface, grabbed the rope, and followed it to the boat, exactly as Sam had ordered. She was thin, lightweight in spite of her wet clothing, and he had no trouble hauling her into the boat.

"That was gross!" was her comment as, gasping, she fell onto the floorboards. "That water is filthy!"

Chad's girlfriend, Lisa Dane, followed Pinky. Chad and Dominic hung back, wanting to see the girls to safety before they made their try.

But Becka refused to jump.

chapter
18

The decision to dive in search of Carmel O'Connor wasn't as easy for Callie as it appeared. She hadn't realized until she toppled into the water how dangerous it had become. It was the roughness of it that kept her off-balance, the way the water surged and whirled and boiled. Like ocean surf.

Fully submerged, swimming furiously, eyes open for signs of Carmel, she had only been under a minute or two when an arm bumped against her, the fingers on its hand clawing at her frantically. Callie grabbed the arm. Hung on. Swam upward, pulling the arm along with her.

Carmel came up to the surface gasping for breath.

"Don't try to swim," Callie instructed, glancing around for Abby and Geneva. She could vaguely see shapes ahead of her struggling valiantly toward higher ground, which as far as Callie could tell, wasn't visible yet. How far were they all going to have to swim before they found a dry spot where they could rest? "If you try, and you panic, you'll drag us both down. Just hold onto me. Put your arms around my neck. I'll get you across."

Callie hoped she wasn't promising something she couldn't deliver. She had no idea how many streets the flood had swallowed up. How far was she going to have to swim in all this filth with Carmel's weight on her back?

By the time she had swum with her soggy, clinging burden across the avenue and then across three more parallel streets, all completely submerged beneath at least six feet of water, Callie had lost sight of Abby and Geneva. All she saw around her, when she gathered up enough strength to look, was darkness and the sheen of black water. Large and small objects bobbed around her, and at one point a packing crate popped up out of the water, smacking her in the cheek. It hurt.

"Didn't you see that coming?" she called over her shoulder to Carmel. "You could at least play lookout back there and give me some warning!"

Carmel's only answer was a half-sob. Her arms around Callie's neck felt like chains. The girl seemed to have gained twenty pounds, and Callie felt a sob of her own catching in her throat. She was so tired. Completely, thoroughly exhausted.

I never should have stepped one foot outside

that drugstore, Callie thought, her strokes weakening slightly. Or I should have just saved myself and left these two bratty girls to Abby. Carmel isn't *my* sister. Why isn't Abby doing this?

Because Abby couldn't have saved her, came the answer. Callie found some comfort in that. In fact, she found a *lot* of comfort in it. Everyone who knew Abby O'Connor liked her, even loved her. The same couldn't be said for Callie Matthews, could it? But who exactly *was* it out here in this wild cesspool risking her neck for Carmel O'Connor? It sure wasn't Abby.

Dry land was blocks away, several blocks past the avenue, past the center of town, past a cluster of darkened homes with water up to their second stories. It seemed likes miles. But Callie made it, with Carmel clinging to her back the entire time.

Abby and Geneva, standing on the sloping lawn of a house that sat high and dry, far above them at the top of a hill, urged Callie on with screams and shouts, from the moment the two were spotted in the water. When they were close enough, the water diminishing to no more than two feet deep, Abby ran to pick up Carmel, and waited to help Callie to her feet.

Together, the four climbed to the top of the hill. If there had been any signs of life in the house, they would have knocked until someone answered. But the house was clearly deserted, and there were no cars in the driveway or, when Abby checked through the window, in the garage. Empty.

She would have broken in and used the telephone to call her mother, but Callie pointed to a tree down in the side yard amidst a tangle of wires. "Wouldn't do you any good," she said. "Those look like telephone lines."

Too tired to trek over to the house next door, which looked equally deserted, they all climbed up on the front porch and collapsed under the shelter of the porch roof. Huddled together, they were asleep in minutes.

They were awakened some time later by the unmistakable sound of a boat's motor approaching from the north.

Help was on the way.

It was Will who awakened Susannah. He knelt beside her, touching her hand and speaking her name quietly. She stirred and rolled over on the tweed couch, opening her eyes quickly, as she always did upon awakening. "What's wrong?"

He knelt beside her. "A rescue crew just came in from the South Side. They said your dad's fishing lodge was underwater. Only the roof is showing. I thought you should know."

Susannah sat up, rubbing her eyes, knowing her mascara had probably streaked, but not caring. "Sam?"

"I don't know. They picked up an elderly couple, but there wasn't any sign of Sam. They're going to take another run down that way, but they said it's getting pretty dangerous out there."

"Did you rest at all?" Susannah asked Will. Her eyes felt gritty, she knew her hair had to be matted from lying down, and what little makeup she'd been wearing had long ago faded from existence.

"Yeah, I did." He waved toward a worn, flowered chair opposite her couch. "I sacked out there." He grinned. "You look good asleep. Not everyone can say that. Some people, their faces look like putty when they're sleeping. Nothing stays where it's supposed to. I've seen lots of patients who look like that when they're asleep. But not you. Everything stays in its own perfect place."

Too flustered to accept the compliment, Susannah failed to acknowledge it. Instead, she asked as she stood up, "Has anyone heard from Kate? Or Abby?"

"I don't know." His voice had turned cool. "I told you, I was sleeping."

She knew she should have at least said thank you. What he had said to her was nice, not the kind of thing a girl heard every day. And she'd ignored it. But he'd picked a terrible time to say it. She wasn't in the mood.

"I did hear, though," he added in a more normal tone of voice, "that we had two more fatalities. Before I came in here. Two drownings, at a low-water crossing. A man and his wife in a car. Their kid survived. Ten-year-old boy. He was in the backseat of the car, and got out through a window. The parents were trapped, and the car was swept away."

"That makes six," Susannah said, horror in her eyes. "Six dead. And it's not even morning yet."

Will glanced down at his watch. "Yeah, it is. It's after five. Twenty after. Think any of the day shift'll make it in at seven?"

"I don't know. I can't believe I slept that long. Is it still raining?"

Together, they went to the window to check. It was still raining. Heavily.

Becka never did jump from the veranda. Chad, acknowledging a signal from Sam via eye contact, reached out finally and gave the terrified girl a shove. She tumbled over the railing and into the water. Chad was right behind her. The minute he came back up to the surface, he grabbed the collar of her shirt and hauled her over to the boat.

"You'll forgive us someday," Sam told her as he pulled her in.

When they were all in the boat, he cut the rope with his penknife and turned the boat around to head upriver, toward the city. It would have been easier traveling in the opposite direction, with the current, but he was afraid that if they got too far away from the city, hope of rescue would lessen. His plan was to head straight for the arched stone bridge in the center of the city. Unless he was mistaken, that bridge should be level with the water right about now. He could drive the boat right up to it and they could all step out onto the safety of the bridge. Even if the bridge happened to be completely underwater by now, they'd still have a better chance of running into a bigger rescue boat if they went toward the city instead of away from it.

"Hang on, everyone!" he shouted. "This is going to be the ride of your life! And keep your eyes out for junk in the water, okay? Yell when you see anything larger than a doorknob."

Sam wished, as he spurred the boat into action, that he'd been able to locate life jackets in the boathouse. He hadn't been able to see well enough, and there hadn't been time to hunt.

No one in the boat was wearing one.

"I'm surprised to see you down here," a nurse said to Sid Costello, who was sitting in the doorway of Rehab's makeshift shelter, a pile of white towels in his lap. "Surprised in a nice way, of course. You're all dressed. You look nice. Who helped you? I didn't even know you were gone.

I'm curious about what got you out of that mood you were in."

"Tiger helped me." Tiger was a big, friendly orderly Sid knew and trusted. "He got me out of bed and helped me dress."

"You didn't answer my question." The noise level in the room had increased. The nurse had to raise her voice, even though she was still standing beside his chair. "It's really great to see you rejoining the real world, even helping out, but what got you going?" She smiled. "I'll bet it was that girl. The one you wanted me to call. I tried, but I couldn't get through. Sorry." She glanced around the room. "Is she here?"

"No. She isn't." Disappointment hardened Sid's voice. "And I came down because I was sick of that stupid room, that's all. It didn't have anything to do with her."

"Um-hum. Well, if you're tired, I can take you back upstairs now."

"I'm not tired. I'll stay."

"Well, okay then. Just keep doing your thing, handing out those towels, okay? Your friend will show up sooner or later. The electricity is still on in north and west Grant, so the hospital put out a call on radio for volunteers to come and help out here."

Sid brightened. She'll come, he thought. Abby will come if she hears.

Sid wheeled his chair around and set it in motion toward the door to greet new arrivals with clean, still-warm towels.

Jeremy was not that far below Kate. The water, bringing Jeremy with it, had risen almost to the second-story window.

"Jeremy," she called down from her perch at the edge of the roof, "what are you going here?"

"Looking for you. I've been looking for you all night long. I would have been here sooner, but I was attacked by a street sign. Probably would have drowned if the water wasn't so damn cold. It revived me, fast!" He was clinging to the windowsill, his legs floating out behind him. She thought his teeth were chattering, but she couldn't be sure. "How did you get up there?"

"I came by way of the drainpipe. Just checking on the shingles up here," she added lightly, "seeing if they'll hold up under the storm. I repeat, what are you doing here?"

"I came to get you."

That struck Kate as almost funny. Get her? And do what? How was he going to get her to dry land, if there was such a thing left somewhere in the city? "Jeremy, I can't swim."

She could tell by the sudden silence that he was shocked. In Jeremy's world, everyone swam and skied and played tennis almost from the moment they were born. *"You can't swim?"* He said it in the same tone of voice he might have used to say, "You can't read?"

"No, Jeremy," Kate answered sarcastically, "I just never did make it to the country club for those lessons."

"You can't swim," he repeated. After a moment, he said, "Well, okay. I'll just go get us a boat. I know where they are."

"A boat? Jeremy, there isn't time! The water's going to be up to the roof soon."

"I'll be right back, I promise. Don't go away."

chapter
19

—⌁⌁⌁⌁⌁⌁⌁—

Abby and her sisters and Callie were taken by boat to ambulances waiting on dry ground, and then to ER, in spite of Abby's protestations that they were all fine and just wanted to go home.

"Speak for yourself!" Callie snapped as they were helped up into an ambulance. The idea of being fussed over at ER appealed to her. Her father wouldn't have left the hospital that night during an emergency situation. He'd still be there. They'd call upstairs and tell him his daughter had been brought in, and he'd come rushing down to ER. Maybe they'd even tell him she saved someone's life. Because she *had*, hadn't she? And she wanted every single bit of credit that was due her. Otherwise, what was the point?

Abby hadn't even said thank you yet.

"Thank you, Callie," Abby said. She was sitting on one of two ambulance cots with her arms around both her sisters. All three were shivering, and Carmel had been seized by a coughing spasm. One of the paramedics began checking her for signs of acidosis, common among near-drowning victims, but quickly realized that Carmel hadn't come that close to drowning.

Thanks to *me*, Callie, lying on the second cot, thought. To Abby, she said, "You're welcome. But you owe me big time." Although she wasn't feeling sick, just tired, she didn't argue when the second paramedic wrapped a blood pressure cuff around her upper arm. If she looked too healthy, they'd just send her home. They wouldn't even bother calling her father. That wasn't going to happen if she could help it.

"How are things at Med Center?" Abby asked the paramedics. "Awful, I'll bet. Any fatalities from the flood?"

She was shocked by the answer. Six. *Six?*

"And that doesn't count actual flood victims," he added. "We don't know about those yet. There are still people missing. Actually," he told Abby, "your mother reported *you* missing. You and your sisters."

"But not me?" Callie asked, disappointed. She knew why, though. Her mother, who never stayed awake late because of her illness, would have tired of waiting for Callie to return from the drugstore and fallen asleep. And her father, of course, thought she was safely at home in West Grant with her mother.

Still, it would have been nice to know that she couldn't stay out all night in atrocious weather without *someone* going ballistic.

"You all live in West Grant?" the paramedic asked. He hadn't inquired about what they'd been doing near the riverbank. Abby was grateful. She nodded in answer to his question. "Well," he continued, "if you can't get through to your house by phone when we get to ER, and you all check out okay, we'll see that you get home. Your parents must be frantic about now."

But only Geneva and Carmel went home. Abby was able to get through to the house, quickly explaining that they were all fine, that she was sending her sisters home, but she would be staying. She was needed at Rehab. Her mother was too relieved to be angry. That would come later, Abby knew, when things had returned to normal.

Callie didn't go home, either. She felt fine, although she let the nurses and doctors in ER fuss over her. Her father did come downstairs to the treatment room where she lay on a table. But once he had ascertained that she was in no danger, all he wanted to know was what on earth she had been doing out on a night like last night? When he was positive she was okay, he retreated back to his office complex on the tenth floor.

Dr. Lincoln saw the look on Callie's face and said sympathetically, "He's really got his hands full this morning, Callie. It's been a horrible night."

"Yeah, hasn't it?" Callie slid off the table. Her

moment in the spotlight hadn't lasted very long. Still, she could see that this place was where the action was. Why go home and be bored to tears when the excitement was right here? Anyway, her mother would sleep until ten or so, and it was only seven-thirty now. The visiting nurse lived in West Grant and shouldn't have any problem getting to the house. So why go home?

But since Callie could imagine the look on Abby's face if she said she was staying for the excitement, what she said instead was, "I want to help at Rehab."

"You *do*?"

Did she have to look *that* surprised? Hadn't Callie just saved her sister's life? O'Connor was an ungrateful wretch! "Yeah, I *do*," Callie replied acidly. A really good-looking young doctor passed them in the hallway. Callie flashed him a brilliant smile. Staying was an even better idea than she'd thought at first. "Is that so weird, O'Connor?"

Abby, her cheeks windburned, her wet hair curling around her face, said hastily, "Oh, no, I didn't mean that, Callie. I just thought you'd be really tired, that's all." She had changed out of her wet clothes into a borrowed nurse's aide's uniform and a pair of white shoes. "Of course you can help. They need all the help they can get."

"Are there any more of those dry uniforms

around anywhere?" Callie asked sharply. "Maybe in red? It's my best color."

Rolling her eyes, Abby pointed her in the right direction, and Callie hurried off.

"You didn't see Kate or Jeremy out there anywhere when you were wandering around in the rain, did you?" Susannah asked Abby anxiously. Susannah had never been as relieved in her life as she had been when that ambulance pulled up and Abby stepped out. Wasn't *carried out on a stretcher*, but stepped out. She was soaked and pale and shivering, but she was okay. And she had found her sisters, who were also okay.

Abby shook her head. "No. Why?"

Susannah explained.

"Kate couldn't possibly still be at the library," Abby said. "That whole area is flooded now."

Kate was lying prone on the edge of the roof. She was so thoroughly drenched, water ran from her ears. Dawn had come quickly, brightening the sky only slightly. She could see now, and what she saw was that Jeremy had not returned with the promised boat. Morning had brought no other activity on the street below her. The houses still looked deserted, the shops along Market Street were still closed, and there was no traffic, boat or otherwise, on the flooded streets. She could hear distant sounds . . . voices shouting . . . a boat's motor, she thought, though she

511

couldn't be sure . . . the faraway wail of an ambulance. But the usual morning sounds of cars starting, buses chugging past her house, the whistle of a train, radios blasting through open windows in Eastridge, people calling to each other as they carried the trash to the curb . . . those sounds were absent. Instead, her vigil on the library's roof was accompanied only by the dull roar of the harsh, steady wind, the slapping of the rain on the shingles, and the hungry lapping of the water now no more than a foot and a half below where she lay on her stomach.

She raised her head, looked around her, and saw nothing moving but the tree branches over her head. If I have to, she vowed, I will climb that tree, clear up to the top branches. But I don't *want* to.

"Jeremy!" she shouted, "where *are* you?"

The arrival of morning, gray and dismal as it was, hadn't done Sam much good. Visibility had increased only slightly, and it seemed to him the wind had picked up. His back and shoulders ached, his eyes burned from constantly battling a fierce wind and the steady spray of dirty water hitting his face, and he'd never been so tired in his life. Twice, the current had yanked the boat into a cove, not shallow enough for anyone to jump out and swim to safety, but so debris-laden, he'd had to fight to get the boat back out into the swollen river again.

The five others were crouched in the bottom of the boat, bailing steadily with bait cans. Becka looked wet and tired, but she never once stopped slopping the water out of the boat. All of them looked pale and drained.

When Sam spotted what was still visible of the arched stone bridge spanning the Revere in the center of the city, he thought at first he was hallucinating. Even though it never should have taken them all night to reach the bridge, even though he'd expected to arrive at this point hours ago, when he did see his goal approaching, he still couldn't believe it.

"There it is!" he shouted, "there's the bridge! We made it!"

His exhausted passengers swiveled their heads to look.

They were still too far away to see exactly how much of the bridge, if any, was still dry. Even if only the stone railing was clear, he could steady the boat against one of the pillars while everyone climbed on to the railing and crawled or walked along it to Massachusetts Avenue on the other side. If the avenue was underwater, they'd have to swim it until they reached high ground. But at least they were back in civilization again.

It hit Sam, then, how alone he had felt trying

to steer this boat back to the city. True, everyone had bailed, everyone had shouted their support, no one had complained. But they were his guests, they had come into the South Side at his urging, and he alone was completely responsible for getting them back to safety.

He had done that. Well, almost.

Keeping his eyes fixed on the curve of the bridge, Sam steered around the flotsam and jetsam floating in the water.

It was Chad who jumped to his feet. Later, he would admit that he knew better. Growing up, he'd spent long hours on the family boat, much bigger than this little craft, on the river. He knew about boats. He even knew about floods, and dangerous water. His excuse was, he'd become so excited at the thought of rescue when Sam shouted that they'd reached the bridge, that he'd forgotten everything he'd learned about boats and water. And he jumped to his feet.

In spite of the steady, arduous bailing, the bottom still held an ample supply of rainwater. When Chad stood up, the boat rocked. All of the water in the bottom immediately slopped to his side of the boat, tilting it precariously.

But it still wouldn't have tipped over if Becka, and then the other two girls in the boat, hadn't become caught up in Chad's enthusiasm and followed his example. Because they had both been sitting on Chad's side of the boat, their sudden motions as they jumped up, combined with the slop of the water that hadn't yet been bailed, tilted the boat so far over on its side that the Revere, accepting the invitation, rushed right in.

"Sit down!" Sam screamed, knowing it was too late.

It was.

The boat went over quietly, spilling all six occupants into the turbulent, muddy water.

chapter
20

Samuel Grant II, dapper as always in a black trenchcoat, a black hat over his white hair, strode into ER as if he owned the planet. Almost, Susannah thought. His ancestors had founded Med Center, the University, the refinery, and Grant Pharmaceuticals. As far back as Susannah could remember, her father had walked with that distinctive, authoritative stride. She couldn't imagine him slowing his pace long enough to smell any roses along the way.

"Where is your brother?" he demanded when he reached Susannah and Will. They had just come from trauma room three, where Jeremy's father, head of Cardiology, had, against all medical odds, revived a seventeen-year-old who had been found lying under a wrecked pick-up truck, her face submerged in six inches of thick, gooey mud. She had nearly suffocated. She was in bad shape when they brought her in.

Susannah knew the girl, she realized, when the face had been hastily wiped clean for resuscitation efforts. She was also a student at The Hannah Rose Grant Day School. Cheerful and friendly and very smart. Treasurer of their class. Her name was Daphne Underwood, and Susannah was sickened by how close she had come to a horrible death.

Technically, Daphne *was* dead when they rushed her into ER. The paramedics had had no luck reestablishing a heartbeat. She had no pulse, and her lips were blue under the thick coating of mud.

But Dr. Barlow, as always, had refused to give up. He had eventually cracked the girl's chest open and massaged the heart manually until it began beating again, something Dr. Izbecki, Susannah knew, didn't approve of. Said it seldom did any lasting good.

And maybe it wouldn't this time, either. Maybe Daphne wouldn't make it. Her chances weren't very good. But when Susannah and Will left the trauma room, Daphne was alive, thanks to Dr. Barlow.

Seeing Daphne lying on that table, her mouth and nose and eyes covered with thick, black, gooey mud, had shaken Susannah to the core.

Now, standing in the lobby as her father waited for an answer to his question about Sam, Susannah was still too shaken to think of an answer. In the past, she had sometimes fibbed for her twin. If he knew ahead of time that he was going to be coming home from a party later than he was supposed to, he occasionally asked her to cover for him; to make something up, and sometimes she did. Their father wasn't as strict with Sam as he was with his daughter, which, although unfair, Susannah had accepted, but he did have rules for Sam. Since she knew Sam wasn't really up to anything horrible, she had fibbed for him.

But not tonight. She was too tired to fib. And besides, she was worried sick about her brother. Her father could find out faster than she could exactly where Sam was and what he was doing, and if he was all right. Her father, unquestionably the most powerful man in town, had ways of finding out such things.

Susannah leaned against the reception desk and told the truth. "Sam's at the fishing lodge. At least, he was. He was holding a party down there."

Although Samuel Grant's hair was snow-white, his face was young, evenly tanned, and unlined. It tightened now with anger. "The lodge? He's on the South Side?"

"Maybe he left," Susannah said hastily, "when he saw how bad the weather was getting." But they both knew that if he had left while it was safe to leave, he would have been home by morning. Sam stayed out late partying, but he had never stayed out all night.

"Then why isn't he home where he belongs?"

Samuel Grant removed his hat to shake it dry, then put it back on his head, saying sharply, "That boy ought to have his head examined! If I find him, I'm taking him straight to the Psych building!" Then he turned on his heel and left the hospital.

"Whew!" Will said in awe. "Sam's really in for it, isn't he?"

Susannah made a rude sound. "Are you kidding? My dad'll be so glad to see him when he finds him, he'll probably buy him something new. Won't be a car. The van's too new. Maybe new skiing equipment, or a computer. Something."

"He sounded mad."

Shrugging, Susannah said, "Well, he is. Right now. But he and Sam are tight." She wasn't aware of the note of wistfulness in her voice, nor did she notice Will's eyes on her in sympathy. "Dad will forgive Sam anything. He likes to think of the two of them as pals. Anyway, he always sounds madder when he's worried, and he's worried now. I can tell. So am I. That paramedic who came in with Daphne said the South Side is completely underwater now. Everyone's been evacuated. But the lodge is so isolated. There isn't a neighbor around for miles. Unless Sam had the portable radio on, he wouldn't have known about the evacuation order. And I'd bet he had his stereo on instead."

"He can see water rising, can't he?"

"Not if he's too busy partying to pay attention."

Will reached out to brush a strand of fair hair away from Susannah's cheek. "He'll be okay."

"That's what we said about Kate, and we still haven't heard from her," she answered, tears in her eyes. "I'm going to ask her mother straight out if she's heard from Kate. I don't know what else to do."

"No," Astrid Thompson answered when Susannah posed the question. "I haven't heard anything." She was filing medical charts. Susannah noticed that her hands were shaking slightly, although her voice was composed. "I tried to call the librarian at home, but his phone is out. Kate's not on any of the rescue crews' lists, and all I know is, she hasn't been brought in here injured. That's a good sign, don't you think?"

"Yes," Susannah told Kate's mother in a firm voice, "I think that's a very good sign. I'm sure Kate is fine." She was, of course, lying.

When Kate awoke, the first thing she was aware of was her astonishment that she'd actually fallen asleep on the roof. The second thing she became aware of was that the rain had stopped. It was still drizzling faintly, a fine mist, but to the north, the sky was slowly beginning to turn a paler shade of gray mixed with a watery, translucent blue.

She sat up. Her muscles, stiff from lying on the rough shingles, groaned a protest. The water had risen to less than a foot below the roofline. She could have washed her hands in it without stretching if she'd wanted to. She didn't. It was filthy, a brackish brown, littered with debris.

But it was no longer rising. And it had quieted. The bubbling and boiling had stopped. The water lay still now, an ugly, foul-smelling, brown blanket spread over much of the city of Grant.

The flooded street showed no signs of life. And Kate heard no sound but the chirping of a few birds. Of course they're chirping, she thought sourly, brushing a loose strand of dark hair back from her forehead, because they can fly *over* all this mess. I never wanted wings before, but they'd come in handy right now.

Jeremy hadn't returned with the promised boat.

Not that she'd really expected him to. Jeremy was decent enough, in spite of his moodiness, but he wasn't Will. Will would have returned immediately with a boat. Sam probably would have, too. Jeremy's problem was that he let himself be intimidated by his father. Impossible to measure up to such perfection. Of course, everyone else who knew Dr. Barlow found him intimidating, too, so she didn't really blame Jeremy. He should have gone to San Francisco with his mother, made a fresh start with people who didn't even know Dr. Barlow. She knew why he hadn't gone. Because he thought his mother wasn't going to have any money. Jeremy liked having money. Personally, Kate thought, Jeremy would be better off with less money and more independence. He'd never have either living with his father.

Dr. Barlow would have been back with a boat by now, too. Maybe two boats. With caviar and champagne on board.

Kate sat back on her heels. Her sweatshirt and jeans were cold and clammy, her hair felt stiff and matted, and the morning was much colder than yesterday, when she'd dressed. She could have used a sweater or two. She was freezing.

"Well, if I'd known I was going to end up on a roof," she murmured crankily, trying in vain to smooth her hair again, "in the middle of a flood on a freezing cold morning, I'd have dressed for it!"

She was so lost in discomfort and cold that she almost didn't hear the slapping of oars in the water as the boat approached. When she did hear it, she leaned forward, close to the roof's edge, and let her eyes survey the quiet, brown lake spread out below her.

And there he was, rowing toward her with great effort through the debris-laden water, steering cautiously around trees poking up out of the water, steering around buildings. "Kate?" he called as he got closer. She saw him craning his neck, trying to catch a glimpse of her. "Kate, are you still up there?"

His blonde hair was plastered against his head, his sweatshirt was filthy, his face smeared with mud. He looked exhausted.

But Jeremy Barlow had probably never looked as good to anyone in his life as he did at that moment to Kate Thompson.

"Yes!" she shouted, rising to her knees. "Yes, I'm still here! Where else would I be?"

Because Abby was wearing a nurse's aide's uniform, Sid didn't notice her when she entered Rehab. After her sisters had been thoroughly checked out by Dr. Lincoln, they had been dried off, warmed up, and given the okay to go home. Immediately afterward, Abby had left ER to hurry through the passageway to Rehab. Callie was at her side, complaining that white made her look "washed out."

Callie never did help. She spotted a friend when they entered the building, and hurried off, eager to start spreading the news that she was a heroine.

Abby might have protested if she hadn't been

completely caught off-guard by the sight of Sid, sitting in his chair at the entrance to The Ballroom. He was wearing a sweater instead of his usual plaid bathrobe. He looked, Abby thought, very handsome. There was a pile of white towels in his lap, a piece of paper and a pen in his hands. Taking names, Abby decided. Sid was actually handing out towels and taking names instead of brooding up in his room. She could hardly believe it.

Since Sid hadn't noticed her, she stood in the doorway, watching him. He looked so different. It wasn't just that he was dressed in street clothes, the first time she'd seen him out of his robe since she'd known him. It was more than that. He seemed to be sitting up straighter than usual. And if she hadn't known better, she would have sworn he had just smiled at a little boy clutching a catcher's mitt who'd stopped to talk to Sid on the way in.

Nah. Not Sid. Couldn't be. Wasn't smiling against his religion or something?

Then he glanced over his shoulder and saw her standing in the doorway. He didn't recognize her at first, because of the uniform. He looked away, then did a great double take, jerking his head around a second time to take another look. And then he *did* smile, a big, genuine, man-am-I-glad-to-see-you smile that sent a delicious shiver down Abby's spine.

Well, surprise, surprise! she thought as she left the doorway to move toward him. And isn't *he* gorgeous when he smiles! When Abby had first met Sid Costello, she had fantasized that *she* would be the one to change his attitude, give him a reason to live, help him see that he had a future, after all. In her fantasies, she had been the one to show him that he could still be useful.

Now, there he was, fully dressed in street clothes, handing out towels, functioning perfectly fine. And she hadn't even *been* here. Couldn't take any of the credit.

Shame on you, Abby O'Connor! she scolded mentally. You should be thrilled that he's not hiding up in his room. Don't be so selfish.

She *was* thrilled. Besides, she hadn't been getting anywhere with him, anyway. Must have been her bedside manner. She'd have to work on that.

He was still smiling. It didn't bother her that when she reached his chair, the smile disappeared and he said in the same rude tone of voice she was used to, "Well, where the hell have *you* been?"

Instead of answering, she bent down and planted a firm, earnest, no-nonsense kiss on his mouth. She wasn't sure why. He'd never acted the least bit interested in kissing her. But, the thing was, *she* felt like kissing *him*. So she did.

And if she was going to kiss him, she was going to do it right. The kiss lasted at least a minute, and during that minute, she could feel him responding, first with surprise, then with what was unquestionably enthusiasm.

When the kiss ended and Abby straightened up, smiling, an equally enthusiastic round of applause sounded from The Ballroom. Everyone in the crowded room had been watching, and all were smiling.

"What'd you do that for?" Sid asked, a healthy flush in his strong-boned cheeks.

"I just wanted to cheer them all up," Abby answered lightly, smiling as she reached down to take half a dozen folded towels from his lap. "They've had a really bad night." Her eyes met Sid's. "You don't mind that I used you to entertain them, do you?"

He didn't look away, not this time. "No," he said, his eyes staying on hers. "I don't mind at all. I'm here to help."

Abby laughed.

chapter
21

———�ᴧ₶ᴧᴧ———

Sam's first thought as he hit the turbulent water was Becka. She didn't swim well. She had to be tired from the long night behind them. She'd been soaked through and shivering with cold even before she hit the water. She wouldn't have much strength to fight the current.

When he spit himself out onto the surface, he glanced around anxiously for some sign of her. He found the other four right away. They were clinging to the overturned boat. But he saw no sign of Becka.

"Where is she?" he shouted, and Chad waved toward the bridge.

Sam saw her then. She was struggling, fighting more valiantly than he'd have expected, given her exhaustion. She hated deep water, he knew that. Swam only in pools, and never in the deep part where she couldn't touch bottom.

No way was he going to let Becka die. He was the one who had talked her into heading for the South Side. She hadn't complained, and she'd kept bailing when he knew her shoulders had to be on fire from the constant motion. She was going to come out of this okay. He'd make sure of it.

Becka's eyes were wild with fear when he reached her. When he clutched her around the waist, she panicked. Her arms flew out and fastened around his throat in a grip so tight, sharp knives of pain scissored their way up into his scalp.

"Let go!" he shouted. "Becka, let go! Let me do it! Let yourself go limp. I'll get us both back to the boat. We can hold on there until a rescue boat comes by." He sounded far more optimistic than he felt. Hanging on to her was hard enough. How was he going to hold on to Becka *and* the boat?

Had anyone else come after Becka, she might have continued to fight. But she trusted Sam to save her. He could see it in her eyes, and then she stopped struggling and let herself go limp.

His chest aching, Sam swam with her back to the boat.

The six of them hung there like barnacles, bounced around and battered by the churning water, waiting for rescue.

It stopped raining.

"Took you long enough," Kate grumbled, climbing off the roof and into the boat Jeremy had pulled alongside the library. "Where'd you go to commandeer this fine craft, Barlow?"

Gray-faced with fatigue, he answered hoarsely, "Sorry. Actually, I was only gone ninety minutes. Took me forever to get to where the boats were. Too much junk floating in the water." There were countless scratches on his face, some of which were deep and bleeding in thin rivulets. When Kate was seated, she reached out to gently swipe at a cut on his chin. Jeremy winced. "Got sideswiped by a saw," he explained as he began rowing again, this time north, toward drier streets. "Good thing it wasn't a power saw."

"Wouldn't have mattered," Kate said, swaying slightly on her seat as the boat turned. "Electricity's off."

Jeremy laughed. "Anyway, when I finally got to the boats, they were all gone. I had to wait for one to come back. The guy didn't want me to take it, but I told him there was a pregnant lady in one of the houses about to give birth, so he gave in."

"I'm supposed to be a pregnant lady?"

"Yeah, well, it worked, didn't it?" He steered around the top section of an old oak tree. "It's a mess out there, Kate. Out *here*. I've never seen so much water in my life. And if Med Center wasn't up on that knoll, it'd be flooded, too."

They sat in somber silence as Jeremy rowed up

the flooded street. "It's so deserted," he commented then. "Nobody's out, except the rescue boats and police. They have to collect people in the boats and then take them to the ambulances waiting in the north and west parts of the city. Takes too much time, but there's no other way."

"Is Sam all right?" Kate asked after another few minutes of silence. The only sound they heard was the swishing of the oars and an occasional clink as one of them collided with a floating object. "He was on the South Side, right?"

"I haven't heard. Are *you* okay? You look . . . well, kind of out of it."

Kate laughed weakly. "Out of it? I wish I *had* been out of it. Out of the storm, out of the library, out of the flood. Safe at Med Center, that's where I wish I'd been." Then, more seriously, she added, "I think I might be suffering from mild exposure. I can't stop shivering, but I feel hot inside. Might have a fever. We'd better go to Med Center, have Dr. Izbecki or Dr. Lincoln check me out. I can't afford to get sick. Anyway, I can't go home. I don't even know if my house is still there. Was my mother still on duty the last time you were in ER?"

Jeremy nodded. "Yeah. She looked beat, but she was still there. And I think the rest of your family's out on the sandbag lines."

"Yeah, they would be." Concern in her voice, Kate said, "I think you should get checked out, too, Jeremy. You look as bad as I do. And you need dry clothes, like right away. You can borrow a doctor's surgical greens." Kate reached out again to gently wipe a smear of blood from a cut on his cheek. He had risked his own life to save hers. He could have just told the rescue crew where she was, but he hadn't. He had come for her himself.

Spurred on by her remarks, Jeremy got them to the waiting ambulances without smashing into a street sign or overturning the boat.

When Susannah heard the announcement over the PA system of six incoming rescued from floodwaters near the bridge, she knew Sam would be one of the six. She had no idea why she believed this. Sam hadn't *been* near the bridge. He'd been on the South Side. And he'd probably had far more than only five people with him. Still, the feeling that he would be one of the six was so strong, she ran to the doctor's locker room and borrowed a set of whites from one of the interns, hoping with all her heart that her twin would need nothing more than dry clothing. No stitches, no casts, no EKG to find out if his heart was functioning, no oxygen, no X rays. He'd be wet, as anyone pulled from the river would be, but that . . . was . . . *all*!

Her prayers were answered. He wasn't even lying on a gurney when he was brought in, but running along beside Becka's, who looked very much as if she hadn't been as lucky as Sam. He and his other four friends, although thoroughly drenched as anyone pulled from the river would have been, seemed to be intact.

"She's breathing, but not very well!" he gasped when he saw Susannah. "She was fine at first when I got her back to the boat, but I think something in the water cracked her on the head just before the rescue boat arrived. She made a sound, and then she went limp. She went under and I had to dive for her. I think she's swallowed a lot of water."

Becka also had a nasty cut on her forehead. The blood had been washed away, but the laceration was jagged, the flesh around it swollen and purplish. "What did she hit her head on?" one of the paramedics asked as the gurney reached trauma room five and entered.

"I didn't know she hit it on anything. Something must have slammed into her while we were hanging on to the boat. There's so much junk in the water." Sam looked at Susannah. "Is it serious?"

She shook her head. Becka wasn't completely limp. In fact, she was beginning to stir restlessly on the gurney. That was a good sign. "I don't know. Maybe not." She knew how Sam would feel if Becka didn't make it. He'd blame himself. And how would he ever tell Becka's mother?

Dr. Izbecki and Dr. Lincoln were each taking a much-needed nap. The doctor on duty was one Susannah didn't know well. He was young, energetic in spite of the fact that he'd been up all night, and wasted no time administering care to the injured girl. His decision was that she didn't need a tube in her lungs, and ordered X rays just to be sure.

Becka began coughing, then, almost choking, and vomited up volumes of brown liquid.

Sam looked alarmed, but Susannah said quickly, "No, that's good. She needs to get rid of it. It's okay, Sam."

"I should call her mother," he said morosely. "God, I dread it!"

"I'll do it," Susannah offered, somewhat reluctantly. "I'll try to call her mother." It was a call she didn't want to make, either. She could have waited and let a doctor or nurse do it, but that didn't seem fair. And she had no idea how long they would be working on Becka. "Were the phones out at the cabin?" she asked Sam.

He nodded.

That meant Becka's mother hadn't heard from her all night. The woman had to be crazy with fear. "I'll call her," Susannah said, and hurried from the room.

Mrs. Downing's phone was still in operation, and she handled Susannah's call well. "I'll be right there," she said, and hung up.

Susannah dreaded returning to the trauma room. What if Becka hadn't responded?

I'll know the minute I walk in there by the look on Sam's face, she thought, her steps slower than usual as she returned to the crowded cubicle. Becka was hidden behind a row of white uniforms, but Sam breathed, "She's going to be okay," as Susannah reached his side. "She's breathing better."

She was not only breathing better, she was far more responsive now than little Louie Murphy, who had been transferred to Women's and Children's Hospital in the complex and was still in a coma. Every cough from Becka lifted Susannah's spirits further.

The doctor, however, was concerned about the head wound, and sent the shaken, shivering girl up to X Ray for a CAT scan, calling a neurosurgeon to meet the gurney upstairs.

"You're sure she's going to be okay?" Sam asked one of the nurses as the gurney disappeared.

"Looks that way." The nurse fixed a critical eye on him. "This hospital wouldn't be nearly as crowded tonight," she told him tartly, "if people like you had stayed home where you belonged."

Sam raised his hands in mock self-defense. "You won't get any argument from me," he said. "Thanks for helping Becka."

The nurse thawed a little then, adding, "She

was lucky, that's all," as she left the room.

"Here, put these on," Susannah said, handing Sam the dry whites. "And you'd better call Mom and Dad. He was here looking for you. He was *not* happy when he found out where you were."

Sam groaned. "You *told* him?"

Now that the crisis is over, Susannah realized, and he has saved Becka's life, he's back to worrying about his own neck. Well, that's Sam. "Yes, I told him. And I hope he hangs you from a beam in the family room. I've been worried sick about you all night long. You and Abby and Kate."

"Kate? What about Kate? She was at the library."

"It flooded. Jeremy went looking for her, but . . ." Before Susannah could finish the sentence, Will stuck his head in the doorway and said, "Susannah! Kate and Jeremy are here!"

Susannah turned and ran.

Kate was a sorry sight, but she looked beautiful to Susannah, who ran and hugged her. "Where on earth have you been?" She ran to the cabinet to grab a blanket, running back to wrap Kate in it. Kate clutched it gratefully.

"On a roof, where else? It's the *only* place to be on a night like this. You should try it sometimes."

"No, thanks." Susannah put an arm around Kate's shoulders. "Come on, let's have you checked out. Jeremy, you, too! You look almost as bad as she does. What happened to your face?"

As they walked, Will on one side of the couple, Susannah on the other, Kate and Jeremy both began talking at once. Susannah felt a knee-weakening sense of relief. Abby was okay. Sam was okay, and his friends. Now, Kate and Jeremy were finally back, and both were intact and breathing.

And they were all safe at Med Center, where they belonged.

"You were on a *roof?*" she asked happily.

At Rehab, Sid and Abby were helping pass out breakfast trays in the main room, now packed wall to wall with pallets and mattresses and cots, with people and their belongings. Volunteers moved back and forth offering food and hot drinks. It was crowded and noisy, but Abby was too busy to notice. The flood refugees looked so lost and bewildered. The hot coffee and food seemed to help.

She had spoken to her mother on the telephone and been given permission to spend the day at Med Center if necessary, now that her younger sisters were safely at home. The last thing her mother had said to her on the phone was, "I'm very proud of you, Abby. When I think of what could have happened . . ."

"Well, *don't* think of it," Abby had said. "I'm

not going to. Ever. I'll call again later when I know what time I'll be home."

"So, I hear you're a hero," Sid said as they passed out trays of scrambled eggs and toast. "People are talking."

"It was really Callie," Abby said, handing a small boy a carton of orange juice. "She's a better swimmer than I am."

He grinned. "Yeah, I heard *that*, too. From Callie, of course. To hear her tell it, you're going to owe her for the rest of your life. She's probably in the office, printing up a bill right this minute. And from what I know about Callie Matthews, you'd better pay up, or *else!*"

Abby laughed. "Yeah, I know that about her, too. Everyone does. Just the same, she did save Carmel. And I *do* owe her. Anyway, probably all she'll want is a date with some hunky football player." The instant the words left her mouth, she was aghast. How could she have said that to Sid?

Her face white, she half-turned to face him, dreading the expression of fury he would have on his face. Or of pain.

She was amazed to see that he was regarding her calmly, his dark eyes on hers. She saw no sign of anger or pain. "I'm . . . I'm sorry," she stammered. "I forgot."

He nodded. "I know." He shrugged. "That's okay with me. It'd be neat if everyone would forget the old Sid. You know, all that football-hero stuff. It'd make it easier."

Abby nodded. "I guess it would." Then she added boldly, "Callie Matthews would be lucky to date someone like you. I mean, I know you've been down here since last night. Susannah told me. You have to be really beat. But you're still here." She turned all the way around to face him fully. "There are heroes, and then there are *heroes*, right?" Holding the tray under one arm, she clapped her hands. "That round of applause is for you, Sid Costello."

"I liked the other applause better," he said boldly, turning his head to grin up at her. "I mean, I liked the reason for it better. Anyone can hand out towels. Not just anyone gets a kiss from Abby O'Connor, right?"

"This is true. I'm *very* particular about that."

He nodded soberly. "I knew that about you. Think you could spare one more? I mean, if you *really* think I'm a hero. They always get kissed in the movies,"

"This is not a movie, Sid." Abby knew everyone was watching them. She didn't care. "And you *have* been rude to me. I haven't forgotten."

"It'll never happen again."

"Sure it will. People don't change that much in one night." Abby pretended to think seriously. "But . . . these people *do* look depressed again. And I *am* a volunteer. If another kiss will cheer them up the way it did before, I should give in."

"Force yourself."

Actually, it took no effort at all on Abby's part.

This time, there was loud cheering as well as applause.

chapter
22

The worst was still ahead for the city of Grant and its residents.

First, they had to wait for the water to recede. Then they prayed for the sun to shine, to do its part in drying up the oozing mud and smelly silt. And then they began the cleanup.

The hardest-hit areas were south, east, and central Grant. Volunteers went into all of those areas, helping merchants and homeowners sift through the devastation for their belongings. People from north and west Grant, for the most part unaffected by the flood, showed up in droves to help with the cleanup. Sam and his friends were there. As well as Susannah's parents, looking very young in jeans and matching plaid shirts. The only occasions on which she'd ever seen her parents in such casual clothing were when her mother gardened and her father went fishing. They looked more . . . approachable in jeans.

There were twelve dead. Less than the last serious flood. And as Abby pointed out to Susannah while they picked through layers of mud in Eastridge, helping Kate and her family pick out and clean off cherished possessions, "Only four of those died at Med Center. The three burn patients, and the cardiac case. Pete Dawes, Curtis Brock, and the two parents trapped in the truck were already beyond hope when they arrived in ER. The others, the flood victims found in their cars or along the riverbank, never had any hope. A lot of people lived because of Emsee."

Susannah gingerly lifted a glass vase out of the mud surrounding the small yellow house. "That's true. Little Louie Murphy went home yesterday. No brain damage, thank God. Becka's going home tomorrow. The pregnant woman we were all so worried about is okay, and expects to go to full-term. Callie's fine, especially now that her picture's been in the paper, along with Sid's, in that story 'Heroes of the Flood.' I've never seen Callie so thrilled. Even her father seemed impressed. He was showing it to everyone in ER."

"Well, she does deserve it," Abby said. "If it hadn't been for Callie, Carmel could be . . . well, Carmel might not have made it. So whatever fuss is made over Callie suits me fine."

"Well," Susannah said, "Callie wasn't the only hero. There's Jeremy, saving Kate from that rooftop. And," she continued with a sly grin, "then there's that boy at Rehab. What's his name? Sid something, isn't it?"

Abby's cheeks deepened in color. "Sid Costello."

"Oh, yeah, Costello, that's right." Susannah hauled a wooden footstool up out of the debris and began wiping it with a wet rag. "You know, it's weird, but he told me you were *his* volunteer." The sly smile spread. "Imagine that? Go figure. As if you'd ever treat one patient better than another. I mean, we *were* warned about that, remember?"

Abby, her head bent, seemed to be concentrating intently on wiping completely clean two pieces of silverware she'd unearthed. "Yeah, we were," she muttered. "Wouldn't want to break any rules, would we? Not even if someone needed us to. I mean, *really* needed us to."

Susannah laughed. "I heard about the kiss, Abby. Everyone did. And he *is* cute. His manners are rotten, though."

Abby lifted her head. She looked relieved, and was grinning. "Yeah, well, I'm working on that."

At least a dozen times that day, someone said, in the midst of all the filth and muck and debris, "It could have been much worse."

Susannah knew they were right. It could have. If it hadn't been for Emsee, there would have been a lot more deaths.

It was Sam's idea, of course, to throw a Flood Cleanup Party at Rehab. When he suggested it that night in front of Will's house, to a group of filthy, exhausted volunteers, Susannah laughed. "Another party? Oh, honestly, Sam, you just never stop, do you?"

But she loved the idea.

And she had a wonderful time. Half the city came. Callie Matthews spent the entire evening telling all who would listen the graphic details of her harrowing rescue of a small child in floodwaters, embroidering the story further each time she told it. There were other, truer stories of rescues, but Callie's voice was the loudest and the most insistent, not to mention the rudest whenever someone became bored and turned away from her.

Ignoring Callie's shrill voice wasn't easy, but Abby managed, dancing the night away with Sid. She sat on his lap, her arms around his neck, as he spun the wheelchair around. They laughed a lot.

Susannah and Will danced past Kate and Jeremy, sitting at a table arguing about her refusal to take swim lessons at the Y. "But I don't want to!" she was saying, and Jeremy, to Susannah's surprise, responded matter-of-factly, "Well, I can't be there to save you every time there's a flood."

Becka hadn't recovered enough to attend the party.

"I'm not sure she would have, anyway," Sam told Susannah. "Couldn't blame her if she stayed home. Maybe she hates me."

"Not in a million years," Susannah said. "She's nuts about you, like practically every other female in this city." She glanced around the room, telling herself silently that she'd been one of the lucky ones. She hadn't lost someone close to her to the floodwaters. There was Will, in a corner talking to Abby and Sid and Jeremy, and Kate was dancing by in the arms of some tall, lanky boy Susannah didn't know. Her parents had just arrived, her mother in blue silk. And her twin brother was standing right beside her. There were people in Grant who hadn't been as lucky. "Anyway," Susannah added, watching as Will left the others and began walking toward her, "you could always remind Becka that you saved her life."

"And she could remind me that I was the reason she *needed* saving in the first place," Sam said. "Wouldn't blame her." Then a small, pretty blonde girl came along and claimed him.

Will returned to Susannah's side a moment later. He looked very handsome in khaki pants and a red turtleneck sweater.

"About that clinic," Susannah said, smiling up at him. "I have some questions."

"How about," he said, taking her hand, "I answer them while we dance? I think better to music."

He took her in his arms and rested his cheek on the top of her head.

That suited Susannah just fine.

An exciting excerpt from *Fire*, Med Center #3, coming next.

On the grounds of Grant Petroleum Products, a sprawling complex of oil tanks, office buildings, and warehouses, the darkness and quiet of a basement closet was broken by a sudden sharp, spitting sound, followed by a duller hissing noise. Then a shower of golden, fiery sparks, like a cluster of fireflies, shot out of a large black electrical box fastened on one wall.

When the sparks and the hissing had died, there was silence again in the dim enclosure.

But minutes later, a tiny puff of smoke curled out from under the edges of the big black box on the wall. The box serviced one of several office buildings on the site, which spread across thickly wooded acreage in the city of Grant, Massachusetts. The office building, tall and wide and constructed entirely of red brick, had been built close to one of the huge, round oil tanks.

"Shouldn't be puttin' a building this close to

the tanks," one of the construction workers had been heard to mutter while working on the site years earlier. "If old Titus Grant wasn't so tight with money, they'd be spreadin' this place out a little more, keepin' all the buildings away from the tanks. Me, I been around refineries all my life. Ain't seen one yet that didn't have a fire at least once a year. This one won't be no different. Shouldn't be puttin' no buildings this close."

But no one paid the slightest bit of attention to his objections. Although the refinery complex had grown over the years, the office building had stayed where it was, side-by-side with the cluster of oil tanks.

Now, the tiny puff of smoke grew. At first, it stayed close to the black box, trailing around its outside edges like a curling, gray vine. Then, fueled by oxygen in the air, it blossomed. Eager to explore its surroundings, it left the black box and began lazily easing its way up the basement wall toward the ceiling. As it did so, a small, bright, orange-red flame stabbed its way out of the box, looked to see where the puff of smoke had gone, and decided to follow it.

The smoke and its tagalong partner, the flame, seemed to be in no particular hurry. They took their time easing along the wall, like children exploring new territory.

But as they went, they grew in size.

Miles away, in the center of the city, in another sprawling complex of taller, newer brick buildings known as Med Center, the staff settled in for a Saturday of meeting every kind of medical emergency and rendering every kind of medical care. They were blissfully unaware of the refinery's lazy, trailing smoke and its companion, the flame. So they had no way of knowing what horrors were in store for them on this unusually balmy, windy Saturday in late October.